A WEDDING TAIL

A WEDDING TAIL

A Rescue Dog Romance

CASEY GRIFFIN

CHARMING FROG
PUBLISHING

ISBN: 978-1-990470-14-1

2nd Edition Paperback: October 2021

Published by Charming Frog Publishing

www.CharmingFrogPublishing.com

JOIN CASEY'S PACK

Casey Griffin's newsletter followers get access to exclusive content such as free stories, fun gifts, and random shenanigans (who doesn't love those?). They're also the first to hear about her new books.

SIGN UP AT CASEYGRIFFIN.COM

Chapter One

TOP DOG

Zoe stood in front of the doors of St. Dominic's Church, greeting each wedding guest as they arrived, cheeks aching from her fake smile. She was so practiced at appearing poised that she could act like she was going for a facial while a zombie apocalypse broke out around her. But internally, she paced and bit her nails, cringing at each new arrival who wasn't her fill-in groomsman, Levi Dolson.

She checked her watch: fifty minutes until "I do" time. She just wished that when Levi finally arrived, he would be on the back of a white stallion. Not because she secretly desired a Prince Charming—that fantasy was ludicrous—but because the horse she'd booked to carry the happy couple into the sunset after the ceremony had canceled. After that first call of the day, everything that could go wrong did. Zoe really needed a win.

She took a deep breath. It would all be okay. No. It was going to be *perfect*. She wasn't the best event planner in San Francisco for nothing. And after all the extra challenges this event had presented, she would prove it—to herself, to her meddling mother, to everyone—by pulling it off without a hitch. Well, that anyone would know about, anyway.

1

"Code red! Code red!" a woman shrieked.

The disembodied voice carried around the side of the building and into the foyer. The bride's grandparents, who were shuffling up the church steps, exchanged worried glances.

Inwardly, Zoe cringed. *Now what?*

With barely a flicker of an eyelash, Zoe maintained her poise. God, her cheeks hurt. "Don't worry," she told the elderly couple. "Everything's fine. That's just my excitable assistant, Natalie. I'm sure it's nothing. Please, remember to sign the guest book on your way in."

A moment later, a curvaceous blonde careened around the corner, ponytail swinging behind her. As three more guests filtered inside, Zoe gave Natalie a subtle quirk of her eyebrow. When her assistant noticed her expression, she visibly gulped. Straightening her skirt, she entered the church with reverence.

Tucking a stray jet-black lock of hair back into place, Zoe motioned to Natalie and ducked into a quiet vestibule out of earshot. The epitome of serenity, Zoe rearranged a bouquet of roses on a carved wooden table. However, her insides had cinched together like corset strings.

"We can't handle a code red right now," she told her assistant. "We already have an MIA flower girl, a sick priest, in-laws at each other's throats, busted air-conditioning during a heat wave, and a wild, four-legged ring bearer. Not to mention we're still waiting on Levi Dolson to replace our food-poisoned groomsman."

"This tops everything." Natalie practically vibrated. She took a few deep breaths, but it only made her hyperventilate. "It's the dress."

Zoe froze. "What about the dress?"

Natalie gnawed on her lip. "It doesn't fit."

The rose stem in Zoe's hand snapped in two. The words echoed through her mind as it emptied of all other concerns. Family feuds she could squelch, flower girls she could track down, rampant dogs she could bring to heel, but this … And with *this* bride of all brides?

"What do you mean?" Zoe hadn't moved, but something in her voice made Natalie take a step back. "How can it not fit? It was made for her."

"I-I mean, it won't zip up."

Zoe's back straightened. "We'll see about that. I'll make the dress fit if I have to staple her into it."

The Fisher-Wells wedding was one of the most extravagant weddings she'd planned, with a commission to match. Once it was over, she would finally have the down payment to buy a place to call her own, proof she could support herself without a man—no matter how often her mother insisted otherwise.

Zipping down the front steps, she skirted around the outside of the church. Natalie remained close on her heels. The pitter-patter of her assistant's sensible flats matched the quick beat of Zoe's heart. The afternoon sun beat down on them. And it was only one o'clock; it was bound to get hotter. Hopefully the industrial fans she'd tracked down at the last minute could keep up.

"How is Juliet doing?" Zoe asked.

Natalie groaned. "Total bride meltdown."

Zoe had figured as much. She remembered the day the gold-embossed invitations had arrived and Juliet's name had accidentally been placed last to read *Wells-Fisher*. To say the least, Fisher was not *well* that day. Somehow, it had set the tone for their entire marriage—something about feeling inadequate and her mother-in-law's strawberry rhubarb pie. It all became incoherent once she'd broken down into full sobs.

But a wedding dress that didn't fit? Despite Juliet's bridezilla personality, no one deserved a crisis like this on their big day. Having experienced a catastrophe on her own ill-fated wedding day, Zoe had vowed to never let it happen to anyone else.

She mentally reviewed her to-do list.

- *Double check on bride's uncle (last seen nursing flask)*
- *Find flower girl*
- *Cough drops for priest*
- *Leash for Juliet's golden retriever*
- *Replacement horse*
- *Levi Dolson*

She added a new item to the list:

- *Get bride into dress*

Zoe's shoulders relaxed beneath her stylish cobalt blazer as everything fell into place in her mind. She could get through this day. Heck, the year before, she'd thrown a party where someone had kidnapped a bunch of her guests—the four-legged variety, but still ... After that, she was officially experienced with any disaster an event planner could face. Only, before today, she'd never faced so many at the same time. And what was she going to do about that horse?

As Zoe and Natalie approached the small office building acting as the bride's room, a peal of muffled swear words drifted through the door. Natalie's face paled as she reached for the handle.

Zoe figured they didn't both need to endure the impending abuse, so she stopped her. "On second thought, could you please call around and find a horse for after the ceremony? Do whatever you can. Get me a zebra, if you have to." She absently wondered about the weight restriction on miniature horses, if it came to that.

Natalie's eyes rolled skyward in relief. She nodded, her ponytail flicking, and scrambled away as fast as she could.

"Oh, and Natalie?" Zoe called after her. "If Levi Dolson turns up, send him to me right away."

Standing in front of the "bride's room," she reached inside her bridal utility bag. Truthfully, it was a fanny pack, but it had saved her butt more times than she could shake a bouquet at.

Her fingers brushed against super-soft polyester fur, and her worries melted away. Who could be upset when they were holding an adorable, lovable, huggable Fuzzy Friend?

The collectible line of stuffed animals topped every child's Christmas list, and apparently the list of stressed-out thirty-year-old Japanese American women too. Or maybe just Zoe's. The cuddly sack of beans acted as a private solace to her during the worst of times—while doubling as her most embarrassing secret.

Predicting a strenuous day, she'd come armed with Pretty Puppy. Old and well loved, it resembled her late dachshund, Buddy. As she gave her Fuzzy Friend a final squeeze, she took a deep breath and knocked.

"What?!" came a sharp reply.

Zoe cracked open the door to check for airborne shoes or bouquets aimed at her. The coast was clear. She poked her head inside the little office and found a cluster of brightly colored bridesmaids, one for every color of the rainbow.

"Can I come in?" Zoe asked.

At the sound of her voice, the women turned in unison. The rainbow parted, revealing a billowing white tulle cloud: Juliet. However, when the bride spun away from the mirror to face Zoe, her expression looked as tempestuous as a hurricane. And she appeared like she'd been through one too.

Mascara ran from a pair of puffy eyes, leaving black streaks down her flushed cheeks. Wisps of hair escaped her veil and clung to her sweaty neck. Her dress sagged off her body, half zipped up. Her maid of honor struggled to hold it up while Juliet's body convulsed with sobs.

Zoe didn't skip a beat. "Look at you!" she gushed. "You look beautiful." Which was probably the biggest lie she'd ever told in her life, and in a church, no less.

"No, I don't!" Juliet wailed, wiping her reddened nose on a

tissue. "I can't go through with it. I'm calling the whole thing off."

"Why? What's wrong?" Zoe dared a few steps into the room. She needed to defuse the situation, brush it off as though this kind of thing happened all the time—which, unfortunately, it did. But why, oh why, did it have to happen today?

Juliet spun to face the floor-standing mirror, elbowing her maid of honor out of the way. "Just look at my dress. It's a disaster! It doesn't fit."

Zoe crossed the office full of tense bridesmaids. "I'm sure the zipper's just stuck. Let me have a look."

"See? I told you it was the zipper," Juliet snapped at the woman in the orange dress.

Zoe grabbed the two pieces of fabric at the back and pulled them together. Extra hands joined in the battle, tugging on the dress. As they struggled, beads of sweat formed along Zoe's brow.

Juliet sucked in, flushing red, then purple, then blue. When she'd turned every color of her bridesmaids' dresses, Zoe admitted defeat; it wasn't going to close.

She frowned at the gown. "Hmm."

Juliet eyed her in the mirror. "Hmm? That doesn't sound like a good 'hmm.'"

"The zipper's not the problem. But it will be all right," Zoe added quickly. "We'll just have to make some emergency modifications to the design. How do you feel about a corset-style back?"

She dug through her fanny pack and drew out a roll of thick, white silk ribbon and a small pair of scissors. Fanny pack to the rescue!

Juliet's hopeful look darkened. "You want to ruin my dress?"

"Would you rather cancel the wedding and wait for a few months? What's more important about today? The dress? The perfect ceremony? An equal number of groomsmen to brides-maids? This specific location?"

"But it *had* to be this church," Juliet whined. "My parents got married in this church."

"I know. I totally get it." Grabbing a wet wipe from her fanny pack, Zoe dabbed the mascara streaks on the bride's cheeks. "And we made it work, didn't we? Now we'll make the dress work too. Today isn't about the details. It's about getting married to the man you love. This is only the first day. It's the rest of your lives that matters."

Whenever Zoe put it that way, it usually brought any errant bride back down to earth. Juliet's eyes, however, burned with an argument. Like when she'd argued to keep the same venue even with the heat wave and lack of air-conditioning. Like she'd argued to push her already-strained budget to accommo-date three more tiers on the wedding cake. Like she'd argued against the first two dresses that seemed perfect but she'd ulti-mately sold on eBay.

Zoe could sympathize, though. There was once a time when she'd gotten caught up in the fantasy of it all: the silk dress, the gardenia arrangements, the old familial tortoiseshell kanzashi comb passed down by a proud mother. But at the end of the day, there was just a man and a woman, and no amount of planning, organizing, and dreaming would force him down that aisle if he changed his mind.

Despite her best efforts, there were some things in life she couldn't control—like when her groom didn't show. But it was for the best. She should thank him, really. She'd walked away a stronger person, more levelheaded. Because of it, she could organize the best damned wedding a bride could ever dream of —at least *that* was in her control.

Finally, Juliet let out a breath like a deflating balloon. "Fine. I suppose. Do what you need to do."

Zoe checked her watch: thirty-nine minutes until go time. Her fingers flew, cutting holes on both sides of the zipper,

7

beneath the folds of the ruching detail. With long, deft fingers, she threaded the silk ribbon through the cuts, crisscrossing them in corset style.

When she pulled it through the last hole, she instructed the bridesmaids to hold the bride steady. "Brace yourself," she told Juliet.

Heaving on the ribbon, Zoe cinched it tight, sucking the bride into the dress. Juliet gasped. Zoe grunted. She yanked and pulled, maintaining tension until she could tie the bow. At the last second, she added a double knot.

Wiping her brow, she stepped back to admire her handiwork. "There. That's better, isn't it? I think it adds a certain sexiness to it, don't you?"

The bridesmaids parted so Juliet could scrutinize her reflection in the mirror. Her narrowed eyes roved up and down the laced ribbon, eventually softening. She beamed, and the bridesmaids released their held breaths.

Zoe had to admit, it looked pretty damn good. As she stared at her bride in self-congratulations, she glimpsed something white soaring past the window: a white dove. And considering her day so far, she just knew it was a white dove meant for the newlywed's grand exit.

She rubbed her temples. *What else can go wrong?*

The door burst open. Natalie practically fell into the room, gasping for air. Her wide eyes fell on Zoe, and she made an attempt—however poor—to act naturally.

Zoe suppressed an eye roll. Her assistant needed some acting lessons in cool.

"Sorry to interrupt, but—"

Zoe held up a hand before she could finish; the white feather stuck in her hair said enough. "Perfect timing. Can you please touch up the bride's hair and makeup for me? We've only got …" She checked her watch again. "Thirty-three minutes."

Natalie clung to her arm. "But the—"

"I know." Zoe plucked the feather out of her hair. "I've got everything under control."

Ready to deal with the next disaster, she yanked the door open. A flash of white. Violent gusts of wind flapped in her face. Feathers tickled her cheek and stirred her long hair.

She cried out and threw her hands up. When the flurry dwindled, she cracked an eye open to watch two more doves escape down Bush Street.

"What's wrong?" Juliet spun just as Natalie held the eyeliner to her lid, leaving a thick ebony streak across her face.

If the bridesmaids had noticed Zoe's feathered attacker, fear of Juliet's reaction kept their mouths shut.

Zoe rearranged her shocked expression into fake outrage. "Who put the rose topiary out here?" She gestured to the front steps. "This isn't where it should go. Do I have to do everything myself?"

Juliet rolled her eyes at the dramatics. "It's okay. They're just flowers. You know, you're kind of high strung."

Zoe gritted her teeth. *Look who's talking.*

"Everything is perfect," Juliet sang, the perfect example of a blushing bride. "So long as you have the horse for after the ceremony, that is. You do, don't you?"

Zoe quirked her eyebrow at her assistant in question. But Natalie gave a subtle shake of her head. Zoe's smile only wavered a little.

"Absolutely," she said. "You can count on me." Though, how she was going to pull it off, she wasn't sure.

As she slipped out the door, Natalie called out, "Oh, Zoe! I almost forgot. Levi Dolson is waiting for you in the foyer."

"Thank you. I'll take care of it." Shutting the door, she went to go wrangle a seriously late groomsman and some unruly birds. Yet another thing to put on the list for the day: bird herding.

Zoe took a shortcut through the sanctuary and nave. Her

heels clicked steadily on the hardwood floor, echoing off the vaulted ceiling.

How could Juliet call her high-strung? She was nothing if not levelheaded, cool, and collected, emotions always in check. At least, they had been ever since her own wedding day. That day itself, however, was an entirely different story. But who could blame her?

Since then, she'd vowed never to let herself lose control like that again. Especially not over a man. Instead, when her temperature rose, her emotions bubbling to the surface, she pushed them down. Deep, deep down. She imagined bottling them up and screwing on the top. Which sounded perfectly healthy, right?

Zoe never let her bottle-o-crazy get too full, however. She had a way of safely releasing the built-up pressure. That was the benefit of being a Pure Pleasure sex toy representative: an arsenal of free merchandise at her disposal to "test." What better way to prevent herself from blowing her top than … well, blowing her top?

To everyone else, she appeared tranquil beneath that layer of ice. No one could make waves in waters they couldn't touch. More than one bitter man she'd rejected over the years had called her an ice queen. And because she was so cool, they never knew how much it hurt.

Marching through the church, she shooed doves down from curtain rods, off St. Mary's shoulder, and away from the topiaries. So far, she'd counted twelve feathered fugitives. The more she chased out an open window or door, the more Zoe's cool thawed.

At least her substitute groomsman had finally arrived—and not a moment too soon. But when Zoe reached the foyer, chasing yet another dove away, there was no groomsman.

There was, however, a man in his mid-thirties, wearing ripped jeans and a wrinkly T-shirt. His blond hair stuck up in a tangle of gelled curls, mashed on one side.

He turned at the sound of her footsteps. A dreamy smile lit up his unshaven face like he'd just stumbled out of his bedroom and not into a church.

For a second, Zoe hoped the man was just sleepwalking and needed directions back to his bed, but then he said the words she dreaded to hear.

"Zoe Plum? I was told you're looking for me." He held out a hand. "Levi Dolson."

Chapter Two

STOP THE MUSIC

Zoe stared at the rumpled man in front of her. Her eyebrow twitched with annoyance as she took in his careless style, his bedhead hair, his half-closed eyes. The kind of look a woman dreamed about waking up next to, but at that moment, it was her nightmare.

"You're not Levi Dolson," she said.

He arched a pierced eyebrow. "I'm not?"

"You can't be. The Levi Dolson I'm expecting is a groomsman in a wedding. Not a candidate for a sleep study."

He ran a self-conscious hand over the stubble on his square jaw. "Hey, give me a break. I just woke up forty minutes ago. At least I brushed my teeth."

"Too bad you forgot your hair," she said, only half-jokingly. The other half was dead serious. This was the last thing she needed. "Late night?"

"You could say that." He grinned. "You gotta grab life by the balls while you can, right?"

She pursed her lips at the cherry red lipstick mark on his cheek. "Looks like life wasn't the only one who had its balls grabbed last night."

When his forehead creased in confusion, Zoe dug into her bridal utility bag and pulled out a makeup remover to-go cloth.

She waved it in question. "May I?"

He nodded, so she reached up and wiped the red smudge off his cheek. She showed it to him, and he shrugged sheepishly.

"Nice shade," she said with a smirk.

Zoe produced a travel hairbrush and held it up. When he nodded again, she fixed his honey and caramel hair as best she could. The sides were short, but there was plenty of length on top to give it some style.

"Why are you so late?" she asked. "Were you planning on sleepwalking down the aisle in your Snoopy slippers?"

"I don't have Snoopy slippers. I'm a man, not a child. I have Batman slippers." He chuckled. "Besides, I only got Owen's text that he wanted me to fill in a half-hour ago. I came right away."

"But you RSVP'd as a guest. Why weren't you already here and showered?" She gave his curls a final ruffle and nodded appreciatively. He had nice locks. If only he'd done them before he came.

"Let me see?" He tapped his chin. "Attend the stressful wedding of a guy I knew back in university or sleep in after a late night? Tough call. Besides, I was going to attend the reception. No big deal."

"Well, it's a big deal to the bride and groom. And it's a big deal to me. You're pushing us dangerously behind schedule." She checked her watch. She couldn't stand tardiness.

Levi's attention shifted, focusing above Zoe's head. *The nerve of this guy,* she thought. He wasn't even paying attention to her. He opened and closed his mouth a couple of times before he figured out exactly what he wanted to say.

"Are there more birds in this church than usual, or is it just me?"

Zoe gasped. "The doves." Spinning on her heel, she raced

for the front entrance. "Come on! We need to take a detour, and I'm not letting you out of my sight."

She found it strange that Natalie hadn't checked on the birds herself. After a year of working together, her assistant still hadn't learned to take a little initiative. Today, however, she was worse than ever. Instead of rising to each challenge, she added to it. How could so many things possibly go wrong with one event?

On the way past a replica painting of the *Last Supper*, she spotted Juliet's tipsy uncle slouched in a velvet chair. She stopped at the refreshment table in the corner and filled a Styrofoam cup with black coffee. Sneaking up on him, she wrestled the flask out of his hands before he could fight back.

"I think you've had quite enough of that," she said.

His bloodshot eyes opened halfway, blinking out of sync before landing on her chest. "But I'm celebrating."

"Save the celebrations for later. They're not married yet." She shoved the coffee into his hand, along with a Tic Tac from her utility bag.

Zoe mentally ticked that item off her to-do list and returned her focus to the top priority. She weaved through the last guests who were filtering into the stuffy church to take their seats. As she saw another dove soar by, she resisted the urge to sprint out the front doors.

Levi tugged on the neck of his T-shirt. "Why is it so hot in here?"

"The air-conditioning broke."

"And they're still having the wedding here? Don't they know there's a heat wave going on right now?"

She threw him a smile over her shoulder, glad someone saw it her way. "You're pretty sharp for a man who just woke up at the crack of midday."

He returned the smile. "I try my best."

Descending the steps, she rounded the corner to where the caged doves awaited the end of the ceremony. A small devil in lace and braids, disguised as an adorable six-year-old flower girl, crouched in front of them. She reached for the latch on the next birdcage.

Zoe fixed her with a hard stare. "And what do you think you're doing?"

The girl jumped and blinked up at her. "They were sad. They wanted to come out and play. The lady said I could."

"What lady?"

The flower girl shrugged and jiggled the latch impatiently.

"I'm sure whoever they were told you to look at them, not let them out." Zoe crouched down, ready to spring into action. "If you want, you can help me let them out to create the grand finale. How does that sound?"

"Grand finale?" After a moment of serious consideration, the girl nodded.

Zoe clapped her hands together. "Great! Why don't we find you a little dessert to keep you busy for a while?"

Her eyes lit up. "Dessert!"

Taking the girl by the hand, Zoe led her into the reception hall. "But you have to promise to behave and carry the flowers down the aisle like we talked about."

"Uh-huh," she said around the forming drool.

Levi drew close and muttered under his breath. "Do you really think she could use more energy?"

Zoe snorted. "No, but I just need to get through the next"—she checked her watch—"twenty-four minutes until the ceremony. Sorry. This won't take long."

"No rush. I've got nowhere to be."

She glared at him over her shoulder and saw his mischievous grin. Was he actually egging her on at a moment like this? Did he take anything seriously? He acted like his friend's big day was "no big deal." But it was a big deal. Her entire job involved organizing "big deal" celebrations.

"Dessert!" the girl demanded.

"Okay, okay." Zoe steered her toward the kitchen at the

end of the hall and swung the door open. "The food is just in here."

Smack!

Zoe's head whipped to the side, face stinging like someone had slapped her. Cream cheese icing slid down her cheek and onto her silk blouse.

She blinked the sponge cake from her eyelashes in surprise. "What the hell?"

The flower girl gasped. "You said a bad word."

"You did say a bad word," Levi said in mock seriousness.

Zoe stared at him. "What?"

The little girl grinned and yelled, "Hell!"

"Don't say that." Zoe pinched the bridge of her nose. This day was so not going according to plan.

Levi peered inside the kitchen. "Holy crap."

"Crap!" the girl cried.

Zoe scowled across the kitchen at the father of the groom —or FOG. Wedding cake coated his right hand, frosting smeared up to the elbow of his suit jacket. By the looks of the mangled fifteen-hundred-dollar, seven-tiered cake, he'd tried a few times to hit his target: the MOB, or mother of the bride. She, however, remained relatively cake-free but for a few globs of icing clinging to her permed hair.

"I'm so sorry," the FOG told Zoe. "I didn't mean to." He wheeled on the MOB. "This is all your fault. You'd drive a priest to violence! Before I met you, I had a full head of hair."

"Right." The MOB scoffed. "And I'm the Queen of England."

"Is that why you're such a *royal* pain in my ass?" He jabbed an accusing cream-cheesy finger at her.

"You want pain?" The short woman somehow grew taller with her fury at the balding man. "I'll show you pain."

The MOB grabbed the engraved cake knife from the tray while Mr. Wells scooped a chunk of cake from the next tier and balled it up in his hands.

Zoe lunged between them. "Whoa! Whoa! That's enough."

They froze at the tone of her voice, eyes darting from their enemy to her. Neither seemed ready to lay down their weapon and yield.

"This day is not about you or how much you hate each other," Zoe said. "It's about your children and their happiness. So, if you aren't willing to support them or be quiet witnesses of their love and happiness today, then you can leave."

Mrs. Fisher's glower didn't falter. She looked scarily like her daughter when she lost her temper. Her knuckles turned white as her grip tightened around the knife.

Zoe dared a step forward. "Or do I need to call the cops?" She held out her hand. "Now give me the knife."

Mrs. Fisher blinked rapidly and stared at the hand clenching the knife like it belonged to someone else. After a moment, her fist relaxed, and she passed the two-hundred-dollar cake knife over.

Zoe took a deep breath as she set it aside; another potential crisis averted. She shooed Mr. Wells away. "Now, you go wash up. The bride walks down the aisle in exactly …" She checked her watch. "Seventeen minutes."

"Cake!" the flower girl cried.

Zoe spun in time to watch the girl ram a fist into the bottom layer of the cake, effectively destroying the remains of the red velvet monstrosity.

Levi considered the ruins. "Maybe you can still save it. You could, like, put a flower here." He pointed. "And here. And here." He swiped a finger over the icing and licked it off. "If it's any consolation, it tastes great."

Sighing, Zoe pulled out her phone to scroll through her list of cake bakers. When she found one, she sent Natalie a text to order an emergency replacement cake from Gimme Some Sugar Shop.

That done, she turned to Mrs. Fisher. "Can you please take the flower girl and get her cleaned up and to the doors ASAP?"

The MOB nodded and herded the sticky girl out of the kitchen. Before the doors shut behind them, Zoe yelled out, "And keep her away from those birds!"

She lifted her wrist to check her watch. However, Levi placed a hand over it before she could see.

"Don't worry. It will all work itself out."

She gaped at him. "Work itself out? Things don't just work themselves out because you want them to. Things will work out because I make sure they do. I am in complete control," she said, as though to convince herself.

Unconsciously, her hand found its way into her bridal utility bag. As her fingers brushed fur, her shoulders relaxed. When Levi examined her a little strangely, she pulled her hand out, afraid he'd discover her secret. But his funny expression remained fixed in place, something between amusement and, well, she wasn't sure what.

His hand rose to her face. Zoe flinched. She didn't realize she'd taken a step until her back hit the refrigerator.

She swallowed. "What are you doing?"

Levi chuckled and closed the gap between them. Pressing herself against the fridge, she recoiled as his hand caressed her cheek. His thumb gently brushed her skin. It felt a little rough, callused, but his touch was warm and gentle.

When he pulled away, her eyes fluttered open. When did she close them?

Belatedly, she slapped his hand away. "What do you think you're doing?"

He showed her his thumb that was covered in cream cheese icing. "You still had cake on your face."

His mischievous eyes held hers as he sucked the icing off his thumb. Her gaze fell to his lips, watching his mouth. She gawked at him as though he'd licked the icing right off her body.

"You didn't think I was going to kiss you, did you?" His nose wrinkled.

"What? No." Actually, she didn't know what she'd thought. They'd met only fifteen minutes before, and he'd already touched her face. Well, she supposed she'd touched him first. In fact, she'd sort of styled him. But that was different.

Levi hadn't backed off yet. "I've never met someone so afraid of a kiss before."

She scowled at him. "I didn't think you were going to kiss me. And I'm not afraid." But then why was she shaking?

It wasn't like Zoe was a prude. She sold sex toys as a side business, after all, and hosted Pure Pleasure Parties to educate and empower. She was practically a sexpert. Except, of course, for one tiny detail: she didn't have sex.

But she still touched people. She hugged her friends and her mom, shook hands with strangers. Pigs in bars thought slapping her butt was a reasonable substitute for a cheeky pickup line. Heck, she touched herself all the time. So, what did it matter if he touched her cheek?

Levi stood so close. She couldn't stop studying his lips now. Mentally shaking herself, she pushed him away. That's when she caught sight of her watch.

She gasped. "We've got only fourteen minutes to get you ready."

"Well then, you'd better stop trying to make out with me."

"I'm not …" She groaned. Could he be any more exasperating? "I wouldn't kiss you."

"Really?" His pierced eyebrow shot up. "Challenge accepted."

Rolling her eyes, she spun and headed for the sanctuary. She couldn't bring herself to turn around to check if Levi followed her, in case he mistook her flushed cheeks as an invitation of sorts. Which it wasn't. She was simply stressed. And as the day went on, the church absorbed more of the afternoon heat. That was it. She was hot. And *not* for Levi.

"You seem to have a pretty good handle on things." He waltzed up, falling into step beside her.

"That's because I don't just let things work themselves out," she said, taking the next corner as fast as she could without running. "That's what a good event planner does."

"So, you plan more than weddings?"

"I do anything, really," she said, mentally running over her list once more. "I even throw Pure Pleasure Parties on the side to sell products."

"What kinds of products?" he asked.

"Sex toys."

His steps faltered, and he stumbled to find his footing. She grinned to herself, happy she could catch *him* off guard for a change.

"Sex toy parties?" His cheeks darkened but wrinkled with a smile, eyes practically twinkling with curiosity.

"If it's a party, I'm there," she said. "I plan it all. But soon, I plan to do mostly weddings."

"Why's that?"

"The Wedding Expo takes place next weekend. It's the best place to promote your business for the upcoming season. I hear you walk away from it with more clients than you know what to do with." *And more than enough money to help me pay down my new house.*

Levi slipped his phone out of his pocket, typing away as they neared the nave. "Maybe I should try it out. I'm in the entertainment business too."

She gawked at him, nearly tripping. "Y-You can't just 'try it out.' This kind of thing takes planning. I've been preparing for months. Advertisements, promotional material, pitches—"

"There," he said. "I'm all signed up."

Zoe came to a stop so fast that he ran into her. "You're what?"

He showed her his phone. A message flashed across the screen: *Thank you for your participation.* "I've booked a booth at the expo."

Her eye twitched. Was this guy trying to get on her last nerve?

She ducked through the doors into the nave. Most of the guests already sat in the pews. The priest waited front and center, coughing into the sleeve of his vestment. Up in the choir loft, the organ player stretched her arthritic fingers between songs. Zoe vaguely wondered if she was the same organ player who had performed for Juliet's parents.

Zoe skirted around the outside of the nave, past the pews jammed with hot guests waving the decorative fans she'd picked up earlier. Bright colors flashed as the folded paper moved back and forth in front of flushed faces, wafting the muggy air around.

She'd arrived early that morning to discover the air-conditioning had blown up the night before. Unfortunately, due to the heat wave, there wasn't an available repairman in the city. Several phone calls later, she'd scrounged up a few industrial fans for rent that ended up blowing the toupee right off the groom's grandfather.

Reverently, Zoe led Levi to the vestry where the groom and his groomsmen waited to take their places at the front. She knocked softly on the door. A moment later, which seemed like forever with eleven minutes to go, the best man opened the door. She slipped into the room, waving Levi inside.

After greeting Levi, the groom and his six groomsmen resumed their positions in a quiet, anxious circle. Zoe zeroed in on the groom, Owen. Despite the hiccups so far, he looked like he should, like this was the best day of his life.

She automatically straightened his bow tie. "How are you feeling? Are you ready?"

"Absolutely." He beamed. "I can't wait for us to be husband and wife."

She patted him on the shoulder like a coach before the big game. "Good, because she's just about ready for you. You don't want to keep her waiting." She clapped her hands. "All right, gentlemen. Take your places."

As they filtered out, she grabbed a tux from a hook on the back of the door. She thrust it at Levi. "Hurry. You've only got six minutes."

"Can do." Reaching for the hem of his shirt, he pulled it over his head.

She blinked, and her eyes grew wide. Maybe the guy wasn't the slacker she'd assumed, because he must have worked hard to get a body like that. He grinned at her, but she was done letting him put her off her game.

Tucking away that mental image for later, she kept a straight face as she asked, "What are you doing?"

"You said to hurry. You can stay for the rest, if you like." He winked. "It only gets better."

Zoe snorted like she wasn't impressed, but heat ran up her neck—make that down her stomach to between her thighs.

She locked eyes with him. "If I thought there was much to see, I'd stick around for the show."

He cringed, and his lips formed an "o" like he was in pain, but then he flashed his pearly whites and reached for his fly.

There was a knock on the door. Zoe turned reluctantly; it had been a long time since she'd viewed "the rest" in person. Six years, to be exact.

Natalie poked her head inside. "Sorry to interrupt, but—" She hesitated when she spotted Levi, probably wondering what exactly she'd interrupted.

"Oh, God. What now?" Zoe asked.

After tearing her eyes away from Levi, Natalie pulled a face. "We're down an organ player."

"What? She was just there. I saw her." Zoe stepped out the door and peered up at the choir loft as though she didn't believe it.

But because it was that kind of day, the elderly organ player had vanished, and the congregation now sat in silence.

"What happened to her?" she asked.

"She got an emergency call."

"Great. Awesome." Zoe took a deep breath. "I need to find an organ player in exactly … three minutes. I can do that. No problem."

Natalie just stared at her, as though waiting for instructions. Zoe gave her a wave, and she scurried off.

Her fingers itched, craving the touch of Pretty Puppy, but she resisted a grope in her utility bag. She spun to face Levi and suddenly had to fight the urge to grope something else because he wore nothing but a dress shirt. He stared down at the ends of the bow tie around his neck, frowning.

She cleared her throat, trying to keep her eyes on his face. "Need help with that?" she asked casually.

"Depends on what you're referring to." His eyebrows waggled teasingly. "But actually, I think you might need my help."

Zoe couldn't resist glancing down this time. The length of his shirt hid anything important, but by the way the fabric bulged at the front, she suspected he'd be an excellent help.

Her eyes lingered only a second—okay, maybe two—before refocusing on his face. "And how can you help me?" Her voice grew thick, layered with the double meaning.

She couldn't help herself. As much as his attitude irritated her, he was too tempting to resist flirting with.

He responded in kind. "I can *play your organ*."

Something about Levi's voice, the timbre, the warm rumble, melted her taut insides. Oh, boy, the material this guy was giving her for later … That is, until his actual meaning hit her.

She shook her head, clearing her one-track mind. "You play the organ?"

"Well, I'm more of a piano man, but I've dabbled here and there."

Her heart, which had risen at first, sank a little. "I don't really think dabbling will do in this situation."

His shoulders straightened like he was being all heroic or something. "I'll give it a shot. No big deal." He returned to fighting with his bow tie.

Zoe tried to remain patient, with only two minutes, no … make that one minute and fifty-nine seconds to go … Fifty-eight … "A shot? No big deal?"

"Sure." That way-too-adorable smile brightened, like the angels in the glowing stained-glass window were shining down on him.

"No offense, but the bride's grand entrance hinges on you giving it 'a shot.' It actually is a big deal."

Stepping into him, she took the bow tie and arranged it with practiced fingers. She could feel him gaze down at her while she worked. Despite her Japanese mom topping out at five-two, Zoe was five-foot-eleven. Yet, Levi had a good half a foot on her, even with her heels on. She loved a tall man. It meant she had to tilt her face up, rather than down, to kiss him. Not that she was imagining kissing him …

Levi pressed his lips together as they curled into a smile. She realized she was staring at them again. He chuckled because he knew it too.

With a final tug on the bow tie, she backed away. She didn't want to go down that mental path. Not when Levi was half naked in front of her. And certainly not at a time like this.

He slipped his pants on. As he tucked in his long dress shirt —and *himself*—she noticed he hadn't just skipped a hairbrush that morning, but underwear too. She hadn't been that close to a wiener since Buddy had died.

"Relax." He shrugged himself into the vest, buttoning it up. "Life's too short to stress about the little things. I'll go jump on the organ now. It will all work out."

Relax? The little things? Zoe gawked at him. Did he expect to simply jump on the organ and give it a whirl? Yup, he was opening the door. Now he was headed for the unoccupied organ.

Feeling the seconds tick by and her anxiety level rising, she stormed after him. "Maybe someone else here knows how to play. I'm not about to leave something this important up to chance."

"It's not chance," Levi said. "I'm a musician. I'll just wing it."

"'Wing ...'" She pinched the bridge of her nose and squeezed her eyes shut. When she opened them again, he was ascending the stairs to the choir loft.

Climbing up after him, she found him already seated on the organ bench. She grabbed his arm—his surprisingly toned arm. "Okay, enough playing around. We've only got ... one minute before go time."

He gazed up at her pleasantly. "Then I guess you'd better *go*."

She pursed her lips. This was so not part of the plan. So far, she'd averted every disaster the day had thrown at her, kept everything going perfectly to schedule. But this guy was more than a challenge with his "just go with the flow" attitude.

Hesitantly, Levi tapped a couple of keys. It sounded like a cat walking across the organ. Zoe flinched.

"You'd better hurry." He grinned up at her. "You only have fifty more seconds to go."

She checked her watch. He was right. There was no helping it; Levi was going to play the organ.

"By the way," he said offhandedly, "are we going with the old 'Wedding March?'"

She sighed. "You can't play 'Wedding March' in a Catholic Church. The bride requested 'Arioso.' But, at this point, I'd be grateful if I got 'Chopsticks.'"

"Okey dokey."

Gritting her teeth, Zoe headed back down the stairs, wincing with each incorrect note he played as he tried to "wing" it. Before she left the nave, she ran over and tossed the priest a cough drop. After that, she found the bride and her entourage in the foyer. Makeup back in place, hair artfully rearranged, Juliet resembled a picture-perfect bride, smile and all.

"You look wonderful," Zoe said. And this time she meant it. "Are you ready?"

Juliet squealed in excitement. It appeared as though she'd done a complete one-eighty. "Absolutely."

"Good," she said. "Your future husband is waiting for you. Let's go."

The bride nodded and took her place at the end of the procession line, next to her father.

Zoe leaned close to Natalie. "Nice job on the makeup, by the way."

"All the fires put out?" she asked.

"Not out, just maintained. Make sure the doves are by the front steps for the end. Oh, and we need that new cake for the reception."

"I'm all over it."

A quick scan of those gathered outside the doors told Zoe the devil flower girl had made a break for it. She was probably bouncing off the walls somewhere from all the sugar. But at least they still had Juliet's other niece to sprinkle rose petals.

The rainbow of bridesmaids lined up outside the doors. Zoe checked her watch one last time just as it struck one o'clock. Ducking into the nave, she peered up at the organ.

Levi was hanging out, staring off into space. Didn't he know how critical this was? Or was everything "no big deal" to him?

Zoe furiously waved her hand. He finally noticed her and waved back. She moved her hand in a circular motion, cuing him to begin. He gave her a thumbs-up and raised his hands above the keys.

She resisted the urge to stick her fingers in her ears as she held her breath for the first note. But when his fingers hit those keys, it actually sounded in tune. And as they drifted over the organ, it formed an actual song. *Canon in D,* she realized. Levi was playing a classical song.

How does one simply "wing" Pachelbel?

She watched in amazement. People rarely caught her off guard, but this guy had. And that irritated her. He was flaky, laid-back, unpredictable. She couldn't plan for unpredictable.

Her skin suddenly prickled like she was being watched. Starting, she blinked at her surroundings. The entire congregation faced her expectantly while she ogled the groomsman. A finger tapped her shoulder.

"Zoe," Natalie whispered next to her. "We should begin."

"Oh, right." Jumping to action, she ran back and opened the doors wide before backing out of the way.

She turned to the first person in line: the MOB. "You're up first. Looks like everything is going perfectly."

Mrs. Fisher's heavily eye-shadowed gaze fixed on hers. "You'd better hope so."

Zoe's eye twitched, but she ignored the implied threat. Stepping aside, she gestured for the woman to enter the nave. As she glided by at a measured pace, Zoe spotted a few pieces of red velvet cake clinging to her curls and smiled to herself.

All her hard work and planning came together in that moment. The parents marched first, followed by the bridesmaids, a perfect rainbow arching down the aisle. The flower girl tossed her petals, and the ring-bearing dog was actually bearing. Finally, the bride slipped her arm through her father's, and she gave Zoe a nod.

The harmonious humming from the organ inside altered in an improvised segue. It ended in "Arioso." Zoe didn't believe her last-minute organist just winged that either. But she didn't have time to puzzle over it as she signaled the bride forward.

The room hushed as Juliet glided toward her future husband. Suddenly, the cake wouldn't matter, the horse was going to be a minor hiccup—Zoe hoped—and the ill-fitting dress was forgotten. Because in that moment, the only thing the bride and groom could focus on was each other.

And that's why Zoe did what she did. She took satisfaction in helping two people get the day she never got. Because no one should have to go through what she did on what was supposed to be the best day of their life.

Zoe snuck in and sat in the back row. She always stuck around for the ceremony in case anything went awry. Over the years, she'd had a fainting pastor, a narcoleptic photographer, and a father of the bride with a heart attack. By now she was prepared for practically anything a wedding day could throw at her. She'd developed some pretty mean photo and video skills, and she'd taken advanced CPR and first-aid training. She was even ordained—just in case.

By the time they got to the end of the ceremony, she thought this disaster might actually work out. She zoned out for a few seconds, already running through the afternoon's to-do list in her head. By the time she tuned back in, the groom had stepped forward to kiss the bride. Then Zoe realized it was too early for that. She blinked and focused on the couple.

It wasn't the groom. It was the best man.

"Stop the wedding!"

A chorus of gasps and murmurs rose from the congregation.

"No, no, no," Zoe muttered.

Her body tensed with the instinct to sprint up there and tackle the best man. Her job was to give the couple a perfect day, to sort out any issues, iron out the kinks. But this was one problem she couldn't fix. One problem that had nothing to do with the wedding planner.

The best man took a deep breath. "I'm in love with Juliet."

The scene froze. The priest looked confused, the bride shocked, the groom furious. As Juliet opened her mouth to respond, the double doors burst open, and Juliet's uncle stumbled in.

His glazed eyes cast over the room before he yelled out, "Congratulations!" He raised a bottle meant for the wedding party table and took a deep swig.

Juliet full-on ugly cried. The groom seemed torn between comforting her and punching the best man's lights out. But whatever he said next to Juliet was drowned out as the FOG and the MOB picked up where they'd left off. Their screams echoed off stone walls and could be heard over the church bells that rang at the exact time the ceremony was *supposed* to finish.

Zoe jumped to her feet, not sure what else to do other than usher the couple into the vestry to give them a moment alone. Or call the police to prevent a murder.

As she pressed her way into the aisle, she watched the MIA flower girl scamper through the open doors and down the aisle screaming, "Hell! Hell!"

The flock of remaining doves flew by her like she was the profane Pied Piper of birds. It seemed she'd freed the rest of her feathered friends. And her timing couldn't have been better because, as the bride came sprinting down the aisle, the groom hot on her heels, Zoe realized the wedding was, in fact, over.

One dove flew overhead and landed on a chandelier, its poorly timed evacuation landing squarely on Mrs. Fisher's feathered fascinator—maybe in an animal cruelty protest, of sorts. Excited by all the commotion, the ring bearer started humping a guest's fake-fur purse.

Zoe stared at the chaos in disbelief. How did this happen? More importantly, how could she fix it?

Reaching into her fanny pack, she found her fuzzy strength. With a deep breath, she gathered her wits and compiled a mental list.

- *Tie up the dog*
- *Shoo the birds out*

- *Stuff cake into the cussing flower girl's mouth*
- *Kick the best man in the balls*
- *Coax the bride and groom back in front of the priest*

While on her way up the aisle to grab the dog's leash, Zoe noticed people clearing out. Probably because the doves lingered dangerously overhead. She held her hands up and addressed the congregation.

"Don't worry, everyone!" she yelled in the most confident voice she could muster. "This is just a little hiccup. Please remain seated, and we'll be underway again in no time!"

But Juliet's partially deaf grandmother obviously never heard her, because she shuffled out of the aisle. She bumped into Zoe, cane crunching down on her foot.

Yelping, Zoe hopped aside and accidentally bumped into another guest. When she spun around, she found herself face to face with Levi.

"Well, I'm glad I didn't sleep through this wedding," he said like he was making casual conversation. "How can I help?"

The last thing she needed was a guy who believed this was all no big deal. "Just stand up at the front and be ready for a wedding." She dragged the overexcited golden retriever down the aisle.

"I can help," he called after her. "Really."

"I've got this," she said. "I have a plan!"

But as she wrangled the dog with the promise of treats, she spotted the bride race out the front doors. A cab pulled up outside, and Juliet waved it down.

Zoe ran outside after her. "Juliet! Come back!"

But her voice couldn't compete with the loud *hee-haw* that blurted nearby.

A man blocked her path down the steps. He yelled into the church doors like he was delivering pizza to a college rec room.

"I have a donkey here for a Zoe Plum!"

Zoe gaped at the animal wearing an oversized party hat. Looking bored, it chewed on her shabby chic sign directing wedding guests into the church.

"Horse, Natalie. I said horse," she muttered under her breath. Smelly donkey just didn't have the same romantic feel while riding into the sunset.

"Hee-haw!" it said.

If only Zoe could talk to Juliet, she could still save the day. So it didn't go as planned. So what? It was about the end result, right?

Before she could push past the donkey, the cab's tires squealed. Burning rubber, it sped off. The train of Juliet's dress, which was shut in the door, dragged along Bush Street behind it, flapping in the wind. Owen chased after her, his dress shoes clicking on the pavement.

Zoe watched in disbelief. How could things have gone so wrong so fast? She thought she'd prepared for everything that could go wrong. She just never expected for *everything* to go wrong at the same time.

She sensed someone come up beside her. For a moment, she expected Natalie or maybe even Levi. But the smell of bourbon and coffee invaded her nostrils before she even turned around.

A wobbly Uncle Wally raised his bottle of wine at the retreating cab. "You win some, you lose some." He bent over and vomited on her rose topiary.

Chapter Three

DOG AND PONY SHOW

Welcome to the Wedding Expo!

The giant letters scrolled across the digital sign above the Hilton Hotel. Zoe gripped the steering wheel in excitement as she pulled her van into the underground parking lot. Keeping an eye out for a free spot, she wound farther and farther down. There were already so many vehicles there, which meant so many potential clients.

When she finally found a free space, she pulled in and parked. Grabbing her phone, she texted Natalie.

Just arrived at the expo. Are you here?

Normally, she wouldn't have worried. However, Natalie had grown increasingly distracted over the last few weeks. Letting things slip, showing up late, making personal phone calls while on the clock.

She leaned back in her seat and waited for a response, mentally going through her to-do list. The song on the radio faded out, replaced by the news on the hour.

"Our top story today: the San Fran Slayer has struck again. Last night, at approximately eight-thirty P.M., an up-and-coming local jewelry designer was found stabbed to death in her shop. Police say the murder

occurred just before the shop closed for the day. Anyone with information about the crime should call the police. In other news ..."

Zoe frowned as she turned the radio down. The serial killer had been on a spree for a couple of years now. The lead investigator on the case was Bob Samuels. He was dating the manager of the dachshund rescue center where Zoe volunteered regularly. While he didn't let on much about the case, she knew the Slayer kept the precinct busy; the entire country was watching.

Ding.

Zoe checked her phone, but it wasn't Natalie. It was an email from Zoe's seamstress; her client's Vera Wang wedding gown was ready. She squealed, as excited to see it as the bride was, because this wasn't just any dress, and it wasn't just any bride. It was her best friend, Piper Summers.

She replied, saying Natalie would pick it up that day. She cc'd her assistant on it and hit *send*.

Sighing, she resigned herself to setting up the booth on her own and got out. As she rounded her van, she admired the new decal she'd recently invested in. A giant blushing bride beamed at her as she tossed a bouquet around the back of the van. She'd dropped a lot of money on it, but it screamed professionalism.

Loading up her moving dolly with supplies, she pulled out two mannequins dressed as a bride and groom. She set them on their feet and gave them the once-over. They looked ready to walk down the aisle. In fact, she'd looked exactly like that on her wedding day since the blonde mannequin wore her dress and veil.

Zoe studied the tulle ball gown with the scalloped lace edging and bateau neckline. Since it had never even made it down the aisle, it had seemed a shame to throw it out—or burn it like she'd originally wanted to.

Slipping the groom's top hat onto her head, she propped the mannequins on the dolly and headed for the elevator. The rest she'd come back for: bouquets, place settings, photo albums, centerpieces, and fabric swatches. She had everything, right down to two silver chairs with cute *Bride* and *Groom* signs. Her booth would be a miniature version of the big day.

The hotel lobby was already choked with expo guests hoping for the early bird specials, the best deals, and the yummiest baked samples. As Zoe shuffled through the excited throng, the guests eyed her bag of samples greedily.

She followed the map from her orientation package down a couple of levels, past rooms lined with eager vendors and wedding circuit professionals. She noted a few stalls she would have to visit later: handmade décor suppliers, invitation designers, and allergen-free flower alternatives. And later, there was a panel discussion on *Wedding Traditions: Obligation or Obsolete?*

When Zoe reached the Grand Ballroom, she steered her dolly under a thick arch dripping with flowers. The fresh scent filled her nose. A wide aisle runner spanned the length of the room, softening her footsteps. Expo guests would feel as though they were already walking down the aisle on their big day. And today was Zoe's big day.

The expo presented a fresh start for her. The Fisher-Wells wedding lay behind her now, and she had to focus on booking new clients to make up for waiving part of her commission fees. As hard as she'd worked for the couple, she'd hoped the gesture would soften the blow of the day's outcome and prevent Juliet from badmouthing her. However, because of that, Zoe had indefinitely canceled her appointment with the real estate agent until she could replace the funds. But once she did, she hoped to finally show her mother she was just fine on her own.

She had her own business, her own money, and soon, her own home. Once she signed her name on that mortgage agreement, she'd have everything she needed in life. As much as her mother believed Zoe needed a man, she felt satisfied, complete, all on her own.

Although Zoe's mother had lived in the United States for over thirty years, her family's traditional Japanese beliefs were as ingrained as a thread in a zanshi weaving. Such old-school ideals baffled Zoe, who had been born and raised in America. She wasn't sure she'd ever find common ground with her mom.

She followed the highlighted area on her map to the main aisle, the highest traffic area set aside for the biggest names in the industry. She'd been lucky enough to snag one of the tables set aside for up-and-comers to help give their businesses a boost. It was probably that piece the local paper did on her after she planned the San Francisco Fire Department's Christmas fundraiser.

Zoe didn't consider herself new to planning by any means, but she'd only officially opened her business a few years ago. Before that, she'd helped plan friends' parties and weddings. It was one of those rare instances when people complimented and celebrated her meticulous nature instead of rolling their eyes. So, she'd decided to put her special talents to good use and get paid for it.

Her gaze flitted around the unoccupied spaces, scanning the place cards for her own company's sign: Plum Crazy Events. But her excitement gradually morphed into confusion. None of the open stalls displayed her name.

Something rustled beneath Zoe's next step: a discarded place card. The tape clung to her black suede heels.

She peeled it off and was about to throw it away when the words caught her eye. *Zoe Plum. Plum Crazy Events.*

"What the …?"

"Zoe?!" a shrill voice called out. "Is that you? Oh my gosh, it's so good to see you."

She turned to find a familiar brunette approaching her. Chelsea Carruthers, her rival—a term Zoe used loosely. And here she'd been in such a good mood.

"Rival" was more of a self-proclaimed title Chelsea had given herself. Maybe because she burned with jealousy that

Zoe held more notoriety in the wedding circuit despite putting less time in. Maybe because Chelsea hoped to bully her out of the business. Or maybe because she just wanted to make Zoe's life miserable.

"Hello, Chelsea. It's nice to see you." Zoe gave her a smile that would never be mistaken for a real one.

A haughty look puckered Chelsea's pinched face as she took in the bride and groom mannequins. Zoe wondered if that was her natural expression or if the tight bun at the back of her head had stretched her skin too tight.

"I see you brought your friends along," Chelsea said. "But if you want to make your booth look popular, these two won't fool anyone. Because let's face it. You're not that popular." She tittered at her own joke. "My booth, on the other hand, will be the talk of the expo. People will line up all the way to the lobby."

She waved a hand at her own setup. A garish banner hung over the booth, screaming *Enchanted Events* at anyone who passed by. The backdrop of sequined curtains dripped with glittering hearts and streamers, oozing a cheesy, high school dance atmosphere.

Zoe tuned her out as she studied her map. By her second time counting the tables, there could be no doubt. "This is supposed to be my booth."

Chelsea's penciled eyebrows shot up to her hairline. "Oh, no. How embarrassing. Didn't anyone tell you? You've been relocated."

Zoe narrowed her eyes at the woman. "To where?"

"Oh, I don't know. Somewhere way, way, way over there in the back corner." She gestured vaguely.

Zoe gritted her teeth. She should have expected Chelsea to pull something. But this was bold, even for her. "Funny that the person taking my place just so happens to be you."

"The event coordinator told me first thing this morning. I'm just cooperating." She fluttered her eyelashes. "I guess they decided to give the better space to the better planner." She pointed to her chest in case it wasn't clear who she meant.

Zoe half hoped Chelsea would accidentally stab herself with one of her ridiculously pointy gel nails. She spun her dolly around to head back to the main lobby. "Well, I'll just go find him and straighten this all out."

"Good luck," Chelsea said casually. "I'm sure it's just a simple mix up. Make sure to ask for James. James Carruthers."

Zoe tripped on the aisle runner as the last name sank in. "Carruthers?"

"Yeah, that's right. As in my cousin. What a weird coincidence, right?" She snickered like they were two besties sharing a good joke. "But don't let that stop you. I'm sure he'll side with you over his favorite cousin."

Zoe kept her face straight, except for a sharp eyebrow arch. However, her insides twisted. Something about Chelsea ruffled her calm, orderly feathers.

She quickly pushed the annoyance back down, screwing the cap tight on that bottle-o-crazy. The prime spot wasn't worth fighting over. The doors opened to the public in an hour, and she still had to find and set up her booth by herself. She'd win over her clients because she could offer them more talent and skill than Chelsea ever could. Besides, who could ignore her incredible display replete with a bride and groom?

"Oh, Zoe." Chelsea clicked her tongue as she took in the bride's wedding gown. *Zoe's* wedding gown. "The dress is a bit outdated, isn't it? You know, you should put your best foot forward for these kinds of events. They'll make or break you."

"It's a classic style." She wasn't sure why she was defending her taste to the likes of Chelsea.

"Not with this lace it isn't," she said. "My dress is Chantilly. Nothing but the best." Her eyes sparkled with a secret.

Zoe realized she didn't mean for her display but for her own trip down the aisle. "You mean you've actually found someone to put up with you? Congratulations. I didn't think it possible."

Chelsea bit her lip like she wanted to say more, but she held back for some reason. Instead, she fingered the dress's fabric with distaste. She shuddered. "Is that polyester?"

Zoe tugged the dress away. "Hands off the merchandise."

"You'd better hurry. You don't have long to set up, and it's a very long walk to your booth." She wiggled her fingers. "Bye-bye."

Zoe raised her chin. "You're right. I don't need to waste my time with you. Eventually, your actions will catch up to you. You'll get yours."

She steered her dolly to the other end of the Grand Ballroom. Way, way, way to the other end. After wandering around for what seemed like forever, she located a table with her name hastily scribbled on a sticky note. She set her bride and groom down, dumping the rest of her supplies onto the floor before going back to her van for the rest.

Three trips, six smug looks from Chelsea, and fifty minutes later, Zoe added the finishing touches to her decked-out booth. Combing the wig on her bride's head, she stood back to appreciate the scene. After a moment, her skin prickled with the sense that someone was watching her. Her eyes shifted to the table beside hers.

Reclined in a plastic chair, a guitar resting on his chest, was Levi Dolson.

She gaped at him. "You've got to be kidding me."

He grinned. "Miss me?"

"When …? How …?"

Raising his phone, he snapped a photo of her. "You know, after watching you keep your cool at the wedding last weekend, I thought nothing could catch you off guard. But now I have evidence. It's a good look on you."

He flipped his phone around so Zoe could appreciate the

stunned version of herself. She frowned at the flabbergasted expression on her face.

"What are you doing here?" she asked.

"You knew I signed up for the expo."

She gave him a look. "I mean, right here. This isn't your booth, is it?"

"Why else would I be here? You don't think I'm stalking you, do you?" He winked.

"At this point? Yes, that's exactly what I suspect. It's a strange coincidence that out of all these conference rooms and halls and the hundreds of expo participants, we're assigned to booths side by side."

"So weird, right?" Levi batted his eyelashes at her. "It's like fate or something."

Zoe looked at him sidelong, thinking fate probably had nothing to do with it. "If this is your booth, then where's all your stuff?"

"This is it." He waved a hand over his reclined body. "What you see is what you get."

Actually, what she saw surprised her. He wore T-shirts and crinkled jeans to a wedding, so she expected him to show up to the expo in pajamas. On second thought, he seemed more the au naturel type. That would explain why he'd shown up to the wedding without his tighty-whities. Not that she was imagining him naked ... again.

But Levi had stepped it up. His close shave highlighted his full lips, and the slate gray button-down shirt—with only a few wrinkles—made his blue eyes pop. But as she looked closer, that wasn't the only thing accentuating his eyes; black eyeliner ringed his thick lashes.

Levi's fingers picked at the guitar strings in a random tune, nails black with chipped polish. His hair stuck up as though a windstorm whirled around him. Zoe was certainly blown away. He looked like a rock star who'd just walked off stage. And was that eyebrow always pierced, or had it been the other one?

After tearing her attention away, she faked indifference. "You might want to improve your sales pitch or add some incentives." Though secretly, what she'd seen so far gave her more than enough incentive.

Since she'd met him, every time she pulled out her toys for a little stress relief, her mind kept wandering back to the vestry in St. Dominic's Church. To Levi standing there with nothing but a shirt on. She wondered what he'd done to deserve that red lipstick kiss, what kept him up so late, and what lay under that shirt. She'd get closer, and closer, and then … nothing. Her vibrator remained full of energy, yet she kept fizzling out.

Of course, she tried to imagine something else, anyone else. But Levi's face kept popping back into her head.

It's just curiosity, she told herself. If she could only satisfy it, then she could finally, well … satisfy *herself.*

Zoe mentally slapped herself. She couldn't let him keep her off guard. Today was her big opportunity. She had to remain focused—and not on the sexy musician.

Tapping the edges of her pamphlets, she set them perfectly in line with her display. She sensed Levi watching her from the next table, but she was far too busy to pay any attention. She wasn't aware of his blue eyes running up and down her long legs. And she didn't care why, out of all the tables in the twenty-thousand-square-foot venue, he'd ended up next to her. Nor did she let the fact that he seemed at ease bother her.

"Don't you have to get ready?" she asked. Okay, so she was paying attention to him. "The expo's about to begin, and you're just sitting there."

"That's not true. I'm warming up." He plucked a few strings as he walked over. "I was thinking … maybe we should team up. I can sing romantic songs while you go through your sales pitch. Like background music. It will help put people in the moment, you know?"

Perching on the edge of her table, all dramatic-like, he played a couple of riffs. He gave her a goofy grin.

Zoe pushed him off the table but laughed at the image of him serenading her clients. "You can definitely stay out of my moment."

Wandering through her booth, he popped the top hat off the mannequin's head and slipped it on his own. "Why are you so worried about today, anyway?"

"I'm not worried. Everything will go perfectly." She snatched the hat off his head, placing it back on her groom. "I'm prepared, I'm confident, and my reputation is known throughout the city—despite the wedding from hell last weekend," she added. "The expo will be the boost I need for my business."

"If you're not worried, then maybe you should have a seat and relax."

Zoe exhaled a breath she didn't know she was holding. "You're right."

She flopped into her chair just as a voice boomed through the speaker system overhead.

"Attention. The doors will open in five minutes."

Zoe watched Levi poke around her display, reading pamphlets and smelling the rose-scented candles.

"Why did you really sign up for today?" she asked him.

"It's lovely to see you again too." And his pleasant grin supported that claim. "I'm a musician. Weddings are my bread and butter. You know, until I make it big." He said it like it was only a matter of time.

"I haven't heard you play anything but an organ," she said, "but I'll admit you did … pretty good."

He considered her reserved answer before nodding. "I was pretty amazing, wasn't I?"

Zoe laughed, but it was true. He'd totally saved her butt. However, she wouldn't tell him that. He didn't need any more encouragement than he found on his own. Okay, so maybe she encouraged him by flirting back too much. But in a very dry, so-not-impressed way. Well … maybe she was impressed, a lot, but she wouldn't let him know that either.

No more flirting, she told herself. It wouldn't be right. She'd only lead Levi on. Besides, once the expo ended, she'd never see him or his rock-hard abs ever again.

Just then, a well-timed distraction arrived: her first customer. She turned on her best you-can-count-on-me expression. However, it turned out to be just her assistant. Zoe's look melted into her no-nonsense business face.

"I am so sorry I'm late," Natalie said. "My car broke down, and I had to get a boost."

"The tow truck delivers flowers now?" Zoe asked, indicating the giant arrangement Natalie set on the table—right on top of her pamphlets.

"Oh yeah. I broke down next to a flower shop, so I bought our booth a nice centerpiece to make it up to you."

"Peonies. Very nice." Zoe's irritation shrank a little.

She spotted the business card tucked into the blooms. Pushing Daisies, a florist she often used on 16th Street. However, she knew Natalie lived in North Beach. She wouldn't have gone anywhere near that florist on the way to the expo.

"Thanks for the flowers, but next time, I expect a call or text." Noticing a young couple approaching, Zoe set the rest of her "boss" speech aside for later and greeted them. "Hello."

"Hi." The young woman gave a timid wave. "My name is Jessica, and this is Cole." She laid her hand on the chest of the young man next to her. "We're getting married."

The sparkling princess cut set in white gold made that obvious enough. But the way she'd said it, kind of shyly, told Zoe they only recently got engaged and were still getting used to the idea. The woman gazed up at her fiancé like he was the only man on earth.

Zoe had looked that way once, before reality set in. She smiled warmly at the couple. "Congratulations. That's exciting."

"We're thinking of hiring a wedding planner," Jessica said.

Before Zoe could respond with a sales pitch, someone cut her off. "Then the last thing you want to do is hire Zoe Plum. Or you might not get married at all."

The bride-to-be's wistful expression vanished. Natalie shrank in her seat, a wide-eyed, groom-with-cold-feet look on her face. Zoe turned, and when she saw who it was, her stomach somersaulted.

"Juliet," she said between clenched teeth. "What are you doing here?"

The ex-bride glared at her. "Just preventing people from making the same mistake I did in hiring you."

Juliet's hair tangled in a nest of curls and grease, almost as though she hadn't washed it since her wedding day. In fact, she probably hadn't. Zoe noticed she still wore her wedding jewelry —but she was missing one teardrop earring, and her tiara sat askew.

Dark circles ringed her eyes. When she narrowed them hatefully, it looked as though she was sporting two black eyes. Had she slept at all since her wedding day?

Traffic in their far corner was picking up. People browsing booths paused to ogle every bride's nightmare come to life.

As gasps and murmurs whirled around her, Zoe wanted to reach into her purse for her Fuzzy Friend. This was so not what she needed today. Instead, she drew on her years of stuffing unwanted emotions into her inner Zen bottle.

"I'm sorry you're unhappy with how your wedding day turned out, but—"

"Wedding?" Juliet's nostrils flared. "You call that a wedding? It was a circus. And you were the ringleader."

Zoe pressed her lips together to stop herself from saying Juliet had been the clown. "I know things didn't turn out the way you wanted them to, but sometimes we need to be more flexible as in the case with, well … many of your requests."

"It was your job to make my dreams come true!" She jabbed a finger at her, nail bitten to the quick.

"No," Zoe said calmly. "It was my job to give you the wedding you asked for. And I did my job."

"Then why aren't I married?!" Grabbing the vase of flowers off the table, she raised it above her head and threw it on the ground.

The vase smashed at their feet. Natalie screamed. Glass scattered over Zoe's heels.

Water sprayed Jessica, and she inched closer to her fiancé. Both of them seemed too shocked to move.

Levi jumped up from behind his table, hands up like he was approaching a wild animal. "Juliet. It's me, Levi. Owen's friend. Why don't we go somewhere and talk about this?"

Her body shook, stray wisps of hair falling around her face like Medusa. She let out a frustrated, three-year-old's-tantrum scream. It sounded hoarse, like she'd drowned herself in hard liquor since the ill-fated day.

Jessica shifted, dragging her fiancé away. "Maybe we should go."

Zoe held up her hands. "No. Please. It wasn't how she's making it sound."

"It's all true." Juliet's eyes bulged. "I didn't get married because of *you*."

Zoe had had enough of the ex-bride, her demands, her accusations, and her crappy treatment for over a year. She wasn't under contract anymore. It wasn't her job to keep her happy or sugarcoat things.

She raised her chin. "Because of me, you got everything you asked for. Every ridiculous, over-the-top demand. I bent over backward for you. I did everything I could to get you down that aisle. All you had to do was say 'I do.'"

At some point, the young couple had slipped away and disappeared into the expanding crowd. The onlookers gathered closer out of curiosity and some in mild horror.

Maybe it was the appearance of the distraught bride, still sporting her wedding jewelry and bedazzled shoes, frozen in the moment every bride fears might happen: the moment it all falls apart. By the icy stares fixed on Zoe, she could tell the crowd sided with the bride, naturally. However, for her, the situation had brought back memories of her own wedding day, of being left at the altar.

By running away, Juliet had done to Owen what Zoe's ex-fiancé had done to her all those years ago. And because of that, she couldn't find any sympathy for Juliet. The woman obviously had some issues to work through, but she needed to work through them somewhere else.

Juliet's chin quivered, but her lip curled viciously. "How could I possibly say 'I do' when I was distraught over the mess you caused?" She pulled an already used tissue from her purse and blew her nose. "I should sue you."

"Sue me for what? Out of sympathy, I waived a portion of my own fees." Which was more than Juliet deserved after the way she'd treated Zoe.

"I'll sue for the cost of the wedding. Not to mention emotional damage."

Zoe wanted to say the former bride was damaged long before she'd come along, but she bit her tongue to avoid inflaming the situation.

Further down the aisle, a giant man in dark clothes pushed his way past people. A security guard. He looked rather menacing for such a joyful event. Zoe vaguely wondered how often wedding expos got out of hand. Levi waved him over—as if anyone could miss Juliet.

"Is there a problem here?" the security guard asked.

Juliet's appearance made the "problem" obvious. He marched up to her and crossed his arms. However, considering the differences between Juliet and the security guard, he didn't need to turn on the intimidation.

"I'm going to have to ask you to leave," he told her.

"I'm not the problem. She is!" She scowled at Zoe. "I came to warn everyone that hiring Zoe Plum as your wedding planner is the worst decision you'll ever make!"

"All right," the guard said. "Let's go."

But Juliet wouldn't go that easily. She dodged, kicked, and hit the guard. Grabbing a fistful of pamphlets from Zoe's table, she threw them at his chest. Once he cornered her by the tux rental booth, she wheeled on Zoe with a look that said "This isn't over" before going limp.

The security guard barely caught her before she hit the floor. He dragged her out, dirty silk bridal shoes scraping along the floor. A few hundred eyes tinged with pity watched her go.

Once Juliet had disappeared from sight, Natalie slumped in her chair. "That was scary."

"So much for the Fisher-Wells wedding being behind me," muttered Zoe.

"Don't worry," Levi said. "There are so many people attending the expo that it won't even matter. It will work out. You'll see."

"You're giving me the 'It will all work itself out' speech again? It didn't work out so well the last time." Zoe let out a heavy breath. "But I hope you're right." She gave him a grateful smile.

Only the people in their corner of the room had witnessed Juliet's blowup. Within a couple of hours, all-new expo guests eager for her business would replace the witnesses. Even now, she could see curious faces wandering in time to the music from the overhead speakers, like a game of musical chairs. Someone was bound to end up in her silver bride and groom chairs.

A woman passed by her table and picked up her business card. Zoe sat straighter; things were already turning around.

She opened her mouth to greet the woman, but the music was suddenly interrupted, replaced by a female voice. A voice that had Zoe reaching into her purse for her Fuzzy Friend, Darling Dolphin.

"Testing. Testing. I have an announcement to make," Juliet declared. *"Zoe Plum is the worst wedding planner ever. She ruined my wedding day. Don't hire her. She's—"*

"Give me that," a male voice demanded.

"Hey!" she yelled.

"Stop … Don't."

Sounds of a struggle and muffled banging continued for another thirty seconds. A loud electronic squeal pierced the air. Everyone in the ballroom covered their ears. A wild scream blasted through the speakers.

"Ouch!" the male cried.

"Don't hire Zoe Plum …" Juliet's voice trailed off as though she was being dragged away.

Zoe's potential customer turned her attention back to the card in her hands. She blinked at the name before dropping the card on the table and walking away. Levi gave Zoe a sympathetic look.

With a click, the overhead speakers went dead—as dead as her schedule for the upcoming season was going to be.

Chapter Four

LEADER OF THE PACK

Zoe marched down the aisle to the beat of Prince's *Kiss*, flanked by her two besties, Piper and Addison. She noticed everyone's heads turn as they passed. Thankfully, it wasn't because of Juliet's public service announcement. Their attention wasn't on Zoe, but on the woman of the hour, Piper, the bride of the most anticipated wedding of the year: the Summers-Caldwell wedding.

It was time to put Juliet's botched wedding behind her. So what if everyone at the expo heard about the matrimonial mess? So what if they avoided her booth?

Zoe focused on the future—specifically, Aiden and Piper's. Their epic wedding would boost her promotion power by gossip and word of mouth alone. Juliet Fisher who?

Hands reached out as they passed each vendor's stall, thrusting Venetian veils, reception-playlist demos, personalized place cards, and everything a wedding planner could need.

But Zoe declined all the free swag and samples. She already had everything she needed to pull off the most legendary wedding of all time. After all, she'd practically started planning it the day Piper met Aiden, the young CEO of Caldwell and Son Investments.

The couple met when Aiden bought the old dachshund rescue center and Piper was juggling three jobs to put herself through veterinarian school. When she'd lost two of those jobs, Aiden had offered her a position as his dog walker. And the rest was history.

Okay, well, it wasn't quite that simple. But it had all worked out in the end. They got a beautiful new rescue center where Piper could give proper care to sick pups, and the happy couple was now tying the knot.

Reaching into her purse, Zoe pulled out her tablet to consult a numerical, color-coded, categorized list labeled *Piper's Dream Wedding.* She swiped down the exhaustive list with a manicured finger.

With only two weeks left to go, she had mapped the seating, ordered the flowers, and booked the caterer and informed him of Piper's sesame seed allergy. All that remained was to fill the annoying last-minute cancellation by the salsa instructor who broke his leg.

"Zoe!" Piper called out to her.

She turned to find her friends lagging. Not only was she a woman on a mission, but she stood considerably taller than her friends; her long strides always left them in the dust during their shopping trips. Which wasn't a bad thing when a flash sale popped up and time was of the essence.

Piper took a deep breath when she caught up. "Can we slow down?"

"I second that." Addison squeezed past two women fighting over the last wedding cake sample from a bakery vendor. "My feet are killing me. These are new shoes I'm breaking in. Fifty percent off. I just couldn't say no." She grinned sheepishly.

The backpack strapped to Piper's shoulders shifted and writhed until a black-and-tan head snaked out of the open zipper. She never went anywhere without her doxie, Colin. He furrowed his tan eyebrows at Zoe, tired of her quick pace too.

His look seemed to say, *What's the deal? I'm trying to nap in here.*

"Sorry," Zoe said. "But we don't have time. We've got a schedule to maintain. There are too many entertainers to interview." She brought up her list. "Four gymnasts, eight dancers, including belly, flamenco, ballet, and jive. Not to mention eleven artists, a magician, two acrobats, and one fire breather."

Piper blinked. "Fire breather?"

"I threw that one in as a wild card. I wanted you to have options. And besides." She winked. "He performs shirtless. His abs have abs. It's really just an excuse to check him out."

Piper's eyes wandered, taking in the endless booths. "What if we just perused the entertainment section? Maybe something will jump out at me."

Zoe snapped the cover shut on her tablet and locked gazes with her. "Look at me. Stay focused. It's a battlefield out there. If you have any ideas, I'm all ears, but it's best if we keep our blinders on and stick to the original plan. Besides, the longer we wait to book someone, the fewer options we'll have. We need to make our move now, before it's too late."

Piper swallowed. "You make it sound like war."

"It is," she said. "The wedding industry is cutthroat. It's not for the weak-hearted. Now, let's get a move on. I'm sending Natalie to pick up your dress from the seamstress in an hour." She released Piper and made sure Addison was close by. "Are we ready, soldiers?"

Addison and Piper saluted.

Flicking back her auburn hair, Piper fanned it out to hide Colin from sight. He disappeared into the depths of her backpack, probably sniffing out any remaining treat crumbs.

Zoe opened her list again and scanned the alphabetized notes. "Okay, we'll work through the entertainment section systematically. Let's start on the right-hand side and—" She glanced back up and saw a balloon artist distracting Piper and Addison.

Rubber squeaked as the man twisted and spun a long white balloon into several bulges and placed it around Addison's neck like a pearl necklace. Next, he fashioned Piper a wiener dog, resembling the one poking his head out of her backpack to investigate the squeaking sounds.

Zoe frowned and tucked her tablet away. She followed the bride-to-be as she haphazardly zigzagged her way through the aisles.

The bride's happiness was always a planner's priority. If they wanted a hot-air balloon for their wedding, they were going to get it. If they wanted a jousting competition, Zoe would buff the lance herself.

By the time they'd finished wandering the endless rows of booths, Piper still hadn't decided. She said no to the dancers, no to the artists, and no to the acrobats. Finally, they arrived at the Plum Crazy Events booth that Natalie was looking after.

"What about the fire breather?" Zoe asked.

Piper gave her a look. "Definitely no fire breather."

She sighed extra dramatically. "Oh, but those abs. You're missing out."

Levi appeared in front of her. "Talking about me, I see. You know, if you want to see my abs again, all you have to do is ask."

Addison nudged her. "Again?"

Levi grinned childishly as he plunked his guitar strings in a playful tune.

Zoe pursed her lips. "We were talking about finding an entertainer for my friend's wedding." She gestured to Piper.

His fingers froze, the strings humming off key. "What about me?"

She stared at him. "What about you?"

He sidled closer until she could smell his spicy cologne—it smelled like Christmas. "I've been told I'm very entertaining." His voice lowered with insinuation.

"I can't argue with that," she said, not unkindly. One would even say it bordered on flirting.

No flirting, she reminded herself.

Piper's gaze flitted from Zoe to Levi. She crossed her arms with an amused look. "Okay. Show us what you've got."

"Pipe." Zoe widened her eyes in a secret message. An entire hour perusing San Francisco's best collection of entertainers, and *now* she showed interest? In *him?*

Her friend gave her an innocent eyelash flutter as he cleared his throat dramatically and strummed his guitar.

> *"Oh, Zoe Plum!*
> *You make my legs go numb.*
> *My brain goes dumb.*
> *When you're near, my heart goes ba-ba-bum-bum.*
>
> *Ever since you saw me half nude,*
> *I don't mean to be crude,*
> *But you've got me in the mood,*
> *Despite your cool attitude.*
>
> *Miss Plum, you drive me plum crazy.*
> *You make my eyes go all hazy,*
> *And I don't need glasses to see.*
> *My eyes are 20-20.*
> *No-o-o-o! It's because you drive me plum crazy.*
> *Miss Plum Crazy."*

Levi made it up as he went along, but the short pauses sounded dramatic, like they were on purpose. To top off the cheese, he strummed out a hardcore guitar solo that just didn't have the same effect on an acoustic guitar. He finished with a rock star pose, his tongue sticking out, Gene Simmons-style.

Clapping erupted around them. Zoe jumped. A small crowd surrounded them. She hadn't noticed people pause to listen to Levi serenade her. At least they weren't shooting daggers at her like she was a wedding wrecker anymore.

She caught Addison observing her and Levi with the same expression she reserved for their annual viewing of *Love Actually*. It radiated hope and romantic optimism. But Zoe wasn't about to fall as easily as her hopeless romantic friend— emphasis on the hopeless.

"You know, she's the bride-to-be." Zoe indicated Piper with her thumb. "You should be trying to impress her. Not me."

"Oh, you're definitely the one I want to impress." Levi waggled his eyebrows, and his piercing flashed.

She pretended to yawn. "Is that all you've got?"

"The show's only just begun. I'm still warming up." Reaching into the messenger bag behind his table, he drew out a card and handed it to Piper. "This is a download card with a code, so you can get our latest album for free. Keep us in mind."

She checked out the photo on the card. "Thanks. I will."

Zoe snatched it out of her hand and gave her a firm look before slipping behind the table. But as her friends took a seat in her *bride* and *groom* chairs across from her, Levi handed Piper another one.

Zoe turned to Natalie. "Thanks for looking after the booth for me. How did things go while I was gone?"

"Pretty good," she said. "I handed out almost two-dozen business cards to interested people."

"That's great." However, Zoe wondered if Natalie was lying to cheer her up. By the looks of her decorative card-holder display, not a single one was missing.

She was about to toss Levi's download card aside, but then she spotted the picture on the front. In a bold typeface, the words *Reluctant Redemption* scrawled across a photo of the band. Four men leaned against a graffitied brick wall, dressed in your stereotypical rock and roll uniform: leather, jeans, faded shirts, tattoos. Levi stood in the center of the group.

Levi Dolson wasn't just a cheesy wedding singer-slash-organ player. He was the lead singer of his band. She had to admit, it was kind of hot. But the man flashing her a silly grin from the next booth was at odds with the dark, hardened man in the photo. Something didn't fit.

Piper leaned over the table and lowered her voice. "Why can't we hire this guy? Maybe having a wedding singer would be fun. We can cancel the DJ and hire Levi."

Addison nodded her head enthusiastically. "Besides, he's really cute."

Zoe gave her a look. "You're in a committed relationship, remember?"

"I'm not talking about for me," she said. "I'm just looking out for you."

"I can look out for myself, thanks." Zoe acted busy, rearranging the pamphlets on her table.

Even after all these years, she hadn't let on to her friends the extent of her reluctance to date. Of course, they'd heard her talk about men, watched her flirt with them and accept their numbers. But when it came to the details—of which there were none to share—she kept them in the dark.

She suspected they assumed what most people assumed: that she had *relations* without having relation*ships*. Which was fine with her. It kept them from wanting to "help" her. She was fine just the way she was.

Addison grinned. "I think he likes you."

"Who? AC/Chee-Z over there?" Zoe's eyes flitted to his table.

She giggled. "Yes. Who else?"

Zoe smiled mischievously. "Well, of course he does."

"Come on," Piper said. "Admit it. He's adorable."

"He's annoying." She waved it away, but heat crept over her cheeks. He was annoying like a puppy, too adorable to resist.

Addison flipped through some Plum Crazy Events

pamphlets with a wistful look on her face, probably imagining her own inevitable wedding to her boyfriend, Felix. "He isn't annoying. I think he's the kind of guy that gets under your skin if you *let him*."

She huffed, unwilling to entertain the idea. "Yeah, gets under your skin like a tick. He's persistent, I'll give him that."

"You know what they say," Addison sang. "Persistence pays off."

"Well, not for him," she said with finality.

Her friends shared a meaningful glance, but they dropped the subject.

Zoe and Addison didn't exactly see eye to eye when it came to love and relationships. Despite her history of poor luck with men, Addison still maintained her idealized fairy tale view about happily ever after. And since she'd recently shacked up with her boyfriend and his daughter, it had worked out well for her.

However, Zoe was too practical for that, too realistic. And then … there was the real reason she didn't want to hire Levi: the way he made her feel scared her. He got a rise out of her—both her emotions and her libido.

Used to hiding her feelings, sometimes the good ones would get bottled up with the bad. Some days, she'd even forget to laugh, afraid something else would slip out of her bottle-o-crazy with it. But Levi's corny stand-up comedy show made her feel good. Which was bad. So very bad.

"We'll find something else," she assured Piper. "You are the future Mrs. Caldwell. You deserve nothing but the best. Besides, it's getting too late to make all these changes now. It's bad enough we need to find a new entertainer at the last minute."

Piper frowned. "But you have to admit, he's pretty good. And it might be fun to have live music at the wedding. We wouldn't even need an entertainer."

She crossed her arms. "Look. You hired me to plan you a

wedding fit for the swanky guests Aiden will be inviting. And that means no cheesy wedding singer. I promise, you'll have the classiest wedding in town, or I'll quit the whole damn industry."

"But—"

She held up her hands. "Trust me."

"Do I detect trouble with the Summers-Caldwell wedding already?" A high-pitched voice cut through the air like a spoon clinking a glass at a reception.

Platinum blonde hair flashed among the crowd. Zoe caught a glimpse of a pink-lemonade pantsuit.

Over the hush, someone hissed, "Is that Holly Hart?"

The Holly Hart from Channel Five News emerged from the gathering crowd. Her hand rose as though inviting applause that never came. The other hand held her shivering Chinese crested canine, Jasmine. The dog's pink, hairless skin blended in with Holly's outfit, and the white tuft of hair matched her owner's over-processed locks.

Nearby, a woman cried out as Holly's cameraman nearly knocked her over. He struggled to keep up with all the equipment strapped to him, sweat rolling down his flushed cheeks.

Zoe didn't actually know the cameraman's name. Although she'd had a few run-ins with the local news team, she'd only ever heard Holly call him "Hey You." Not that she cared to get to know the guy. The only time she'd ever spoken to him was to utter explicit threats to his nether regions because he and Holly were harassing Piper.

Holly's eyes landed on the three friends. Her hand flew to her mouth, and she gasped in shock. "I don't believe it. Piper? What a complete coincidence to see you here," she said in a way that made it clear it wasn't a coincidence at all.

She'd written stories about Piper's fiancé long before she became a legit news reporter. Back when she'd worked for the gossip mag *The San Francisco Gate*, she'd followed Aiden along his trail of sordid escapades—pre-Piper, of course. But that wasn't him anymore. He'd found the woman he wanted to settle down with and was ready to give Holly the shake, once and for all. But she had other plans.

Ever since the wedding announcement in the paper, the local reporter had hounded Zoe for details. Obviously, she was getting desperate because she'd tracked down Piper herself.

Holly sidled closer. "How is the future Mrs. Caldwell?"

"I was thinking of hyphenating," Piper mumbled, clearly not pleased to see her.

As though Colin could sense a disturbance in the force, he growled inside the backpack.

The reporter ignored both of them. "So, the countdown begins. Only two weeks until the big day. Tell me, Piper. Any pre-wedding jitters? Cold feet perhaps?"

"No. Just a cold shoulder." She turned her back on the reporter.

Zoe shared an eye roll with her friends. "Why don't you get out of here before this gets ugly? I need to get back to work anyway."

Ready to play defense so her friends could escape, she stood up. A second later, a weight settled on her shoulders as Levi slung his arm around her.

"Aren't you going to introduce me to your friend here?" He indicated Holly with a chin thrust.

Zoe flung his arm off her. "Why would I do that?"

"I thought we were a team."

She rubbed her temple. "We're not a——"

He lunged forward, holding his hand out to Holly. "Levi Dolson, front man for the band Reluctant Redemption." He gave her a winning smile. "You've probably heard of us. And before you ask. Yes. I'd be happy to do an interview."

The Chinese crested in her arms growled, its teeth flashing. Levi pulled his fingers back an inch.

She brushed his hand aside. "Never heard of you. And no one wants to hear about your little a cappella group."

He frowned. "Rock band. Been around for years. On the precipice of breaking out. Nationally. No, globally." He spread his hands through the air. "We just need a little exposure, is all. You want in on the action?"

"I can find my own action," she told him.

He shoved his hands in his pockets. "Your loss."

She wrinkled her nose. "I don't think it is."

"Trust me," Zoe said to Levi. "You don't want to get mixed up with Holly Hart."

"Ouch," Holly said in mock hurt. "And here I thought we were friends?"

Zoe crossed her arms. "Friends?"

She held a hand to her chest like she'd just been shot. "Addison, who helped you get your business back on track when you were accused of stealing all those show dogs last year?"

Addison scoffed. "You were the one who accused me of stealing them in the first place."

The reporter had taken the accusations of a few angry dog owners and run with it, turning San Francisco against Addison. It took only a two-minute-long smear segment, and her dog-spa business and promising Fido Fashion line had faced obliteration.

Holly barely skipped a beat. "Any publicity is good publicity. Besides, you got your boyfriend Francis out of it all."

"Felix," Addison corrected.

"Whatever." She waved away the detail. "And Piper, you got all those donations for your precious dachshund rescue center thanks to my amazing reporting skills and enormous viewership." She gave her a light punch on the arm, chuckling genially. "You're welcome, by the way."

"That's true," Piper relented. "But your enormous viewership is thanks to us and your exploitation of our misfortunes." She slipped on her backpack, preparing to leave.

"Now, no one likes a bragger." Holly held up a finger.

"Let's not quibble about semantics. So, Zoe, what do you say about an exclusive?" She nudged her with a chummy elbow. "A sneak peek of the wedding? You know, a few spoilers of the happy couple's big day?"

"I'm a contender for the entertainment," Levi offered.

"Is that so?" She faced him with a flash of interest.

"No, he's not," Zoe said.

She threw her hands up. "Then give me *something*."

Zoe raised an eyebrow. "I don't think so."

"Oh, come on," she persisted. "Think of the mutual benefits. Maybe a couple segments leading up to the big day. Imagine the promotional opportunities for your event-planning business." She plucked a pamphlet off the table and flipped through it.

Zoe rounded the table and snatched it back. "My business is doing just fine, thanks."

Holly frowned. Or rather, it would have been a frown if not for all that filler and Botox. She looked pointedly around at all the clients *not* lined up for her booth. "Well, remember, it's tit for tat. You scratch my back, and I'll scratch yours. You know where to find me." With a snap of her fingers, she beckoned Hey You and disappeared into the crowd with her dog.

Addison watched her go. "After what she did to my business last year, I'd never trust her. She'd as soon stab you in the back as scratch it."

Zoe replaced the pamphlet on the table. "Trust me. The last thing I need is to tango with Holly Hart. Good PR be damned."

"I appreciate it," Piper said. "Aiden and I have taken up enough real estate in the papers and on gossip sites lately. We want to keep the wedding as quiet as possible."

She crossed her heart. "Absolutely. Low-key. Private. Everything will be perfect. I promise."

"I know." Piper wrapped an arm around her. "Because you're planning it."

Zoe gave her a grateful look, ready to do everything in her power to live up to Piper's faith in her. Especially after what they'd been through over the years. When Zoe's father died, Piper had been her rock. After all, she'd gone through it herself, so she understood what Zoe was experiencing. She was there to help her through every rough moment of it.

Now came Zoe's turn to be there for her, to show her exactly how important their friendship was. To give her the perfect wedding. "I won't let you down. I promise."

"Oh …" Addison sniffed as tears welled in her eyes. She pulled them in for a hug.

"I love group hugs." Levi pretended to lean in. "Oh, you mean just the three of you. Okay. That's cool. I'll be over here."

The girls laughed. Even Zoe. Addison was right; the guy was persistent.

Just as Zoe relaxed, thinking the weekend might still turn around, she spotted Holly farther down the aisle. The reporter pointed to her own piercing eyes, and then at Zoe, in an "I'll be watching you" gesture. This wasn't over.

Chapter Five

SAME SONG AND DANCE

Ding!

The Hilton logo on the doors parted in front of Zoe to reveal a blissfully empty elevator. It had been a long day with little to do in her far, far, far corner at the expo. By the time most people had reached her booth, they'd already found a wedding planner.

Stepping inside, she hit the button for her parking level. Leaning back, she rested her head against the mirrored wall. The doors slid closed, but they jerked to a stop at the last second.

Her eyes flew open. A hand poked through the nearly closed doors. When they slid apart, Levi stood on the other side, his guitar bag strapped to his back.

He looked as tired as she felt, but when he saw her, his face reanimated. "Hey."

"Hi," she said. "I thought you went home already. How was the rest of your day?"

"Great," he said. "I worked the room. You know, wandered around the place, serenading random people. Got a few contacts, some interested clients. How was yours?"

Zoe blew out a breath, watching the floor numbers light up

as they descended. "I didn't sign a single contract. I need a new plan. Today was a complete bust."

"That's not true," he said. "You got to see me again."

"Of course." She smirked. "How could I forget that? Considering you were strangely assigned to the table next to me. Somehow. Randomly ..." she fished, hoping he'd shed some light on the situation.

But he wasn't biting. "It's true. I'm unforgettable," he said humbly.

"You are that. But mostly because you never go away." She grinned mischievously as they got out of the elevator to let him know she was kidding. Which was a first, really.

Mostly when she told men to screw off—and that was often —she meant it. But Levi was different from most guys who hit on her. Sure, he flirted with her a lot, but in an entertaining way. It wasn't the smarmy propositions she received any time she and the girls went out on the town. It was respectful and ... cute.

"Well, you'd better get used to me hanging around," Levi told her. "Because once you listen to my album and discover how amazing I am, you'll hire me."

"Don't hold your breath."

She headed for her van, and he walked with her. She doubted they'd parked next to each other—unless he'd somehow set that up too.

"That's okay. I'm a patient man," he said.

"You'll be waiting a long time, my friend," she threw back at him.

"I know when something's worth waiting for."

She laughed. "Do those lines work on the women at your gigs?" She imagined, for some women, all he had to say was "I'm in the band" and their clothes would magically fall off. Well, she wasn't like them.

Zoe didn't want to hurt him, but he couldn't take a hint. She wasn't interested. In *anyone*. Sure, she'd considered doing the no-strings attached thing on more than one occasion. In fact, Levi made her reconsider that as an option. But maybe that was her built-up sexual frustration talking because, ever since she'd met him, her usual toys weren't working. Just one more reason to leave the guy in the dust. So things could get back to status quo.

"What have you got to lose?" he asked. "Just give me a shot."

She gave him a sly grin. "Are you talking as a man or as a musician?"

"Both."

"I'm sorry, but we don't need a musician, just the entertainment. We've already hired a DJ."

He beamed like she'd just given him the best news. "So, Levi the man has a chance."

Zoe snorted, but she didn't know what she could say that wouldn't give him the wrong idea, wouldn't lead him on. Because that's not what she wanted. Was it?

As she approached her van, she shook off the doubt. Of course she didn't want that. She'd been sure of it for years. That didn't change just because some sexy musician walked into her life. Or because she couldn't satisfy herself without imagining them back inside St. Dominic's vestry with the door locked. It didn't change a thing.

"Well, this is me," she said, already taking her keys out.

She waved goodbye and tried to get to her van, but a group of hotel guests lingered in the middle of the parking area, blocking her path. After a long day with nothing better to do than ogle Levi, she wanted to put some distance between herself and the rocker, to get some perspective. Out of sight, out of mind, right?

"Excuse me." She squeezed through a couple of people. "Sorry. Excuse me." She maneuvered through the crowd, weaving through them. They didn't seem to be doing anything. Just standing around.

A woman on her phone noticed Zoe and covered the mouthpiece. "Is this your van?"

"Yes …" A bad feeling crept over her.

"Don't worry," the woman said. "I'm already on the phone with the police."

"What for?" Frowning, she pushed forward to get a better look.

People finally noticed her and moved out of her way. Their feet kicked up something white that fluttered over the pavement like fresh snow. Zoe looked closer: silk flowers. *Her* silk flowers. They decorated the pavement as though a herd of flower girls had paraded by.

Her heart raced as she followed the trail. The last of the gathered looky-loos made way for her, opening up the scene like curtains drawing. But it was a tableau of a tragedy.

Zoe's jaw dropped, and she stepped closer. Her van's back doors gaped open. The contents spewed out as though it had vomited a wedding day: torn table runners, broken photo props, shattered crystal vases, bent candle holders, and shabby chic décor—now too shabby to ever be chic again.

But the worst thing, the thing that made her heart stop dead in her chest, was the white gossamer and lace fabric hanging out of the back and down the bumper like a dead body. Piper's wedding dress.

"No, no, no." Zoe automatically reached out for it.

Someone grabbed her hand and held it back. It was Levi.

"Don't touch it," he said. "The police are on their way. You don't want to disturb the crime scene."

Instead of pushing him away, her hand tightened around his. "But the dress," she breathed. "It's ruined."

"It's okay," he said. "You can order another one."

"No. You don't understand. Wedding dresses are ordered months, sometimes a year in advance. The wedding is in two weeks."

Piper's dress drooped lifelessly, the tattered shreds dangling on the greasy pavement. It had been perfect. A Vera Wang. There was no replacing that dress. Not with only two weeks left to go. To get a dress in that time frame, Zoe's best friend would have to resort to getting a dress—she gulped—off the rack. It was a disaster.

What bad luck. Why did the dress have to be ready that day? Why did she have to send Natalie to pick it up?

The telltale click of a camera going off on someone's phone tickled Zoe's ears. She searched for the source. Holly Hart hovered next to the scene, snapping off photos of the wreckage with her phone.

"That wouldn't be Piper Summers's dress, would it?" She grinned like a kid on Christmas.

Zoe swiped at the phone. Holly danced away before she could grab it, her fingers moving in a blur as she typed something on the screen—probably a new post about how Zoe just ruined her best friend's wedding.

Zoe's fists clenched as she marched after her, but Levi blocked her path. "Ignore her. She's going to write about it either way."

She glared at the reporter but relented. "You're right. I don't want to give her more material against me."

Shoulders slumping, she turned back to her van. Her body ached to take action, to do something, but there was nothing she could do until the cops arrived. As the crowd slowly dispersed, she compiled a mental list of dress shops to call on Monday morning. After a few moments, she sensed Levi hovering next to her.

Zoe checked her watch. It was past eight o'clock on a Friday night. Surely, he had some gig to get to or band party to attend.

"Don't feel obligated to stay," she told him. "The police are on their way."

He shrugged, his usual easygoing response. "I thought you could use a ride."

She blinked at him. Only five minutes ago, she'd rejected him, and he was being so nice. "That's a kind offer, but I imagine I'll be here for a while with the cops."

"They could take a bit to get here. In the meantime, you look like you could use a coffee."

The corners of her mouth turned down.

"Dinner?" He tried again. "How about a drink?"

She laughed humorlessly. "I could definitely use a drink, but it will take more than a couple to end this day on, so I'd best wait until I get home."

"Great. I'll drive." He proffered his arm for her to take.

She let his arm hang there. "You don't give up, do you?"

"Should I?"

She frowned. "What?"

"Do you want me to give up?" he asked. "Because you pretend like you do, but I can't tell if that's just an act, since you flirt back. You strike me as a pretty direct person, so give it to me straight."

Zoe opened her mouth, but no sound came out. Hadn't she basically rejected him both personally and professionally? Wasn't it obvious enough? Okay, so maybe she'd flirted with him far too many times. And now, for some reason, she couldn't find a simple answer, like "Yes, give up."

Her phone rang, saving her. "Hold that thought."

She glanced at the screen before answering. She didn't recognize the number, which made her worry all the more; it was just one of those days.

"Hello?"

"Hello. Is this Zoe Plum?" a male voice on the other end asked.

"Yes, this is Zoe."

"You're listed as the emergency contact for a Junko Plum."

The name rang in her ear. Her heart clenched as everything else melted away, replaced by a torrent of worst-case-scenario visions.

She took a steadying breath and said, "She's my mother. What's happened?"

"She's had an accident. She's in the emergency department at San Francisco General Hospital."

"I'll be there right away. Thank you."

Zoe threw her phone into her purse and, without thinking, headed to her van. The sight of it brought her up short. She hesitated, shifting from foot to foot. All she could focus on was the fact that her mother was in the hospital. *The hospital.* She needed to get to her right away.

When she spun around, Levi was there. He took in her expression, and his face transformed. For the first time since she'd met him, he looked dead serious.

"Can I give you that ride now?"

Chapter Six

DOG DAYS

The emergency room reeked of antiseptic, bleached linen, and cool indifference. Zoe hated that her mother was in there, being taken care of by strangers. Her legs twitched with impatience, but Nurse Derrick led the way at a glacial pace.

Her phone buzzed: a private number. Probably the police wondering where she'd gone. She'd left before they'd arrived at the scene. She ignored the call; they could wait. Funny how a phone call from the ER could shift priorities in an instant. Vera Wang who?

Levi had been really sweet on the drive to the hospital, trying to distract her with small talk like everything was cool, no big deal. But she could tell he was rushing because his van's tires squeaked around the corners, and a few lights turned red before they'd cleared the intersections.

Maybe that was just his way. The more serious things got, the more relaxed he became, balancing out the situation. At least, he'd helped to balance Zoe out on the way there.

Once they'd arrived, he'd insisted on staying. And to Zoe's surprise, she didn't argue. Knowing someone was there made her feel less alone in her moment of need, even though she barely knew him.

The nurse paused at a privacy curtain pulled across an exam bay and peeked inside. "Mrs. Plum, your daughter is here."

Too anxious to wait for an answer, Zoe grabbed the curtain and whipped it aside. When she saw her mother lying on the gurney, it brought her up short. At least, the person hooked up to the various beeping monitors and whirring machines resembled her mother. However, at the moment, Junko Plum appeared so small and helpless, suddenly older. Her cropped, graying hair hung lifeless and unkempt, and she wasn't wearing a stitch of makeup, which was why her swollen black eye stood out starkly against her pale skin.

After a stunned moment, she rushed to the bedside. "Okaasan."

"Zoe." Her mother reached out a hand.

She took it and squeezed tightly. Was it her imagination, or did her mother's hand feel smaller, frailer?

She grabbed the plastic chair next to the bed and dragged it closer before sitting. "How are you feeling? Are you all right?"

Junko waved away her daughter's concern. "Daijoubu."

She frowned. "You're not all right, Mom. You're in the hospital. What happened?"

"Zoe." Her eyes flicked meaningfully toward the nurse, who was swapping out her empty IV bag for a fresh one. "Nihongo de."

She gave her mom a look. "It's fine. He's the nurse. We can speak English."

Her mother's mouth pressed into a firm line. Gripping the stiff hospital sheet, she pulled it up to her chin like it could protect her from prying ears.

"Nihongo de." She widened her eyes.

"Okay," Zoe replied in Japanese. "What happened?"

"I just had a little fall."

"You fell? How?"

"I felt tired and must have tripped," she said. "I'm fine."

"You're not fine. Look at this shiner." Zoe touched a gentle thumb to the dark patch around her mother's eye, and her mother flinched.

It was as though her mom thought she could hide what was going on, as if the ambulance attendants who brought her there hadn't caught on or the tests they ran wouldn't have told them everything. The IV dripping into her arm, the monitor displaying her vital signs … it was all just a misunderstanding.

Zoe rubbed a rough hand over her face. "Ever since dad passed away, you've had ailment after ailment. And last month, you accidentally locked yourself out of the house for five hours."

Junko's eyes crinkled at the mention of her late husband. "Your father kept me young."

"Dad's not around anymore," she said. "You can't keep going on like this. I'm worried about you."

The nurse slipped out, but Junko continued to speak in Japanese. "It's you I'm worried about." She placed a hand on Zoe's cheek. "One day, I'm going to be gone, and you'll be all alone. You're well into your thirties—"

Zoe rolled her eyes. "I just turned thirty."

"—And are unmarried," she said like she didn't hear. "Who is going to take care of you?"

"I can take care of myself. This is the twenty-first century. I don't need a man." Zoe leaned back in her seat, annoyed at having the same old conversation at a time like this. "And how did this become about me?"

Her mother picked up the spare blanket at the foot of the bed and folded it. "I had hoped Sean was the one."

"Well, he wasn't," she said.

"He almost was."

"Almost? It's not like there's a fine line between showing up for your wedding day and leaving your bride at the altar. It's pretty cut and dry."

"Zoe." Her mother fixed her with a hard stare. "I am your mother. You will listen to what I have to say."

She straightened in her chair. Conversations with her mother were usually puzzling, a minefield of poorly masked guilt and jokes that weren't really jokes. Yet today, Junko's candor surprised her. Maybe she was too tired to put on a false pretense. Or, maybe, Zoe worried, it was because her mother knew something about her health that she didn't.

Junko's chin rose. "It's time we discussed the deal we made after your father died."

She frowned. "What deal?"

"You agreed that if you were still single by the time you turned thirty, you would consider letting me set you up."

She gaped at her mother. "You're lying in a hospital bed right now, and you want to set me up on a blind date?"

"Not at all."

Zoe slumped against the stiff plastic backrest. "Good."

"I was thinking more of an arranged marriage."

"What?" she choked.

Her mother's expression remained firm beneath the oxygen tube running below her nose. Zoe's heart sank as she remembered that she had, in fact, made that promise—more or less.

It had been two weeks since her father's death. Zoe had checked in on her mother and found her wandering restlessly around the house, looking like she didn't know what to do now that he was gone. The normally fastidious home was a mess, and so was her mother.

To have found her like that, alone and lost, had stirred something in Zoe. On top of her own sense of loneliness without her father and the rejection at the altar less than a year before, fear had gripped her. Fear that maybe she would end up alone, that she'd struggle through the rest of her life without a partner to get through it with.

Her usual resolve had wavered, and her defenses had lowered. This had made her vulnerable to her mother's poking and prodding, her little lighthearted comments and jokes about being single—though Zoe understood her mother well enough to know she wasn't really joking.

When Junko proposed an arranged marriage, the idea had freed Zoe of the fear. If her prospects in life didn't improve by the age of thirty, then it guaranteed she wouldn't end up isolated and alone.

Of course, time heals all wounds, and she soon forgot her promise. Forgot her terror of being alone. In fact, it became easier to trust in that loneliness. If she never found a man, she'd never be susceptible to abandonment, either by choice or by death. She couldn't grieve for something she'd never had.

But as a master of manipulation, her mother knew how to take advantage of situations, even laid out in a hospital bed. It was all out of love, of course. She was looking out for her daughter's best interests. Or rather, her own version of it. Surely, she didn't expect Zoe to make good on a promise she'd made five years ago.

"His name is Taichi Kimura," Junko said.

Zoe's insides clenched. Apparently, that's exactly what her mother expected.

"Your aunt in Kyoto is good friends with his mother. He went to university here in America and is moving to San Francisco to open his own architecture firm."

Zoe ran her hands through her hair. Her mother actually had someone picked out. "Arranged marriages are archaic."

"They are still practiced," she said matter-of-factly.

"Maybe in Japan."

"You're Japanese. Or am I so unwell that I'm hallucinating and you're not my daughter?" Her mother giggled.

Zoe didn't find it very funny considering her current state. "I'm also half American."

"And you're also thirty," she said. "And single."

They'd come full circle. This was the kind of roundabout conversation Zoe was used to having with her mother. She wanted to point out that thirty and single wasn't unusual in America. People married later and later all the time—she was an expert on weddings, after all. But she didn't use that argument, since she didn't plan on marrying at all.

"Whatever happened to marrying for love?" she asked evasively.

"Love can grow in time," Junko said. "But you need a good partner if you want to build a strong foundation for that love."

"But you married Daddy for love. Weren't you happy?"

Her mother's face softened. "Very happy. And I got a wonderful daughter out of it. Most days," she joked—sort of.

Zoe rolled her eyes.

"Give it a chance. You don't want to go through life alone. It's comforting to have someone who will be there for you."

"Ah-ha!" She held up a finger. "Technically, I agreed only if I couldn't support myself by the time I was thirty. If my prospects and situation hadn't improved from when Sean left me."

She remembered her promise had nothing to do with romance, with craving male company—those had been the last things on her mind after Sean.

Her mother's lips puckered thoughtfully. "And what is different about your life now compared to five years ago?"

She took a breath, preparing to give her a long list of all the ways she'd become more self-sufficient, more financially stable, more independent. She had her own thriving business now, after all. Well, it was supposed to be thriving, but ever since the Fisher-Wells wedding, things looked bleak. And since she'd waived part of her commission fees, who knew when she could afford to buy a home. The expo didn't exactly look promising …

The silence dragged out, the rhythmic beeping from her mother's monitors marking the passing seconds like a count-down timer. When Zoe took too long to answer, her mother laid a hand on her arm.

"You've tried very hard," she said. "But this marriage will be beneficial. You will see. Don't think of it as a marriage. Think of it as a partnership. A business relationship."

She spoke like it was a done deal. How did she always turn these conversations around?

Zoe opened her mouth to say she didn't want either of those things. Not from Taichi Kimura. Not from anyone. But the curtain swished open, interrupting them.

A woman in a lab coat stepped into the partitioned space. Her thick brown hair sat atop her head in a sloppy bun. A pair of glasses slid down to the end of her nose as she read a tablet screen.

She glanced up and noticed Zoe. "Oh, hello. You must be Junko's daughter, the wedding planner we've heard so much about."

Zoe eyed her mom, wondering how much she'd told them. "That's me. Zoe." She held out a hand.

"Dr. Neilson." The doctor shook it. "Your mother said it would be all right if I update you on her condition. Would you mind stepping outside with me for a moment?"

"Sure." She looked back at the bed before following, but her mother averted her gaze.

Zoe followed the doctor, dodging nurses and physicians who rushed from one curtain to the next. Dr. Neilson found a quiet corner before turning to Zoe.

"Your mother had quite the fall outside her home this evening," she said. "A neighbor called the ambulance. We're still doing tests, but I'm fairly certain the cause was a transient ischemic attack or TIA for short."

"What is that?"

"Like a miniature stroke, a temporary lack of blood flow to a part of the brain."

Zoe swallowed hard. "A stroke?"

Something was really wrong with her mom; she had an actual diagnosis and everything. It felt far too real. Her mother couldn't leave her too. Who else would guilt trip her about men?

"With TIAs, the symptoms are usually temporary," Dr. Neilson said reassuringly. "Your mother's symptoms have mostly resolved, but this is a warning sign. If things don't change, she could have a stroke."

Zoe wanted to grip her by the collar and yell, *Well, do something!* "What happens now?"

"I've ordered a few more tests to determine the cause. I suspect it's partially due to her high blood pressure, but her readings could be off because she seems anxious."

Zoe nodded. "Yeah. She's not comfortable here."

"I understand, but to get a better picture of what's going on, I'd like her to stay in the hospital over the weekend. However, she seems resistant to the idea." By the look on her face, Dr. Neilson probably meant something more like "stubborn as a mule."

Zoe cringed. "My mother is very private and doesn't like to be a bother to anyone."

"If you can convince her to stay, that would be my recommendation."

She nodded, ready to strap her mother to the bed if she needed to. "I'll try. Is there anything else I can do?"

"There will be the long-term care to consider," Dr. Neilson told her. "It's important she follows doctor's orders, takes her medications, makes changes to her lifestyle, that sort of thing. She'll need a lot of support."

"I pop in regularly," Zoe said. "Maybe a few times a week. Do you think I should stay with her for a while?"

The doctor pursed her lips before making a vague sound. "It's hard to say. If she's independent and able to take care of herself, then I don't see why you would have to. Every situation is unique."

Nurse Derrick approached. "Sorry to interrupt, but the patient in bed five returned from medical imaging."

Dr. Neilson gave a curt nod. "Thank you." She turned back to Zoe. "For now, the best thing you can do is ensure she remains as stress free as possible."

"No stress," she assured her. "I can totally do that. Thank you."

"I'll be in touch. Excuse me," she said, already moving away.

"Sure."

Zoe returned to her mother's bedside. When she slipped through the curtain, Junko's eyes were closed, her breathing deep and slow. She must have been tired if she could sleep through all the racket in the emergency department.

As Zoe took a seat in the cold plastic chair, she stared at her mother's bruised face. Anxiety tugged at her insides. The possibility that she could lose the only family she had left felt too real.

That old fear of being alone crashed over her. As she focused on taking deep breaths, she knew that if she were hooked up to her mother's monitors, alarm bells would be ringing. Her hand slid into her purse and wrapped around Darling Dolphin, and just as quickly as it had come on, the uneasiness washed away.

Junko stirred, groaning as she shifted beneath the rough hospital blankets.

Zoe leaned over her. "Okaasan. Daijoubu?"

"I'm okay." The corners of her mouth turned down, and she held a hand to Zoe's cheek. "I only worry about you, dear. If only I knew you'd be okay when I'm gone, I could rest easy."

"Okaasan …"

"It's okay," she replied in Japanese. "I won't be around much longer to worry about you." She closed her eyes, as though she was ready to cross over right then.

Zoe tugged on a lock of hair. As worried as she was about her mom, she wanted to strangle her for playing up her illness. A classic Junko manipulation.

Stress free, the doctor had told her. Zoe gritted her teeth.

Before she had time to think about it, she blurted out, "I'll do it. I'll go on a date with Kimura-san."

Junko's eyes fluttered open. She searched Zoe's face, squinting as though she couldn't quite see her from two feet away. "You'll consider the arranged marriage?" she asked weakly.

Zoe took a deep breath. "Yes. I'll consider the arranged marriage, if you'll stay here and let them take care of you."

"Oh, well, it means nothing to me, but if that's what you wish," her mother said offhandedly.

She shut her eyes again. After a moment, she appeared to be sleeping. However, it was clear she was faking it because of the satisfied smirk on her lips.

Annoyed, Zoe left before she began ripping those cords out of the wall at random. *No stress. No stress. No stress.* Instead, Zoe was the one who felt stressed.

But as she returned to the waiting room to find Levi, she knew her mom was right—but she'd never admit it out loud. If she allowed herself to dwell on it, she'd been lonely ever since her doxie, Buddy, had died.

She knew something needed to change. That did not, however, mean she needed a man. What she needed was to figure out a way to turn around her recent bad luck and book some clients, make some money, and buy a house. Once and for all, she had to prove to her mother she was fine on her own. Before she wound up walking down the aisle.

Chapter Seven

WELL, DOG MY CATS

The dark streets of San Francisco went by in a blur outside Levi's van. Zoe stared out the passenger window, distracted by the memory of her mother lying in a hospital bed, not to mention thoughts of her upcoming date with her potential future husband.

It was ridiculous. It was absurd. Her chest tightened. Her fingers wrapped around the door handle like she might dive out of the moving vehicle and run away as fast as she could. The moment she reconsidered the entire setup, an image of her mother's black eye popped into her head. With a sigh, she resigned herself to the date once again. At least until her mother was better.

"How is your mom doing?" Levi asked as they approached the Financial District.

The break in silence made Zoe realize she'd barely said two words on their drive back to the Hilton. Guilt stirred inside her; he'd been so nice to stick around and give her a ride.

"She's okay," she said. "It was a mini stroke. The doctor says she'll be all right with treatment, but it will take some major changes in her life. I'll be there to help her through it."

"That's good," he said. "You seem close with your mom."

"She's the only family I have. I've had to look out for her since my dad passed away from a heart attack five years ago."

"I'm sorry."

They'd stopped at a red light. She could sense Levi assessing her from the driver's seat, but she avoided his gaze. "Thanks."

It felt so easy to talk to him, to open up. However, she worried that if she cracked open her emotional bottle, it might all come spilling out. She didn't want to take their relationship there. *No*, she reminded herself, *I don't want a relationship at all.*

"Mom relied pretty heavily on my dad, so I had to take on a lot of his jobs. It sounds like I'll be taking on a bit more until she gets back on her feet. Maybe I'll even move in for a while."

"Sounds like you've got your work cut out for you. I'm sure she'll appreciate your help."

Zoe cringed, wondering how her mother would turn the situation around. First, her plans to buy a home had been delayed. Now, she was moving back home at the age of thirty. Yeah, that looked great. Just what every independent woman strives for.

Levi pulled into the Hilton's underground parking and began the downward spiral to her van. When it came into view, strands of leftover police tape dangled from it. The officers had stuffed most of her belongings back inside and wedged the doors closed.

Before she'd left the hospital, she'd returned the officer's call. He'd understood why she'd taken off and had told her to go to the station the next day to give a statement.

Levi eyed her vehicle as they drew close. "Strange that only your van was hit."

"It wasn't a coincidence. I suspect it was Juliet. Maybe even her mother." Zoe couldn't forget the implied threat Mrs. Fisher had made before walking down the aisle. Maybe she agreed with her daughter and blamed Zoe for the wedding falling apart.

"You think they're capable of doing this?" he asked.

"There's no way to know for sure. On the phone, the police said that no security cameras are aimed this way." She frowned. "With all the extra traffic from the expo, there are a lot of potential suspects. Hopefully, they can narrow it down using the time it was reported."

"You don't think it could have been a random attack?"

"No way." She shook her head. "That dress was a Vera Wang, worth over eleven grand. This is a wedding expo, so chances are, whoever did this must have known its worth or at least had some idea. Instead of stealing it, they mutilated it. They wanted to send a message."

He parked in the space next to her vehicle and leaned back, considering what she'd said. "You think someone out there is trying to sabotage you?"

Her response caught in her throat. The word "sabotage" had her second-guessing her revenge theory. Could it have been a rival? The first person who came to mind was Chelsea.

"Maybe," she said at last.

"Well, from what I saw at the wedding last weekend, something tells me you'll be able to handle whatever's going on."

She pushed aside the questions weighing on her for now and sat up straight. "You know what? You're right. I can handle anything."

"Anything?" His eyebrows shot up before a slow smile crept over his lips. "Can you handle me?"

Zoe snorted. "Oh, I think it's you who can't handle me, rock star."

"Try me." His voice rumbled, deep and low, like when he sang. He leaned in, daring her to "try."

Levi's easygoing nature coaxed her to open up, to tell him things she hardly discussed with her friends. But as he gave her that daring, seductive look, the one he probably used to make his groupies swoon when he was on stage, she could feel herself opening up in a whole new way, tempted toward things she normally avoided. Maybe Addison was right. His persistence might pay off.

Would it be so bad to give in just for one night?

Zoe bit her lip. Levi glanced down to watch her mouth, his own lips parting as though he wanted to do the biting.

The mere thought of him the night before had left her vibrators inadequate, as though her body was telling her it needed the real deal. But it was such a slippery slope. Could she stop after one time? Or would she crave him again and again? And how many times before the lines blurred, before they grew comfortable with each other, stayed the night, met each other's family?

No. She shook her head, chuckling. "Sweetheart, I'd leave you singing the blues."

Zoe opened her door and hopped out. Levi got out, too, as though to walk her all of four feet to her van. And she was going to get in and leave. Really, she was. She planned to drive away from him as fast as she could, to put space between them, so she could get her head on straight again.

But suddenly that space between them grew smaller until they were in each other's arms. She wasn't sure who reached out first, just that she couldn't seem to pull away.

His hands slid over Zoe's hips, and her knees buckled. She braced herself against the van like everything was cool. She was cool. Not at all affected by that cocky smile or the feeling of his hands on her.

Levi's gaze darkened beneath his charcoal eyeliner, and he lowered his face to kiss her neck. His five-o'clock shadow tickled her, deliciously scraping against her skin. Leaning her head back, she closed her eyes and imagined how it would feel rubbing over her body, down her stomach, between her legs.

Warning bells alarmed in her head. She tried to shake off these sudden urges, to push him away. And yet she couldn't stop herself from sliding down the slippery slope that would surely end in Levi's bed.

He smelled amazing. She inhaled him like something she wanted to devour. His lips worked across her neck, her jaw, moving toward her mouth. All she had to do was turn her face and kiss him. To grab him. To tear off his clothes in that parking garage.

Zoe's breathing quickened. Her hands ran up his torso. A second later, he was stumbling back, a surprised look on his face. As surprised as she felt. Without meaning to, she'd pushed him away.

She stared at her hands as though they belonged to someone else. *What was that?*

Maybe it was instinct after so many years. Maybe she wasn't even capable of letting herself have sex anymore.

Belatedly, Zoe laughed like she was being playful and wasn't totally screwed up. "Thanks a lot for the ride. I really appreciate it, but I think we'd better stop."

She fished out her keys. Turning her back on him, she rushed to unlock the driver's door.

"Do you want me to?" he asked.

"What?" She glanced back at him, still dazed, torn between her body's need for Levi and her decision to remain unattached, to keep things uncomplicated. Safe.

"Do you want me to stop?" Levi slipped his hands into his pockets, waiting patiently. "Because you never answered me before. And now, I'm more confused than ever."

As persistent as he was, he hadn't been pushy, overbearing, or handsy like some guys could get when they flirted with Zoe. He hadn't pushed further than she'd allowed him to, than she'd invited with her own behavior. And he wasn't pushing now. He just wanted a clear and final answer. He *deserved* an answer.

All she had to do was say "no," and she knew he would back off. *No.* Zoe had said the word a hundred times to a hundred guys before Levi. It was easy. *No.*

And yet, as his open invitation for rejection hung between them, the word just wouldn't come to her lips. Instead, she opened her door and hopped behind the wheel. "Thanks for the ride."

He chuckled. "That's not a no!" he sang.

She slammed the door shut, grinning to herself as she started up the van. She wasn't sure why she allowed their back-and-forth flirting to go on. Maybe because it had been so long since she'd allowed herself to bask in a man's attention.

But it's wrong, she told herself. It wasn't going anywhere, and she couldn't keep stringing him along. Tomorrow, she would have to be absolutely, 100 percent clear with him.

When the radio tuned in, it was barely a whisper, but the familiarity of the voice coming through her speakers caught her attention. It was Bob. She turned it up. He was making a statement about the most recent San Fran Slayer killings.

"... can assure you we are doing everything we can to bring the person to justice before they hurt anyone else. We encourage people to keep calling with any information that might help us solve this case. Thank you."

Zoe turned down the volume. Bob hid his emotions well while he hung out at the rescue center, but as an expert in masking her emotions, she knew the case was getting to him. She thought about all those poor people lost. Their families just wanted closure, and Bob was desperate to give it to them.

As she drove out of the parking space, she saw Levi pull out after her. He followed her out of the parking garage and up to street level. When she slowed to turn onto Washington Street, her foot hit the pedal wrong. It took a second too long to come to a stop. She regretted not changing out of her heels before getting behind the wheel, but she didn't live far away.

At the first crossroads, the light turned red. This time, when her foot came down on the brake pedal, she realized the problem wasn't her footwear. The brake gave a little resistance before slowly sinking to the floor under her foot.

Her van crawled beyond the stop line like it had a mind of its own. Zoe's heart thudded against her rib cage. She pressed harder. But it was metal on metal. She held her breath as she entered the intersection.

Lights glared through her side window. A car sped through the green light. Tires screeched as it slammed on its brakes. A horn honked.

Zoe braced for impact. Her fingers tightened around the wheel, the leather squeaking in her grip. The car skidded to a stop inches from her door.

It was too dark to see, but she imagined the person yelling and swearing at her inside their cab. She waved her arms frantically at them. But even if they could decipher her gestures, what could they do?

She focused on the path ahead. Her breath turned to lead in her lungs as the severe downward slope opened before her. She instinctively pumped the brake a few more times, but she might as well have been tap dancing. The metal clicked against the floor.

As she coasted toward another red light, she remembered the parking brake. She lifted her foot and applied it steadily. Nothing happened.

"Oh, my God."

She squeezed her eyes shut as she sailed through the intersection. A skipped heartbeat later, she blew through unharmed.

Options flashed through Zoe's mind. For a panicked moment, she considered diving out of the van while it was still cruising slow enough, but in the time it took her to think of it, the van's speedometer rose ten miles per hour.

She wondered if she should crank the wheel and pull a quick U-turn. *No*. At that speed, it would probably roll the van.

Staying the course and slowing down at the bottom wasn't an option, either. Too many crossroads, too many possible T-bones. And this was San Francisco. Who knew when the hill would taper off? The Financial District may have been quiet on the weekend, but it was only a matter of time before she ran out of less-busy streets. And luck.

Farther down the hill, bright lights, colorful banners, and dangling lanterns caught her eye. Chinatown. Headlights whizzing through intersections told her it wasn't a quiet Friday night. But when was it ever?

"Come on, Zoe." She gritted her teeth and gripped the wheel tighter.

Ahead, she spotted a figure silhouetted by the lights: someone crossing the street. She laid on the horn. The pedestrian's head whipped toward her. She saw the whites of their eyes before they leaped out of the way.

Zoe drifted the van closer to the line of cars parked along the street. She nudged the steering wheel, planning to graze the next car. Just a gentle kiss would help slow her down. But when the van connected, it was more like a wham-bam-thank-you-ma'am.

Metal scratched against metal. Plastic siding crumpled. The van jerked, throwing her to the side. Her head cracked against the side window, and stars burst before her eyes.

The wheel jumped beneath her hands. She clamped down and braced for the next vehicle, and the next one. Each time, it threatened to throw her off course. She held it steady, glancing the van off each one to create friction—not to mention a long list of insurance claims.

Gradually, her vehicle slowed, but not quickly enough. The busy streets of Chinatown approached. Erratic shadows and flickering lights hinted at crowded crosswalks.

The next intersection came too soon. Another red light. A long delivery truck passed through, and she was on a direct collision course with it.

No other choice. At the corner, she cranked the wheel for a sharp right turn.

Rubber chirped on pavement. Her body slammed against the door as she felt the tires lift off the ground. For a heart-stopping moment, she thought the van would roll. Then the wheels set down again, slamming her back into the seat.

The steering wheel tore out of her death grip, the van taking off with it. Her world spun. When it came to a stop, she was staring at the grill of the approaching delivery truck.

A deep horn reverberated through her brain. The truck's tires skidded, rubber smoking, the cab juddering.

Zoe's hands flew up. She cringed, expecting glass, flying debris, or a whole truck to come crashing through her windshield. The moment dragged on forever. And then they connected.

A sharp jolt, some rocking. She kept her eyes shut, afraid to open them and find herself in the hospital. But when she finally focused on her surroundings, she marveled at the delivery truck's grill kissing her mostly intact van.

Trembling, she leaned forward and glanced up through her windshield at the truck driver in his cab. He removed his *Sharks* ball cap and ran a hand through his thinning hair. For a moment, maybe longer, they stared at each other in silent communication like "Did that just happen?"

The oddly serene silence broke when her door squeaked open.

"Zoe!"

She jumped at Levi's voice. Had he followed her all this way?

"Thank God." He leaned into the cab, automatically reaching out for her.

Rattled and confused, she moved into his embrace, only to realize he was reaching for the gearshift. He threw the van into park and turned off the engine.

His wide eyes searched her face. "Are you okay?"

"I-I don't know," she stuttered. "I think so. The brakes wouldn't work."

"Come on. Let's get you out of here."

Zoe didn't argue as he unbuckled her and helped her out of the van. Her limbs felt as sturdy as cooked ramen noodles. Her knees buckled, and she slid to the ground.

Levi caught her, wrapping his arms around her. She let him support her weight until they were safely on the sidewalk. Sinking to the curb, she sat with her head between her knees and focused on taking deep breaths.

Something heavy fell around her shoulders. She looked up to find Levi wrapping a leather jacket around her. She hadn't noticed she was shivering, but now the cold set in. Which was strange; the city was trapped in the middle of a heat wave. Numbly, she realized she must be in shock.

Turning her face to the side, she inhaled the cologne imbedded in the jacket's silk lining. The combination of cinnamon and wood smelled strangely comforting. So did Levi's touch as he swept her hair to the side so he could zip up the jacket.

He grasped her trembling hands in his hot ones, and it felt like tucking them into her mother's freshly baked anpan bread. With his scent lingering in the air and his jacket hugging her, she could imagine being in his embrace again.

"Put your hands inside the jacket," he said. "Keep them warm. I'll be right back."

Something in his expression sent heat creeping over her cheeks. His look softened, as if she were something fragile to be coddled, not the strong, independent woman she was. Obviously, it annoyed the heck out of her. However, instead of taking charge, she realized that, for now, maybe she should let someone take care of her. It felt … nice.

Her mother's words popped into her head. *It's comforting to have someone who will be there for you.*

After a moment, Zoe took a deep breath and stood. She stumbled slightly and had to brace herself against a signpost, but she felt a little less like a weakling.

People crowded around, getting out of their cars to help. Or maybe they stopped because they had no other choice— Zoe's van and the delivery truck blocked the entire street.

She watched as Levi weaved through the people and jogged

back to her van. Easing himself onto the ground, he wormed his way along the pavement until his upper body hid beneath the vehicle.

Someone holding a cell phone to their ear stepped out from the crowd. "Hey! You should wait for the police to come," he told Levi, even as the sirens wailed in the distance.

"I'm not touching anything," he called back from under the van. "I'm just having a look." Slipping his phone out of his pocket, he shone the light around the dark undercarriage.

The truck driver approached Zoe, looking as shaken up as she felt. "Are you okay?"

She nodded. "I think so. You?"

"Yeah. You scared me half to death." And she could believe it because he looked a little pale. "What happened?"

"That's the question of the day." She attempted a smirk, but it felt more like a grimace.

Levi got to his feet. He wiped his hands on his jeans and returned to the sidewalk. As his eyes held Zoe's, his brow furrowed, and his mouth screwed up.

"What's wrong?" she asked him.

That concerned look was back, stronger than ever. For a moment, she wondered if this time he really would hug her. In fact, she yearned for it. Especially after his next words.

"Someone cut your brake lines."

Chapter Eight

HOWLING MAD

Zoe tapped her blank notebook with a pen that was becoming gnarlier by the minute with her anxious bite marks. She consulted her watch again. The expo doors had opened an hour ago. Saturday was supposed to be the busiest day of the weekend, and yet no one who had found their way to her far, far, far little corner had shown interest in her booth.

Overnight, her hopefulness for a successful weekend had turned into desperation. The expo had started out as a means to gain more work so she could buy her own home, could be the responsible grown-up she tried to convince her mother she was. Now, all her desires had mutated into needs.

Zoe *needed* to buy a home to prove to her mother she was a success. She *needed* to get out of that arranged marriage without causing her mom stress. She *needed* to undo the negative word-of-mouth created by Juliet's wedding. She also *needed* to find out who was trying to sabotage or possibly kill her.

Things weren't a total bust, however. Natalie had said she'd handed out a ton of business cards the day before. Maybe one of those interested people would pop by that morning.

At the thought of her assistant, she checked the time again.

Ten o'clock and still no sign of her. Zoe knew she needed to have a serious talk with her. Either that or she was going to have to get a new assistant. She added it to the growing list in her head.

- *Talk to Natalie*
- *New dress for Piper*
- *Buy new wedding supplies*
- *Find out who's trying to kill me*

Zoe stared at nothing in particular, the beats of her pen growing louder and faster. The strum of a guitar interrupted her thoughts. Levi perched on the edge of her table, directly in her line of sight. She jumped.

"Zoe's eyes sparkle like the bay.
A smile from her blows me away.
But I don't get one today.
Because she seems kind of gray.
Hey, hey, hey ..."

Zoe cut off his crooning. "Did anyone ever tell you that your tunes are cheesy?"

"They're not cheesy." He laid a hand over his wounded heart. "They're honest."

"If you say so."

Considering the ease with which he played around on his guitar, she suspected a lot of talent hid beneath his cheap rhymes.

He plucked the strings as naturally as one might tap their foot. "Did you listen to my album?"

"I didn't exactly have time between visiting my mother in the hospital, nearly dying in a car accident, and answering police questions until one in the morning."

He heaved a dramatic sigh. "Well, I'll forgive you. This time."

"Now, if you'll excuse me, I have a booth to run." Zoe turned as though she expected someone to approach at any second. It was mostly so she wouldn't get sucked into another flirt session with Levi.

That morning, she'd woken from yet another steamy dream about the musician. Maybe it was all the emotions she'd stuffed into her already-too-full bottle, but for some reason that she couldn't—or refused to—explain, her one release was, well … not *releasing*. Not even Ryan Reynolds was doing it for her. Everyone's face ended up transforming into Levi's.

She felt ready to explode. She just needed to get through that weekend and everything in her life would go back to normal. Without Levi Dolson.

He peered both ways down the aisle, taking in the complete lack of potential clients vying for her attention. "Don't you have an assistant to help you?"

Zoe pulled a face. "I'm supposed to, but she's been unreliable lately."

A woman in a cardigan approached their quiet corner. Her eyes shifted over the row of booths before finally landing on Zoe's. Recognition passed over her face, and she headed that way.

Zoe sat straighter. "See? There. A customer," she told Levi in an "aha" tone of voice. "Now, if you'll excuse me."

He shrugged and returned to his chair, guitar resting on his chest as he strummed at random.

As the middle-aged woman approached, Zoe smiled. "Hello. Can I help you?"

Her focus darted around the booth. "Actually, I wanted to talk to the other wedding planner who was here yesterday."

So did Zoe, but she imagined for different reasons. "Actually, I'm the wedding planner for Plum Crazy Events. That would be my assistant you were speaking with. I'm sure I can take over where she left off." She gripped her pen and held it eagerly over her notebook. Then she wrote the date, just to make it official.

"Plum Crazy?" The woman frowned. "Actually, I want to hire the woman who works for Enchanted Events. I spoke to her here yesterday. Natalie, I think her name was."

Zoe blinked, scrambling to make sense of what she was saying. "Natalie is the name of my assistant, but I can assure you this is the booth for Plum Crazy Events. If you're looking for Enchanted Events, that booth is somewhere over there. Way, way, way over there." She gestured vaguely to her original prime location. "But my services are quite competitive. I can give you a quote for comparison's sake."

The woman narrowed her eyes like Zoe was playing some kind of trick on her. "No. I'm certain this was the right booth. I remember that ugly wedding dress." She pointed at the mannequin.

Zoe's eyebrow arched in annoyance, but she kept the smile on her face, hoping to gain at least one new customer that weekend.

The woman rifled through her purse and pulled out a pink business card. "Here it is!" She waved it in the air like "I told you so." "Natalie. Natalie Evans."

Zoe gaped at the card. After a second, she reached out. "May I see that?"

She handed it over. Zoe could sense Levi read over her shoulder, but she didn't care. The words on the card were all that mattered.

Natalie Evans
Enchanted Events Wedding Planner

She read the silver-embossed lettering three times before it sank in. Her hands shook, and the words blurred.

"See? She was at this booth offering her services yesterday."
The woman tapped the table insistently. "Are you a smaller affiliate or branch company?"

Zoe's eyelashes flickered at the unintended slight. A sort of cold calm blew over her, but it felt more like the eye of a storm.

Natalie hadn't been lying when she said she'd handed out two-dozen cards. They just weren't Plum Crazy Events cards. Natalie was jumping ship. And not just to anyone's ship, but to Chelsea Carruthers's.

She recalled the day before, when Natalie showed up late with a bouquet from an odd area of town. Had her car really broken down or had she placed an order for a wedding she was planning? And she'd used *Zoe's* florist.

She didn't know why that fact cut at her the most. People were free to use any florist they wanted. But Zoe had used that one exclusively for years in exchange for a VIP discount. And Natalie was probably benefiting from that discount since they knew she worked for Zoe—or rather, *used to work* for her.

Zoe had taught Natalie everything she knew, showed her the best retailers, how to get the cheapest deals, all the industry secrets. And she'd taken those secrets and run straight to her competitor with them.

The betrayal hit her like a garter toss to the heart. It stung.

Her mind ran over the last couple of months. Natalie's private phone calls, her tardiness, the weddings she hadn't been available to assist for. Zoe's fist clenched around the pink card, crushing it.

"Hey," the woman complained. "I need that."

"Trust me. You don't." Zoe tossed it in her purse before slinging it onto her shoulder. "Anything would be better than Enchanted Events. And everything Natalie knows, she learned from me." She jumped to her feet, knocking her chair over. "Now, if you'll excuse me. I have to go find someone."

As she stormed off, she dug desperately into her purse for

the solace of her Fuzzy Friend. Hatred for Chelsea consumed her until she couldn't focus on anything else. She was hardly aware of the booths she passed, the potential clients watching her storm by, or Levi following close behind. He was saying something, but she couldn't hear over her anger. All she saw, all she knew, was red.

When she turned down the main aisle and Chelsea came into view, Zoe squeezed the life out of Gentle Giraffe. But it had little calming effect at the moment. She drew close to the Enchanted Events booth, and their eyes met. Her rival appeared as furious as Zoe felt, which was pretty difficult since she was irate.

"You!" she said like it was an accusation. "You're trying to ruin me."

Chelsea planted her fists on her hips. "Really? And how exactly am I doing that?"

Zoe risked letting go of Gentle Giraffe to count on her fingers, if only to keep her hands busy so they didn't find their way around her rival's neck. "First you stole my booth. Then you stole my potential clients. And now you've stolen my assistant."

"Oh, that." Chelsea brushed it aside like old news. "Obviously, she wasn't happy with you. She moved on to greener pastures."

She started. Natalie not happy? It was hard to imagine. Zoe had treated her less like an employee and more like a friend. She'd gone to her grandfather's funeral to show her support, and she'd even helped Natalie move when her boyfriend cheated on her. Zoe gave her regular raises, Christmas bonuses, and paid vacations.

Confused by the sudden betrayal, Zoe narrowed her eyes. "What did you say to her? What did you offer her?"

"Just some independence," Chelsea said. "You've been smothering her talents. I've given her a position as a wedding planner. She's overseeing one as we speak."

"Natalie's not ready for that," Zoe said. "She can barely show up for work on time." Heck, she couldn't tell the difference between a horse and a donkey.

The memory of Juliet's wedding brought her up short. She recalled what the flower girl said when Zoe caught her releasing the doves. *The lady said I could.*

At the time, she'd assumed the girl was lying, but now she realized who that "lady" had been: Natalie. Now it made sense how so many things could go so wrong.

She inhaled sharply. "Did Natalie sabotage the Fisher-Wells wedding?"

Chelsea lifted a bony shoulder. "How would I know about that? I was nowhere near it."

Zoe's body stiffened. If that wasn't an "I can't be held culpable" statement, she didn't know what was. But how could she prove Natalie had set her up, if that's even what happened? Her assistant could have accomplished it in so many ways, without leaving a shred of evidence behind.

Chelsea crossed her arms. "So, is that why you retaliated? To get back at me for stealing Natalie?"

"Me?" Zoe forced a laugh. "What did I ever do to you?"

Before she could answer, someone nearby gasped. Excited whispers drifted around them.

"Oh, my gosh!" someone said. "Is that Holly Hart?"

Zoe scanned those gathered for her least-favorite person. The reporter swept down the aisle as though she could smell a story brewing. Held within her arms, Jasmine the Chinese crested sniffed the air like she could smell it too.

Holly's sights homed in on Zoe and Chelsea, her sharp gaze flicking between them. The moment interrupted, Zoe realized she wasn't the only one paying close attention; their argument had attracted quite a crowd.

"My drama radar is going off," Holly sang. "Do I detect a story here?"

Chelsea ran to her side and grabbed her arm. "Miss Hart, I'm so glad you're here."

"Watch the suit." Holly brushed her off. "It's Gucci."

Jasmine growled, bearing her fangs like *Back off.* Her personality matched her owner's.

Chelsea patted the bun on top of her head, making sure every hair was in place for the camera that invariably followed Holly. "Have I got breaking news for you."

"I'll determine what's breaking news." Holly soothed Jasmine. "What happened here?"

"Sabotage. That's what. By Zoe Plum." Chelsea's face burned with triumph, as though this were the moment she'd been waiting for.

Zoe rolled her eyes at her rival's antics. But the confidence in Chelsea's expression made her a little afraid of what came next.

"Sabotage?" Holly licked her lips. "Ooh, delicious." She twirled her finger in the air, and Hey You materialized with his camera.

Chelsea jerked a thumb in Zoe's direction. "Little Miss Perfect here couldn't handle her jealousy of me. Look what she did to my booth last night." She waved her arm awkwardly, as though on some kind of game show. She stood aside and invited the camera to take a panorama.

"What?" Zoe took a step back. "What are you—"

For the first time since her tunnel vision had cleared, she caught sight of the Enchanted Events booth. Or rather, what should have been *Zoe's* booth.

The ostentatious banner, ripped in half, dragged on the floor. Sparkling hearts littered the aisle runner, crushed like someone had stomped on them. Décor samples and photo albums lay in shreds.

Zoe shook her head. "How could I have done this? I've been nowhere near your booth. I've been over there." She pointed to the corner. "Way, way, way over there. Remember?"

"It happened sometime last night," Chelsea said. "I spoke to security, and they said you came back to the hotel late after the expo closed. The cameras caught you leaving the parking garage around eleven o'clock."

Zoe planted her hands on her hips. Not exactly the image of sweet innocence, but, well, she *was* innocent. She didn't need to pretend. "I came back to pick up my van. So what?"

"So you probably snuck in here and destroyed my booth," Chelsea snapped. "You threatened me yesterday. You said, 'You'll get yours.'"

Mutters rippled throughout the crowd. Hey You snuck closer until the camera practically pressed against Zoe's cheek. She shoved the lens away.

"I was there," a woman manning a nearby table piped up. "I heard her say that."

"Yeah. Me too," said another vendor.

Zoe groaned. "I was talking about karma. I didn't mean I'd do anything myself. Why on earth would I want to do this?" She gestured to the ruined booth.

Chelsea threw her hands up. "Because you're jealous of me."

Zoe rubbed her throbbing temples. "What would I have to be jealous of you for? You're a terrible wedding planner."

She heaved a sigh as though weary of spelling it all out. "Not because of my wild success. Because of my recent engagement."

Zoe shrugged. Like she gave a damn. "Congratulations. You finally found someone to put up with you. I wish him good luck."

She wasn't wasting any more time, or room in her emotional bottle, on Chelsea's crap. She spun to return to her booth. However, the camera stuck with her, Hey You backpedaling in front of her.

"Obviously, I'm more of a dream than you," Chelsea called to her back. "Because he left you and traded up."

Her steps faltered. "Traded up?"

"What? Don't tell me you didn't know." Chelsea laughed, each giggle hitting Zoe's back like tiny little daggers. "I'm about to marry the man who left you at the altar."

The world fell out from under Zoe's heels, and she had to hold on to a nearby table for support. Her breaths came faster and faster until the edges of her vision grew dark, and the room tilted. She reached back into her purse, hoping Gentle Giraffe's comforting power would take effect quickly.

Slowly, she spun back to face her rival. "What did you say?"

Chelsea spoke her next words very slowly and clearly, in case Zoe might miss one heart-wrenching word. "I'm the future Mrs. Sean Wilson."

Zoe took these words and, using the last ounce of patience she had left in her, she stuffed them deep down. "You two deserve each other." And she meant every word—but not in a good way.

Chelsea glowed like a joyful bride-to-be, coming in too close for anyone else to overhear her. "You're right. We do deserve each other. Obviously, *you* didn't deserve him, or you'd be with him right now." She chuckled, her cheerful expression at odds with the venom behind her words. "I guess things really do happen for a reason. If he'd actually showed up to your wedding day, he'd be stuck with you right now. Instead, he's marrying the woman he belongs with: *me.*"

Gentle Giraffe's head popped off in Zoe's hand. Beans spilled to the bottom of her purse, the same way she could feel her emotions spill out of that carefully sealed bottle.

Her fists clenched, and her body shook. Her breaths released in hard pants like a bull about to charge. Someone screamed, a fierce, painful wail from the gut. Distantly, Zoe realized it was her. Her self-control slipped away, just like on her wedding day.

The day had been a culmination of months of wedding stress—the planning, the calls, the meetings, the details—that had exploded out of her in one epic moment of grief and anger. All that work was meant for one joyous purpose: a celebration of her and Sean's love, of their eternal union. But it had all been for nothing.

Instead, the purple-and-chartreuse theme had seemed to mock her. She'd felt like a fool. When she couldn't take it out on her fiancé, she'd taken it out on all her pointless planning, shredding the freesias, tearing paper lanterns from the ceiling, and throwing cupcakes. And she'd done it all in front of the entire congregation with their pitying looks and whispers. Zoe had lost her mind. No. Worse. She'd lost her heart, like a part of her had vanished when she'd heard the words "He's not coming."

And now, standing in front of a gloating Chelsea and all those people, that day rushed back to her. She felt the sharp stab of rejection anew. Sure, it was duller now, but Chelsea's announcement felt like a silk bridal pump crushing that old scar in her chest where her heart had been ripped out.

The murmurs from the crowd rang in Zoe's ears like the congregation's whispers on her big day.

"How scandalous."

"How awful."

"Poor Zoe."

She wanted to fight back, to reject the idea that she was weak, "poor" Zoe. She was strong, and she wouldn't take it lying down. Nor was she going to stand for Chelsea's accusations or poisonous attitude.

Legs that didn't feel like hers moved toward her rival. As though she floated outside her body, she watched as everything she'd pushed deep down inside herself erupted. Her hands balled into fists. She didn't know what she was going to do, and it frightened her.

Suddenly, arms wrapped around her from behind, restraining her. She struggled against them, but they wouldn't budge. They felt firm, yet so gentle. A strong hug holding her together, preventing her from falling apart.

"Zoe," Levi's deep voice hummed in her ear. "Just let it go."

It had been so long since a man had hugged her. In fact, she couldn't remember being in a man's arms since her father had died. The touch unarmed her and then instantly infuriated her. Not because he was touching her, but because of what it did to her.

Zoe's eyes stung. She didn't need a man. And she definitely didn't need Levi.

She ripped free and pushed him away. "What are you doing?"

"Trying to help you." He held up his hands and backed off.

"I don't need your help."

"Obviously, you do," he said calmly. "She's just egging you on. Walk away. It's not worth it."

"Oh, yes, it is."

But she felt more aware of herself now and of everyone watching her lose control—something Zoe didn't do. She'd moved beyond that now. Beyond caring. Beyond being hurt, especially by her ex-fiancé, Sean.

"Oh, what a fabulous story," Holly purred from the sidelines.

Zoe bowed her head, humility weighing down her rising emotions. "No story. Just ancient history."

Holly waved a dismissive hand. "Well, it will have to do. It's been a slow weekend at the expo. Too much lovey-dovey crap for me."

She snapped her fingers in the air. Hey You returned to her side in an instant, lugging his equipment through the crowd. He handed her the mic, and she stood next to Zoe as though about to interview her.

But Zoe wasn't sticking around. All she wanted to do was run, to disappear for the rest of the weekend. She turned for her booth. Maneuvering through the curious onlookers, she nearly stumbled into a bakery booth with a precariously balanced five-tier pink cake.

"Hey, where do you think you're going?" Holly's nails dug into Zoe's arm as she tugged her back. "You're not going anywhere. You're my story. Like it or not, it's happening."

Zoe ran her hands through her hair, eyes searching for an escape route. She just wanted to get out of there.

Levi wedged himself between the two women. "I'm still available for that interview, if you'd like. You know, we've got a big tour of California coming up."

Holly scoffed. "The people don't want to hear about your little boy band."

"Rock band," he corrected.

She swept him aside. "They want Zoe's misfortunes."

"But I didn't do anything," Zoe said. "I couldn't care less about Chelsea and her sad personal life. And I didn't vandalize her booth." She glared at the reporter. "And if you think for one second that I'm going to let you ruin my reputation like you did with Addison, then you've got another thing coming. I'm not as nice as Addison."

But Holly wasn't deterred. "One way or another, I need a story out of this boring weekend. So what story am I running?" She pretended to think, fluffing up the little tuft of white hair on Jasmine's head. "Maybe something like 'Always a Wedding Planner, Never a Bride.' Think of the damage control you'll have to do. How can you plan other people's weddings when you can't even make it through your own?"

Zoe closed her eyes. *Great*, she thought. *What else can go wrong this weekend?* "Please, don't." Her voice sounded weaker than she'd meant it to.

Holly looked her up and down before grinning

mischievously. "Well … there's only *one* other story I'm more interested in. And that's the Summers-Caldwell wedding."

"Of course." She laughed humorlessly. "I see your angle now."

"An angle? Little old me?" Holly bit her lip and fluttered her eyelashes innocently.

"I'm not throwing my best friend under the bus."

"No, no, no. Nothing as scandalous as that. People just want to feel connected, like they're involved in the monumental occasion." She inched the microphone closer to Zoe's mouth. "Just a tidbit. A morsel. Nothing more. I promise." Another eyelash flutter.

Zoe eyed Chelsea. She was no longer alone. A man with a boss-like arrogance hovered anxiously next to her. A gold name tag flashed on his lapel. She heaved a sigh and laid a dramatic head on his shoulder.

Zoe assumed he must be her cousin, the expo coordinator. Despite her overly visible anguish, when Chelsea's gaze locked with Zoe's, she found a triumphant grin just for her. Zoe scowled back.

The coordinator barked orders at the beefy security guard who had dragged Juliet away the day before. The guard scanned the crowd. When his eyes landed on Zoe, they narrowed, and his nostrils flared.

Her heart skipped a beat. Her instinct for flight or fight kicked in. She automatically glanced over her shoulder, but another security guard closed in on her from the other end of the aisle. She was trapped.

"Tick tock," Holly said. "Hey You, are you ready to catch the takedown?" she asked her cameraman. "I want the best angle for the five-o'clock news."

The decision pulled at Zoe's insides. Piper had said she wanted to keep the wedding as quiet as possible.

She cringed. "Just a tidbit?"

Holly nodded eagerly, mashing the microphone against Zoe's lips.

But she pushed it away. "Off the record."

"Of course." She snapped her fingers, and Hey You lowered the camera, backing off.

Zoe chewed the inside of her cheek, but on seeing Beefy charge her way, she said, "Fine. The dress is, *was*, a Vera Wang."

Holly pursed her lips. "But it's a goner now. I was there, remember? I already got that scoop. So, what else have you got?"

"The theme is pink and navy blue." *The colors aren't a big deal*, she reasoned with herself. It wasn't critical or anything. Not like the location.

"And ..." Holly coaxed.

"And the dogs are their ring bearers." That factoid wasn't so terrible, either. It only made sense; they were dog lovers.

She glanced nervously at the approaching security guards. "Happy?" she asked the reporter.

Holly's mouth twitched, neither a smile nor a frown. "For now." With a wiggle of her fingers in farewell, she backed off to the sidelines for a good view.

Chelsea drew closer for a front-row seat as the security guards converged. She wore a self-satisfied look on her pinched face.

Beefy crossed his thick arms, towering over Zoe. "Are you going to come quietly, or do I have to call the police?"

"Oh, I'll come," she said. "But I won't do it quietly."

Chelsea snickered at her. "You just can't admit defeat, can you?"

Finally, Zoe's usual calm settled over her. "No. I just figure, if I'm getting kicked out, it's going to be for a good reason."

Reaching for the bakery table next to her, she jammed her hand into the pink sample cake. Before Chelsea or the security guards could react, she cupped a handful of the dessert and slapped it across Chelsea's smug face.

Her rival gasped and sputtered, wiping the icing from her round, shocked eyes. "Screw you, Zoe Plum! I'll get you for this!"

Zoe licked the remains off her fingers. *Mmm, pink champagne cake.* "There. Now I'm ready."

Chapter Nine

TAIL BETWEEN THE LEGS

I know what you did. You're fired.

Zoe reread the words before texting them to Natalie. There'd be more to come eventually, but she needed time to wrap her head around the situation, to deal with the hurt, so she could act semi-professional when she finally confronted her. Unlike earlier that day.

At the moment, she wasn't sure what else to say that encompassed the betrayal she felt, the anger for all the lies and deceit over the last few weeks—maybe even longer. She now understood why Natalie had been acting extra skittish recently. It was guilt.

Clutching her phone, Zoe hit *send* with a flourish. But really, the firing was just a formality. The only one rejected was Zoe.

The bride and groom in her booth leered at her with their plastic expressions of marital joy. They were mocking her, turning their perfect noses up at her failure.

Annoyed, she ripped the tiara and veil off the bride and tossed the combo into a box, but the couple remained indifferent to her feelings. Now they were just trying to piss her off.

She frowned at her dismantled booth, disappointed at how the weekend had gone. The expo had been her chance to break out. And Zoe had blown it.

Security had allowed her to return to gather her things once the expo had closed for the day. At least everyone had gone home by now. It meant fewer people to witness her walk of shame even though she didn't think she'd done anything to feel ashamed about.

Okay, so she did smash pink champagne cake in Chelsea's face. But, well … that was satisfying and totally worth having to pay for the cake—even if it had cost three hundred dollars.

Zoe gripped the bride's head and ripped it clean off the body. It pulled out of the socket with a pop. She tossed it over her shoulder, and it landed in a box.

"Whoa. Is that any way to treat a lady?" a man's voice asked behind her.

Startled, she spun. Levi gave her a lopsided grin, pink frosting on his lips. He held two plates of cake. He placed one on the table and slid it toward her. The pink icing glared up at her judgmentally.

"Can you believe they were just going to throw this away?" He shoveled another bite into his mouth. "It's delicious."

She gaped at it. "You're eating the cake I threw at Chelsea?"

"No. That would be disgusting," he said. "I'm eating the part that you didn't throw."

A surprised laugh bubbled out of her, which she supposed was his goal. "Oh, well, I can't have my cake this weekend, but it turns out I can still eat it."

She picked the plate up and dug in. It tasted pretty good. She needed a little pick-me-up after the day she'd had, as ironic as the choice in dessert was.

They ate in silence for a while before Levi asked. "So, what was that all about earlier? Why does that woman hate you so much?"

"Usually, it's just a little industry rivalry," Zoe said. "It all began when one of her clients grew tired of her poor service and asked me to plan their wedding instead. Ever since, Chelsea's hated me. She bad-mouths me to people in the business."

"And today?"

"That was definitely something else."

It suddenly occurred to her that maybe he didn't know what to think about her run-in with Chelsea. Security had escorted her out before she'd had the chance to talk to him. Maybe he thought she was as unbalanced as, well … as how she acted that morning. Heck, maybe she was a little unbalanced.

"I didn't ruin her display. You know that, right?" She didn't know why it was so important that he believed her. Once she packed up and left the expo, she'd never see him again. But for some reason, she couldn't walk away without him knowing.

He gave her a look over his mound of pink icing. "If I thought that, I wouldn't be here eating cake with you."

"I guess not." She smiled, happy to have one person on her side.

As Levi took another bite, his expression grew serious. "You said Chelsea's booth location was originally yours, right?"

"Yeah, why?"

"Your company's name would have appeared on the original expo map layout."

Zoe's fork froze halfway to her mouth. "You think the vandal might have intended to trash my booth, not Chelsea's?" She grew quiet as she considered it. "Well, I suppose if the lights were off in the ballroom, they wouldn't have noticed the banner wasn't for Plum Crazy Events."

"And it would tie in with the damage to your vehicle." He gestured with his fork.

"So maybe the van wasn't a onetime thing." She gnawed

on her lip. "Maybe they're not done. Great. That makes me feel so much better." She took another comforting bite.

"It's not a great theory, but it might help you get closer to figuring out who it is."

She nodded. "You're right. The last thing I want is for anything else to happen. Any information I can give the police is a good thing."

All afternoon, she'd run scenarios through her head, reviewing everything that had happened over the last couple of weeks. Months, even. After learning of Natalie's betrayal, she wanted to point a finger at her for anything that had gone awry. But could she be responsible for everything?

The very thought of her assistant had Zoe reaching for her Fuzzy Friend. Then she remembered it lay in a pile of beans at the bottom of her purse.

But as much as she wanted to blame Natalie, she couldn't imagine the timid thing with a crowbar in her hands, exacting violence on her van. Or, for that matter, knowing where to find the brake lines to sever them.

Natalie didn't exactly strike her as the cold-blooded killer type. Shoving a metaphorical knife into Zoe's back, however, was a different story. She had no problem doing that. Besides, if Levi's theory was right and the same person was behind all of it, Natalie was off the hook; she knew the location of Zoe's booth.

Done torturing herself enough for one day, she shook off that line of thinking. "Thanks for earlier, by the way," she told Levi. "I'm glad you stopped me from doing anything I'd regret."

He waved away her appreciation. "You were understandably upset."

"No kidding." She laughed humorlessly. "Chelsea can be antagonistic, to say the least."

"Are you sure that's all it was?" he asked. "Is it possible

your reaction had something to do with Chelsea marrying your ex?"

The way he studied her made the cake in her mouth turn thick. His stare, usually so cheesy and silly, cut right through her. Past the mask she put on every morning, deep down to where she hid everything she didn't want people to see.

"Oh, that?" She swallowed hard. "It's ancient history. It was years ago. I'm over it."

"It didn't seem that way to me."

She pulled an incredulous look, but her mask felt a little stiff. "It's not that I'm jealous, or anything. Chelsea just hit a sore spot."

Levi took another bite of cake, regarding her as he chewed. "If you say so."

She huffed. She didn't know why she wanted to explain herself to him. It's not like it would matter once they finished their cake and parted ways. But still … something in his look compelled her to expand. "Sean left me standing at the altar."

He whistled. "That might leave a sore spot. Maybe more like a gangrenous festering wound."

"Ew." She wrinkled her nose. "No. It's healed by now. That's just not something you forget, you know? It stays with you. The questions, the doubts. I guess when Chelsea told me they were engaged, it caught me off guard." She shook her head as the news hit her for the tenth time that day. "God, Chelsea of all people. You can't help but make comparisons. He didn't want to marry me, but he wants to marry her? *Her?* What does that say about me?"

"It says you're too good for him," Levi said.

"Thanks." Zoe hadn't meant to fish for a compliment, but there it was. And it felt good. Being around Levi felt good.

Of course, Piper and Addison told her the same thing all the time, in a hundred different ways. But friends were supposed to say those things. It was right at the top of the friendship contract.

However, Levi didn't know her. He didn't owe her anything, so it felt less of a contractual obligation and more truthful.

"For what it's worth," he said. "I would have been standing at the other end of that aisle."

Her mouth opened, but before she could reply, a voice drifted around the corner. She couldn't mistake the owner of that high-pitched voice: Holly Hart.

Zoe winced. "Crap."

Levi pulled a face, maybe a little pouty. "Okay, well, I might not be what you're looking for. But, you know, I'm not exactly the bottom of the barrel. I have a lot of things going for me and ..."

He continued to mope, but Zoe didn't have time to correct him. She searched for an escape route. The last thing she wanted was to endure another onslaught of questions about Piper's wedding. But her booth was backed up against the wall; no way out.

With footsteps approaching and Holly's voice growing louder, Zoe dove for the only thing large enough to hide her—the headless bride. Hoisting up layers of semi-transparent fabric, she peeked beneath it.

Levi was still talking. "… I mean, I've been told I have a certain old-school gentleman quality to me, but—"

"No, no. You're great. Shh." She lunged for him and pressed a hand to his mouth. "I mean, 'crap, Holly Hart is coming this way.'"

"Holly Hart?" he asked a little too loudly.

Clearly eager for his fifteen minutes of fame, he craned his neck to peer down the aisle. She grabbed his hand and yanked him to the floor. Lifting the dress's hemline, she shoved him under the billowing tulle and scurried in after him. The wide skirts created a tent, the mannequin's legs its center post.

"Why are we—" he began.

She held a finger to her lips as the voices became clear, and he trailed off. Even through the multiple layers of tulle, she could make out two figures passing in front of her stall. One was definitely Holly because she wouldn't shut up.

Zoe crossed her fingers, hoping they would move on, but they came to a stop right in front of their hiding spot. She could sort of see them, so if they looked hard enough, they'd probably notice Zoe and Levi.

"… so get over it," Holly spat.

"But you were supposed to interview me, not her. This wasn't some crappy episode of *Everybody Loves Zoe*."

Zoe's fist clenched as she recognized Chelsea's nasally voice.

"She ruined my booth, and you treated her like some kind of star. The focus should have been on me, not the person responsible for the damage."

"What can I say, sweetheart?" Holly said. "No one cares about your little lemonade stand."

"Do you have any idea how long I've waited for this weekend?" she asked. "How hard I've worked? This is the biggest promotional opportunity for wedding planners, and Zoe not only ruined my chance to get my business noticed, but then she overshadows me in the media?"

With a click of her tongue, Holly spun to face her. "Who are you? You're a nobody. My job is to give the public what they want. And since I've been doing my segment, *Holly Hart's Hounds*, it's clear the public wants Zoe Plum and her friends. Piper Summers is about to marry San Francisco's most eligible bachelor. That's what the viewers want to know about. Not you."

A high-pitched grumble started up, like a mini motorcycle idling. It was hard to see through the dress, but Zoe assumed Holly's Chinese crested sat in her arms.

There was a heavy *thump*, like Chelsea had stomped her foot. "This is bullshit. I'm the victim here."

But Holly wasn't paying attention. Her gaze scraped over Zoe's booth.

Clearly, she'd been on a stakeout ever since the expo closed or she wouldn't still be there. It was as though she could sense Zoe's presence, could smell her nearby. Even hidden beneath the dress, Zoe shrank in on herself.

"A crime was committed," Chelsea continued. "It's your public duty to tell the truth. This is an injustice."

After a moment that dragged on forever, Holly huffed and turned away from their hiding spot. "I'll tell you what's an injustice," she said. "That dress."

Zoe gritted her teeth.

Chelsea banged on the table. "Pay attention to me, damn it!"

"Then do something worthy of attention."

"But …"

Holly reached into her purse and drew out something white. "Here's my card. Call me if you have any real news to report." She handed it over. Casting one last glance over Zoe's dismantled display, she left.

Chelsea dipped her head to read the card. "Hey! This is a coupon for the Dog and Bone." Tossing it aside, she stomped after the reporter.

Zoe waited until she was certain the coast was clear. Lifting the wedding gown's unwieldly skirts, she crawled out and held them up for Levi.

He popped up to his feet and wiped his brow. "It sure gets hot in there."

"Try wearing it for a whole day."

Before Holly could come back, Zoe stacked boxes to take out to the van she'd rented after the tow truck picked hers up for repairs. She was ready to put the weekend behind her. When Levi grabbed the box of brochures, she frowned.

"You don't have to help," she said. "I'll be fine."

"I know, but I have to burn off the cake calories somehow. Unless you have some other way to help me burn them off." He gave her a suggestive eyebrow waggle.

"You bet I do." Her gaze scraped over his tall, fit body. Then she stacked another box on top of his already-heavy one. "There."

He grunted under the additional weight. "Yup, that'll do it."

As they rounded the corner, she discovered the security guard hadn't gone far; he'd been waiting for her like he suspected she might destroy someone else's booth. He followed them to the lobby and hit the elevator buttons for them.

"So, what are you still doing here?" she asked Levi. "Not that I don't mind the company. Or the cake. But the doors closed to the public almost an hour ago."

He tilted his head noncommittally. "I'm just hanging out."

"Because you have nothing better to do on a Saturday night?"

"What could be better than spending time with you?" He grinned at her over the boxes.

When the elevator stopped at her parking level, they got out. The security guard waited for them to return for the rest of Zoe's things, watching them struggle with the heavy boxes all the way to the van.

After her long day, she got straight to the point with Levi. "You know you're barking up the wrong tree, right?"

"What could you possibly be talking about?" he asked airily.

She blew out a breath. Apparently, he wasn't going to make it easy. "I'm not sure if you waited for *me* or because you want to get hired for my friend's wedding, but neither one is going to happen."

He grunted as he shifted his hold on the boxes. "Damn. You mean I'm out twenty bucks for nothing?"

As they approached the rental van, she unlocked it. "What do you mean?"

"I paid the guy who originally had my booth to swap with me."

Zoe nearly dropped her box. "I knew it! I knew it couldn't be a coincidence." The confession annoyed her, but a second later, she had to set her box down as she doubled over with laughter.

"Where was your original booth?" she asked when her giggles died down.

"Center aisle."

Her head whipped toward him. He'd given up a prime location just to be next to her?

"Oh well, I tried." Levi's expression was unapologetic. "You want to get some dinner? My treat."

"I'm not going on a date with you," she said, but with a hint of an amused smile. She supposed those were the hints that made him question if she really wanted him to stop pursuing her. She bit her lip to hide it.

"It's not a date. I figure we should probably get to know each other better," he said, way too casually. "We could talk business. We'll be working together, after all."

"Right." She laughed. "What makes you think I'd do business with you?"

"Because your big-shot client said you will."

Her smile faded. She narrowed her eyes. "Piper wouldn't …"

"She called me about an hour ago." He waved his phone in front of her like it was hard evidence. "Apparently, she liked our music."

She dug her phone out of her purse. As though Piper had read her mind, a message popped up on the screen.

Hey! Aiden and I listened to Levi's music. We think the band would be fun and much more "us" rather than a DJ. I've already let him know. Talk later. Lots of love!

However, Zoe wasn't feeling much love at the moment. Except from maybe Levi, who beamed at her.

"Looks like you and I will be spending a lot of time together."

And by the way he said it, she wondered if her vibrators would ever work again.

Chapter Ten

PUPPY DOG EYES

Zoe pulled up to the San Francisco Dachshund Rescue Center in her rental van. The sun was out in full force, shining down on the pineapple yellow home. She'd always loved spending her free time volunteering at the center, but ever since Aiden had purchased the early 1910 farmhouse and renovated it to suit dogs, it truly felt like coming home.

Time spent with her four-legged friends was one of those rare occasions when she felt her emotional bottle open and some of the contents pour out harmlessly. Of course, since her own doxie, Buddy, had passed on, that solace didn't come nearly often enough.

So, with everything that had happened recently, she looked forward to an afternoon with a bunch of wieners not fashioned out of silicone. Besides, she'd already tried _that_ again, but she was still batting zero. Levi had definitely thrown her off her game.

Zoe hurried up the flagstone steps to the wraparound porch. Thick floral scents enveloped her like a hug. As she pushed open the French doors to the reception area, the little brass bell above them rang, announcing her arrival. The Bee

Gees greeted her, playing through the speakers wired into the ceiling.

Marilyn, the manager of the center, pored over adoption records behind the desk. She sported a zebra print sweater over a hot pink top. Ever the saucy dresser, she especially favored animal prints. While she adored dachshunds most of all, she loved all things furry. Zoe supposed that meant she literally wore her heart on her sleeve.

The older woman glanced up at the pleasant jingle. "Oh, hi. I didn't expect you today."

Addison was mopping the vinyl flooring. She did a double take when she saw her friend. "Zoe?"

Naia, the five-year-old daughter of Addison's boyfriend, sat on a wingback chair, putting together a puzzle on the coffee table. She waved. "Hi, Zoe!"

"Hi, Naia." Zoe waved back.

It wasn't unusual to see her there on the weekend. Addison often brought her along to play with the dogs. It gave Felix a chance to catch up on sleep after working late on Saturday nights at the bar he owned.

Piper came up to the front, carrying a piebald doxie in her arms. "Hey! What are you doing here?"

"Why are you guys so surprised?" Zoe asked. "This is my normal shift."

She tossed her purse behind the reception desk, pretending she didn't understand everyone's reactions. Like what else would she possibly be doing? You know, other than repairing the damage to her business's reputation, preparing for her mother's return home, planning a wedding to a man she'd never met, or figuring out who cut her brake lines.

Something rolled across Zoe's foot. Marilyn's blue dachshund, Picasso, raced around the reception in his wheelchair. While he suffered from a severe case of intervertebral disc disease, the little doggy wheelchair helped him to get around pain-free.

She bent down and scratched under his collar where he liked it. "Hi there, Picasso. How's it rolling?"

She noticed her friends share a look. Obviously, they weren't going to drop the subject that easily. She'd filled them in on everything the night before, including the bad news about the poor Vera Wang dress.

Piper fed the doxie in her arms a treat. "I figured with everything going on, you might skip today. Not that we don't want the help," she added hastily. "But we can manage without you if you need the day off."

"You mean because someone wants to kill me?" She waved it away as casually as she could. "There's not much I can do until the police finish their investigation. Right now, they have no idea who cut my brake lines, so I can't protect myself from everyone and anyone."

"What about your mom?" Marilyn asked. "Doesn't she need help?"

"I already visited her this morning. She doesn't get released until after the weekend. And since I'm no longer in the expo, I had some spare time."

Zoe signed into the logbook as though that settled it.

Checking the chore list, she saw the fish hadn't eaten yet. She ticked it off and grabbed the food. It was easier for her to do since she was the tallest of the bunch. The aquarium took up the entire wall behind the reception desk, and no one else could reach the opening without a step stool.

After sprinkling the food into the water, she turned around. Everyone focused on their tasks like chores were the most important thing in the world, like they weren't all silently conversing behind her back.

Marilyn started wiping down the counter. "The girls told me about what happened with that woman yesterday. Sounds like your ex has his hands full with that trollop. And in my opinion, your ex deserves what he gets."

"Marilyn, I'm shocked. Such language." Zoe teased her, as she usually did for her English expressions.

"Well," she sniffed, "no one hurts my girls. And if that woman can get a rise out of my Zoe, then she must be a real piece of work."

"Exactly," Addison agreed. "You're the coolest cucumber I know."

Zoe watched the exotic fish dart around the tank; they looked like someone had dropped a box of colorful confetti in there. "I guess she just hit the right buttons, and I saw red." She snorted. "Or rather, pink champagne cake."

"And who could blame you?" Marilyn asked. "I'm sure it hurt to find out she's marrying Sean."

"That's not it. I don't miss him or anything." She laughed extra hard to prove how ridiculous the idea was. "I'm not jealous, if that's what you mean."

Finished with the floor, Addison plopped the mop back into the bucket. "You may not miss him, but maybe you miss …" She searched for the word. *"It."*

"'It?'" Zoe arched a suggestive eyebrow. "Oh, I get plenty of *it* on my own."

Addison threw her a sour look. "Not pleasure. *Love.* It's been a long time since you've had a boyfriend."

Piper frowned. "Come to think of it, I don't think I've ever met any of the men in your life."

That's because there's never been any. But Zoe kept that to herself.

She wasn't lying to her friends, just keeping information from them. Information that, if they knew it, they wouldn't drop until they "fixed" her. Like they knew what she needed. What Zoe needed was to be left alone. Besides, she already got enough lectures from her mother.

"I'm not missing something just because I don't have a serious man in my life right now." *Or ever.*

Piper clicked her tongue and set down the piebald doxie.

His toenails clicked on the floor as he explored the room. She sat on the settee next to the fireplace, as though settling in for a good, long talk.

"You know what we mean," she said.

"We?" Zoe's gaze flitted around the room. All her friends had stopped working, their focus on her. *What is this? Some kind of romance intervention?* She crossed her arms. "No. I don't know what you mean."

"How can you not be lonely for companionship?" Piper asked her. "For something more?"

"Because I have everything I need. I have your friendships, my mother, my businesses." She plucked the piebald doxie off the ground, cradling him in her arms. "Besides, what better companionship can you get than from a loyal dog?"

A dog loved you unconditionally. They appreciated your affections and returned them with lots of kisses, cuddles, and tail wags. They'd never leave you.

The doxie gave her a kiss as though proving her point. *Nice to meet you,* he seemed to say.

Addison sat on one of the wingback chairs, joining the intervention. Naia automatically scrambled onto her lap— because apparently everyone was in on this.

"But you don't even have a dog," Addison argued. "Not since Buddy passed away."

It was true. Buddy's death had left a wiener-sized hole in Zoe's life. She'd assumed she'd move on by now. It's not like she didn't have an endless source of dogs to choose from at the center, but more than a year later, she was still returning to an empty home.

"I'm getting there," she said. "I just haven't found the right dog."

"And maybe you haven't found the right man," Marilyn said.

Zoe laughed. "Isn't that an oxymoron? Do those even exist?"

But Piper didn't think it was funny. "Remember who you're talking to. You don't have to be Miss Always-In-Control with us."

"I'm acting in control because I am in control." When they continued to give her a look, she relented with a sigh. "I guess the news about Sean's wedding kind of caught me off guard. But I'm okay. It's not about him."

And it wasn't. Maybe it wasn't even about Chelsea. But Zoe's reaction had to do with someone, and she feared it was more about *herself* than anyone else. Her bottle was getting too full to keep a lid on it.

"Well, I appreciate you coming in, Zoe," Marilyn said, thankfully changing the subject.

She grabbed her purse from the closet and checked her hair in the antique mirror above the fireplace. "Now that you're here, I might visit the usual centers to check for some guests."

Zoe knew "guests" meant stray dogs, but the British manager liked to think of them as only staying for a short time before finding a family. A trip to other centers around the city meant she would return with at least ten new guests. Zoe put prepping spare kennels on her mental to-do list.

The centers filled up fast, and while San Francisco's claim to fame was its anti-kill efforts, abandoned pups didn't do so well cooped up in a strange place. It didn't take long before they simply stopped thriving, and Marilyn couldn't walk away knowing that. That's why the center's volunteers worked so hard to find forever homes for their guests as soon as possible.

The intervention officially over, Piper got up from the settee. "We're already dirty from chores, so Addy and I will start baths." She took the doxie from Zoe to carry him to the back. "Do you want to cover the desk?"

"Sure thing," Zoe said.

For the next hour, she puttered around the center, picking away at the chore list. She'd just started inventory on the dog food when her cell phone rang. Craving a drama-free day, she wanted to ignore it, but she worried it had something to do with her mom, so she answered.

"Hello?"

"Hi, Zoe. It's Amber."

Zoe straightened, shifting to planner mode. Amber was a client. Her wedding was still four months away, but her voice sounded halting; something was wrong. Zoe always made her brides a priority, even when it meant turning her back on her own problems.

"Amber. How are you?"

"I'm okay," she said, but she didn't sound okay.

"You sound upset," Zoe said. "What can I do for you?"

"I-I wanted to call to, well … to let you know I've decided to go another way."

She frowned. "What do you mean?"

"I mean …" Amber took a breath. "I've signed with another wedding planner."

Zoe stared at the phone, checking the call display as though this must be a wrong number. Finally, she found her voice. "Did I do something wrong?"

"No, no. You've been great. Perfect, really. You've always been there for me," Amber gushed. "It's just that our finances have kind of changed with Dean getting laid off, and we've had to re-evaluate our budget."

She pulled her tablet out of her purse. "But you're still going with a wedding planner? We can always take another look at cheaper flower options or combining the venue for both the service and reception to save some money."

She'd already put so much time and effort into planning their wedding. To lose them now would be a huge hit. Of course, they had a contract, but Zoe didn't want to point that out with their recent job loss. You couldn't get blood from a stone.

"I'm sorry," Amber said. "But it won't be enough. Another planner contacted us and offered us a lower rate."

"By how much?" She opened Amber's file, already calculating how much of a discount she could give them.

"Half."

Zoe nearly dropped her tablet. Her rates weren't outrageous, but she couldn't compete with that price. But who possibly could? Who would undercut her by that much?

"I'm sorry to hear that," she finally said. "Do you mind if I ask what planner you're going with?"

Amber kind of whimpered on the other end. "Natalie."

She gripped her phone until it squeaked under the pressure. But she'd let her emotions get the best of her enough lately, so she reached inside her purse and gave her Loyal Lion Fuzzy Friend a good pat. "I wish you and Dean all the best."

"Thanks. Again, I'm sorry."

Zoe ended the call and rubbed her temples. She put her phone back into her purse, automatically seeking the comforting touch of microfiber fur.

So, Natalie had come out guns blazing. Her introductory prices would build her client list and make a quick name for herself. Just not in a good way.

The wedding circuit was a small world. Soon enough, word would get around about Natalie's cheeky tactics and substandard pricing. She wouldn't make many friends that way, least of all Zoe.

The front bell rang, interrupting her thoughts. Abandoning the inventory, she headed for the front desk. When she got there, a man tapped his fingers on the wood countertop as he looked around.

"Can I help you?" she asked.

He jumped, as though she'd caught him doing something wrong. "Yes. I spoke to a woman named Marilyn on the phone earlier. She's expecting us."

"Us?" She glanced behind the man, looking for the rest of his party.

The man bent down, disappearing behind the tall desk. When he reappeared, he held a wirehaired dachshund. He placed the dog on the counter in front of Zoe.

His wild boar coloring was a beautiful mix of brown and black with a bit of gold sprinkled over most of his body. Stiff tan fur circled his mouth like a goatee, matching the color on his paws and legs.

"Hello, there," she said. "What's your name?"

"Freddy," the man offered.

"Hi, Freddy. It's nice to meet you."

Two tan eyebrows quirked up. Freddy tilted his head to the side, as though sussing her out. His oversized ears rose quizzically as he padded a little closer and gave her hand a sniff.

He was still a pup. By the disproportionate body, he looked less than a year old—not that one could ever accuse doxies of being proportionate with their stubby legs and stretched torsos. But that's what made them so darn cute.

Once he finished sniffing, he gave her a lick of acceptance before exploring the rest of the counter. She ran a hand over his coarse fur, keeping a protective eye on him as he checked things out.

"I'm sorry," Zoe told the man, "but Marilyn stepped out. Maybe I can help you."

"Oh, okay." He frowned, tapping his fingers on the counter again. "Well, Freddy will be staying with you for a while."

She'd assumed that's why he was there—that would explain his guilty behavior. Not many people waltzed in to show off their beloved dog and then take them back home. They were a rescue center, after all. However, his evasive words chafed at something inside of her.

"You mean you're giving him up," she clarified.

"We're not parting ways by choice," he said. "I have to. I'm moving into an apartment that doesn't allow pets."

"Of course." She nodded understandingly. "It wouldn't be because Freddy's moving into a place that doesn't allow humans."

His forehead creased. "What?"

"Never mind." Her eyebrows drew together. She bit her lip to stop from saying more; it wasn't her place.

Anytime she admitted new guests, she tried her best to think of Marilyn and how she would deal with it. The manager always preached the importance of welcoming new guests warmly and to not criticize their owners. Everyone had their reasons for giving up their pets, and some of them were even good ones.

Maybe the guy had lost his job, and he had to downsize. He could have moved in with his girlfriend and she gave him an ultimatum—it was her or the puppy. Maybe his kid was allergic to dogs.

Zoe took out one of the record books and opened it to a new admission form. "Is there anything special about Freddy that we should know? Has he had all his shots? Any health concerns?"

"I already gave Marilyn all the information." He jingled his keys impatiently like he had things to do, or maybe the situation made him uncomfortable. "He's a good dog. A bit stubborn, maybe."

She snorted, flipping through the completed intake papers until she found Freddy's. "He's a dachshund. That's to be expected."

"Right." He rubbed a hand over the back of his neck. "Well ... thanks. See you, buddy." The man gave Freddy a scratch behind the ears before he walked out the door and out of the pup's life forever.

Freddy whined a little as he watched his former owner leave. He shifted from paw to paw as though he wanted to follow him right off the countertop. Zoe picked him up before he got any funny ideas.

When the door swung closed behind the man, the doxie squirmed in her arms. She murmured sweet nothings to him, petting him slowly. He tilted his face up, giving her actual puppy dog eyes. Dachshunds were fiercely loyal to their owners. Too bad some owners didn't share the same trait.

"How about we find you a treat?" Whether it was the excitement in her voice or he understood the word "treat" well, his tail slapped her side. It beat to the rhythm of Justin Timberlake playing on the radio.

She plied him with comfort treats as she entered Freddy's information into the computer. He was a healthy dog with up-to-date shots. He'd been tagged and clearly groomed regularly. A great option for someone to adopt.

Once she finished up, she snapped a few photos of him to post on their website. Thanks to Holly Hart's news segments about the center the year before, they'd gained a lot of local notoriety and support. Most of their guests quickly found families through the center's adoption page, which Zoe maintained and kept up to speed.

While she worked, Freddy explored his new surroundings. He sniffed at the fireplace, tested the plush sitting room furniture, and ventured a step or two upstairs. Most of the time, he seemed content to stare up at the massive fish tank. His big chocolate eyes followed the tropical fish back and forth.

When Zoe went to the kitchen, he shadowed her. Making herself a cup of coffee, she stepped out onto the farmhouse's wraparound porch.

The view opened onto a beautiful sanctuary nestled in a small, wooded area hidden away from the city. A huge fenced-off green space sprawled in the center, where the guests could enjoy it at their leisure. They came and went freely from the little doggy doors that led into the converted horse barn with spacious kennels.

Naia ran around in the middle of the enclosure, surrounded by a writhing mass of excited fur balls. She squealed as the dachshunds chased her until she threw a tennis ball across the field. Their deep barks echoed through the yard as they raced for it, rolling in the grass as they fought.

"Do you wanna play?" Zoe asked Freddy.

He watched his group of peers romp, as though deliberating. After a moment, he huffed and walked over to join Zoe, his tail tucked between his legs.

Some dogs took longer to warm up to the center. Then again, the man he trusted most in the world had just abandoned him. That wouldn't exactly instill a lot of confidence.

"Don't worry." She bent down and gave him a scratch under the chin. "I know exactly how you feel."

His paw jiggled, slapping the wood planks. *Oh, yeah. Scratch that itch.*

Taking a seat next to him on the top step, she gazed out at the yard and sipped her coffee, U2 playing softly in the background. They watched Naia chase the dogs and get chased in return. After the weekend from hell, the moment settled over Zoe like a calming breeze. She petted Freddy absently, sharing a wordless conversation with him.

Maybe her friends were right about missing companionship in her life. She missed having someone to go home to, to watch TV with, to talk to, a breathing body on the other side of the bed. Maybe it was time to move on. And who better to move on with than a dog? Dogs could fulfill all those roles.

"What do you say, Freddy?" she asked. "You want to come home with me?"

Freddy licked her hand like he could understand her. He was so well-behaved and calm, exactly the soothing countenance she needed in her life. The perfect match. They would be the best of friends. She could just feel it.

Her phone vibrated in her pocket. She pulled it out to find a text message flash across the screen.

Hi, Zoe. It's Levi. Would you like to get together tonight and run over the playlist for Piper's wedding?

There was *one* role, however, a dog couldn't fill. And since Levi Dolson had fallen out of bed and into her life, she'd failed to fill that void on her own. And now that they were working together, it was about to get even harder.

After six long years, she wondered if she should give into that temptation to scratch her own itch. Maybe it was finally time.

She hit reply.

It's a date.

Chapter Eleven

LOVE ME, LOVE MY DOG

"Whoa! Stop! Heel! Bad dog!"

Zoe raced around the next hallway of Levi's apartment building in pursuit of Freddy, who, since the moment she'd stepped out of the rescue center with him, had seemed possessed.

She passed by a large yucca plant with a curious puddle next to it—even though she'd tried to get him to pee outside. The trail of shredded newspaper he'd probably stolen from in front of someone's door told her which way he'd gone.

"Freddy!" she hissed.

Trailing him through the halls, she kept her voice down. However, one of the building's tenants must have heard because an industrial-style metal door at the end of the hall slid open. Freddy took this as an invitation and veered toward it.

Zoe lunged for the leash dragging behind him, scraping her knee on the hallway floor. The leash grazed her hand, but her fingers clamped down on thin air. He slipped into the stranger's apartment and disappeared.

She cringed. The building might not even allow animals, and here he'd invited himself into a random apartment. She was still on her hands and knees when the door slid open the rest of the way.

She glanced up. "Levi?"

Zoe had considered being in this position for him more than once in the last week. In fact, she'd hoped for it all day. With much less clothing on, of course. When he gazed down at her, his look said the thought had crossed his mind too.

He held up his hands. "All right, all right. You don't have to beg. I'll go out with you."

She laughed and got to her feet. "I'm sorry. My dog's out of control."

"Is that the dark streak that flew through here?" He gestured over his shoulder.

"That would be him." She rubbed the bruise forming on her knee. "We're still getting used to each other."

He chuckled, stepping aside. "Come on in."

"Thanks." She slipped by him and into the apartment.

The space looked like the rest of the building: industrial origins, tall ceilings, exposed ductwork, glossy concrete floors, exposed metal beams. Warehouse-style windows consumed an entire wall, floor to ceiling, adding to the spacious feeling.

The open loft flowed from one end to the other with a set of spiral stairs leading up to a dark area. She suspected that's where he slept. Beneath that space sat a collection of instruments spaced out in a semi-circle.

A rare loft like this in San Francisco didn't come cheap. Levi had said weddings were his "bread and butter." By the looks of his place, he must have raided a bakery.

"Business must be good," she said appreciatively.

"I get by."

He led her to the sitting area, where Freddy tore around the oversized area rug. It was like he'd ingested a V6 engine on the way there—along with the mints in her purse, and, come to think of it, part of her purse too.

"What did you feed him?" Levi asked. "Jet fuel?"

"I think he's just overexcited. He was dropped off earlier today at the dachshund rescue center, where I volunteer. It's been a big day for him."

Freddy took another spin around the carpet, pausing at her feet. His tongue lolled out as he stared up at her. A few pants later, he took off again.

Zoe sighed wearily. "I thought it was love at first sight."

Levi laughed. "Hopefully it won't turn out to be a one-night stand."

She smirked to herself. *Funny he should mention that.* "I hope you don't mind that I brought him here. It was an impromptu decision today, and I didn't want to leave him alone on the first night. I'm taking him home for a two-week trial run to see if we're a good fit. He acted much calmer at the center. I don't get it."

"Don't worry about it. I love dogs."

"All right, shall we get started?" she asked, wanting to get down to business. So hopefully they could *get down to business.*

"You can't just snap your fingers and ask me to perform. You have to immerse yourself in the experience." He gestured to the sofa. "Please, have a seat."

"All right." She sat on the edge of the leather couch. Crossing her legs, she waited patiently.

He gave her a funny look. "You can relax."

"I am relaxed," she said.

"No. I mean, really relax. Or do you not know how?"

She arched an eyebrow. She supposed he was the expert, Mr. Relaxed himself.

Okay, so maybe she was a bit nervous. All day long, she'd imagined how their little meeting would go. Imagined what she would say to him, how she would broach the subject of a no-strings-attached arrangement. It's not like she propositioned guys often. Or ever.

"I know how to relax," she said. Wiggling back on the

cushion, she leaned back but then slid down a few inches when her tight skirt slipped on the leather upholstery.

He snorted. Walking over to the coffee table, he picked up a piece of paper and handed it to her. "This is the list of songs that are big hits at weddings."

She scanned the list, pausing on one song in particular. "Sir Mix-a-Lot?"

"It's a beautiful song about a man's love."

"For big butts?"

He grinned. "Yes."

She gave him a flat look. "No."

"But it kills at the right moment. Usually about ten drinks in. I'll show you." He picked up a guitar from a stand in the corner and perched on a chair across from her. He gave a slow, romantic strum of the strings, then began singing about his passion for voluptuous derrieres. He pulled an emo boy-band face as he drew out the so-not-romantic verse.

Zoe giggled at the serious look on his face. "Absolutely not."

"Freddy seems to like it." Levi nodded to the center of the carpet.

The doxie sat at his feet, staring up at him expectantly. He barked as if to say he was impatient for the next song. *Encore!*

She frowned. "That's weird. I guess he finally burned off all his energy."

Levi considered the dog for a moment. "Okay. Let's see if he likes this one."

He strummed a new tune. At first, she didn't recognize it, but once he sang, it turned out to be Adele.

As he ran through a couple of examples from his list, he didn't simply regurgitate the same old pieces. He made them his own, speeding up or slowing down, shaping them with his style. Freddy seemed to approve. Head resting on his paws, he listened intently, as captivated as a groupie.

Zoe had to admit, Levi's voice blew her away. Smooth and

low, with a rumble that vibrated through her body, massaging her from the inside. He sang until every little knot in her back melted, and she actually did relax.

For the moment, she put aside worries about someone trying to hurt her, arranged marriages, her shrinking savings, and Piper's wedding dress. Everything washed away until only his voice lingered.

A hand squeezed her shoulder. Her eyes flew open, and she blinked at her surroundings. Levi stared back at her with that lazy smile of his.

"Good morning."

"What?" She jerked upright. "I slept all night?"

He chuckled. "Kidding. You just fell asleep."

"Sorry. I don't know what came over me. I guess it's been a busy weekend." She yawned, rubbing a hand over her face. She froze when the scents of parmesan and oregano tickled her nose. "What's that smell?"

"I just finished making dinner."

"What? How long did I sleep?" She glanced at her watch.

"An hour."

"Oh, wow." Tucking her hair back into place, she straightened her clothes. "We can go over the rest of your playlist another day. You can stop by my office, if that works for you."

"Or we can try again after we eat. I made dinner for two," he said. "Besides, I've already taken Freddy outside for a walk, so you've got time."

Zoe scanned the apartment to find the doxie curled up on one of the armchairs. "I see he's still his calmer alter ego."

"He got a little excitable, so I threw on some music, and he calmed right down."

She tuned into the soft background music. "Jazz?"

"Classic. Duke Ellington, to be exact. Freddy's been napping ever since." He held out his hand. "Would you like to taste my meatballs?"

"What?" She gaped at him. Her eyes automatically dipped

to his crotch. Did he know what she'd been thinking when she came over? Did she talk in her sleep?

"Spaghetti and meatballs." Levi gave her a cheesy smile "That's what's for dinner."

He held out a hand. Dazed, Zoe took it, and he helped her to her feet. When she followed him to the dining area, she saw he'd already set the table. Steam rose from the dishes of served spaghetti.

"You didn't have to go through so much trouble." Secretly, she wondered if he didn't sneak someone in there to prepare it while she slept.

"No trouble at all." He pulled out her chair.

She sat down as he pushed the seat in behind her like a real gentleman. Frowning, she observed the table setting, the music, the wine, the candles.

"Did you trick me into a date?"

"Date? Me? Nah. We're just two people eating a meal together." Levi shook out his napkin—a fabric one, not paper —and placed it on his lap.

She narrowed her eyes. "Sure. If you say so." Twirling her fork into the pasta, she took her first bite. "It's not bad."

"Something I just threw together."

She peered over at the kitchen, searching for the empty cans of prepared pasta sauce. But she only spotted the remains of diced vegetables and spices. "You made this from scratch?"

He held an offended hand to his chest. "Don't sound so shocked. I can cook."

She took another bite and nodded. "You can cook pretty well. You struck me as a takeout kind of guy."

His brow furrowed. "I don't know what that means."

She laughed. "Me neither, I guess."

"So, how did you get into wedding planning?" Levi asked her while they ate.

Casual small talk, Zoe noted, the getting-to-know-you type of conversation. Now it definitely felt like a date. It wasn't exactly why she'd come, but her stomach was twisting with hunger, and they would need their energy if she had her way.

"Originally, I just wanted to plan parties," she said. "It sounded extravagant, nothing but fun and cocktails and fancy dresses. I never expected to plan weddings."

"Why not? You don't enjoy the buildup, the excitement, all the mushy girly stuff?"

She shrugged. "Maybe it's like that for the bride, but all weddings are the same after a while. For me, it's just business. I already let myself get caught up in all that once before."

He sipped his wine. "I suppose it would have put a bad taste in my mouth too, if I'd had your personal experience."

"So why do you work the wedding scene?"

"Because I like the mushy girly stuff." He winked. "Call me a sucker, but I think weddings are nice. Sometimes you witness some pretty romantic things."

Zoe eyeballed him over the homemade dinner and candles as slow jazz played in the background. Where had her rock star gone?

When she said nothing, Levi continued. "It's also because weddings are where the steady money is. In a perfect world, our music would take off and the band would fill the big venues. For now, I've got to be flexible."

She nodded. Now that she'd eaten and woken up a bit, the real reason she'd come over nagged at her. Ever since she'd received his text at the center, she'd flip-flopped about giving into her temptations, her desires fighting with her instincts to run far, far away.

She'd avoided men for so long that it felt unnatural to spend the night with one. However, after a climax-scarce week, she was more than ready to give into him. He'd certainly seemed up for the job. But now, strangely, instead of acting like a flirtatious, cocky rock star with a woman in his apartment, he wanted to wine and dine her. How the hell was she going to get him in the mood?

"Sex in a pan?" Levi asked.

Zoe blinked. *That's more like it.* "I prefer the bed, or maybe a shower, or we can do it on the couch if you like."

He snorted. "No. I mean dessert."

Grabbing their dishes, he carried them into the kitchen. When he returned, he brought two plates loaded with layer upon layer of chocolate, whipped cream, pudding, and some kind of nutty base.

"Sex in a pan." He gestured with the plate. "Well, it's not in the pan anymore, but it was."

"Looks delicious."

"Shall we eat in the living room?"

He carried the dessert to the coffee table, and she followed him. When she took her first bite, "delicious" didn't even come close. The man knew how to cook.

Zoe couldn't stop observing him while he ate. He still radiated rock star: faded T-shirt and ripped jeans, chipped black nail polish, the piercing—which she was sure had been on the other side. Yet, Levi acted like a regular Martha Stewart.

"Dinner seems a little less impromptu than you made it sound," she said.

"What?" He started guiltily. "You mean you don't have sex in a pan sitting in your fridge all the time?" When she gave him a look, he held up his spoon. "Okay, you caught me. I hoped you'd say yes to dinner."

"I'm glad I stayed." She moaned in pleasure as she took another bite. "You make good sex."

"Thank you." His voice dipped low. "I knew I'd have you moaning in no time."

Zoe put her plate down, hoping the dessert she'd really come for was finally ready. She leaned in close. Close enough to smell his aftershave, close enough to run her nose across his stubbled cheek.

"And tell me," she whispered, her lips grazing his earlobe. "How do you plan to make me moan?"

Levi groaned before turning to face her. His lips hovered inches from hers. "First, I'll get you comfortable on this couch."

He leaned closer, pushing her back until she lay down. The cool leather caused goose bumps to rise on her skin. Or maybe that was his hand gliding up her thigh. He toyed with the hem of her skirt, pushing it up an inch or two.

Her lips parted. "And then what are you going to do?"

"Well," he said, "being a musician, I'm pretty good with my hands."

"Is that so?" She shifted restlessly, desperate to find out just how good.

His fingers crept higher. Shutting her eyes, she reveled in the touch of a hand other than her own for once.

She inhaled sharply. "Where are you going to put them?"

"I'm gonna put them all over your ..." His fingers trailed along the lace of her thong. "Feet."

Zoe's eyes flew open. "Huh?"

"I know how to give the most amazing foot rubs." Levi's voice rumbled against her throat as he ran kisses up her neck.

Okay, she thought, *maybe he's a foot man.* She could do kinky. "I was kind of hoping you'd rub something else."

He pulled away slightly. "Like your back?"

Her hips squirmed greedily toward his touch, but his fingers went no farther. She grunted in frustration. Her vibrators never teased.

"Or we could always skip the foreplay," she said hopefully.

Zoe couldn't take it anymore. She adjusted herself on the couch until she was on top, straddling him. Popping the top button on his jeans, she unzipped his fly. When she tugged his pants down over his hips, he wore boxers. They only gave her a teasing hint of what bulged beneath.

Greedy for more, she reached for the waistline of his underwear. Before she could pull them down too, he grabbed her wrists and drew her close for a kiss. As his lips grazed hers, she recoiled in surprise.

Kissing was for romance. If she'd wanted romance, she would have stayed at home and watched a chick-flick with Addison.

"We can't skip the foreplay," he said. "That's my favorite part. And I'm good at it."

"Yeah? What did you have in mind?" She bit his chin playfully, feeling his stubble scrape against her teeth.

"Like flirting."

"Mmm," she groaned. "You're good at that."

Reaching for the bottom of Levi's shirt, she tugged at it, ready to rip it right off him. Sliding it up, she exposed the smooth, hard abs she'd previewed in the vestry—and had imagined touching ever since. She ran her tongue along his hairless skin.

"And talking," he said, but his voice sounded a bit rougher.

"Yes." Zoe panted. "Talk dirty to me."

"And hand-holding."

Her lips paused on his tight stomach. "Umm. Yeah … okay."

"And texting thoughtful messages throughout the day."

"Like sexting?" She wrinkled her nose.

She was done with the talking now, with the torture. Since the day they'd met, Levi had pursued her. He'd claimed to be the kind of guy who reached out and grabbed life by the balls. And now that she'd decided to do the same, he was playing hard to get.

Tired of the games, she took a page from his sheet music. Reaching out, she grabbed those balls—literally. *His* balls.

Levi jumped. "Whoa! Wait. What are you doing?"

"Grabbing life by the balls. Was I too rough?" She gave his ear a nip. "You strike me as a guy who likes it rough."

He laughed but gently held her away so he could meet her eyes. "I think you've misunderstood the ball-grabbing theory."

"What are we waiting for?" she asked. "You're ready. I'm ready."

"Ready for what?"

"Sex."

"We're not having sex," he said. "At least not tonight."

Though, by the way he took in the sight of her straddling him, she thought he must be kidding.

Zoe shook her head as though the sex fog clouding her brain had affected her hearing too. "What?"

"It's too soon for that."

She slid off his lap and back onto the leather. "Are we on some kind of schedule I don't know about?"

Levi straightened up on the couch to face her. "We should get to know each other better first. Hobbies, likes, dislikes, family. That my childhood's pet name was Jujube ..."

Zoe leaned closer, running her hands up his chest with a coy smile. He couldn't be serious. "Why get into all that when we're clearly attracted to each other. Let's just have some fun."

"I'm trying to. But I want more first." He grabbed her hand to hold it.

She pulled it back as if he'd burned her. "How much more?"

"Like a date. A few of them. Dinner at a restaurant, maybe a movie. That new rom-com just came out. I could take you to see it on Friday night," he said hopefully.

She sneered. A rom-com? Was this a joke? "Okay, rock star. Let's cut the crap, shall we? I'm offering you sex with no strings attached. Except, if it's good, maybe I'll want to do it again."

Levi leaned back and gave her a hard look. "But I don't want that."

"Then what do you want?"

"I want *more*." He gestured to her like he meant specifically more of her, not just her body.

"I don't *do* more. I'm not the relationship type. To be

honest, I don't even do this." She pointed at the couch. At them.

"We're not doing anything." He laughed like she was acting ridiculous.

Her back straightened at the sound of it. She'd practically thrown herself at him, and he was laughing?

"You're right," she said. "We're not doing anything." Tugging her skirt back down, she stood and gently picked her sleeping puppy off the chair.

"Wait a minute," Levi said. "What's going on? You seemed interested. I thought we had something going on here."

"Yeah, so did I." Zoe grabbed her purse and made a beeline for the door.

He laughed again. "Then what's the problem?"

"I don't want any of this romantic stuff." She waved a dismissive hand at the dinner, and the candles, and the jazz music. "Come on. What's with the thoughtful texts and foot rubs? You're supposed to be Mr. Rock Star. You stay out all night and wake up with lipstick on your cheek in the morning. Are you being serious right now?"

He crossed his arms and scowled. She'd offended him. Maybe as a rock star. Maybe as a romantic at heart. "I'd like to be serious about you. But unless you want the same thing, then we're done here."

"I agree. Come on, Freddy."

Zoe wrenched open the sliding metal door and stormed out of the apartment. It clanged shut behind her.

She didn't know what consumed her more: the humiliation of rejection or the frustration of knowing her vibrators would prove useless when she got home. Either way, she wasn't getting any with Levi or herself that night. In a pan or otherwise.

Chapter Twelve

SINGING THE BLUES

Zoe pulled out of the Monday morning traffic and into a free space on Folsom Street in front of her office. She killed the engine, and the radio shut off. Freddy whined from the passenger seat, annoyed by the silence. Or maybe he wondered why she just sat there, staring listlessly out the window. Then again, he could have to pee. Or he was hungry. Or he was simply being Freddy.

With his two-second attention span, he hopped down from the passenger seat. He sniffed his way into the back, which was loaded with the new supplies she'd bought to replace her damaged stuff. A few seconds later, a *thump* made her jump in her seat.

She spun around. Freddy buried himself beneath a pile of clean, pressed cloth napkins—or at least they *had been* clean.

He dug at the pile, burrowing like a true doxie before worming his way into the hole he'd built.

Zoe tutted. "Freddy."

The pile shifted and twitched until a tan face nudged out. His eyebrows twitched up innocently. *I did nothing.*

She rolled her eyes. She couldn't argue with that. Just like she couldn't argue when he'd torn apart her pillow that morning, toilet papered her living room, or peed on her dining table leg. She knew puppies took time to train. But the more time she spent with him, the more she was convinced this wasn't a puppy. He was Satan's spawn.

However, she had to admit, he had his moments. He'd behaved during the drive to her office, but now he wouldn't sit still. Maybe he liked car rides. Or Levi's theory could be right, and the dog liked to jam.

As he fidgeted again, she turned the key until the radio tuned in. It took only a few moments for Freddy to stop his relentless and destructive burrowing. Laying his head down, he kicked back, chilling to some soothing Jack Johnson. Zoe wished she could do the same, but she had a lot of damage control to do.

The moment she pulled the key out of the ignition, the doxie got up and snooped for something to chew on. As she reached to open her door, a figure popped up next to the van, rapping sharply on the window.

Zoe jumped in her seat. Freddy barked like the devil himself wanted in. Then she spotted the bright pantsuit and over-processed blonde hair and thought his assumption wasn't far off: Holly Hart.

Howling, Freddy tore to the front, knocking over a box of blank thank-you cards. Picking him up off the floor, Zoe soothed him until his barks subdued into muttered threats.

Her fingers twitched toward the keys to start the engine and peel out of there like she hadn't seen the reporter. However, Holly read her mind and jumped in front of the van. She slipped her oversized sunglasses onto the top of her head and motioned for Zoe to roll down the window.

Heaving a sigh, she hit the button. "What are you doing here, Holly?"

Bleached teeth flashing, the reporter leaned through the window. "Darling! It's so good to see you. I was in the neighborhood and thought I'd pop in for a little girl chat." She gave

Zoe a not-so-subtle wink. "What do you say we go grab a coffee and catch up?"

"We have nothing to catch up on." Zoe opened her door, using it to shove Holly out of the way.

She pouted. "Now don't be like that. We were like old pals at the expo, remember? Now, where were we?" Her friendly smile melted, and she fixed a don't-mess-with-me look on her plastic face. "Oh, right. I did you a favor by not running a super-embarrassing story, and you were about to tell me all about your friend's upcoming wedding. Now go ahead and gush. It's just us girls."

Zoe ignored her and went to grab supplies from the back, but when she rounded the van, Hey You shoved his camera in her face.

She scowled at him and threw Holly a sour look. "Just us girls?"

"Oh, right. And him. But don't be shy. It's for note-taking purposes only." She waved him away like he was simply air. "Ignore him. I do."

Zoe could have sworn she heard him huff, but he never stopped recording for a second. She turned her back on them and wrenched open the van doors.

Holly took a seat on the bumper, crossing her legs casually. Now Zoe couldn't get rid of her without physically tossing her aside or slamming the door closed on her—which were both tempting options.

"Listen up," Zoe said. "I have nothing more to give you on the Summers-Caldwell wedding."

Picking up her bag, she slung it over the arm not burdened by a wriggling doxie. She tried to close the van doors, hoping the reporter would take the hint.

Holly didn't move an inch. "Don't hold out now, Plum. Remember? It's tit for tat."

Her teeth clenched. "Yeah, I remember."

While Zoe didn't want to give her any sort of tit, she

needed Holly's tat. Not only had she failed to gain new clients at the expo, but her run-in with Chelsea had probably cost her some reputation points for the next season. However, she also wasn't about to go against her best friend's wishes to keep her wedding on the down low. She'd given away enough info already.

"Look," she began, "I appreciate you not running that story on me—"

"Then show your appreciation and give me some facts." Holly made a "gimme-gimme" motion with her manicured hand. "It's not a big deal, you know. If I search hard enough, I can easily dig up the same info. But it would take a few annoying phone calls," she said as though it was, like, the hardest thing to do in the world.

Zoe scoffed. "To who?"

"To florists, seamstresses, caterers." She groaned, and her eyes rolled back into her head from the effort of listing them off. "Eventually, I'd find the right ones. But that sounds incredibly boring, so why don't you save me some time? No one has to know it was you."

Zoe cocked an eyebrow at the camera. "I bet."

Holly stood up and waved away the cameraman. The red light on the front dimmed, and he lowered it.

"Just give me some meaningless tidbits to satisfy my fans," she persisted. "The venue, perhaps?"

Zoe laughed, slamming the van doors and locking them. "There's no way you're getting the venue. Or anything else, for that matter."

"Oh, come on," she whined. "You can tell little old me."

Zoe spun, towering over the sleazy news reporter. "I can't, *I won't* tell you. If I did, the place would be crawling with curious looky-loos. Or worse." She narrowed her eyes. "*You.*"

"Fine. What about the florist?"

She chewed on her lip as she considered it. There didn't seem any harm in it, not if it would get Holly off her back.

Besides, her florist was an artist. And she strongly believed in cross promoting her contacts in the wedding industry. It was all about building a reputation. And what goes around comes around. Tit for tat, she supposed.

Finally, she relented. "It's Pushing Daisies on Sixteenth." With that, she made a break for the building, where she could put an office door between her and Holly.

However, the reporter leaped in front of the door, blocking her path. "And the person performing the ceremony?"

"I think you've got enough intel already. I don't need you harassing the justice of the peace."

Her eyes lit up. "Oh, so they're not going the religious route then?"

Zoe cringed at the slip. "Now, if you're done harassing me, I need to get to my office."

"What do you mean 'harassing'?" Her mouth dropped open. "I don't harass. I investigate."

Zoe threw open the door. It hit Holly's back, and she stumbled out of the way. Slipping inside, Zoe let the door close behind her.

The reporter yelled through the glass. "Great talk! We'll do it again soon."

Freddy barked over Zoe's shoulder. *Goodbye!* His tail whipped against her blouse like *Wasn't she nice?*

Thankfully, Holly never followed her inside. Maybe she worried about harassment charges or some trespass law associated with reporting.

Zoe carried Freddy up the four flights of stairs. There was an elevator, but it was slow and kind of sketchy. She could afford an office in a newer building, but she liked the quirks of the converted early 1900s hotel. It had a certain charm. During the renovation, the painting on the side of the brick facade, advertising rooms for rent, had even been restored.

When she reached the fourth floor, she set Freddy down. The building manager had allowed her to keep Buddy there during office hours, so she knew it would be all right to bring Freddy to work. Then again, he wasn't quite the well-behaved dog her last one was.

This wasn't the calm, well-mannered dog she'd planned on adopting. What if he never settled down? If he continued to act like a toddler on espresso throughout their two-week trial period, she wasn't sure it would work out between them. Maybe they were just too different.

She supposed that's why all adoptions from the center came with a two-week trial run; they didn't always go to plan.

Freddy trailed behind, sniffing dubiously beneath random doors. Thankfully, no one came out to see what all the snorting at their door was about. He would be a handful. Remembering his love of music, she pulled out her tablet and made a note to pick up some speakers for her office. Then she spotted the time at the top of the screen. She was running way behind her usual schedule—probably because she'd stayed up late, dwelling on her evening with Levi.

For some reason, compared to everything else, the rocker's rejection consumed her the most. She'd actually enjoyed spending time with him. He'd helped her forget her mounting stress, even for just a little while. And she'd hoped he'd help her relieve a little more, but he'd shot her down. And now all her brain wanted to do was fantasize about him.

Zoe whistled, calling Freddy as she approached the office at the end of the hall with the purple sign: *Plum Crazy Events*.

Her appointment calendar was sadly clear that morning, so when she reached her door and a man appeared from around the corner, she gasped in surprise. Then she recognized him, and she took a wary step back.

"Owen. Hi … How are you?"

The jilted groom's lips curled into a smile, but the rest of his face didn't join in. "Good. You know, all things considered."

"Still haven't patched things up with Juliet?"

He shook his head. "She won't return my calls. I've sent her texts, emails, flowers, but she doesn't want to see me."

"I'm sorry to hear that. Sometimes these things happen," she said, apologetically. Because she was sorry—for him, not for Juliet. "The weeks and days leading up to a wedding can be so stressful. Tension builds, adding to anxiety and fears. It can put a lot of strain on a relationship. Maybe her running off was a blessing in disguise," she suggested hesitantly. "I mean, if it's not meant to be, then it's better to know now rather than once you're married, right?"

Owen's eyes dropped. "But then why doesn't it feel that way?"

Zoe took a moment to give this shell of a groom a once-over. His bloodshot eyes studied his feet. His ball cap hid a head full of greasy hair. He looked as terrible as Juliet had at the expo.

"So, what can I do for you?" she asked.

He cringed. "Actually, I'm here about Juliet. Or maybe on behalf of her."

"Oh?" she said. "I thought she wasn't talking to you."

"She's not, but I've spoken with her mother. She tells me Juliet's been in trouble with the police over some vandalism."

Zoe tilted her head noncommittally. She was beginning to see why he'd really come. "There was some damage to my van."

So, he was there to convince her to … what? Not pursue it? Not press charges? The guy had gone through a lot recently, but despite everything, he still cared for his bride. He was only guilty of being blinded by love.

"She didn't do it," Owen said simply. "She couldn't have."

Zoe straightened, wondering if it was time to call her lawyer. "She publicly threatened me earlier that day, and then I found my vehicle vandalized. It's hard not to draw conclusions."

"I know it looks bad, and Juliet can sometimes be a little …"

"Frigging intense?" She decided to skip the expletives.

"Well, yeah," he relented. "But she doesn't mean it. She's like a cute little Chihuahua." His smile was genuine this time, kind of boyish. "She's all bark and no bite."

She scoffed. She'd had enough experiences with Chihuahuas to know they could bite pretty hard. "Sorry. But I'm not convinced. And there's nothing I can do about it anyway. It's in the hands of the police now. If she's truly innocent, then she has nothing to worry about, and their investigation will turn up nothing."

He glanced at Freddy, who rolled onto his back to ask for a belly rub. Owen gave in, squatting down to pet him. The doxie writhed and wormed to soak up all the love and to give Owen's wrist a lick at the same time. Like his slobbery kisses were fair payment.

"I suppose you're right," he said. "It's just … I can see she's angry and hurt. I wish I could do something for her." Gnawing on his bottom lip, he stood up. "Well, I'd better go. Thanks for hearing me out. I'm sorry to bother you. I know your day didn't go exactly as planned either."

"It wasn't my day. It was yours," she said. "And again, I'm sorry."

His head sank as he trudged down the hall, feet scuffing like he didn't have the energy to go on.

Zoe couldn't understand what he saw in Juliet, but she couldn't ignore a problem. She loved a challenge, and Juliet was nothing if not challenging. Heaving a sigh, she jogged back down the hallway after Owen.

Freddy jumped and barked at her heels. *Why are we running? Are we going somewhere? I like going places. I like running too.*

When she reached the top of the stairs, she called out. "Owen?!"

A second later, his head poked around the corner.

"Try a box of truffles from the shop at the ferry building," she called down to him. "Juliet requested them for your honeymoon suite after the wedding."

"Really?" He smiled like she'd just thrown him a morsel of hope. "Thanks. I will."

"I hope she likes them."

He gave her a wave, and as he continued down the stairs, his footsteps sounded a little lighter.

She shook her head. *To each their own.*

As Zoe headed back toward her office, Freddy paced at the top of the stairs, hoping Owen might come back for more belly rubs. Eventually, he abandoned his post. Zoe kept an eye on him as he trailed behind, double-checking the doors.

Maybe he wasn't so bad, she told herself. Maybe he was actually super smart, monitoring for danger, protecting her. A real guard dog.

As he passed the next door, his tail whacked against the wood, making a knocking sound. He spun around and barked at it.

Then again, maybe not.

Zoe took out her key and approached her office.

BANG.

Scorching heat slapped her in the face; light blinded her. An invisible battering ram punched her gut, and she sailed backward.

Thud.

A wall. Pain shot through her shoulder. Her head smacked a door frame. Agony.

She blinked. Stars danced across her blurry vision.

In a daze, she glanced around. She lay on the floor. Freddy frantically licked her face. His mouth opened and closed, but she couldn't hear his bark over the ringing in her ears.

Zoe pushed herself upright. She gazed at her office—or what remained of it.

The door hung awkwardly from the hinges. Flames licked

around the frame. Smoke billowed out into the hall, reaching toward her.

She stared for a few stunned moments until reality set in, hitting her like … well, an explosion.

Her office had just blown up.

Chapter Thirteen

BLOW THIS HOT DOG STAND

Zoe watched the little light go up and down, then side to side. As it drew back, she blinked away the white spots in her vision and focused on the ambulance attendant.

"Your reaction looks good," he said. "Pupils equal and reactive."

As he jotted a note on his clipboard, the tiny flashlight shone on her lap. Freddy scrambled out of her arms and dove for it. He barked and dug at Zoe's thighs. It might have tickled if everything didn't hurt so much.

The moment the EMT shut off the light, Freddy spun on Zoe's lap to face her, his tail patting her leg. *I just saved your life.*

"I already told you I didn't lose consciousness," she told the attendant. Not that she could recall, anyway. But then again, she wasn't sure she would remember a thing like that. "I'm not going to the hospital, so you might as well give me that waiver to sign now."

With her luck, she'd end up in the same ward as her mother. Wouldn't that be an adorable mother/daughter bonding experience? Lying side by side in a hospital room. How would she convince her mother she could take care of herself then?

"Are you sure you don't have a headache?" the EMT asked her. "No nausea?"

"No. Just the ringing in my ears."

He made a couple more notes on his sheet. "Okay, if that persists, make sure you see your doctor. And as for the rest of the symptoms—"

"I'll monitor them and head to the emergency room if I have any concerns. I promise."

Finally, he smile-frowned, handing her the waiver and a pen. He pointed to the bottom. "Sign here ... and here."

She did as he asked before sliding off the stretcher with Freddy. "Thanks for the help."

"You didn't let me do anything," he said teasingly, and maybe a bit fed up with her stubbornness.

She supposed she had that in common with her mother. And doxies, for that matter.

She waved over her shoulder. "Thanks anyway."

Zoe hopped out of the back of the ambulance and glanced up to the fourth floor of the office building. The window on the end had been blown out. Black char marks surrounded the brick facade around it. Rivulets of soot mixed with the water the firefighters had used ran down the side of the building, reminding Zoe of a bride who forgot to wear waterproof mascara.

Thankfully, no one in the surrounding offices had sustained injuries; the blast was confined to her office.

If she'd arrived a few seconds earlier, she and Freddy would have been smack dab in the middle of the explosion when it went off. Her knees trembled, and her hands shook. She held Freddy tighter.

When the police had interviewed her in the ambulance, they hadn't exactly been forthcoming; she was on a need-to-know basis. However, she'd heard one or two building occupants hovering outside the police tape complain about a gas leak. Zoe wouldn't have seen it coming.

For some annoying reason, she could hear Levi's voice in her head. *Life's too short.*

She held Freddy close as she watched the police officers discuss the wreckage, taking photos of blown-up bits of taffeta, silk flowers, crystal headpieces, and chunks of silicone from her inventory. Lots and lots of colorful silicone. While she'd answered most of the police's questions already, she assumed that would raise a few more.

"Zoe!"

Over the ringing in her ears, she heard her name. For a second, she wondered if she'd imagined Levi's voice again. Then she turned to see him farther down the sidewalk, waving at her. With a glance back at the remains of her business, she went to meet him.

He ran up to her. "There you are. Are you all right? I was worried when I saw all the emergency vehicles."

She stared at him. Why was he even there? He eyed her like he wanted to hold her, to comfort her. After what had happened—or rather, what *didn't* happen—between the two of them the night before, she couldn't understand why.

"That's your office building, isn't it?" He pulled out her business card and checked the address on it.

"Yes," she said. "And that giant charred hole at the top is my office. Or it *was* my office."

His mouth popped open, and he moved closer. "Your office blew up? How?"

Her heart thudded in her chest, and she took an automatic step back. She squeezed Freddy tighter, hiding behind him. "I'm thinking combustion."

Levi flinched at her dry tone. "Obviously. Snap out of it. It's not funny. You could have been in there when it happened."

Startled by his dramatic reaction, her mask slipped. Her legs wobbled as her true feelings seeped through her calm exterior. But she couldn't fall apart. Not here. Most especially not in front of Levi.

Zoe shoved her rising anxiety into that overfilled bottle inside and reached into her purse to grope Merry Monkey. "Yeah, but I wasn't. I was about to go in when it blew up. I only got thrown around a little."

He reached out to her. Taking another step back, she brushed his hand aside. But as his fingers grazed her arm, she felt his touch like a call, a need to lean against him like she'd wanted to after her van had lost control.

"Well, it looks like you're just fine without me. I'm sorry to bother you with my concern." He wiped the emotion from his face before he turned and walked away.

She scowled at his back. Where did he get off being mad at her? Wasn't he the one who pushed her away in his apartment?

She marched after him. When she caught up, she grabbed him by the sleeve and spun him around to face her.

"What happened to laid-back Levi, the go-with-the-flow rock and roller? You're getting awfully worked up. I didn't realize you cared so much."

He threw his hands up. "Cared whether or not you blew up?"

"You seemed pretty indifferent when you kicked me out of your apartment." Okay, so maybe it was a little extreme to accuse him of not caring whether she lived or died. Maybe that was her hurt pride speaking.

Levi tossed his head back and laughed, but he obviously wasn't amused. "I believe you left of your own free will after I asked you for more than what you were offering."

"If you didn't like what I was offering, then why are you here?"

Had he reconsidered? She wasn't sure she would sleep with him now that he'd rejected her. But she couldn't deny what his touch had done to her the night before. Even now, she could feel those talented fingers on her skin, his deep, melodic voice echoing through her. Her body wanted him, all right. She couldn't deny that—at least not to herself. To Levi, she would deny it to her grave.

"You told me to come by to finish going over the playlist," he said. "Remember?"

"Oh." She'd completely forgotten about that. "I just hadn't expected you so soon."

"I guess I was a little eager."

She wasn't sure if he was eager to play at Piper's wedding or eager to see her. Since she wasn't sure which answer she wanted, she didn't ask.

Zoe had been honest with him the night before. She didn't want to get romantically involved. She couldn't offer him *more*. And he clearly wasn't interested in just sex. What else was there to say?

"So, what happened?" Levi interrupted her thoughts.

She rubbed a hand over her face. "Nothing happened. This is just the way I am. I don't want a relationship with anyone. It's not you. It's me."

"Really? You're giving me the whole 'It's not you. It's me' line?" He laughed. "I meant what happened in your office?"

The way he smiled at her made her blush. She'd been doing that a lot lately. Pieces of her Pure Pleasure merchandise surrounded them, scattered all over Folsom Street, and yet she felt embarrassed because a guy had a crush on her. Go figure.

"Oh," she said again. After a moment, she turned to the building to hide her blazing cheeks. "I heard it was a gas leak, but I don't know. That seems so …"

"Made up? You think someone bombed your office," he said more than asked. "I take it you have some suspects in mind."

"Chelsea, for starters. Either her or Juliet."

Levi stared up at the fourth story. "Can you really see either of them doing something so extreme? I mean, Chelsea struck me as a mean girl from high school all grown up. This seems a little out of her league."

It was true. Her rival preferred the mental head games. But then Zoe recalled her threat at the expo.

Screw you, Zoe Plum! I'll get you for this!

Was this her revenge? Holly had told Chelsea that if she wanted to get noticed by the media, then she should do something worthy of attention. Maybe this was her seeking attention, or at least bringing bad attention to Zoe.

Then there was Juliet, aka Bridezilla. She had that twitchy, teetering-on-the-edge quality. Lots of potential there for something to snap, despite what her jilted fiancé thought.

Her conversation with Owen rushed back to her. She frowned and spun to Levi. "When I arrived today, minutes before the explosion, I had a visitor waiting outside my office."

"Who?"

"Owen Wells."

"You're kidding. Owen? You think he could be a suspect?" He cocked his head, probably trying to imagine his college friend as an attempted murderer. "If so, maybe they're more perfect for each other than anyone thought."

She shook her head. "No. I don't think he's capable. He came to defend Juliet over the whole vandalism thing. It's just … weird timing, is all."

"Like maybe he might have been stalling you?"

"Maybe." She grew quiet as she considered him as an accessory to the crime.

Owen struck her as a nice guy. She didn't want to think of him in that light—or rather, darkness. However, if he loved an odd fish like Juliet, maybe it took one to love one.

"I don't know what to think," she said. "But I can't come up with anyone else who wants to kill me this week."

"Got a lot of friends, do you?"

She snorted but didn't reply.

Freddy answered by trying to lick her chin. *I'm your friend. Who are you again?*

Zoe ran a hand through her hair, tugging on it. "I don't know. Maybe I'm overthinking all of this, seeing enemies where there are only shadows."

"Maybe," Levi said. "You know what they say. When it rains, it pours."

"It feels like I'm in the middle of a monsoon."

"What will you do without an office?" he asked.

She forced a chuckle, but it came out like an exhausted sigh. "Can't do much. I suppose I'll start searching tomorrow. My apartment isn't an option right now. It's a disaster. I'm in the middle of organizing for a move that's not happening now. You know, to a house I can't afford anymore, thanks to the lack of steady business."

Levi casually kicked the brick wall next to them. "I know someone with a pretty big flat. He might have some extra space to offer you."

Zoe's mouth fell open. "Why would you do that? Why would you offer me your space after last night? After you were about to walk away just now? I don't understand."

He shrugged. "No big deal. I aim to please."

"It is a big deal. Do you usually aim to please anyone? Or just me?"

"Lots of people. I'm not the worst guy, you know," he said a little defensively. "But especially you."

She'd made it clear the night before. She knew she had. And yet here he stood before her with that hopeful expression on his face.

Part of her recoiled at the sweetness, while something inside her perked up. On the surface, Levi appeared a bona fide rock star. But beneath all the piercings, the dark look, the ripped jeans, he struck her as a sweet, innocent guy. The boy next door all grown up. The guy who, when he told you he liked you, he meant *you*, not your body or what he might want to do with it. He could be one of the good ones. For someone else, that is.

"I don't want things to get complicated," Zoe said. "I don't want to lead you on."

"Who says you're doing the leading?" A boyish grin animated his face.

She locked eyes with him. "You can't change my mind. Many men have tried before you."

"I know I can't. The only person who can change your mind is you." His expression mirrored her own, like maybe she was getting through to him. Or maybe he believed he could get through to her.

She gnawed on her lip. With Piper's wedding coming up and so much work to do, she was in a tight spot. However, she was afraid to accept. "I can't offer you more, Levi."

"This isn't extortion. You need help. I can give it. No strings attached." He gave her a ghost of a smirk, and she knew he'd used her words on purpose.

She couldn't help but smile back. "Okay. I appreciate the offer. It won't be for long, I promise. I'll be out of your hair as soon as I can."

Freddy whined and squirmed in her arms. He probably had to pee since his last walk had been before they arrived at the office. She placed him on the ground. With all the people coming and going, she kept his leash short as he searched for the perfect spot to relieve himself. Then he became distracted by a butterfly, and then a piece of grass, and then his own tail.

Zoe stared at the path of wreckage littering the sidewalk and decorating parked cars. Her eyes followed the ruined remains of her office all the way to the intersection.

On every street corner, people with nothing better to do gawked at the scene. Most of them had their phones out, snapping photos or taking videos. However, one person caught her eye. He had a professional video camera aimed at the chaos.

The man's posture was tense, his attention focused as he

captured a panorama of the area. Finally, he lowered the camera to survey the area, and she got a clear look at his face.

It was, well … Zoe didn't actually know his name. It was Holly Hart's minion, Hey You, as she not-so-fondly called him.

She automatically scanned her surroundings for a sign of the annoying blonde. Hadn't she dragged enough stories out of her for one day? Zoe could just imagine the headlines she'd invent for this one.

"I'll be right back," she told Levi.

Plucking Freddy off the ground, she strode toward the intersection. Hey You spotted her before she caught up to him. He gave a guilty start. Clutching his camera, he made a break for it, diving into the throng of onlookers.

She took off after him. However, without the obvious camera as a giveaway, his muted brown hair and undefined features made him difficult to pick out in a crowd. He was so very extraordinarily ordinary. It was hard to describe him while looking right at him. Heck, she'd never even heard him speak.

Just when she worried that she'd lost his trail, she spotted him racing for an alley halfway down the block. Pausing at the entrance, he glanced back. His eyes locked with hers, and his one free hand reached down and covered his crotch, as though subconsciously.

Zoe grinned wickedly. Obviously, he hadn't forgotten the time she'd threatened him for harassing Piper.

She pushed past a couple of people she recognized from her office building. As she picked up her pace, her head throbbed and new aches and pains introduced themselves.

Biting the inside of her cheek, she pushed aside the discomfort and turned the corner. Ready to grab Hey You by the sweaty shirt collar, she plunged into the alley.

She blinked. *Where is he?* Her eyes caught a flash of his tan jacket just as he rounded the corner at the other end and disappeared from sight.

"Dammit," Zoe muttered.

He ran faster than she would have guessed, but she supposed a person couldn't get involved with Holly Hart for a living and not know how to run for their life—or balls, in his case.

She slowed to a stop. It wasn't like she could catch up to him with her injuries, while wearing heels, and carrying a dog. However, Freddy's legs pawed the air like they were still running. *Let me at him. Let me at him!*

Zoe gave his head a soothing pat. "Don't worry. We'll get him next time."

He stared at her, his big ears rising a little. *Get who?*

Rubbing a stitch in her side, she walked back to the main road. It was still too early for the sun to reach the narrow back alley. The morning chill lingered, crawling over the sweat settling on her skin after her chase. Goose bumps prickled up the back of her neck.

She held Freddy tight, both for warmth and comfort. She still wasn't convinced the explosion was an accident, and here she was chasing a creep down a quiet alley.

Zoe peered back over her shoulder, but Hey You was long gone. With a shiver, she turned back and nearly ran into someone. A tall figure blocked her path.

Freddy barked. She jumped, then hated herself for it. It was only Levi. The pup's tail whipped back and forth, hitting one of the many bruises she'd acquired that morning.

"Are you okay?" Levi asked her.

"Yeah, I saw Holly's cameraman hanging around."

"Really? Is she around here somewhere?" He scanned the crowd eagerly.

She rolled her eyes. Even at a time like this, he was desperate for an interview. Before she could come up with a witty retort, her phone vibrated in her purse. She pulled it out and answered.

"Hello?"

"Hello, is this Zoe Plum?"

"It is." She held her breath, half expecting more bad news.

"This is San Francisco General Hospital. Your mother is ready for discharge."

"Thank you. I'll be there to pick her up as soon as I can."

Zoe hung up and automatically turned for her rental van. But the sight of it stopped her short. Little number tags littered the hood, marking the evidence scattered all over it. No way would the police release it to her.

"Do you have to pick up your mom?" Levi asked like he was just making conversation. "It's a shame you don't have a ride."

He rocked onto his heels, a self-satisfied grin on his face. He wasn't going to make this easy, but Zoe supposed she deserved it. He'd done a lot for her in the last few days, and what had she done? Assumed he was some easy lay, propositioned him for sex, and then got grumpy when he shot her down.

With a deep breath, she swallowed her sore pride. "Levi, would you mind giving us a ride?"

"Why, I'd love to." He batted his eyelashes at her. "You just can't get enough of me, can you?"

"Not that I can help, no." Zoe kept her voice even because she wasn't entirely sure she was being sarcastic.

Chapter Fourteen

PUT A DOG OFF THE SCENT

Zoe unlocked the front door to the Victorian stick-style home in Noe Valley where she'd grown up. "Here we are."

She held the door open for her mother to enter, but Freddy barged in first, already scoping out the joint.

It was another hot day. The air felt heavy inside, despite the fact that Zoe had shut all the curtains to keep the sun from beating in.

"It's nice to come home." Her mother shuffled through the door. "Thank you very much for the ride, Levi."

"It was my pleasure," he said. "It was nice to meet you."

"You too." She gave him a little head bob, like a mini bow, a habit that had never fully faded since leaving Japan.

Taking off her shoes, she put on a pair of slippers and disappeared into the living room. Zoe knew her mother often got cold feet, but she also suspected that it was another lingering habit, even though they had hardwood floors, not tatami mats.

She felt a brief pang of regret. It happened whenever she glimpsed little hints of her mother's Japanese upbringing, a side to the woman she'd never know. Zoe ached to visit Japan, to explore the other half of her family history, to see how her mother grew up. If nothing else, maybe it would help her understand Junko better.

Levi waited until she was out of earshot before whispering in Zoe's ear. "I think your mom hates me."

She snorted, not sure why he cared what her mother thought of him or why he'd tried so hard to change her mind on the drive home. He'd pestered her with small talk and cheesy compliments, such as "I can see where your daughter gets her good looks."

"She doesn't hate you. She's distant with everyone at first," she told him. "My mom is private and keeps to herself. She's probably embarrassed that a complete stranger had to drive her home from the hospital."

He handed Zoe her mother's bag of belongings. Freddy gave it a curious sniff before wandering into the living room.

She started up the stairs. "I won't be long. Or I can take a taxi home if you have somewhere else to be."

"Somewhere better than here with you? Impossible." He waved her on. "Take your time. I'll just be snooping around your childhood home."

She threw him a look. "Then I'll only be a second."

Zoe quickly ran through the house, checking to make sure her mom had everything she needed. However, she'd done most of the preparations the day before. As she went from room to room, she made a list of things to bring the next day. It was routine by now since she regularly popped by a few times a week.

While her mother usually did her own grocery shopping and cleaning, Zoe had to do the heavy lifting around the old house. For being the black sheep of her family and leaving Japan to marry an American at twenty, Junko was still a traditionalist at heart. She'd relied heavily on her husband to perform the "male" roles of the household.

After her dad died, Zoe had to teach her mother how to reset the breaker, start the gas lawn mower, and do things like set mousetraps. And Zoe still ended up doing most of that herself during her regular visits. She felt better knowing her mother wasn't lighting the pilot light on the furnace or changing a burned-out light bulb in a ceiling fixture.

Heading to the kitchen, she pulled out her mother's new medications and organized them all on the kitchen counter. Each label had different instructions. Junko's English was excellent, but even Zoe was confused. She took out a pen and relabeled them in Japanese.

She grabbed the mail from the mailbox. Flipping through the letters, scanning for junk, she joined her mother and Levi in the living room. He hovered in front of the fireplace, a picture frame in his hands.

He waved it in the air. "Your mother says you were quite the gymnast."

Zoe recognized the photo in his hands. A dark-haired little girl balanced on a beam no wider than her body, a giant satisfied grin on her face. She'd been eight.

She swiped it out of his hands and set it back on the mantle. "Stop snooping."

"But I'm getting to know a whole new side to you." He reached for the next photo in line.

She slapped his hand away. "Keep digging, and I'll show you a side you won't soon forget."

He grinned, undeterred. "Cool leotard, by the way."

Junko sat in her recliner and lifted Freddy onto her lap. He flopped onto his back like a baby in her arms. His foot jiggled with pleasure as she rubbed his belly. *I could get used to this.*

"Zoe is a hard worker," she told Levi. "She's always been very talented at whatever she's done. She could have become an excellent gymnast."

"If not for the growth spurt that landed me a foot taller than most boys in my school," Zoe said. "I blame Dad's genetics for that one."

She sifted through the last of the mail. Finding no more

ads, she went to set them down on her father's desk in the corner. That's when one caught her eye. Red letters screamed up at her.

Urgent.

She noticed another stack of envelopes on the desk, unopened. More bold red letters. She picked one up. *Final Notice.*

The envelope trembled in her hands. She spun around, holding it up. "Mom. What is this?"

"Oh, just junk mail." She waved a dismissive hand. "Nothing to worry about."

"Junk mail isn't marked 'urgent' or 'pending foreclosure.'" She tossed it on the coffee table in front of her.

"Shizukani." She switched to Japanese as easily as she might take a breath. "I didn't raise you to speak to your mother that way," she continued in her native language. "Nor do we discuss such matters in front of strangers."

"No, you've just decided not to speak about it at all," Zoe replied pointedly in English.

"In Japanese!" Junko persisted. "What's done is done. It can't be helped."

"Paying your mortgage helps." She rifled through the rest of the unopened letters, all with similar messages and red-lettered threats. "Why? Why haven't you paid your bills?"

"Nihon-go de," her mother demanded.

Levi jiggled his keys in his hand, eyeing mother and daughter. "Maybe I'll go wait in the van."

Zoe gave him a grateful look. "Sorry. I'll only be another minute."

"Take your time," he told her.

She waited until she heard the front door close before asking her mother again, "Tell me why?"

Junko's lips pressed together until they nearly disappeared.

Zoe huffed and switched to Japanese. "Naze?"

"I can't pay them because I don't have the money."

She frowned. "Where is all your money going? Surely Dad had some kind of life or mortgage insurance."

Her mother turned away, speaking to the cold fireplace when she answered. "He had a pre-existing heart condition. A congenital defect. When he died of a heart attack, the insurance company wouldn't pay out because of a loophole. What little money that was left hasn't been enough."

She sank into the chair across from her. "Why didn't you tell me? I could have helped."

"It doesn't matter now. Once you meet Kimura-san, I'm certain you will like him. And he is rich. When you are married, we won't have to worry about all this."

Zoe rubbed her temples as pressure built behind them. "Mother, I haven't agreed to marry him. I might not even like him. He might not like me."

"What's not to like?" she asked. "Everything will work out. You will see. My sister assures me he is a reliable man. He will take care of us."

Because her mother had relied on a man all her life, Zoe understood why she believed that her daughter needed to as well. But Zoe didn't share her view of things. That just wasn't her.

"But Mom—"

Suddenly, her mother clutched her head. She slumped in her chair, moaning as she massaged her forehead.

Zoe jumped to her feet. "Are you all right?"

"Oh, I'm fine." But she didn't sound fine. "I just worry about you. It causes me so much anxiety."

Crouching down beside her, Zoe patted her hand. "You don't have to worry about me."

She stroked Zoe's hair like she did when she was a child. "You're all I have left to worry about."

Zoe remembered the doctor's advice. The best thing she could do was reduce stress—for her mom, anyway. Her own stress was an entirely different story.

"I told you I would meet Taichi. And I will. You don't have to worry."

Her mother straightened in her chair, her dizzy spell miraculously over. "Good, because you have a date with him this weekend."

Her mouth fell open. *So soon? No stress. No stress. No stress.* Her face formed what she hoped passed for enthusiasm. "Great."

Yet another reason to get things back on track with her business. Then she'd prove to her mother once and for all she was fine on her own. She could take care of herself. And now it looked like she would have to take care of her mother too. But with barely any clients left, she wasn't so sure how she was going to pull that off.

She crossed the room and swiped the other letters off the desk. "In the meantime, I'm taking these with me."

Her mother stood. Setting Freddy on the floor, she made as if to take them back. "I'm the parent. You're the daughter. It's not your job to worry about this."

Zoe held them out of her reach, which wasn't difficult, considering their height difference. "Well, too bad. You didn't raise me that way either." She threw Junko's words back at her.

Shoving the letters into her purse, she kissed her mother on the cheek. She headed out to Levi's van with Freddy in her arms. His wagging tail seemed to say, *Wasn't that a lovely visit?*

Chapter Fifteen

LIKE A DOG WITH A BONE

Thud. Thud. Thud.

Levi's metal door vibrated with each beat as though his studio apartment were alive, its heart beating. Zoe raised a fist to knock, but it was pointless; anyone inside wouldn't hear her over the racket—or maybe because of their acquired hearing loss.

Balancing her box of supplies under one arm, she slid the metal door open, releasing the chaotic noise within. It was like stepping into a nightclub from a quiet street on a Saturday night.

Freddy strolled inside as though he had VIP access. He was getting used to being at Levi's. They'd spent more time there than in Zoe's own apartment that week.

The place may have sounded like a club, but it lacked bouncers, drunk friends taking selfies at the bar, and perverts rubbing their junk all over women and calling it dancing. There was, however, a band. A pretty good band by the sounds of it.

Zoe set her supplies down on the table and approached the music room. Levi noticed her but carried on singing. When he hit the chorus, his voice, which had sounded sweet and melodic during the verse, rumbled with extra grittiness. It rolled over her and through her like cool, hard marbles.

She'd heard him sing before, but this was different. She couldn't see any sign of the cheesy serenading boy next door and definitely not Martha Stewart. He wasn't belting out silly lyrics that he'd made up on the spot, rhyming like a Dr. Seuss book.

He was rocking. Hard.

In that moment, everything about him fit the bill: the rocker look, the sexy voice, the way his body moved in time to the music. If she didn't know his silly side, she'd swear he was born backstage at a Led Zeppelin concert and swaddled in leather.

He was practically every woman's dream. A hard exterior with a gooey interior. Not that she'd given it much thought …

It wasn't as though his performance melted her insides like hot caramel or anything. Her breathing wasn't coming faster from desire. She'd just carried her supplies all the way from her newly repaired van after all. And her heart didn't throb with lust. It was the kick drum pulsating through her.

Nope. Levi had no effect on her at all. *I'm so over it,* she thought.

Freddy sat next to her heel, slapping his tail on the concrete floor in time to the beat. He glanced up at her as though he could see right through her. *Liar.*

"Whose side are you on, anyway?" she mumbled. "Remember who feeds you."

Levi held Zoe's stare while he sang. His powerful voice resonated deep inside her like the floor vibrating beneath her shoes. His gaze darkened, and as he sustained his last note, the sensation lingered, sinking lower until it settled somewhere between her thighs.

Singing with his band as a for-real rock star gave him that bad-boy factor. And while she wasn't going to take off her bra and scream like an adoring fan, something about the way he looked behind that mic made her want *him* to take off her bra and make her scream.

As the music ended, she had to take a deep breath. She reminded herself of what he wanted in exchange for sex: *more.*

This was just business. He was giving her a temporary place to store her supplies and a quiet space to work. She just had to resist ripping the clothes off his tall, tight body. She could manage that for a few days until she found a new office. Probably.

"Excellent set, guys." Levi placed his guitar in its stand. "Let's wrap it up for the day."

A jolt of giddiness ran through Zoe as he approached, like he'd picked her out from the crowd. *Don't be ridiculous,* she told herself, focusing on his Star Wars socks. It was just Levi.

"Hey," she said a little breathlessly. She cleared her throat. "Sorry, I just let myself in."

"No worries. Mi casa, su casa, remember? That's why I gave you a key."

The bass player leaned over her box on the table, peeking inside. "What's in here?"

"Toys, mostly," she said.

"Cool, I love toys." He reached inside and then leaped back like a scorpion bit him. "Oh … you mean *those* kinds of toys."

Once he recovered, he pushed aside the cardboard flap with a single finger. His eyebrows rose an inch at what he saw.

"That's nothing," Zoe told him, hiding a smirk. "I've got a van full of boxes outside."

His mouth dropped. Maybe he thought they were all for her personal use.

Levi laughed. "Zoe, this is Brody."

The drummer of the band didn't act as shy as the bass player. He dug through the box, pulling out items. His eyes lit up as though it were Christmas morning at the Playboy mansion.

Levi shook his head. "That lovable perv is Aaron."

"My favorite kind of customer," Zoe stage-whispered. "They tend to spend more money."

Both of Aaron's hands were full of toys, so he waved the furry purple handcuffs in his fist. "Nice to meet you. What else do you got?" He suddenly gasped and dug for the bottom.

The keyboard player hung back. His ears slowly reddened as he watched with a dubious look.

Levi waved a hand at him. "And this is Jett. The only one of us with manners. That's why we leave the PR stuff to him."

"Nice to meet you." Jett shook her hand and then slapped Levi on the back on his way to the door. "You're a lucky man."

She watched him leave, not entirely sure what he meant. Maybe that Levi got to spend time with a woman well versed in sex. Or was it more specifically related to her? Did Levi talk about her with his bandmates?

Brody slung a casual arm around her shoulder. "You know, I've got an extra room in my apartment for an office. I'd be happy to let you play with your toys there." He flashed her a grin.

She snorted. "You wish."

"Goodbye, Brody." Levi shoved his friend toward the door.

He threw his hands up in the air. "What did I do?"

Aaron seemed more reluctant to leave the toy box behind. At the last second, he grabbed something with a chain attached to it. "Can I have this?"

The guy was hilariously unabashed compared to his bandmates, but Zoe would never laugh at someone's sexuality. Heck, she encouraged people to express it for a living. Instead, she pulled a business card out of her purse.

"Only if you tell your friends where you got it."

"Woo-hoo! Thanks!" He followed the rest of his band out.

Groaning, Levi slid the front door shut and locked it as if afraid they'd come back. "Sorry about them."

She chuckled. "They seem nice."

"I've got some errands to run, so I'll let you get to work." Picking up his phone, he tapped the screen a few times until music drifted through the speakers around his apartment. "There. Just in case Freddy gets any ideas." He looked pointedly at the puppy.

Freddy's tail slapped the concrete floor. *Who? Me?*

"Sorry about the mess." She added her new box of supplies to the ever-growing pile of wedding stuff and Pure Pleasure merchandise in the corner. "It won't be for long. Aiden is helping me look for an office to rent. He owns a lot of properties around the city, so I'm sure something will pop up soon." If Aiden couldn't find her a place, then no one could.

"Trust me. There's no rush." He grabbed his keys off the counter and gave her a wave before slipping out the door.

Zoe spent the rest of the morning organizing her merchandise, taking stock of what hadn't been blown into a million pieces or damaged in the van break-in. Once she'd placed a few calls and ordered replacement décor, she set it all aside to sort through her mother's bills. After tallying up the numbers twice, she realized her mother was right: more money went out than came in. San Francisco was an expensive city, and her father's unexpected death had left her with little to survive on.

She crumpled a bill and tossed it into the garbage. Guilt gnawed at her for not intervening sooner. Finances weren't her mother's forte. Then again, when things got tough, Junko Plum tucked into her turtle shell, just like with her health.

No matter which way Zoe worked the figures, there was no easy fix. The house was too much for her mother on her own. She needed help—and not just financially. She'd struggled to live on her own even before the hospitalization. Who knew if she took her medication right or ate as often as she should? Zoe's frequent visits weren't enough anymore.

When numbers blurred together, she popped a couple of aspirin and faced the facts. Junko needed help. She needed Zoe. However, it would mean giving up on her dream to buy her own place anytime soon. It meant she'd have to buy part of her mother's house and move in for now.

She paced for an hour, gnawing on her nails, arguing with herself, consulting with Freddy—who wasn't very much help, really. But in the end, she called her mother and proposed she help take over the mortgage and move back into the house.

"That sounds like a great idea," Junko said without hesitation.

Zoe stared at the phone, double-checking she'd called the right *Mom*. "It does?" She waited for the catch, for a jab to her pride about moving back home. "So, I guess I'll call the mortgage company and start the process."

"Okay," Junko said. "It's only temporary, after all."

She frowned. "Why would it be temporary?"

"Because you have a date with Kimura-san tomorrow night. And once you marry him, everything will be all right."

Tomorrow night? She bit her tongue. She didn't want to upset her mother. Instead, she ended the call and put down the phone to scream into her hands. Before she could pick it up again to call the mortgage company, it vibrated on the desk.

"Plum Crazy Events. Zoe speaking."

"Hey, girlfriend!" Holly's voice screeched through the phone. "Just wanted to catch up. How are things since the big blowup? Were any irreplaceable items for Piper and Aiden's wedding destroyed?" she asked casually.

Zoe's head throbbed at the sound of the reporter's voice. It reminded her of Holly's report about the bombing that aired on Monday's five-o'clock news. Of course, she just had to name Plum Crazy Events in the segment.

Even though another San Fran Slayer tragedy headlined the news—the victim was a pizza delivery boy—it hadn't overshadowed Zoe's small-business misfortunes. She'd already received calls from three weddings, two parties, and five Pure Pleasure Party bookings, wondering if they should cancel her services. Whoever said there was no such thing as bad publicity was out to lunch. Now the entire city knew about her business woes.

Unwilling to give Holly anything to use against her, she said, "Everything is on track and their wedding will be beautiful. You can quote me on that. Otherwise, no comment." She hung up before Holly could argue, then blocked the number immediately.

She slammed the phone on the desk and laid her head next to it. As she closed her eyes, the front door slid open, and Levi strolled in.

He took in both Zoe at the desk and Freddy curled up on the area rug, chilling to the music in the background. "Nap time already?" He flopped down on the couch. "How are things? Making any headway?"

"It's official," she said. "I'm going to be a thirty-year-old woman living with her mother. I'll be taking on half of the mortgage payments in order to prevent a repossession."

"Really?" He studied her for a moment. Finally, he huffed and shook his head. "I'm not sure I could do the same thing. A week living with my parents and I'd move out of the country. I think what you're doing is amazing."

"I guess I never thought of it any other way. She and my father took care of me for the first twenty-some years of my life. Now it's my turn to pay back the favor. It's just happening sooner than I'd expected." She sighed. "I had no idea things were so bad for my mom. She's a very private person, even with me, it seems."

"Maybe she didn't want you to worry," he said.

"Well, it backfired because now there's even more to worry about."

Anxious, Zoe dug through her boxes of Pure Pleasure merchandise, pulling out the items she needed for a party she was hosting that weekend.

Each party paid a couple hundred or more, depending on the information requested and the number of guests. Plus, she received a commission on all sales. While it was just a side gig, the average of two grand a month helped supplement her income—she excelled at selling sex.

After a moment, Levi crossed the room. He hovered over her collection, a curious sparkle in his eyes. She watched him poke at things, his neck flushing pinker and his eyebrows rising higher by the moment.

He recoiled at a pair of nipple clamps. Shivering, he stepped away. "So, why sex toys? What made you want to get into that line of work?"

"I didn't get into it. It got into me." She winked. "That's how it usually works, anyway. I should know since I'm a sexual health rep for Pure Pleasure," she said in mock seriousness. "I have a certificate and everything."

"You're practically a sexpert," he joked. "But no, come on. Really. Why do you like to sell this stuff?"

"Because I believe sex is important to your physical health and your mental well-being. There are cardio machines for your heart and lungs, and weights for muscles and joints." She waved at her collection. "These are machines to exercise a person's sexual health."

Her voice took on the usual sultry cadence she used to sell sex toys. Only, it wasn't the toys she wanted to sell him.

God, she wanted him so badly it hurt.

"And do you get enough exercise?" Levi asked suggestively.

Technically, Zoe didn't get any at all, but she wasn't about to admit she was practically a nun. "What's enough?" she asked vaguely. "That's why I have to supplement."

He chuckled. "Like a daily vitamin?"

She could hear a change in his voice too, a response to her own. Something had altered in the conversation. He shifted his body like he wanted to touch her. His eyes dropped to the low neckline of her blouse.

"You know, if you ever get tired of toys, you can have the

real thing right here." He spread his hands in case she didn't know he meant him.

She narrowed her eyes. "You're a tease."

"I'm not teasing," he said. "I'm completely serious. But if you want me, you get the whole package, not just my"—he glanced down—"package."

Just as she'd thought. Levi talked a big game, but when push came to shove—or at least when she wanted it to—he was the boy next door, the guy you'd bring home to meet the family.

"I'm fine on my own, thank you." She waved at the pile of supplies.

"You don't look fine. You look a little stressed." He began to massage her shoulders, his hands slow and firm. "I could help you with that, distract you for a while. We could have a little … fun."

Levi's breath tickled the back of her neck, and she shivered. His voice was infused with a dare, with lust, and a confidence that guaranteed a good time. She groaned under his touch. She'd dreamed of those hands on her, craved it. He wasn't saying …?

"Mmm," she purred as his hands moved lower. "What did you have in mind?"

He pressed against her from behind. "It's a surprise."

Zoe wondered if that was the "surprise" she could feel against her back. The unknown made her clench with anticipation. Was it really happening? Was he finally giving in? It wasn't often a man had her on the edge of her seat.

"I like surprises." She spun to face him and tugged at the waistband of his jeans, wanting to discover what "surprise" he was hiding from her.

Levi's firm hands ran over her, drawing her near. He brought his mouth closer to her neck, and his lips tickled her skin as he spoke his next words. "So, you're up for whatever?"

A heavy sigh escaped her. She swallowed hard and nodded

eagerly. "Whatever you want."

"Is that a promise?" His pierced eyebrow arched as he held her gaze.

Just what exactly did he want from her? Was it something kinky? It didn't matter. At this point, she'd take anything before she exploded.

"I promise. I'm all yours."

He smiled. Having the control clearly did it for him. "Good."

"Thank God." Her eyes rolled back. "I've been dying for this."

His cheek dimpled. "You have? And here I thought you were just fine on your own."

"I lied. Now take off your clothes."

As she reached for the buttons on his shirt, he grabbed her hand and led her to the door.

She stumbled along in a daze. "What? Where are we going?"

"It's a surprise, remember?" He pointed a finger at her, as though daring her to back down. "You promised."

She stared at him as he grabbed his keys. "But you said ... But I thought ..."

"I said I'd distract you. I didn't say with sex. Whatever gave you that idea?" He shook his head teasingly. "You sure have a one-track mind, Zoe Plum."

As she watched him head out the door, her hope wilted like month-old mitsuba.

Freddy yawned and padded toward her, wondering what all the excitement was about. The moment he spotted the open door, he made a break for it. *Freedom!!!*

Grabbing his leash, Zoe trudged after them, unable to hide her disappointment. She should have known Levi wouldn't give in that easily. There was no denying it anymore: she wouldn't be satisfied until she had him.

She knew it, and now Levi knew it too.

Chapter Sixteen

TUNED OUT

Zoe narrowed her eyes, focusing on that sweet spot, the hole at the far back. A risky move, but she'd get big points for it. And if she played along and kept Levi happy, maybe she'd get what she wanted in return—no matter how many rounds of Skee-ball it took.

Swinging her arm back, she went for it. The ball rolled along the side, popping up into the air, and slipped perfectly into the hole worth one hundred points.

She cried out in surprise, jumping up and down. "I did it! I've never gotten it in that hole."

Levi nodded approvingly, clearly impressed. "Beginner's luck."

"Yeah, right. Let's make it best two out of three then."

"You're on."

Levi dug another coin out of his pocket and slipped it into the Skeeball machine. Their scores reset to zero, and the machine rumbled as it spat out new balls.

Zoe reached down and picked one up. "You know, when you said you wanted to have fun ..."

"I meant I wanted to have fun," he said. "You know how to do that, right? Fun? It's that thing that makes you smile."

She rolled her eyes and gave him a sarcastic look.

"Yeah, kind of like that, but with less contempt."

She laughed. "I know how to have fun. I just assumed you'd put a smile on my face a different way." She bit her lip and arched her eyebrows suggestively. "I didn't take you for an arcade man."

"Me? I'm a kid at heart."

She looked him up and down. "Okay, that I can see."

"Hmm." His eyes narrowed. "I'm going to choose not to be offended by that."

"That's probably best since you drove me here." She gave him a wink. "Okay, show me what you've got. And don't be too sore when you lose."

"Getting cocky, are you? Okay, you're on."

They went shot for shot. It was close, but Zoe beat Levi by ten points.

After they left the Musée Mécanique on Fisherman's Wharf with its variety of antique games, they strolled down The Embarcadero toward Pier 39. The late-afternoon sun beat down on them, but the breeze blowing across the bay made it bearable.

Zoe felt bad for dropping Freddy off at her mother's, but it was probably for the best. Tourists, joggers, and dog walkers crowded the sidewalk. It would have been overwhelming for him. Though, he would have enjoyed the music drifting out of each restaurant they passed. The fish and chips shop cranked an old 3 Doors Down song. It reminded her of Levi's style.

"So why music?" she asked him. "What made you want to join a band?"

"My parents introduced me to music at a young age," he said. "They enrolled me in piano lessons when I was five, violin when I was eight, and clarinet when I was eleven."

"Wow. That's a lot of instruments. You must have been a natural."

"I was lucky it came easily to me," he said. "I think my

parents wanted a one-man symphony. They were obsessed with classical. But when I turned fifteen, I bought my first guitar and broke their hearts with my love for rock and roll."

"And a star was born," Zoe said with awe before cracking up.

Levi shoved her playfully. "Yes, it's true. I've always been this amazing. But because my parents introduced me to a wide variety of music growing up, I appreciated all of it: jazz, swing, classical, hip-hop, blues … I like to blend what I love about each one into my own music."

"I've noticed. You definitely have your own style." And she didn't just mean his musical tastes. "Your parents must be proud of you."

He snorted. "Not really. They wanted me to learn music to become well rounded, not to make a career out of it. They expected me to be an accountant like my successful father. I was supposed to follow in his footsteps, join his firm, and take over the company one day."

"I guess that's not what you saw for yourself."

A man dressed as a sad clown held out a helium balloon to Zoe. She waved it away with a smile, and he tipped his bowler hat to her.

"I tried it their way at first," Levi said. "I went to college, took the courses they chose, graduated with honors."

She gaped at him. "Honors? There's no pigeonholing you, is there?"

"I'm not just a pretty face, you know." He gave her a look that dared her to say otherwise.

She held up her hands. "No argument here."

"But in the end," he continued, "it just wasn't me. I will always have my parents to thank for my gift and my education. They only wanted what was best for me, but I had to follow my dreams."

"But isn't that what's best for you?" she asked. "To do what you love to do, what makes you happiest?"

"Depends on who you ask. My parents thought they knew better."

She snorted. "I can sympathize with that. My mom manipulates my life all the time." Like her date with her supposed "future husband." She'd been dreading meeting him all week, and it was already happening the next night.

The sounds of their footsteps changed as they reached Pier 39. The wooden boards click-clacked musically beneath them.

"So, you went against your parents' wishes and gave into your love of music," Zoe summed up. "Admit it. You did it for the women."

"It didn't hurt." He shoved his hands into his pockets, watching his feet as he spoke. "That's how I met my ex-wife."

Her head snapped toward him. "Ex-wife? You were married?"

Levi suddenly reached out and tugged her toward him. As she stumbled to the side, she realized she'd nearly walked headlong into an antique lamppost.

"As a matter of fact, I was," he said. "You don't have to say it like that. Like, how could I possibly convince someone to marry me?"

"No. No." She cringed at her lack of filter. "I didn't mean it that way. I'm sorry."

When she'd first met him, he'd stumbled into the Fisher-Wells wedding with a lipstick smear on his cheek. She'd imagined he hooked up with groupies and fan girls who'd lingered after last call to get their chests signed. That is, until she got to know his boy-next-door side.

But at one point he'd been the kind of man who had promised forever, who had committed to one woman for the rest of his life—or he'd believed so.

Was he still that man? Maybe that's why he wanted more from Zoe. Even now, she got the feeling he'd roped her into another date. And it frightened her—mostly because she was actually enjoying herself. Usually she could avoid the "more" with men, but Levi hadn't given up like all the others before him.

They climbed a set of steps to the upper level of the pier, where a series of wooden walkways zigzagged over the busy shopping area. It was far quieter above the popular tourist shops and allowed them to talk without having to dodge people taking photos or kids racing into candy stores.

"So, how did you meet your wife?" she asked Levi.

"*Ex*-wife," he said pointedly. "We met at a bachelorette party I performed at. We got divorced five years ago."

"What happened, if you don't mind me asking?"

He leaned against the walkway railing and stared down at the shoppers below. "She wasn't happy. Not from lack of trying, though. She wanted extravagant meals, so I learned to cook. She wanted to travel, so I took her all over the world. Eventually, she wanted nicer things, a bigger house, a more expensive car."

Zoe considered how persistent he'd been with her, a woman who'd rejected him from the start. So he must have gone to the moon and back to make his marriage work. "I take it that bachelorette gigs didn't pay for all that."

He chuckled without humor, shaking his head. "I had to quit music. She convinced me to reach out to my parents. My dad got me a job in his company for a while. Wore a suit and everything." He ran a hand down his faded T-shirt like he was smoothing down a tie.

"You behind a desk?" Zoe tried to imagine him without the gelled hair, black nail polish, leather wrist bands, and the ever-increasing piercings. She frowned. *Were his ears always pierced?*

She shook her head. "I can't see it. So, let me guess, she still wasn't happy?"

Levi sighed. "No. She said she needed space to figure out what she wanted. It turned out what she wanted was my best friend and the trust fund that came along with him. *Ex*-best friend, I should say." He pulled a face. "I guess I just wasn't enough for her."

"I'm sorry." Her heart lurched in her chest. "God, when Chelsea told me she's marrying Sean, it felt like the ultimate slap in the face. But I was wrong. Losing your partner to your best friend … How did you get over that?"

He let out a long breath. "Time."

She nodded, thinking he'd had even less time to move on than she had, and yet he was ready. But for her, time wasn't the issue.

Not ready to talk about that "issue," she nodded toward another set of stairs. Levi followed, maybe ready to leave the conversation behind for his own reasons.

They descended another set of stairs. Back on the lower part of the pier again, the noise kicked up a notch. However, it wasn't because of the extra bodies. Three hundred or more sea lions lounged on the floating docks to the west of the pier. They lined up nose to tail, sometimes thirty of them per dock.

Zoe leaned against the fence and listened to their loud barks carry across the water. They didn't seem at all disturbed by the people snapping photos of them as they basked in the hot sun, enjoying their perfect view. To their left, Coit Tower perched on its hill in the distance, and to their right lay Alcatraz, lonely in the middle of the bay.

After a few moments, Zoe and Levi moved on; it was far too noisy to talk. As they rounded the pier, the barking sea lions and the chatting tourists faded into the background.

He walked up to the ticket booth for the carousel. When he returned, he waved the tickets with an easy smile. "I thought we needed a change of pace. You ready?"

They climbed the carousel's bright red stairs to the second story. Detailed paintings of the most famous sights in San Francisco greeted them. Bright, round light bulbs reflected off the shiny golden poles holding the colorful horses in place.

He gestured for Zoe to go first. "Lady's choice."

She picked a fierce black horse with its teeth bared as it fought its restraints. He hopped on the one next to hers: a docile mare with a pink saddle and bright flowers braided into its mane.

A warning alarm rang out, and the ride jerked to a start. They moved up and down next to each other like the waves in the bay. As they spun around the mirrored center, she caught sight of Levi's expression in the reflection. Despite riding on a carousel, surrounded by giggling children and the cheerful music blasting out of tinny speakers above them, his distant gaze appeared sad.

She leaned closer. "I'm sorry about your wife and your best friend. You didn't deserve that."

He shrugged, but it wasn't his usual easygoing gesture. "It was for the best. It helped me rediscover what I wanted. And that was music. I quit my dad's firm and started the band. Ever since then, I've put everything I've got into it. I guess, I want to prove to my family, and especially my ex, that I'm worth something the way I am. That I don't have to sell out to achieve success."

Zoe watched his handsome face as he spoke. By the way he'd said it, she wondered if he believed it or if he needed to prove it to himself too.

"Plus," he said. "I've always dreamed that, one day, my ex will go through a supermarket checkout and see me staring back at her from the front cover of *Rolling Stone*."

She laughed. "That would be amazing."

She recalled how he'd jumped to get Holly's attention at the expo. Despite how aggravating the reporter could be, an interview with her would boost his career. Now she understood why he wanted it so badly.

"At least I know what I'm looking for in a partner now," he said. "I want my next relationship to work. That means finding a woman who knows what she wants. A woman who's not looking for something or someone to complete them. A good relationship would just be the encore act to make their life perfect."

As he gave Zoe a meaningful look, she realized he meant her. Feeling heat rush through her, she glanced away.

"But that's just it," she said. "I'm happy all on my own."

"How can you truly be happy when you're holding yourself back? You can't live life to the fullest by only living part of it. By hiding from people."

The calm way in which he said it, like some fortune cookie come to life, grated on her like the music blasting overhead.

She shifted in her saddle to face him, sensing the light-hearted part of their date was over. "What is that supposed to mean? I am living life to the fullest. I'm not letting anything or any*one* hold me back. I've told you I'm not interested in a relationship. So why won't you accept that?"

Levi threw his hands up. "Because I don't think you're being honest with yourself. Life is too short to be alone. Everyone wants to find a special person to spend the rest of their lives with."

"I'm not everyone," she said. "I never want to get married."

"There was obviously a time when you did."

"And that was a mistake," she snapped back. "A close call. I'm better off this way. It worked out for the best, really."

He shook his head with an annoyingly insightful look on his face. "You got hurt, and now you're scared to open up. Have you let anyone in since your wedding day?"

His expression shifted to one of pity. And there was nothing Zoe hated more than being pitied.

She rubbed her forehead as the music, the lights, the spinning boomeranged inside her skull. "You can't pretend to know me after two weeks. Because you don't."

He huffed. "That's my point. Does anyone? Or do you keep yourself so guarded that no one knows what's really going on inside your head? Do *you* even know what you want?"

"I know a hell of a lot better than you do," she threw back at him. "Who are you to tell me what I want and what will make me happy?"

Levi leaned closer. "Because I think you know what you want, but for being such a straight shooter with everyone else, you can't be honest with yourself. One minute you're telling me I've got no chance, and the next you're grabbing my junk."

"No. I mean ... okay. I did that." She ran a hand through her hair. "Maybe I've been a bit unclear, but it's not because I don't know what I want. I do know."

"Then what is it?" He touched her hand clasped around the pole. "Because you're sending me mixed signals."

She flicked his hand away. "Maybe because you're pushing me. You're pushing me for promises, for more. You're pushing me for something I can't give you."

"Can't or won't?" His face hardened, and his nostrils flared as he took a steadying breath. "Fine, look me in the eyes right now, and tell me you don't want me. All you have to do is say 'no,' and I'll never bother you again. That's all you've ever had to do. Just be straight. Say it, Zoe."

She glared at him. Her rapid breaths escaped in nauseated pants, her heart thudded inside her chest, and her head ached from the music overhead. But she couldn't seem to form the word.

"What do you want?" Levi asked when she didn't say anything.

"I don't know!" The words burst out of her before she even realized it was true. She didn't know. Was he right? Was she lying to herself?

Things bubbled up inside of her, things she wanted to swallow back down, to tuck away in her bottle. But that didn't seem to work so well anymore. They kept leaking out whenever she was around Levi, like he shook her up, building the pressure inside her like a can of Coke.

She couldn't think clearly. The only thing she wanted right

now was to leave, to get off the ride and run as far away as possible. She couldn't wait another second. The ride needed to be over. *Now.*

"Stop the ride!" she yelled. "Stop the ride! I need to get off!"

But when the carousel kept going and her world kept spinning out of control, she slid ungracefully off her horse. She fell to the metal floor with a *bang* and scrambled to the edge of the spinning platform.

Someone shouted nearby. The ride jerked. Zoe gripped the horse next to her.

Somewhere inside the inner workings of the antique carousel, gears ground together. A motor whined as everything slowed. Finally, the ride stopped.

Lurching to her feet, she staggered to the stairs.

Levi called out behind her. "Zoe!"

She turned to the sound of his voice. He was still on the horse, staring after her like she was a pirouetting elephant. His forehead creased, and he shook his head; he felt sorry for her.

"You were right the other day," he said. "It's not me. It's *you.*"

Swallowing hard, Zoe raced down the steps and away from the carousel. Away from Levi. Because she knew he was right.

Chapter Seventeen

A SONG AND DANCE

Piper swept out of the changing room in a white empire dress. Zoe and Addison watched from the plush Queen Anne sofa with hopeful anticipation. Would this be the one? The perfect gown to replace the mutilated Vera Wang dress?

Fabric swished with each step as Piper glided across the room and stepped onto the raised platform in the center. Zoe crossed her fingers, feeling guiltier than ever that her friend had to go through dress fittings and alterations all over again. And so close to the big day.

She might not have cut up the dress herself, but it had happened because of her. She just wasn't sure why yet. The police still had no leads; it was hard to narrow down suspects from the thousands of people who had visited the Hilton that day. And apparently finding a dress murderer wasn't on the top of their priority list, what with an actual murderer on the loose in the city.

The short saleswoman, Astrid, danced around her high-profile customer like an excited puppy, rearranging her train, releasing any wrinkles. Once she'd tweaked, tugged, and fluffed every square inch, she stood back and spread her hands wide as though displaying Piper. *Ta-da!*

Piper assessed herself in the three-way mirror before spinning around to face her friends. A hesitant wrinkle creased her forehead. "What do you guys think?"

Addison sighed. "You look beautiful. It's gorgeous. Aiden would love it."

Zoe shook her head. "You look awful."

Piper's mouth dropped. "What?"

Addison gasped, cartoonlike. "Zoe!"

"It's true." She held up her hands. "You look beautiful, as always, but the dress isn't flattering. Your breasts are squished, your curves hidden, your torso shortened."

The bride-to-be turned her shocked gaze to Addison, the fashionista of the group. "Addy? Is it true?"

She bit her bottom lip and kind of cringed. "Well …"

"It's only one week until the big day," Zoe reminded Addison. "We don't have time for sugarcoating."

Piper crossed her arms, still waiting for a response.

"It could be better," Addison finally relented. Which was as blunt of an answer as they would get out of her since she was nothing if not coated in sweet sugariness.

"So, this is a no?" Astrid asked in her thick French accent.

"It's a no," Zoe confirmed.

Piper's shoulders slumped, and she headed back to the changing room to try the next one.

The moment the door closed behind her, Addison spun on Zoe. "You don't have to be so rude."

"I'm not rude. I'm honest," she said simply. "We're running out of time, and I will not let this wedding be anything but perfect."

Addison frowned, but eventually nodded. "You're right. Okay. Honesty. I can do that." She took a sip of tea out of the shop's Royal Albert teacup, as though the caffeine would fortify her. "Are you okay? You seem a bit stressed today."

"I don't know why?" she said airily. "There's only one week until Piper's wedding, my business is tanking as we speak, and

I'm moving back in with my mother." And she didn't even want to get into the whole arranged marriage thing. "Oh, and there's that little thing about someone trying to kill me."

By now, she couldn't deny that someone had it in for her. The snipped brake lines had been a tiny hint, the explosion an even bigger one—and she didn't believe the gas leak theory. Despite her repeated follow-up phone calls to the police, they were still feeding her vague answers. Whoever was behind the incidents didn't simply want to hurt Zoe. They wanted to ruin her, destroy her business, her office, her supplies, her life. It felt personal. That was why her first instinct screamed "rival."

Natalie had gone out of her way to cut her down professionally by stealing her clients. She would have known exactly which dress to cut to shreds to do the most damage. Heck, she'd even had a key to Zoe's office to plant a bomb. But could she have gone that far?

Then again, Chelsea had as much motivation as Natalie, if not more. She'd tried to undermine her for years. Or maybe they were both in on it since they worked together now, enacting a master plan to eliminate Plum Crazy Events for good.

Then there was Juliet. And, well … she was a loose cannon. And the apple didn't fall far from the tree. Zoe recalled the mother of the bride wielding the cake knife at the wedding without even a conscious thought.

Rubbing a hand over her face, she leaned against the sofa's backrest. She shoved all those problems into her bottle with everything else and jammed the cap back on.

Already up to speed on her drama, Addison patted her comfortingly on the knee. "Can I do anything to help?"

"Thank you, but I just need a little stress relief." She sipped her tea.

Addison grinned into her cup. "Maybe Levi can help you out with that."

At the reminder, she swallowed hard, nearly choking on

tea. As she coughed and sputtered, Addison gave her a strange look. Okay, so she hadn't updated her friends on *all* her dramas. They didn't know she hadn't spoken to the rocker since she'd run away from Pier 39 the day before.

Thankfully, she didn't need to explain her reaction because the changing room door squeaked open. Astrid held it for Piper so she could squeeze out in a tulle ball gown with heavy beading on the sheer bodice.

She barely made it to the platform before Zoe pointed her back toward the changing room while Addison shook her head —albeit with an apologetic frown.

Piper groaned and spun on her heel, disappearing for round three.

A chime to the tune of "Wedding March" rang throughout the store. Astrid slipped out of the dressing room.

"That'll be the door. I'll just go see who it is. I'll be right back!" Shoving the heavy privacy curtains aside, she headed for the storefront.

The dressing room door opened again, and Piper shuffled out in a shapely mermaid gown. It hugged her curves nicely. She penguin-walked onto the platform and spun to face her friends.

"Beautiful," Addison breathed.

Zoe ran a critical eye over the gown. "I agree. But it's still a no. Too impractical. You need to be comfortable on your big day. If you can't move freely, there won't be any dancing. You'd have to cancel Reluctant Redemption." A hopeful smile crept over her lips. "But if you really want this one, I can call them right now and let them know the bad news."

Astrid's thick accent drifted through the curtains as she returned. "I'm sorry. I'm booked for the day. You'll have to make an appointment and come back another time."

"Oh, it's fine. They won't mind."

Zoe recognized the voice only a second before the heavy pink curtains swished apart and *The* Holly Hart burst in.

"Ladies!" the reporter cried. "What a coincidence!"

Piper gaped. "Holly?"

Zoe shot to her feet to block her from taking another step inside. But Holly had obviously learned to be quick to get all those breaking stories. She dodged Zoe's outstretched arms. Slinking to the platform, she shoved her phone to Piper's mouth, a recording app cued up on the screen.

"So, any talk of honeymoon destinations?"

Piper narrowed her eyes. "Why? Will I find you lurking in the bushes?"

"I don't lurk. I stake out. It's a professional term." She held a hand to her chest. "I'm a professional."

"What are you doing here?" Zoe demanded.

"I didn't think you'd mind, you know, considering our little arrangement." She gave a subtle eyewink. Or about as subtle as Holly could be.

Zoe eyed her up and down. "What arrangement? We don't have an arrangement." Grabbing the reporter by the arm, she tried to drag her out.

"Oh, you remember," she said lightly, like she was used to being manhandled. "I scratch your back, you scratch mine."

Piper's harsh gaze flitted to Zoe. "What is she talking about?"

Her mouth opened, but she didn't know where to begin.

When she didn't answer, Piper stepped down from the platform to get into Holly's face. She crossed her arms below the sweetheart neckline. "What are you talking about?"

Holly rolled her eyes. "Where do you think I've been getting all my delicious facts for my blog articles?"

Piper spun on her friend. "What? Zoe, you didn't."

"I didn't. Well …" She winced. "I guess I did, but—"

Holly gasped and held a hand over her mouth. "Was that supposed to be a secret? Oops. My bad."

Stepping back, she held up her phone to take a photo of

the dress. Addison slapped it away before she could take the shot.

Piper stared at Zoe. "How could you?"

Zoe cringed at the tone in her friend's voice, at the hurt, the betrayal. And she wished she could deny it, but she had let a few things slip. A lot of things, now that she thought about it. But she definitely didn't tell her about their appointment at the bridal shop.

"I'm sorry," she said.

"You knew Aiden and I wanted a low-key wedding. No media, no public, and especially no Holly Hart." She said the name like it was poison in her mouth.

Holly waved. "Hello. Right here. Still in the room."

With a sound of disgust, Piper stormed toward the changing room.

Zoe tugged on her arm before she could slip away. "It wasn't like that. You know what Holly is like."

"Overbearing, obtrusive, nosey ..." Addison counted the amazing qualities on her fingers.

"Again," Holly said. "Right here."

Zoe spun on the reporter, hands balling into fists. "Yes, you are still here. Let's do something about that, shall we?"

She held up her hands in surrender. "Now, now. Let's not be hasty. We're all friends here."

"No. We're friends," Zoe gestured to the three of them. "That doesn't include you."

"Friends?" Piper repeated. "That depends on your explanation as to why you leaked the info."

The shop owner shifted uncertainly. Finally, when the tension was thick enough to jab one of her stick pins into, she clapped her hands. "Shall we try on another dress?"

"Ooh. Yes! Let's." Holly plopped down on the sofa and settled in like she was replacing Zoe in the "friends" category.

And by the fierce expression on Piper's face, it looked like there might be an opening.

"Not you." Addison shoved the reporter off the velvet sofa and onto the hardwood floor.

Huffing, Holly picked herself up and brushed off her coral pantsuit. "I don't have to take this. I'm leaving," she said, like it was entirely her choice.

"Allons-y!" Astrid shooed her out the exit.

They disappeared through the curtains together, and Zoe relaxed as the fabric fell still. A moment later, Holly's head popped through the slit again.

Her eyes narrowed in Zoe's direction. "Tit for tat, remember." She waggled her fingers in farewell. "Ciao!"

Silence fell over the friends like a thick tulle veil. They heard the distant chime of "Wedding March" as Holly left the store.

"Zoe, how could you?" Piper asked again.

Zoe's face screwed up as she searched for an explanation that made sense, but she couldn't find one. "I didn't plan to. I'm sorry."

Astrid returned and ushered the bride back into the changing room, determined to sell a dress. "Next dress. Here we go!"

She shut the door firmly behind them, and a moment later, the frantic swishing of silk and organza drifted out.

"So," Piper called through the door, "if you didn't mean to do it, then what happened? Did wedding details just fall out of your mouth by accident?"

Zoe hovered close to the door, speaking through the louver slits. "The day I got kicked out of the expo, Holly was there with her cameraman. They caught it all on film. It wasn't good." She cringed at the memory. "She threatened to run a smear campaign against my business. Between my assistant stealing clients, Chelsea slandering my name all over town, and Juliet's tantrum at the expo, I couldn't afford the bad publicity."

"So you sold me out."

"No. I mean … yes." She ran a hand over her face, banging her head against the wall. "But I only gave her information that she could dig up herself if she had a mind to, and you know she would have. I didn't tell her anything that would get her anywhere near the wedding or allow her to stick her nose into it."

"Except for my wedding dress appointment," Piper shot back.

Zoe placed a hand against the door. She wished she could talk face to face. "I swear I didn't. I have no idea how she found out about today."

Addison had been listening from the other side of the room, but now she came to stand next to Zoe. "Piper, to be fair, I know firsthand how manipulative Holly Hart is and what kind of damage she can do." She frowned, probably remembering how close she'd come to losing her business the year before.

The changing room grew quiet. Zoe and Addison exchanged a look as they listened to the scratch and swish of fabric against skin.

Finally, Piper replied. "It's not like I don't get it. I do. And I don't want your business to suffer. But I only get one wedding, and if she can ruin a business, then she can ruin our big day."

"I won't let her," Zoe said. "Look. It's done. Holly isn't getting any more information from me. I swear it. Or I'll find you a new wedding planner myself."

"It's not like I haven't had offers," she muttered under her breath.

But Zoe heard every word. "What?"

Piper went quiet for a few seconds. "I didn't want to tell you this because you already have so much to worry about, but …"

"Tell me. What is it?" She resisted the urge to whip the door open.

"I got a call from your old assistant yesterday."

The tea in her stomach turned acidic, eating away at her insides. "What did Natalie want?"

"To be my wedding planner."

Zoe stepped back from the door. "She tried to poach you? With only a week left to go?! You're my best friend."

"Ahem," Addison fake-coughed.

"One of them," Zoe amended, eliciting an angelic smile from Addison.

Astrid stepped out of the changing room, a curious look on her face. "Natalie? Natalie Evans? She's no longer your assistant?"

"No," she said. "She left me for the competition. Enchanted Events."

The shop owner frowned. "That is so strange. She just called here on your behalf this morning to confirm your appointment."

"You're kidding." She laughed in an *I'm going to kill someone* kind of way.

"I guess we know who let the cat out of the bag," Addison said.

Zoe paced the room, eager to take action. Her heels clicked angrily on the hardwood. "Holly must have gone to Natalie after I refused to talk to her anymore. Natalie knows this is one of my favorite shops, especially in a pinch."

The changing room door opened as Piper came out. "Zoe, please do something before she tells Holly any more."

"Oh, trust me, she won't be doing any more talking once I'm finished with her." She turned around and gasped at the sight of her best friend—one of her best friends, that is.

Addison squeaked and covered her mouth. "Oh my gosh."

Piper flinched like she wanted to slink back into the changing room. "Is it that bad?"

Zoe shook her head. "It's perfect."

"Really?" Her face lit up as she rushed to the platform.

Astrid appeared with a shoulder-length double veil. Sliding

the combs into Piper's hair, she fluffed it out to frame her pretty face.

Piper's breath hitched a little, and her eyes glistened: the bridal moment. That had never happened with the original dress.

"This is *the one*," she said.

Addison skipped over to the platform and did a little happy dance. Zoe's relief escaped in a groan as she thanked the wedding gods. Despite all the last-minute roadblocks with the wedding, she might actually be able to pull it off.

She turned to Astrid. "We'll take it."

The woman smiled, pleased with the sale. "Certainly. Let me grab an order form." She turned for the front.

Zoe stopped her. "No. I don't think you understand. We want *this* dress."

Astrid blinked. "You mean the one off the rack? No. No … C'est impossible. We can put a rush order on it. It will be here in three months."

"Three months!" Piper gaped at the woman.

Zoe pursed her lips. "We don't have time for that. Try a week."

Astrid sputtered. She opened her mouth to argue, but Piper hoisted her skirts and hopped down from the platform.

"I'll take *this* dress, please," she said. "Just name your price."

Astrid snapped her mouth shut. Her eyebrows rose, as though in question. Piper responded with a confident nod.

A grin spreading across her face, Astrid slipped through the privacy curtains, calling over her shoulder as she left. "I'll just go ring it up!"

Zoe waited until the drapes swished closed before laughing. "Impressive, Piper. You're practically a Caldwell already."

But Piper spun on her with a firm look, shoving a fist on her hip. "Now promise me. No more Holly."

Zoe crossed her heart. "I promise. And I'm really sorry."

Piper smiled, placated. "Me too."

"Group hug!" Addison threw out her arms and encircled both her friends.

With the dress dilemma solved, Zoe planned a visit to Chelsea's office. Holly's visit reeked of her rival's underhanded guidance.

It was one thing when Natalie had simply left her high and dry; people quit jobs all the time, after all. Before now, confronting the traitor had fallen low on her list of priorities, considering everything going on in her life.

But this time, Natalie had gone too far. Zoe wouldn't stand by while her backstabbing assistant continued to undercut her and hijack her business. Clearly, she needed to remind Natalie who was boss.

Chapter Eighteen

MAKE THE CANARY SING

Zoe stood in front of an office space in South Beach, reading a sign engraved with a delicate script—a nice font for thank-you cards: *Enchanted Events*. She sneered before turning the handle and barging in.

The door swung open and banged against the wall. Natalie, who was pouring coffee at a table in the corner, gasped and spun around. The pot slipped from her hand, dark roast splashing across the table linen. Coffee leaped out of her cup to land on the front of her pale blue blazer.

Then she saw it was Zoe, and the cup dropped from her hands. It broke, and the rest of the contents spilled over her suede shoes and onto the cream area rug.

Zoe stood taller, pleased at the results of her visit so far. She always did know how to make an entrance.

"Natalie." She drew out her name in false affection. "How are you?"

"Zoe!" she squeaked. "W-What are you doing here?"

"I thought we could catch up."

Zoe strolled casually through the office, wrinkling her nose at the over-the-top romantic décor. The place oozed with heart and kiss symbols, cheesy quotes about love and marriage, and stock photography of people holding hands. It was so clichéd, like Cupid had exploded in the room.

Natalie shrank back as Zoe approached. "I've done nothing wrong."

"Then why are you so nervous?"

She straightened her coffee-stained blazer and lifted her chin. "If those clients wanted your business instead of mine, they would have stayed with you."

At least she wasn't denying what she'd done. Zoe had to give her that. "Hard for them to refuse the prices you're advertising. No one in the industry is going to look kindly upon you undercutting every planner in the city."

"This is a cutthroat business. You taught me that."

"I also taught you to make friends, not enemies," she said.

Natalie placed her hands on her hips. "You're one to talk."

Zoe took a step forward and smiled. Natalie automatically backpedaled, bumping against the coffee table and spilling the creamer down the back of her skirt.

It's not like she'd ever hit the poor girl—mostly because it wouldn't be a fair fight; Natalie wouldn't have lasted twenty seconds in a bouquet-toss fray. However, it felt therapeutic to toy with her a little like a cat would a mouse.

Natalie's eyes flitted to the French doors on the other side of the room. The golden letters swirling across the frosted glass said *Chelsea Carruthers*.

Zoe had come for answers, and not just about how Holly Hart learned of their appointment at Love and Lace bridal shop that day. She had bigger questions to ask first. So far, the cops had given her the runaround. If they wouldn't tell her the truth, then she would uncover it for herself.

As much as she disliked Natalie at the moment, she knew her former assistant wasn't capable of blowing up her office or cutting her brake lines. Chelsea, on the other hand, had that vindictive, underhanded, sociopathic vibe to her.

She backed away from Natalie, who now stood in a puddle

of hazelnut creamer. "I'm not done with you." Leaving her to sweat a little, she marched for Chelsea's office.

"You can't go in there," Natalie said, her voice cracking a little.

"Don't worry. I just want to talk."

Natalie took a step after her. "She's not in."

But she was lying because a figure moved behind the frosted glass. "Nice try."

Gripping the handles, Zoe flung the doors open. She strolled into Chelsea's office like she owned the place, a smug smile on her face. Only, Natalie hadn't been lying; Chelsea wasn't in. But someone else was.

The person turned, and, suddenly, she was staring at her past.

"Sean," she breathed.

"Zoe? Zoe, is that you?" Sean got to his feet. "Oh, my God."

She winced as he smiled that brilliant smile of his. Too brilliant, too white, too friendly for how she'd imagined him over and over again during the last six years. She'd remembered him ugly, mean, and not worth missing for even a second. But he looked as handsome now as he did the day he'd dumped her.

"It's been so long," he said. "How are you?"

He crossed the small office and reached out as though to hug her, as though they were a couple of old friends, as though he hadn't turned her life—and her heart—upside down.

Without meaning to, Zoe retreated into the reception area. Her heart stopped, dead. In fact, part of her believed that would be best. Yes. She could keel over right there on the *Live, Laugh, Love* carpet, and then she wouldn't have to come up with something half clever to say.

But when she didn't die soon enough, her heart ached from lack of oxygen. She took a gasp of air. Sean's expression never wavered. He still looked like an old friend wanting to catch up.

She couldn't pretend this was a social call. She wasn't one to hide her feelings at the best of times, much less the worst. And this felt like the worst.

But Sean was good at hiding his feelings. He'd pretended he loved her and wanted to spend the rest of his life with her. Pretended right up until the last possible moment, when it really mattered.

"What are you doing here?" she finally managed.

"Waiting for Chelsea," he said.

"Of course." She nodded, not unlike a bobblehead. "She … She told me you're getting married."

"You must be here to see her. She won't be long, if you wanted to wait." He gestured to the other chair in the office, inviting her to sit with him.

Like she wanted to be in the same room with the two of them. As if Chelsea wouldn't take full advantage of the situation, rub their love in Zoe's face.

She wondered why on earth he thought she'd wait for Chelsea. Didn't he know they were practically mortal enemies? Then it dawned on her. *Of course, he doesn't know.*

Why would Chelsea tell him about their run-ins, about how she'd been treating his ex-fiancée? To get anyone to marry her, she probably had to hide her maliciousness, lie about who she really was.

Zoe turned to leave. "That's all right. I think I'll be going."

Sean lurched forward to stop her. "Wait, please. I think …" He ran a hand through his thick, dark locks—and she'd so hoped he'd be sporting a cul-de-sac by now. "Maybe we should talk. You know. Get things off our chests and out in the open. Find some closure."

She stared at him as though he'd confessed to being a professional wrestler. "Closure," she repeated numbly.

"We can go grab a coffee. Catch up." He flashed a perfect set of teeth.

God, he could be so damned charming when he wanted to

be. But not charming enough for her. Never again. "No. I can't. I'm busy."

"Too busy to catch up with an old friend?" He laughed congenially.

The sound was like a name she'd heard a million times before. It used to sound musical to her ears. Now it reminded her of "Wedding March"—so overdone.

Zoe's lip curled at the word "friend." "Yes. I've … I've got a date."

Natalie snorted. "A date?" She'd remained frozen by the coffee table as she watched the reunion unfold.

Zoe had forgotten she was even in the room.

"*You* have a date?" Natalie asked pointedly.

They'd worked closely together for two years. Hearing no talk of men, Natalie probably assumed she was a hardened spinster. Which wasn't far from the truth—however, Zoe preferred the term *seasoned bachelorette.*

She glared at Natalie, daring her to challenge her story. "Yes. A date."

Sean's eyes took on the look of a hurt puppy, the look that had always prevented her from staying mad at him for long—with the exception of his last screw-up.

"With who?" he asked.

Faced with Sean's undeserved look of betrayal and Natalie's disbelief, her expression hardened into a smooth mask. She wasn't that hurt twenty-four-year-old anymore. She'd gotten over it—sort of.

She raised her chin. "My fiancé."

Spinning on her heel, she marched toward the door. On her way past Natalie's desk, she spotted a turquoise daily planner lying next to her laptop. Her determined footsteps slowed as she considered it for a moment.

It was the same planner Natalie had used while working for Plum Crazy Events. With Zoe's favorite contacts, vendors, and suppliers—including wedding dress shops. It would have had all the info for Piper's wedding in it. Every last detail.

Reaching out, she swiped it off the desk and flipped through it. "Did you tell anyone about the wedding venue for Piper Summers's wedding?" she asked Natalie.

Her pale cheeks suddenly flushed. "Of course not. Being professional means maintaining client confidentiality."

"Except she's not your client, and you haven't acted the least bit professional so far. Did you tell anyone?"

She scowled. "No."

"Good. Keep it that way, or I'll be back for another chat." Zoe waved the planner in the air. "I'll be confiscating this. And if you have a problem with that, take it up with Holly Hart."

Natalie opened her mouth, an argument on her face. Before she could speak, Zoe turned her back on her two exes— assistant and fiancé. Marching out of the office, she slammed the door behind her and went to get ready to meet her future husband.

Chapter Nineteen

PAWS OFF

Zoe subtly checked her phone for the eighth time since Taichi Kimura had picked her up. Eight-thirty. She absently wondered how long a date had to be before it was considered an official date. Or rather, how long it had to be to make her mother happy.

Taichi's pasta-filled cheeks puffed out in a grin across the table. Zoe dug deep for some enthusiasm and gave what she hoped was a passable smile before drinking deeply from her wineglass.

"How is your pasta?" she asked.

"Very good. Thank you." He eyed her abandoned lasagna and then his own nearly empty plate. He ducked his head. "I grew so used to take-out as a college student that I missed American food when I returned to Japan. I guess I'm making up for lost time."

At least one of them was enjoying their date. "That's totally fine. Please, finish. I'm just not very hungry tonight." But that was probably because her stomach was filled with wine to help her get through the date. Or to forget it. She wasn't sure which.

She took another swig from her glass. "So, how is your new job going? Are you settling in?"

"It's great, thank you," Taichi said. "Everyone has been very welcoming."

He returned to his fettuccini, and Zoe didn't know what else to say, so the conversation died off for the rest of the meal. When he finally finished eating his last noodle, and Zoe her second drink, she hoped the date would be over—along with her obligation to her mother. She anxiously scanned the room until she caught the server's attention.

He gave her the head tilt and approached their table. "Will there be anything else for you?"

She opened her mouth to ask for the bill, but Taichi eagerly leaned forward.

"Yes, please. I had my eye on the chocolate cake."

"Certainly." The server turned to Zoe. "And for you, madam?"

The world's largest bottle of wine? she thought. "Make that two chocolate cakes. And another glass of wine, please."

"You like chocolate too? We have that in common," Taichi noted with delight, as though that would have been a deal breaker.

She'd forgotten how boring dates could be. Then again, they didn't have to be. She'd spent a lot of time with Levi lately, and it sometimes felt like they were on a date. And at no time would she consider their interactions boring.

But she wasn't on a date with Levi—not that she secretly wished she was or anything. And because she'd promised her mother she would consider Taichi, she put thoughts of the rock star aside.

The nonexistent small talk slowly ate away at her sense of propriety. It might have been a first date, but she didn't like to waste her time. Besides, they both knew why they were there. Why dance around the subject? Or maybe that was her third glass of wine talking.

"Tell me, Taichi," she said. "Why did you agree to this date?"

"I'm new to town. I thought it would be nice to meet up and get to know you. Your mother said you were beautiful, but her description didn't do you justice."

"Thank you." She smiled. "But you're aware of our mothers' intentions? Of the arranged marriage?"

"I am," he said blankly.

"And you still came?"

"You came as well." He indicated her thereness with a hand gesture.

"Touché, I guess." She frowned into her empty glass. "I'm just trying to understand. You've moved to America. I assume you want to live here because of the lifestyle, the freedom to choose your own life, without the pressure of family obligations."

Taichi shrugged. "That's one reason."

"Doesn't that include the freedom to choose your own wife?" She bit her lip, wondering if she was being too blunt, but she forged on anyway. "Being from a younger generation, I'm surprised you would consider such a traditional arrangement."

His look sharpened, but not because he was offended. He considered her question for a moment. "I enjoy many things about America and look forward to discovering more of it. However, who better to do it with than someone who understands me and my culture as well as American culture?"

Even to Zoe's fuzzy, wine-befuddled brain, his succinct answer surprised her. It actually made a lot of sense. "But why me? I'm more American than Japanese. Not to mention I'm brash, I'm blunt, I swear too much, and I'm stubborn. Don't expect a docile, quiet wife."

What was she saying? He shouldn't expect anything because she wouldn't marry him. Maybe her fight with Levi had got her thinking about marriage. Or maybe it was running into Sean so unexpectedly after all these years. But she wanted to know what Taichi saw in her that was worth marrying, even

207

if he'd only just met her. What did he see that Sean hadn't? That—if Levi was right—*she* didn't see? Was she marriage material?

Taichi chuckled good-humoredly. "In all your mother's descriptions of you, she never used the word docile. You know who you are. You're independent. I like that. We are just two like-minded people willing to come together and form a mutually beneficial union. I'm simply looking for someone to enjoy my life with. So why not you?" he asked simply.

Thankfully, the server came with their dessert, and she didn't have to respond.

Why not her? That was a good question. Zoe thought she was a great catch. But marriage material?

Taichi seemed perfectly pleasant. She could never imagine him mistreating her or leaving her at the altar. As she studied him over her chocolate cake, he looked attractive enough. He had kind eyes and a youthful optimism about him. And to have someone to lie next to every night meant no more vibrators for her.

Scratch that, she thought. Of course there would be vibrators. It only made things more interesting.

An arranged marriage seemed less messy than hopping back into the dating scene again. It made her cringe to think of the uncertainty of it all, the self-consciousness, the doubts, all to possibly end up single anyway. Taichi, on the other hand, would be a sure thing. He already knew he wanted to marry her.

He dug into his chocolate cake. "Why are you considering an arranged marriage? As you say, you are more American than Japanese."

Zoe's candidness suddenly turned around and bit her right in the butt.

A week ago, she would have laughed at the question. Her? Consider marriage? Ha! Not possible. Not until she'd met Levi, until he'd made it impossible not to take a good hard look at her decision to be alone.

He'd made her think about things, feel things she'd assumed she never would again. Things she'd put behind her a long time ago. Or at least, she'd thought she had.

But Levi wanted only to date her. There was still the uncertainty, the possibility it would all fall apart one day. He wasn't a safe bet.

She recalled the way he'd looked at her on the carousel the day before. He'd asked her *What do you want?* And frankly, she didn't know. But she couldn't run away from the question anymore. Not seated across from a man who could be her fiancé.

Taichi was giving her his time, his honesty, and his candidness about marriage. She owed it to him to be honest. With him and with herself.

She took a deep breath. "I guess because it would be nice to have someone there by my side. Someone to share my day with who can respond with more than a bark. Someone to wake up next to who doesn't have doggy breath. An equal partner."

And there it was. The truth. Maybe she didn't have everything she needed. Maybe she wasn't entirely sold on remaining alone forever, just her and Freddy. As she thought more and more about it, there were a lot of holes in her life a dog couldn't fill. But was Taichi the man to fill them?

"Those are good reasons." He nodded. "Partnership, dependability, mutual respect."

Smiling, Zoe tucked into her dessert, allowing herself to enjoy the date for the first time. Later that night, she got home and crawled into her empty bed. And when she cuddled up next to Freddy and her Fuzzy Friends, she knew for certain it wasn't enough anymore.

The only remaining question was, who would be enough?

The man she knew would never break her heart, but might never make it whole again? Or was it the man who had opened her heart, who had the potential to fill it again, but could also leave it shattered?

Chapter Twenty

SINGING A DIFFERENT TUNE

Zoe paced in House of Glass, waiting for everyone to arrive for lunch. She'd chosen Chef Glazier, San Francisco's very own celebrity chef, to cater Piper and Aiden's wedding. Thanks to the groom's reputation—and wallet—the chef had closed his restaurant for a private tasting for all of their friends. And that included Levi … if he showed up.

While she tried to focus on her friends' upcoming nuptials, her mind kept wandering back to Levi. To the things she'd said to him on the pier, to how she'd reacted, when all he'd said was the truth. She just hoped she could apologize in person.

Pulling out her phone, she checked the screen for the hundredth time. He still hadn't responded to her invitation. Maybe he didn't want to hear her apology. Or worse. What if he simply didn't care?

As the servers set up their table, the kitchen doors swung open and closed. The movement released the exquisite scent of gourmet food and the comforting undertones of fish. They wrapped around her like a blanket, and she took a deep breath.

It reminded her of when she was a kid; fish had always been her mother's go-to dish. Junko said it brought back memories of her own childhood growing up in Uji. Today, however, Zoe didn't find it comforting enough.

She made a list, putting her worries about the day in order.

- *Will Levi show?*
- *Will he forgive me?*
- *Does he still want to date me?*
- *Do I want to date him?*
- *Would I marry Taichi?*
- *Do I even want to get married at all?*

She couldn't believe she was even considering these things. Ever since her fight with Levi, or maybe since her date with Taichi, she'd realized how much Levi had influenced her in the two short weeks they'd known each other. She just didn't know to what extent yet.

The front door opened. Street noises filtered in as someone entered. When she turned around, she crossed one worry off her list.

"Levi."

He hesitated in the doorway. "Hi."

He'd cleaned up for the brunch with tie and dress shirt—not tucked in, but somehow it worked for the rocker.

"I'm glad you came," Zoe said.

"Free food? Can't say no to that." He patted his belly. "Sorry I didn't text you. I just finished a jam session with the guys, and we have a no-cell policy while we work. And if I'm being honest, I wasn't sure I was coming until I came in."

"I want to apologize for the other day. I didn't like what you had to say, so I got defensive and took it out on you. I guess I'm used to dishing it out, not receiving it."

"Thank you. And I'm sorry for what I said." He took a step inside.

"Don't be. Never apologize for being honest with me. Because you were right. Maybe I am afraid to let people in. To let them get too close." The words hurt to admit out loud, but she also felt lighter, her bottle a little emptier.

"I get it," he said. "You were hurt. And you're scared it's going to happen again."

"I'm starting to think remaining single might not be the answer." She chuckled. But she'd lied to herself for so long that she'd actually believed it. "You always say life is too short. But maybe it's also too long. Too long to spend it alone."

"It's also a long time to spend with the wrong person, trust me." He glanced down at his shoes. "I guess that makes me scared of choosing the wrong person again."

It felt like a corset had tightened around Zoe's chest. Her breath whooshed out. Did that mean he now thought of her as the wrong person? She wouldn't blame him after how she'd reacted on the carousel. Did she want to be the right person?

She thought back to her date with Taichi and their conversation. "How do you know? Who's the right one?"

"I guess that's the hard part. You don't know. You just have to go for it." He rubbed a hand over his clean-shaven jaw. "It's like when the band and I jam. We have an exercise where we just pick up our instruments and play random notes, tones, riffs and hope it all harmonizes together. Sometimes it works out. Sometimes it doesn't. But when it does, it's a real hit. You never know unless you take a chance."

She nodded, understanding where he was going. "Grab life by the balls."

He smiled, really smiled, like he usually did with her. "Yeah."

She wanted to say more, say something about him. About them. But she didn't know where to start. She couldn't even understand her own feelings right now, so how could she explain them?

The front door opened again, and she lost her chance as Piper and Aiden walked in.

"Sorry we're late," Piper said. "We got stuck in traffic."

"That's okay," Zoe said. "The food is just coming out as we speak."

They gathered around the only table set in the restaurant. Soon, Addison, Felix, and Naia arrived and joined them. When Bob and Marilyn showed up, the soup was served.

Now that they were all seated around the table, their group felt whole. It was generous of Aiden to buy out the restaurant so they could still be together for their usual Sunday brunch, even if they weren't eating pancakes.

Their group was larger than it used to be. All Zoe's favorite women were paired off and in happy relationships. And to her surprise, even she had her own plus one for once. Well, sort of; she didn't know exactly what Levi was yet. But it was the first time she'd ever brought a man around her friends, so it had to mean something.

"Tell me, Levi," Aiden said. "Are weddings big business for live bands these days?"

"It's not too bad. Not steady work, but with other weekend events and gigs at the local bars, we're almost full time." He reached for a butternut squash tart. "We're actually booked to do a week-long tour around California this week. I leave tomorrow."

"Tomorrow?" Zoe nearly dropped her tart. She tried to rearrange her surprised features into one of mere interest. Now that she thought about it, she recalled Levi mentioning the tour to Holly Hart.

"Don't worry," he told her. "We'll be back in town for a gig Friday night, so it won't interfere with the wedding the next day. And, of course, you can continue to use my place to work."

She nodded, but that wasn't what had her worried. She wondered if they'd be able to talk more before he left. Or maybe this was a blessing in disguise. Maybe time away from him was exactly what she needed. Time to think.

"Sounds like you guys are no amateurs," Felix said. "Maybe I should hire you to play at my pub one night."

"That would be cool," Levi said. "I do some solo stuff too, even for the fancy parties. Soirees, fundraisers, black-tie events, that kind of thing. I know a lot of classical and jazz standards. Apparently, I make pleasant background noise."

This got a chuckle out of everyone around the table.

Zoe snorted. "I can't see you blending into the background."

Levi gave her a familiar look. And then it struck her: his looks were *familiar*. That was something new.

"Hey," he said. "I can behave myself, you know. I clean up pretty good too."

"Oh, I remember." But when she recalled how he looked at Juliet's wedding, her mind automatically produced the memory of him with nothing on but his dress shirt.

His eyes crinkled like they were sharing an inside joke. Was it her imagination, or was he thinking about the same moment?

When she finally looked away, there were more familiar looks from around the table. Apparently, they were the entertainment for the meal. Could her friends be any more obvious?

She wanted to throw one of her salad croutons at them, but then she would be stooping to their level of immaturity. So instead, she settled for sticking her tongue out at them when Levi wasn't looking.

Addison set down her glass with a bang. "So, Levi. Why do you want to date our Zoe?"

Zoe gasped, her mouth dropping open. "Addison!"

"What?" She batted her eyelashes. "Normally you'd be the one asking the blunt questions, so someone's got to do it for you."

Levi didn't skip a beat. "Because she's a great catch. But I don't think I need to tell her best friends why she's amazing."

Good answer, Zoe thought. Did it mean he was still interested? He was still there, so she supposed that was a good sign.

Addison nodded, a wry twist to her bright pink lips. "Touché."

"What are your intentions?" This time it was Piper demanding an answer.

"Purely honorable," Levi said.

Zoe heaved a weary sigh. *A little too honorable, so far.*

When the main course arrived, conversation turned to their usual Sunday chit-chat. Levi jumped into the conversation easily, fitting right in. But of course he would. He was so easygoing that Zoe could see him slipping into any situation effortlessly.

Leaning closer to Bob, he struck up a conversation. "Zoe tells me you're with the San Francisco Police Department."

Bob wiped the crumbs off his mustache with a napkin. "Yes. Been there all my working life. I'm an inspector."

He whistled. "Now that's an interesting job. I bet it keeps you busy."

"That's an understatement."

"Bob is investigating the San Fran Slayer case," Zoe told him. "He makes the official statements on the news all the time."

Levi's eyes narrowed as he assessed the older man. "Now I know where I've seen your face before."

Addison glanced at Naia, making sure she was distracted by the game on her dad's phone. She lowered her voice. "I heard the killer struck again last week."

"I saw that on the news," Piper said. "Didn't he kill some jewelry designer?"

"They found a pizza delivery driver the other day," Zoe said.

Marilyn tutted, setting her fork down. "This isn't a discussion for mealtime. Can't we talk about something more pleasant?"

"My ears are burning!" A voice sang out.

Everyone twisted in their chairs to find Holly Hart poised at the entrance.

She waved a hand. "Now don't stop chatting on my account. Go ahead. Talk about how pleasant I am."

Jaws dropped as she grabbed a nearby chair. She dragged it over, metal legs scraping on the floor. Too immobilized by shock, no one stopped her as she took a seat.

Wedging herself between Aiden and Piper, she scooted herself closer to the table like she was one of the gang. She placed her chin on her fist, batting her eyelashes at Aiden.

His jaw clenched. He dropped his fork on the plate, and it clattered noisily. The curl to his lip said he'd lost his appetite for the dessert spread being carried out at that very moment.

Zoe glimpsed the bride-to-be's expression and wondered if she should tell the server to clear the knives off the table, just in case. "What are you doing here?" she demanded.

"Now, now," Holly said. "Is that any way to treat a guest?"

The server hesitated as she set the last of the truffles on the table. "But the reservation was for nine. I'm not sure there's enough food left. I could always go check with Chef Glazier."

Holly held up her hands. "Oh, I don't want to be a bother."

"She's not staying," Zoe said. "The word 'guest' would imply she was invited, and *she wasn't*." She glared across the table at the reporter.

"Oh, but I was." She aimed a conspiratorial wink at Zoe so everyone could see.

Piper's eyes widened, and her head snapped toward her friend. "Zoe. You didn't."

Holly bit her lip. "Oops."

Piper threw her napkin on the table and jumped to her feet. "How could you? You said you would stop feeding her information."

Zoe flinched at the anger in her voice. "I wasn't feeding her information. I gave her a few useless details."

"Except when she showed up at my bridal gown appointment. That hint wasn't so useless."

Zoe got to her feet and leaned over the table. She wouldn't back down. She'd done nothing wrong this time. "I didn't tell her about the dress fitting. Natalie did it. Or maybe Chelsea. I thought you said you believed me."

"I did. But you said you stole her planner, and now Holly shows up at our sample meal?" She threw her hands up. "How did she find out about this one, huh?"

Zoe banged the table with a fist. "I swear I don't know how she found out."

Holly stood now too. "Ladies. Ladies. You know, you wouldn't have to fight about me if you'd just give me an invite already."

Zoe turned her murderous gaze on her. "Why bother when you seem to invite yourself to everything anyway?"

"Don't blame her," Piper said.

Holly placed a touching hand over her heart. "Thank you."

"I blame you." She jabbed a finger in Zoe's direction.

"Oh, drama, drama, drama." The reporter took a seat again, as though getting comfortable for a show.

Zoe gritted her teeth. "I didn't tell her anything. Do you really think I'm lying?"

Piper took a deep, calming breath. "Look. I'm just saying you haven't exactly been on the ball lately." She held up her hands. "I understand. You've got a lot of things on your plate and—"

"So, you don't believe me," Zoe said. "I thought you were my friend."

"Friend?" She scoffed. "You're the one leaking wedding info to the paparazzi."

"I'm not a paparazzo," Holly corrected her. "I'm the people's voice. Their champion. Ooh, are these peanut butter chocolate balls?" She popped one into her mouth and rolled her eyes in ecstasy. She held up the platter to Piper. "You should really try one of these babies."

Marilyn fidgeted in her seat, flinching at all the yelling. Everyone else eyed one another like no one quite knew what to do. How could they possibly choose sides?

Bob placed a gentle hand over Marilyn's, stopping them from twisting in her lap, but he directed his no-nonsense response at Piper and Zoe. "I'm sure there's a perfectly good explanation as to why Holly is here. And if we all settle down, I'm sure we can sort it out."

Aiden rubbed Piper's back. "Let's just sample the desserts, so we can make our choices for the wedding menu and go, okay? This chef has been booked for months and we've been waiting for this appointment. There's no time to come back."

She huffed a breath through her nose. "Fine."

But Zoe had lost her appetite. "I wouldn't want to throw off the chef's numbers. I'll go."

"No, wait!" Addison called after her.

Zoe grabbed her purse and marched out the front door. The summer air hit her, thick and hot after the air-conditioned restaurant. But despite the humidity, it felt easier to breathe. Chin raised, she headed for her van.

The restaurant door squeaked open behind her. Footsteps slapped the pavement as someone followed at a quick pace. They slowed as they came up beside her. It was Levi. Shoving his hands in his pockets, he strolled casually like he'd been there the whole time.

"Well, the salmon was delicious," he said. "A bit salty, but the dill was a nice touch."

Despite her anger, Zoe felt herself smile. He'd walked out of a brunch with the people who'd hired him for a high-profile gig. Not to mention, he didn't even try to stay behind to schmooze Holly Hart for a segment on his band. Instead, he'd chased after her.

Reaching out, she slid her hand into his. It was such a simple thing to do, and yet she felt like she'd just climbed Mount Everest. Thankfully, he didn't make a big deal about it. He just squeezed her hand briefly and continued to chat as though they'd had a perfectly pleasant meal.

"You should have tried the dark chocolate caramel balls. The chef's a genius. I never would have thought to pair sesame seeds with salted caramel."

Zoe's heart lurched. Her footsteps faltered, and she came to a stop. She gripped his arm. "What did you say?"

He frowned. "Caramel balls?"

"Sesame seeds." Her voice was barely a whisper. The air left her lungs like she'd received a punch to the gut. Piper was deathly allergic to sesame seeds.

"Piper."

She spun and raced back to the restaurant. She had to stop Piper from eating them before she wound up in the hospital. Or worse.

Chapter Twenty-One

A BARKING DOG NEVER BITES

Zoe wrenched open the restaurant door and ran back to their table. She stumbled over chair legs and bumped tables decorated with fresh flowers, knocking over their vases. She could hear Levi right on her heels. By the time she got to the private area, she was out of breath.

Her eyes locked on Piper. Chocolate was her friend's comfort food during times of stress, joy, boredom, or any time for that matter, so of course Piper had reached for one of the truffles. A truffle containing deadly sesame seeds.

As she brought it to her mouth, Zoe screamed, "No! Grab that ball!"

She leaped across the table, slapping it out of Piper's hand. The chocolate ball flew across the room, bouncing off Holly's cheek, and landed in someone's water glass.

Dishes slid off the table, shattering as they hit the floor. Marilyn screamed. Felix shielded Naia from flying silverware. Bob shot to his feet.

When everything settled and the last glass stopped spinning on the floor, the moment froze like some bizarre tableau.

Piper's mouth hung open like it still expected the chocolate truffle. Sprawled across the tabletop, Zoe tried to catch her breath. She groaned as lukewarm soup soaked through her dress.

Naia giggled in her dad's arms, entertained by the events. Holly snapped photos from different angles with her phone until Addison grabbed it. Drawing her arm back, she tossed it clear across the room.

"That's the second phone this week," Holly whined.

"Then be a better human," Addison shot back.

Piper finally shut her mouth and glared at Zoe. "Have you lost your mind?" She rubbed at the tomato basil soup sprayed down the front of her dress with a napkin.

Zoe gasped for air. "Sesame seeds … in … balls."

Piper's glare shifted to the chocolate ball floating in the glass. The truffle's dark powder coating floated on the water's surface. After a moment, she backed away from it like it had personally tried to kill her.

"Oh, God," she said. "How—"

"Levi ate one," Zoe explained. "He told me it had sesame seeds in it."

Aiden automatically reached out for Piper. "Are you okay? Did any get in your mouth?"

"No … No. I'm fine." She rubbed her fingers on the front of her dress.

Zoe inched her way off the table, trying to do as little damage as possible, or at least no more than what she'd already done. All manner of desserts and drinks dripped down the front of her dress.

Levi held the table steady so it didn't tip over as she slid off it. "Wow," he said to Piper. "You must really hate sesame seeds."

Zoe wiped herself off with a napkin. "She's highly allergic. Like anaphylactic allergic."

He threw her a look. "Yeah, I gathered that."

Holly marched over, holding her phone up with a voice recording app on the newly cracked screen. "Piper Summers.

Your wedding planner has dropped the bouquet on your upcoming nuptials to rich CEO and ridiculously fit Aiden Caldwell. Is it time to search for a new planner?"

Piper stared the phone down. "Not a chance. I couldn't do it without her. I wouldn't."

Her expression burned with such sincerity that Zoe lunged for her friend, wrapping her arms around her.

"Thanks," she said. "I needed to hear that." And it seemed she'd needed a hug too because she lingered in Piper's embrace a moment longer.

"I'm sorry I didn't believe you," Piper said.

"I'm sorry too." When she pulled away, she glared at the metal doors to the kitchen. "I specifically told the chef no sesame seeds. He knew you had a severe allergy. This is inexcusable." Her fists balled at her sides as the reality of what just about happened hit her. "Excuse me while I go have a few words with Chef Glazier."

As she strode toward the kitchen, she nearly ran into Holly. The reporter stuck the phone in her face, but she pushed her away.

"Don't go anywhere," Zoe told her. "I'll deal with you in a minute."

She gaped. "Me? What did I do? I'm just doing my job."

Zoe sneered at the reporter in disgust and reached for the kitchen door. However, the server cut her off.

"Excuse me, but it's staff only in the kitchen. You can't go back there."

Zoe unleashed the full force of her eyebrow on her. With a quirk and a twitch, the server backed off as though Zoe had physically pushed her.

Sweeping aside the stainless steel door, she blew into the kitchen like a storm, while feeling as thunderous as one. "Chef Glazier?"

She'd had to fire caterers for overcooked vegetables or cold soup before. But this mishap wouldn't have put a bad taste in someone's mouth. It could have killed Piper.

The door swung shut behind her, muting Holly's screeches; someone must have been forcibly removing her from the restaurant. But as silence fell over the kitchen, there was still no answer from the chef.

She strained her ears, but she heard nothing. No signs of life in the spotless kitchen. No clanging dishes or chopping knives.

"Chef Glazier?!"

When she rounded the stainless steel counter, she knew he couldn't have gone far because his station was still a mess: fresh tomato juice ran across the counter, yam peels slid under her foot, the knife he'd used for the steak bites was still covered in blood.

Maybe he was in the restroom. Or maybe he'd heard the commotion and realized his mistake, then took off to let the servers deal with the customer complaints. Well, Zoe wouldn't let him get off that easily.

She spotted the cutting board covered in the dark cocoa powder used to sprinkle over the chocolate balls. However, when she took a closer look, it appeared much darker and chunkier than powder.

Swiping a finger over it, she rubbed the black stuff between her fingers. Gritty, something finely chopped. She tasted it: sesame seeds.

He'd chosen a black seed color, which blended into the cocoa powder. No wonder no one had noticed it.

The garbage was full of discarded onion peels, containers, and mushroom stumps. She grabbed a spatula and shifted the garbage aside. Beneath a watermelon rind hid a half-empty bag of sesame seeds. A small package that one would find in a grocery store aisle.

Had he misplaced her prioritized, itemized, color-coded list of allergies, preferences, and favorites? And just where did he go?

"Renowned chef, my butt," she mumbled.

Zoe wandered farther into the back, where she came across a door labeled *Office*. She brought up a fist and banged on it. No answer. When she tried the handle, the door creaked open.

A quick scan told her the chef should still be there. His coat hung on the wall, and his keys lay on the messy desk. She spotted the deposit check she'd given him months before. It was stuck to the wall with a thumbtack. He might have been a talented chef, but he was a terrible recordkeeper.

Reaching out, she ripped it down. She'd rather scramble to find a replacement caterer than use his services again. She was about to tear it up, but then she thought of something even better. Something that would send a clear message.

She stomped back to his station. After the close call of nearly seeing her friend succumb to anaphylaxis, her body shook with adrenaline. And Chef Glazier wasn't even man enough to own up to his mistake.

She swiped his bloody steak knife off the counter and placed the check on the cutting board with the sesame seed debris. Raising the knife, she stabbed the slip of paper right through the middle.

That should be clear enough.

Zoe left the kitchen, ready to get out of there. She found the others waiting at the front door.

"Did you find him?" Aiden asked her.

"No. Unfortunately."

"I'll have a talk with him when I get to the office tomorrow." He wrapped a protective arm around Piper as they went to leave. "Or maybe my lawyer will."

"Don't worry," Zoe said. "I'll find a new caterer for the wedding. One that's even better. It will be perfect. I promise."

There was that word again, "perfect." But so far, nothing about this wedding came close to it. First the entertainer broke his leg, then someone shredded the gown, her décor blew up, and now this. But so far, she'd met every challenge. And she'd meet this one head-on too.

She and Levi were the last to leave. He grinned at Zoe as he held the door open for her.

She hesitated, suddenly self-conscious. "What?"

"You're a force to be reckoned with, Zoe Plum. One would almost say you're close to finding those balls to grab."

She scraped past him through the door, closer than she needed to, rubbing against him. "Maybe those balls are closer than I thought." She smiled at him. Not seductively to match her innuendo, but earnestly.

He must have understood her meaning because his look softened.

Standing close to him in the open doorway, she realized that despite their steamy encounter on his couch and a couple of accidental dates, they'd never actually kissed.

At first, she hadn't wanted to. It was too romantic, too intimate. But now, she leaned into him, tilting her face up to meet his.

A smile lit his face, and he dipped his head. But before their lips could touch, a noise interrupted them.

Squeak ... squeak ... squeak ... squeak.

Exchanging a look, they searched for the source. It came from a white van parked three cars down. The decal on the side said *Channel Five News.*

Squeak ... squeak ... squeak ... squeak.

It rocked gently on its wheels, increasing in tempo. It could mean only one thing.

Zoe snickered. "Do you think ...?"

Levi wrinkled his nose. "Holly and her cameraman?"

As the noise persisted, changing in rhythm and gusto, they stifled their giggles. Zoe braced herself against the restaurant doorframe, clutching her aching stomach.

Bob and Marilyn lingered nearby on the sidewalk. They caught on a moment later.

Marilyn clicked her tongue. "Well, I never."

The shocked look on the woman's face sent Zoe into a whole new round of giggles.

"Help! Help!" someone inside the restaurant yelled. "Call the police!"

Footsteps slapped the restaurant floor, growing closer. Levi and Zoe pulled apart and rushed inside to see what the commotion was. A moment later, the server appeared from the back and skidded to a halt in the waiting area.

"You!" She pointed an accusing finger at Zoe. "You did it, didn't you? You monster!"

Something red dripped from her hand. And it wasn't tomato juice. It was blood.

"I did what?" Zoe asked. "What's wrong?"

"You killed Chef Glazier."

Chapter Twenty-Two

BAD DOG

The clock on the wall ticked loudly, counting the painfully slow minutes as Inspector Warner examined Zoe from across the metal table. She'd been stuck in the room for six hours already, her mind going in circles as she answered the same questions over and over. Every once in a while, the inspector would leave and come back with a new batch for her. Her head spun like it had on the Pier 39 carousel.

He tapped his fingers on the table and stared at her expectantly. It must have been her turn to take it from the top again.

"Am I free to go yet?" she asked, already knowing the answer.

He inhaled, as though he were seriously considering it. Then he let out a forceful breath. "There's still the issue of a dead chef."

She groaned. After so many hours, the inspector's voice scratched against her brain like cheap lace. "I've already answered your questions. I've told you everything I know. What more do you want?"

He crossed his arms and sat back. "I'm still not satisfied."

She threw her hands up. "You think I killed this guy?"

"I'm the one asking questions around here, Miss Plum." He

228

leaned forward, planting his elbows on the table. "How's business?"

She blinked at the sudden change in direction. "Okay, I guess."

"Now, be honest." He wagged a finger at her. "Your business has suffered recently. You've been losing clients. Isn't that right?"

Zoe rolled her eyes. They must have interviewed Chelsea at some point. "Any clients I've lost have been because of Chelsea and my ex-assistant, who's now working with her."

"So, you admit business is bad," he said like he'd caught her.

She shrugged. "Yeah, but I'll get back on track soon enough."

"Remember that little gas leak at your office?"

"Remember it? It practically killed me." She wondered at his new angle. What did that have to do with Chef Glazier?

"It wasn't a gas leak. It was a bomb, Miss Plum. Someone blew up your office intentionally."

She snorted. "I'd already guessed as much. This isn't exactly news." But the confirmation made her shiver.

"Of course it's not," he said. "That's my point."

Zoe held up her hands. "Wait a second. Are you implying I did this to myself? Why would I blow up my office when I needed everything in there for events over the next couple of months? Do you have any idea how far this has set me back? How much work I have to do to replace everything in time?" She ran her hands through her hair, tugging on her long locks. "Why would I risk my business?"

"Insurance fraud, Miss Plum. Instant cash in hand." The inspector rubbed his fingers together in her face, close enough that she could smell the stale smoke on them.

She wondered if some of his bad-cop routine was aided by him going without a cigarette for so long.

As though reading her mind, he popped a piece of nicotine

gum into his mouth. As he chewed, she saw his extra-pointy incisors, like he was some balding, middle-aged vampire.

He crumpled the gum wrapper and tossed it across the room at the garbage can. He missed. "I called your landlord. He says you've given your notice and are moving in with your mother."

"That's because *her* finances are a mess, not mine," Zoe responded coolly, which was getting harder and harder to do as the hours went by. "That and her health has been failing. She needs help—"

"I called her too." He cut her off. "She says everything is just fine."

She groaned. *Thanks, Mom.* "Of course she said that. She's an incredibly private person. Why would she tell a complete stranger about her life? She barely keeps me informed. Besides, what does all this prove?" she asked. "If you think I'm so hard up for money, why would I do anything else to jeopardize my friend's upcoming wedding, a good-paying gig?"

With a burst of energy, the inspector jumped to his feet, knocking his chair back. He leaned across the table. "You've been losing clients left, right, and center. Your office just blew up, your company van went in for repairs, and you can't even afford your rent so you have to move in with your mother." He succinctly summed up each crappy thing going wrong with her life lately, counting each one on his fingers as he went.

She pretended to check her nails. "And I suppose I cut my own brake lines too?"

"Say you didn't blow up your office—"

"Because I didn't."

"Say you're just down on your luck," he continued like he didn't hear her. "You need this wedding to go well. With all the public exposure for your friend's big, high-profile wedding, it could boost your business again."

He circled the table, walking behind Zoe. She spun anxiously in her seat to face him.

"But everything's not going perfectly, is it, Miss Plum? First the wedding dress, then your office blows up, and now the caterer nearly lands your bride in the hospital. That was the last straw. You lose it. You snap." He snapped his fingers in her face. "You march into the kitchen—"

"But I didn't find Chef Glazier when I was back there," Zoe interrupted.

"So you say." Inspector Warner paced. "Or you found him, and things got out of hand. You argued. It turned physical. You grabbed a nearby knife and killed him. In a moment of panic, you dragged the body to the loading bay, where you stashed it among the storage boxes. Then you went back to your tea party as though nothing happened." His eyes lit up as if he'd just solved the case.

"That's a nice story. It makes me sound pretty devious."

Grabbing his chair, he spun it around and straddled it to face her. "You can't fool me, Miss Plum."

She scowled. "I didn't kill him."

"We found your little deposit check stabbed with the knife."

"The steak knife? So what?" She frowned. "It was a message to let him know I fired him."

"Oh, you sent him a message, all right. It was a little sloppy of you. His DNA was practically still dripping from the knife when we found it."

Zoe's body suddenly grew cold, her fingers and toes tingling. "What?"

"His blood, Miss Plum." He spoke slowly, like she was having trouble following. "The knife was covered in it, along with your fingerprints."

She remembered the blood on the knife. She'd assumed it came from cutting the steak bites. Leaning forward, she gripped the table. Her stomach twisted.

"Oh God. But I-I just found the knife lying on the counter-top. I swear—"

The door burst open. Zoe jumped, tipping over her cup of

water. It ran across the table and spilled onto the inspector's lap. He leaped out of his seat, swearing as he tried to wipe it away.

"I'm in the middle of an interview here," he barked at the officer in the doorway. "What the hell is going on?"

The officer gave an apologetic shrug as a trim woman strode through the door. Inspector Warner's face went slack.

Without waiting for an invitation, she strode across the room, heels clicking on the linoleum floor. "There's nothing going on because you're done here."

When Inspector Warner got to his feet, she towered over him. Fist on her hip, she looked down her nose at him like she ate balding vampires for breakfast. She stood between him and Zoe as though protecting her.

"You've got to be kidding me." The inspector eyed Zoe. "I thought finances were tight. How can you afford an attorney like her?"

She gaped at the attorney like Wonder Woman had just come to save her. "They are. I can't. I have an attorney?"

"Michelle Johnson with Wright Law Office." She held out a hand.

Zoe shook it a little robotically. "How—?"

She winked. "Aiden Caldwell sent me."

Of course he had. She should have lawyered-up once it became clear where the inspector's finger pointed, but she supposed she hadn't thought of it. Why should she need a lawyer? She was innocent. She had nothing to hide. At least she hadn't thought so. However, it seemed they were finding enough dirt on her to build a case.

"Don't say anything more," Michelle told Zoe.

Inspector Warner barked a laugh. "She's said plenty enough already."

"Well, unless she's said, 'I'm guilty,' then I assume 'plenty' isn't quite enough."

He sucked on his teeth. Finally, as though he were agreeing

to a colonoscopy, he waved a hand. "Fine. You're free to go. I'm done with you anyway."

Zoe got to her feet. "Really?"

He pointed a stern finger at her. "Don't leave town."

Michelle gestured to the cup on the table. "Take that with you. They can get your prints off it after you leave."

Zoe grabbed it and followed her attorney out of the room. "But I already gave them my fingerprints." She wondered if she shouldn't have done that. Did she have a choice? She really should have called a lawyer sooner, but she'd used her one phone call to make sure someone checked in on her mom and Freddy.

"That's fine," Michelle said. "But you don't want to give them anything else."

She nodded, assuming the attorney meant saliva or something.

Once they got to the reception area, Michelle gave her a business card. "Go home. Get some rest. I'll speak to you first thing in the morning. Don't discuss the incident with anyone."

She read the card numbly. She liked this woman. Focused, direct, confident. Everything she didn't feel at the moment.

By the time she got her purse back and signed some papers, it was seven o'clock. As she pulled her cell phone out to arrange a ride, someone accosted her from behind.

Arms wrapped around her, squeezing her like bridal under-garments. She gasped and spun around.

"Zoe!" Addison cried. "Oh, my gosh. Are you okay?"

She gripped Addison's sweater, relieved beyond words to see a friend after the hell she'd been through. But instead of admitting that, she said, "Of course. Why wouldn't I be?"

"They didn't try to throw you in the slammer?"

"No." She couldn't help but laugh. "They just interrogated me."

Addison gave her a serious look. "How does it feel, you know, now that you're on the other side of the law?"

"I didn't break any laws, Addy."

"Oh, I know that." Her one eye closed in a ridiculously slow wink.

"No winking. Stop that." She swatted at her.

"I'm totally behind you a hundred percent." She gave another wink. "Let me know if there's anything I can do for you. Just name it. A file baked into a cake, boxes of cigarettes for trade, conjugal visits."

Zoe's shoulders relaxed as she exhaled in a half laugh. "Thanks. I appreciate it. How about we start with a ride?"

"That I can do," she said. "And no law-breaking necessary."

Zoe glanced sidelong at her as they descended the front steps of the precinct. "You forget I've seen you drive."

Addison giggled but didn't deny the insinuation.

"Did someone check on my mom or Freddy?"

"Yes. Freddy is fine but missing you. And Piper went to your mom's earlier, and she's all good."

Zoe frowned. Even if her mom wasn't okay, she wouldn't say anything. "Do you mind if we check in on her on the way to pick up my van?"

"Of course. And don't worry. She knows we were all brought in for questioning but not that you're suspect numero uno."

"Good." She thought the stress of that news might actually kill her mother on the spot.

As soon as she crawled into Addison's Mini Convertible, she called Aiden and Piper and thanked them profusely for the help. When she got to her childhood home—or rather, her future one—her mom seemed to be in relatively good spirits for someone whose daughter was involved in a murder investigation. When Junko asked about the date with Taichi Kimura, Zoe knew why. What had he said?

Maybe it was guilt over being a daughter who gets arrested on suspicion of murder, but she told her it went very well.

Naturally, her mother pressed her about marriage, and Zoe, very honestly, told her mother she was considering it. Which was completely true, just maybe not to Taichi. But she'd give her mother another week out of the hospital before they had that talk.

By the time Zoe had picked up her van and was trudging up the stairs to her apartment, she not only faced possible incarceration for a crime she didn't commit, but if that didn't happen, she'd have to consult the koyomi to set a wedding date to Taichi. She didn't know which fate was worse.

But assuming Aiden's kick-ass attorney could keep her out of jail for the next week, she still had a wedding to plan, which also meant finding a chef—a live one. That's if whoever was trying to take her down didn't get to her first.

She wondered if the sesame seed poisoning was somehow linked to all the other recent incidents. Was this about discrediting her as a planner? To create bad press in the media about her biggest wedding of the year?

The only person who might have sent Holly there at just the right time—or the worst—would have been Natalie. But then there was the whole murder aspect, and there was no way she was capable of that.

Chelsea popped into her mind. Was she capable of murdering the chef? Maybe it had been Juliet Fisher. Maybe everyone was about tit for tat lately.

As she slid her key into the lock, she wanted to fall into bed with Freddy and at least a dozen Fuzzy Friends to keep her company. But when she opened her front door, she had more company than she'd expected.

A figure stood in her dim entryway, waiting for her. She gasped and opened her mouth to scream. The sound was suddenly blocked by a mouth against hers: Levi's mouth.

Her scream turned into a moan as he sucked hungrily on her lips. Not removing his mouth from hers, he pulled her inside.

Shoving the door closed with his foot, he backed her up against it. His body pressed close to hers like he didn't want to leave an inch of space between them. And neither did Zoe.

She'd held him at a distance for so long, refused to let him near. Now she wanted to get her fill of him, gorge like a bride after a hardcore wedding diet.

Zoe ran her hands around the back of his head and gripped his hair, pulling his face, his kisses, closer. He grunted and drove his tongue into her mouth greedily. She met it with her own, wanting to taste him, to have every part of him inside of her. She wanted it all.

She moaned as he rubbed against her, panting as she lost herself in the make out session. Maybe it was the sounds or the way they gripped each other, but Freddy barked wildly, dancing at their feet.

Are you fighting? Do you need help? Don't worry, I'll save you!

Reluctantly, Levi pulled away. Even in the dim entryway, Zoe could see the lust lighting up his eyes. They scraped over every inch of her like he'd worried he'd never see her again.

She sighed. "I've wanted to do that since this afternoon."

He ran a thumb across her lips, biting his own as though he wanted another taste. "I've wanted to do that since the moment we met."

Tired of waiting for his turn, Freddy circled her legs three times before jumping up and pawing at her shin.

She picked him up and welcomed his frantic kisses. She ignored the fact that he'd get excited over anyone and was probably thinking *I feel like we've met before. Do I know you?*

Zoe had never been so happy to come home. And not to just one male in her life, but two.

"How are you?" Levi asked.

"A free woman. Thanks to Aiden." She slipped off her shoes and headed for the living room.

He followed her. "Yeah, I know. I saw him at the station. After the police finished questioning the rest of us, we waited around, hoping they'd release you. When it was clear it wouldn't be that simple, Aiden made some calls."

The news made her feel both guilty that her mess had disrupted everyone's day and grateful for such good friends. "I'm glad he did, or I'd still be in there. I'm suspect number one." With a groan, she flopped onto the couch and put her feet up while she snuggled Freddy.

Levi sat next to her, apprehensive for a man who just had his tongue down her throat. "I hope you don't mind me being here. Piper gave me her spare key to your place. Aiden was dealing with the attorney and Addison was still being questioned. I figured your mom would be more comfortable with Piper than me." He scratched behind Freddy's ears, "Besides, he and I get along pretty well."

As though in agreement, Freddy gave a quiet *woof*.

She cradled him against her chest, soaking in the comfort after her long day. But despite the plentiful kisses he gave her, something told her it wouldn't be enough to comfort her that night.

"I didn't know how long they would hold you at the station, so I thought I'd stay with him," he said.

"I don't mind at all. Thank you for keeping him company."

"Actually, that's partly a lie." He smiled sheepishly. "I also hung around to see you. I wanted to make sure you're all right."

She produced the same lighthearted answer she'd given Addison. "Why wouldn't I be?"

Levi's mouth turned down, and he got to his feet. "Good. I'm glad. Well, I'd better get going. You're probably tired. I'll see you at the wedding?"

Before he could head for the door, she grabbed his hand. "Wait."

Levi was going away with his band for an entire week; she couldn't leave things this way.

She took a deep breath and tried again. "I'm okay, but I could be better."

Hesitantly, he sank back onto the couch. "Can I do anything to help?"

She could see he was trying not to push too hard for more, so if she wanted it, she had to ask for it.

"I don't want to be alone tonight. Stay with me." Zoe held his gaze, pleading with her eyes as though she'd never wanted anything more. In fact, maybe she never had.

He winced like he was in physical pain as he searched for an answer. He squeezed her hand tight. "Zoe, I—"

"I don't mean sex," she corrected. "I just want to sleep. Nothing more."

His expression melted. "That's definitely something more. A lot more. Of course I'll stay."

Chapter Twenty-Three

THREE-DOG NIGHT

Zoe led Levi into her bedroom as though it were the grand tour of a castle throne room. It felt monumental, pivotal, like the moment held a certain reverence. Beyond the odd plumber or repairman, she'd never had a man in her apartment, much less her bedroom. And since Sean, the only wiener she'd had in her bed was of the four-legged kind.

Levi had said he'd wanted more. For her, this was so much more than she'd ever thought she could give again. And it felt good. Maybe good enough to find more of herself to give.

She flicked on the bedside lamp and plopped Freddy down on the bed. "I'm going to get into something more comfortable. And by that, I actually mean something more comfortable. There's a spare pillow in the cupboard over there."

She headed for the bathroom, but then she heard a cupboard door creak, and her stomach dropped.

Levi inhaled. "What the …"

Zoe lunged for the wardrobe. Slamming the door shut, she braced herself against it. "Not in there."

But it was too late. The mixture of confusion and amusement on his face told her he'd already seen what hid inside.

A smile tugged at his lips. She feared he'd burst out laughing. Slowly, he reached behind her and gently pulled on the door until she gave in and stepped aside.

"Are these … Fuzzy Friends? I remember these from when I was a kid." He picked up Happy Hippo. "I didn't even know they made these anymore."

"Well, they're not just for kids, you know," she said defensively, snatching it back. "They're collector's items too."

But he gave her an eyebrow arch that said he wasn't buying it. He picked up Tricky Turtle. "You know they lose their value once you open the package, right?"

"They never came in packages," she said. "And this cupboard protects them from both dust, and UV light, and—"

"Stop. Stop." Levi kind of laughed and sighed at the same time. "Come on. Let me in."

Zoe ducked her head. She was doing it again, shutting him out. Putting on her cool persona, both emotionally and physically. The ice queen. "You must think this is pretty silly."

"No, I don't." His smile was so big it was almost as if he'd grown extra teeth.

"Then why are you looking at me like that?"

"Because beneath that tough exterior, beneath all those layers of armor you've built up, I'm getting a glimpse of that soft, fuzzy, bean-filled center." He tapped her chest. "I'm finally getting through. Not that I'm pushing or anything." He threw his hands up and took a step back. "I'm being pushy again, aren't I? I'm sorry. I just … I really like you. The bits you let me see, anyway."

She opened her mouth, wanting to say something, but nothing came out. It had been so long since she'd let anyone this close.

"How can I get in there?" He tapped her chest again. "See what's inside?"

"Oh, they're called buttons," she said. "See, you slip this round thing through this hole—"

He held a hand over hers to stop her from undressing. "You know what I mean."

Her gaze dropped to her feet. "It doesn't come naturally. Not anymore. Just give it some time."

"Does that mean you're giving me the time?"

"I know I want to try," she said honestly. "I convinced myself being alone was the best thing for me, that I'd be happier that way. But you were right. I was scared. It's something I need to work on."

Levi cringed, and his shoulders slumped. "I'm sorry I pushed so hard. I guess I thought you could take it. You didn't seem like a woman who scares easily. But I should have let you come to that conclusion on your own." He stared down at his feet as he chuckled. "It turns out, I'm not a very patient man."

"You grab life by the balls."

"Exactly."

"But you know," she said, "I'm not the only one hiding behind a mask."

His eyes widened. "What? I know you don't mean me because I've been annoyingly me right from the start."

"Oh, I'll agree to that." She laughed. "Your mask is more literal. The nail polish, the eyeliner, the piercings."

Zoe tugged lightly on his eyebrow ring. Under the light pressure, it came away in her fingers.

She gasped, dropping it in surprise. "I'm so sorry! Are you hurt?"

However, when she assessed the damage, there was no blood. There weren't even holes in the skin. Just two red marks.

She bent down and picked up the metal hoop. A section was missing from the metal circle. She wrinkled her nose. "What?"

"You've caught me." Levi reached up to the spike in his upper ear and pulled it apart like two magnets. "I'm a fake."

She gaped at him. "They're not real?" Now she knew why they seemed to move around his face all the time.

"I'm not a big fan of pain. I know I'll never get a tattoo, that's for sure. But I have used some stick-on ones. They were pretty badass."

Zoe stared at the ring in her hand. "Why do you do it?"

"I guess I'm trying out some new looks," he said. "Seeing what suits the whole rocker vibe. I need to fit the part, right?"

"I don't think your fans care what you look like. They care about your music, and your music is amazing."

"But what if that's not enough?" He bit his lip and sat on the end of her bed, staring at his painted nails. "What if I'm not enough?"

The words tickled at a memory. She recalled what he'd said about his ex-wife. *I guess I just wasn't enough for her.*

Frowning, she pulled the rest of his piercings off impatiently. She tossed them onto her dresser. Setting Freddy onto the floor for safety, she slid her hand into Levi's and dragged him into the bathroom. She dug through the cupboard until she found her nail polish remover pads.

The acetone stung her nostrils as she scrubbed his nails, one by one. Freddy sneezed at the smell and left to search for more interesting things to do—probably like chewing on Zoe's shoes. Levi watched her work with an amused look on his face, but he never said a word.

When his nails were clean, she handed him a makeup remover pad. He glanced at it and chuckled. When she narrowed her eyes, he dutifully faced the mirror.

Wiping away the dark eyeliner, he washed his face and patted it dry with a cloth. When he turned back to her, he looked less dark and brooding, less tortured rocker, but just as handsome. However, now she could see *all* of his handsome face. All of Levi. He might have even passed for the boy next door.

"There," he said. "Are you happy? Is there anything else I should get rid of? Maybe my jeans, perhaps?"

He reached for his fly, but for once, her focus wasn't down

there. Placing her hands on either side of his face, she stared at him for a moment until he shifted uncomfortably. Maybe he felt as naked as she sometimes did beneath his piercing gaze.

"It's more than enough," she said.

"So, what does this mean for us?"

Zoe bit her lip. She wished she could say what he wanted to hear, but she looked away. "I can't make you any promises. I can't tell you I'm a forever kind of woman, that I suddenly want 'til death do us part.'"

He grabbed her arm and gently turned her to face him. "I'm not asking for a promise of forever. Just a promise of more."

She searched his hopeful eyes. "More than what?"

"More than a night."

And it was surprisingly easy for her to say, "I can do that."

"Then that's good enough for me." He held her face. "For now."

She kissed him, relieved they were on the same page, that she could even be on a page at all and for it to feel right. And kissing Levi felt so very, very right.

He pulled back and returned to her bedroom cupboard. "Look. We can pretend I didn't see any of this until you're ready for me to know the stuffed-animal-cupboard side to you." He tossed Tricky Turtle back inside and shut the cupboard doors firmly. "See? What collection of stuffed animals?"

Zoe took a deep breath. Despite her racing heart, she opened the cupboard again. Reaching in, she drew out Courageous Cat. "This was the first Fuzzy Friend I ever received. My dad gave it to me on my first day of elementary school to give me courage. I used to take him everywhere with me."

"You can tell." He rubbed the ratty fur.

She pointed to the back of the wardrobe. "That's Merry Mouse. Dad gave him to me the day I won my first spelling bee. Noble Numbat was for graduation. Lucky Lynx helped me through my grandmother's death." She continued to point out each one as she went. "Broken arm. Passing my driver's exam. My first broken heart. And he gave me this one after my wedding day."

She grew sad as she considered the meaning behind each one. The collection was a furry representation of all the biggest life moments her father had been there for. She swallowed hard before closing the doors.

"My dad was a pretty stoic man, the strong silent type, you know?"

"Yeah, I know." Levi shot her a pointed look.

She relented with a little shrug but continued. "He didn't always know what to do or say, but he remembered how much I loved my first Fuzzy Friend. It became his way of showing me he cared, even long after I was too old for stuffed animals."

She sank onto the bed. He sat next to her, barely blinking, like if he moved, if he spoke, this more open Zoe would disappear.

"When my dad died, I felt so lost in my grief," she told him. "I didn't know how to deal with it. I'd already started shutting people out after my wedding the year before, bottling things up. When I searched for something to help ease my grief, I didn't know what else to do but buy a Fuzzy Friend."

"So, you collect them," he said. "That's not strange at all. People collect all types of things."

"Well, I do more than collect them. Sometimes I use them to help lower my stress or anxiety during situations. I carry them around in my purse and I ..."

She paused, trying to think of exactly what she did or why. She automatically reached out for Kissing Koala and rubbed its soft fur.

"I guess knowing it's there is comforting. Maybe it's my way of remembering all of those other hard times." She gestured to the wardrobe. "Knowing I got through them makes it easier to go through whatever it is I'm currently facing, you know?"

Zoe finally met Levi's intense gaze. He nodded, a look of understanding on his face.

"That sounds exactly like a worry stone. Some people keep a stone in their pocket, and any time they feel stressed-out, they reach in and touch it. In fact," he said, "I always have my lucky guitar pick in my pocket during gigs. I never use it to play. I just like knowing it's there."

"So, you don't think it's childish?"

"Of course not. But you know …" He glanced at the wardrobe and then lowered his voice as though the fuzzy bags of beans could hear him. "You could talk to a real person when you have a bad day instead of a stuffed animal."

She snorted. "I don't talk to them. I just, you know, hold them." She rolled her eyes at the ridiculousness of it. She'd never actually said it out loud before.

But he didn't laugh. "You could talk to me. I'd like to be there to support you."

"I guess that wouldn't be so bad."

He gave her a sidelong look. "You guess?"

"Well, I'll have to see," she said in mock seriousness. "Tonight is your audition."

"Now I'm nervous. And me without my lucky guitar pick." He repositioned himself on the bed, sitting straighter like it was an interview. "How am I doing so far?"

"Not bad, but I think we'll need some snacks. I haven't eaten in hours." She grabbed her stomach. "I'm pretty sure they wanted to starve a confession out of me."

"Snacks. Okay, I can totally support you in this endeavor." He hopped to his feet, ready to snack her.

Zoe gestured to the kitchen. "I've got tons of food in the fridge. Why don't you dish something up while I go wash the jail off me?"

"Are you sure you don't need support in the shower too? Because I'm totally here for you if you do."

Giggling, she waved him away. "I've got this. You get the

snacks."

Levi grabbed her, nuzzling her neck. "But you look good enough to eat."

His stubble tickled her. She squirmed and slipped out of his arms, but she wanted nothing more than to stay wrapped in them, to feel his facial hair tickle the rest of her body. Suddenly, she was afraid that just sleeping together wouldn't be enough that night.

Ducking into the bathroom, she shut the door, smiling to herself, something she'd never have guessed would happen after the day she'd had. Stripping out of her clothes, she jumped in the shower. When her hand reached for the massaging shower head, she turned the water temperature down until she got a blast of cold.

Just sleep, she reminded herself. *Just sleep*. But even that had her breathless with excitement.

Zoe felt like a whole new person. Or maybe just a *whole* person. Levi had strolled into her life and turned it upside down in such a short time. Or maybe right side up. She just needed a push from the right person.

Once the last of her day was washed down the drain, she climbed out of the shower. As she brushed her damp hair, she heard a knock on her front door. Or rather, she heard Freddy bark and howl like a herd of zoo animals was parading through her apartment, so she knew someone must be at the door.

Throwing on a robe, she slipped out of the bathroom. As she made her way to the entrance, she heard Levi open the door.

"Hello," he said.

"Is Zoe home?"

The familiar male voice hit her body like an ocean wave. She stumbled back and steadied herself against the wall. Fighting the desire to bolt, she put one foot in front of the other.

"I'll go grab her," Levi said. "Who can I say is here?"

But Zoe already knew before she came around the corner. "Sean?"

"Zoe." Her ex's eyes briefly ran over her robe before flicking to Levi in an unspoken question.

Levi shifted uncomfortably. "I'll go finish up in the kitchen."

He disappeared around the corner to give them privacy. But it wasn't a big place; he'd still hear them.

Sean reached out. "Zoe—"

She stopped him with a look. "What are you doing here?"

He hesitated in the open doorway. "After I saw you the other day, I don't know … I had to see you."

She crossed her arms, aware of how underdressed she was. "Why? You haven't needed to see me for six years."

"It's not like I didn't try at first." He took a tentative step inside her apartment, like the fact that she hadn't kicked him between the legs was a good sign. "I called, I emailed, I wrote, I popped by. You wouldn't talk to me."

"You left me standing at the altar."

He took another step forward. "But if we could have talked—"

"There was nothing to talk about," she said. *You left me standing at the altar.*

"If you'd just let me explain. I had my reasons."

"Unless pirates were holding you hostage, I don't want to hear it."

But he tried anyway. "I was young and stupid—"

"You got that right," she snapped.

"And I didn't understand what I wanted or what I had." Sean's hands rose as though he wanted to touch her, to hold her.

She flashed him a severe warning look, and they dropped to his sides.

"I took you for granted, and I'm sorry." His forehead

247

creased as his eyes filled with pleading. "I've always regretted that day. I've always wondered what our life would've been like if I'd turned up."

Zoe hugged herself tighter, as if she could hold in all the things he was dredging up again. The things she thought she'd pushed down inside a long time ago. "Why are you telling me all this now?"

"Because I thought that was all in the past, and then I saw you the other day, and it felt like a sign. It all came rushing back to me." He ran a hand through his thick hair. "Look. I know we can't start over, but God ... I don't know, Zoe."

None of this was funny, but she suddenly had the urge to burst out laughing. Or maybe crying. No, yelling. Definitely yelling.

"What about Chelsea? You're marrying her."

He pulled a face. "I called it off." He fell to his knees in front of her. "Please, give us another shot. Just a date. Coffee, even. Some place we can start over."

He inched closer, reaching for the hem of her robe. Freddy began to growl and snarl, hackles raised as he crouched between them. Sean leaned back, hands raised.

Zoe picked up her puppy, amazed they agreed for once. Her shocked gaze was so focused on the prostrate figure before her that she hadn't noticed the man in the hall until he spoke.

"Zoe? What is this?"

She blinked at the newcomer, mouth falling open. "Taichi. What are you doing here?"

"Your mother said you were home. She told me I should come see you." He looked from her to Sean and back again, trying to make sense of it.

Hell, so was she.

Sean pushed himself to his feet, blocking Taichi from entering the apartment. "Well, you'll have to come back, pal. We're kind of in the middle of something."

She glared at Sean. "You don't get to talk for me. Taichi has more right to be here than you do."

Taichi puffed up his chest, staring him down. "And who are you?"

"I'm, well …" He ducked his head and turned to Zoe. "I'm hoping to be her boyfriend." He spun back. "And who the hell are you?"

"I am her fiancé."

Oh God, he said it. She slapped her forehead.

"Fiancé?" A hushed voice asked behind her.

She spun around. Levi stood at the edge of her kitchen with bowls of chips and dip in his hands. Her attention had been so consumed by the two men at her doorstep that she'd nearly forgotten he was even there.

His forehead creased. "You're engaged?"

"Who's he?" Sean and Taichi asked together.

The hurt in Levi's expression faded, concealed beneath a cool mask. "I'm nobody."

"Levi, I—"

He put the bowls down and slipped on his shoes. Without a backward glance, he left.

Zoe's mouth opened and closed wordlessly. She couldn't speak, not to blurt out an explanation, not to beg him to stay. Not even to tell the two men arguing in her doorway to shut up and leave.

Freddy twisted in her arms and licked her face, pulling her from her trance. She pushed past Taichi and Sean, stumbling through the doorway.

"Levi, wait!"

She ran down the hall after him. Her hair clung to her neck and face in wet tendrils. Her robe flapped open, flashing glimpses of her naked body. She hadn't even stopped to put on a pair of shoes.

The woman in the next apartment poked her head out her door. She shushed Zoe as she flew by and then gasped at the sight of her, like Zoe had absolutely lost her mind. Heck, maybe she had. And if she let Levi get into his van and drive away, she worried she might never find it again.

Her footsteps echoed in the stairwell as her feet slapped each step on the way down. She clung to Freddy with one hand while she clasped her robe shut with the other. The doxie's barks ricocheted off the walls, piercing her eardrums.

Wait up! You forgot to play with me!

She rounded the next landing and saw down to the exit. A glimpse of Levi's backside gave her hope that she could catch up. The doors slammed shut before she could yell after him.

Stumbling down the last few steps, she shoved the front door open and lurched onto the sidewalk. She hissed at the cold on her bare feet and the cool night air sweeping around her legs.

The last time she'd felt this desperate, this helpless, had been on her wedding day, when her entire future had blown up in her face. All the plans, the promises, the hopes, and dreams tossed away by the individual she'd trusted most in the world. Like they were garbage. Like *she* was garbage.

That day, however, all those feelings, the grief, the resentment, the humiliation, and rejection had burst out of her because the one person she'd needed most in the world had betrayed her. But now that she'd finally found someone she needed more, *he* felt betrayed by *her*.

Zoe rounded the corner of the alley and spotted Levi climbing into his van. He slammed the door and started the engine.

"Wait!" she screamed out.

She ignored the sharp stabs to the soles of her feet as she pushed herself harder, faster. But then the engine revved, and the van took off.

Zoe watched it disappear around the corner. Suddenly, she was just a pitiful woman wearing nothing but a robe in a dark alley, screaming a man's name.

Chapter Twenty-Four

ALL BARK AND NO BITE

Zoe set Freddy down on the hardwood floor and took in her new office space with pride. The late-1800s Italianate building was on 24th Street with ample parking nearby and a busy shopping area to boost her visibility. Aiden had really pulled through for her. She'd only moved in on Monday, and already it was coming together nicely.

Paper crinkled. She searched for her puppy. She found him unraveling a roll of wrapping paper in the closet. Scrolling through her phone, she cued up a playlist she'd titled *Freddy's Tranquilizer*.

When calming tunes drifted out of her new office speakers, Freddy yawned and found a patch of sun spilling onto the stylish area rug. Flopping down in the middle of it, he exposed his pink belly to the warmth after the walk there from their new-slash-old house.

That was the best part about the location; it was only a ten-minute walk from her childhood home. Although she was still sleeping at her apartment, she'd already moved most of her stuff. Once she and Freddy officially moved in, they could begin every day with a walk to work. Plus, she could run home and check on her mother whenever she needed to.

After gathering piles of paperwork for the lender, they'd added her to her mother's mortgage, thanks to her large nest egg and impeccable credit score. She was officially a home-owner. The feeling was strangely innate and yet foreign. The home reminded her of a time she'd depended on her parents. Only now, her mother needed her.

Zoe checked the time again: nearly 10 a.m. She rearranged her décor in the bay window for the tenth time that morning, fluffing up her wedding dress on the mannequin, angling the groom's top hat just so. Anything to keep busy. To keep from worrying about her first appointment: Sean.

After Levi had stormed out on Sunday night, she'd returned to her apartment to find Taichi and Sean still bick-ering—well, mostly it was Sean. Sending her ex away to cool off for a few days, she'd had a talk with Taichi, explaining that an arranged marriage wouldn't work for her.

Now that she'd had most of the week to calm down, she'd agreed to meet Sean in—she checked her watch again—fifty minutes. And although she'd been imagining their conversation all week, making lists of the things she wanted to tell him, she still didn't know what to say.

To kill time, she perched on the edge of her antique desk, an office-warming present from Piper and Aiden—like they hadn't done enough already. Raising her phone above her, she snapped a selfie, capturing the big bay window and Freddy's sprawled body in the shot. She sent it to the both of them, along with a text.

See you guys at the wedding rehearsal tomorrow night. XOXO.

The office couldn't have come at a better time. Levi's band was on their rock tour, but she didn't feel comfortable using his apartment when they weren't even on speaking terms.

At the thought of him, Zoe picked up her cell and called him. *Again.*

Ring, ring, ring.

She held her breath. After calling him so many times that

252

week, the noise had become as aggravating as the Chicken Dance to her ears.

If she could just talk to him, explain that things weren't how they seemed. But it wasn't the kind of thing she wanted to leave on his voicemail either.

Three weeks before, she didn't know the man existed, but now she couldn't go five minutes without thinking about him. She missed talking to him, missed hearing his voice. She'd even downloaded his album and played it on repeat to hear him sing.

Surprise, surprise, there was no answer. She waited until the voicemail kicked in to hear his voice.

"This is Levi Dolson with Reluctant Redemption. Sorry I missed your call. Please leave your name and number, and I'll get back to—"

She quickly hung up before it finished, as she always did. Or else, like some creepy, mouth-breathing stalker, she'd have left ten silent voicemails by now. Okay, maybe fifteen … or twenty.

Yup, nothing ruffled about Zoe Plum. She was as cool as a cucumber.

Someone knocked on the door. Freddy sprang to his feet like he'd received an electric shock and danced around the carpet, barking his head off. A thrill of excitement hummed through Zoe. Her first customer in her new office.

But when she swung the door wide with a welcoming smile, she nearly slammed it shut again.

"Zoe!" Juliet Fisher squealed. "It's so good to see you."

She gaped at the woman beaming in her doorway. Expecting a setup, she took an automatic step back and tried to close the door. However, the ex-bride wedged herself inside.

"I wish I could say the same to you and …" Zoe did a double take. "Owen? What are you doing here? Together?"

She remembered the last time she'd seen him—right before her office blew up. Her eyes flitted to the window, her nearest exit. Scooping Freddy off the floor, she held him protectively to her chest.

Freddy's tail wagged. *Oh good. Visitors. Are they here to play with me?*

"Look." She held a hand up. "I already told you I'm not responsible for the cost of your wedding. You can check our contract."

"No. No." Juliet's titter sounded so sweet it hurt Zoe's teeth. "We're not here for that."

Zoe's heart raced. This ubersweet side of Juliet freaked her out more than her usual bridezilla one. "Then what is it? Because I'll call the cops if you try anything funny."

"About the expo," Juliet began, "I'm sorry. I was hurt and angry and hadn't slept in days. I lost my mind without my munchkin." She pinched Owen's cheek.

Zoe wondered if the chocolates had won her over. "I see you two have worked things out. When did this happen?" She hoped she sounded casual enough as she dug for information to feed the police.

"Just the other day," she said. "Monday, I think. Wasn't it, pookie?"

Monday. So, she was still pissed off at Zoe on Sunday when Chef Glazier died. Which meant she wasn't out of the running for potential suspects.

Zoe's eyes narrowed. "When you say you're sorry about the expo, are you talking about the van?"

She shook her head. "No. I'm sorry for yelling at you and making that announcement over the PA system. The van wasn't me. I swear."

"Right, well, I think that's best for the police to determine." Zoe casually inched closer to her desk, where her feathered pen stood next to an inkwell. It was purely decorative. However, the pen's metal tip would make an improvised weapon if needed.

Juliet didn't seem to notice. "I came here because I wanted to put all that behind us. To move on."

Zoe tilted her head. "Move on to what?"

She slid her hand into Owen's, batting her eyelashes up at him. "To our wedding, of course."

Zoe gaped at the two of them. "Your wedding? You're going to try to get married again?" This time she spoke directly to Owen.

He beamed at his fiancée. "We won't let one bad day ruin what we have."

"Well, congratulations. I'm thrilled you two worked things out." She went to the door and held it wide open, hoping they would take the hint.

"So, you'll do it?" Juliet asked hopefully.

She glanced from bride to groom. "Do what?"

"Plan our wedding, silly." Juliet squealed.

"Plan your … No way. I can't possibly." Zoe backed up, ready to leave her own office just to get away from them.

Juliet grabbed her arms, squeezing hard like she was desperate. Or maybe she wanted to rip Zoe's arms off and beat her with them. Freddy licked Juliet's hand like they were all such good friends.

"But you already know our tastes and our must-haves." She squeezed harder. "It would be a piece of cake."

"I'm actually booked solid," Zoe lied.

"But it's not for another year. We'll offer you double."

Not even for a million dollars, she thought. "Yup, sadly booked for the next two … make that three years."

Juliet's hands dropped in disappointment. "Oh, that's too bad."

"If you want my advice," Zoe said, "elope. So much cheaper." Suddenly, a better idea came to her. "On second thought, I know of someone who could help you."

She ran to her purse and dug her way to the bottom. Things had been so hectic that she hadn't had time to clean it out since … Yup, there it was. Natalie Evans's scrunched-up business card from the expo. Straightening it out as best she could, she handed it over.

"Natalie Evans?" Juliet read. "Isn't she your assistant?"

"Natalie works for Enchanted Events now. And she worked closely with me on your wedding, so she understands all your needs." *As in everything under the sun.* She gave the couple a cheerful wave as they finally headed out her door. "Tell her I sent you."

"Thanks. I will!" Juliet called back.

"Good luck, you crazy kids." *Emphasis on the crazy.*

Freddy barked after them. *You forgot to play with me!*

Zoe rushed over to her bay window. Freddy licked the pane as she watched the couple walk down the street, shaking her head in amazement. At both the fact Juliet actually believed Zoe would plan her wedding and that there would *be* another wedding.

"Can you believe them?" she asked Freddy.

He whined. *Play now?*

Once they'd disappeared from sight, she put Freddy down and shut the door. She locked it, just in case they came back. Grabbing her phone, she found the number for Inspector Warner to let him know the couple had popped by. She didn't know if it meant anything, but the more information she could gather to absolve her, the better.

Her finger hovered over the call button just as someone knocked on the door. She gasped and spun to face it. Freddy howled wildly and spun in circles. She groaned, hoping he would eventually get used to clients coming and going.

Thanks to Freddy, she couldn't pretend she wasn't there, so she sidled closer to the door. "Who is it?"

"It's Sean," came a muffled response.

Now her heart raced for a whole different reason. With a shaking hand, she flicked the deadbolt. Gripping the handle, she took a deep breath and opened the door.

Sean wore a grin from ear to ear and clutched a bouquet. He handed it to her. "For your new office."

"Oh." She blinked down at the roses in surprise. "Thank you. You're early."

"Sorry. I was just eager to see you. I'm so glad you called." When Freddy jumped up, pawing at his shins, Sean patted him on the head. "Is this Buddy 2.0?"

Zoe scowled; she wouldn't replace one dog with another like a pair of shoes. "No. This is Freddy."

"Hi, Freddy." He scratched him under the chin. "Can we go somewhere? Maybe grab a coffee? Some lunch?"

"Look, Sean. I wanted to talk to you about Sunday night. What you said—"

"Was all true. Every word of it." He grabbed her hands in his, squeezing them. "I was a fool to ever let you go."

"You mean stand me up." She tugged her hands away. "You didn't let me go. You didn't respect me enough to be upfront with me. You just ran away."

"I know. I owe you an explanation."

"No. Don't." She held up a hand. "I don't want to hear it. I don't care anymore. All I wanted to say is that you can't just show up at my apartment. You can't just come waltzing back into my life unannounced. I don't know you. You don't know me. Not anymore. I'm a different person."

Maybe he'd forgotten how blunt she could be, or maybe she'd grown less subtle over the last six years, but his smile withered.

"I know," he said. "And I want to get to know that person."

Zoe reminded herself there was a time she loved this man, and that, despite the sheer absurdity of it, he'd come because he clearly still had feelings for her.

Uncrossing her arms, she softened her tone. "But that person doesn't want to get to know you. I've moved on. I'm over it."

Walking over to her desk, she slid open the top drawer and

grabbed the ring box she'd dug out of her closet that morning. She'd never been able to get rid of her old engagement ring—she supposed in the same way she'd never let go of her wedding dress. Or that day.

She handed it back to Sean. "I've moved on with my life. You should too."

He didn't quite know what to say after that. Hell, neither did she. Her revelation surprised her as much as it probably did him. Maybe more so.

Zoe had dreaded this moment all week and, in reality, for much longer than that. It was as though she'd been afraid of the memory of him.

And yet, as he stood in front of her after all these years, she found she was tired of wasting her time on him, on their past, on her memories and fears. After six years of letting one day control her life, she didn't want to waste another minute on it.

She held the door open for him. "Thanks for stopping by. And for the flowers."

Sean took a deep breath and nodded. "Take care of yourself."

"Thanks. I will," she said, and meant it. And when she finally closed the door on that chapter, she knew the first place to start.

Picking up a pair of scissors from her desk, she took care of that hideous old wedding dress, once and for all.

Chapter Twenty-Five

FACE THE MUSIC

Zoe, Piper, and Addison strolled down Folsom Street like they owned the town. Heck, with all the properties Aiden owned, once Piper became Mrs. Caldwell, maybe she would. And by the way the men lingering outside the SoMa bars eyed them, the girls were owning their dresses.

And why not let them look? That's what a bachelorette party was for. Saying sayonara to all the single men. Giving them one last look at what they'd missed out on. After the rehearsal dinner, the girls had raided Zoe's closet for the sexiest, slinkiest numbers while Addison worked her magic on hair and makeup.

Zoe glanced at Piper in her red cocktail dress and thought the men of San Francisco would weep that night. And Addison? Well, she was taken too, but she loved any excuse to doll herself up.

But Zoe had nothing in her way. No memories of Sean, no fear of getting hurt, and definitely no Levi. By ignoring every single one of her calls, he'd made it clear she was the last thing on his mind. And she wanted to prove he was the last thing on hers.

There was no holding her back tonight. She felt six years

259

of repressed emotions and desires ready to burst out of her. Or maybe those were the shots they'd had at Felix's pub talking.

Piper dragged her friends into a club with a bouncer who had multiple piercings in his lips. Zoe gave him a wink as he swung the door open for them.

A wave of stale booze hit her nose like a sucker punch. The heavy bass pulsated through the floorboards, thumping inside her chest.

It wasn't exactly the kind of club she'd envisioned for Piper's bachelorette. Since it was the night before her big day, Zoe had suggested a few rounds at a classy wine bar, something relaxed and subdued. This dive was neither of those things. In fact, among all the ripped jeans, leather, and chains, their sexy cocktail dresses stood out like the only single woman at a bouquet toss.

She sidled closer to Piper. "Are you sure about this place?"

"I'm definitely sure," she said. "Besides, this is the last place Holly Hart would look for us. And I'm tired of dodging her."

"True," Zoe relented.

A guy walked by and smiled at them. The black lights glowed off a row of teeth filed to points.

"But maybe that's also a bad thing," Addison said. "Because no one will think to look for us here if we, you know, don't turn up."

"Oh, come on. It will be fun." Piper grabbed their hands and dragged them deeper into the crowded club.

Zoe eyed up a guy dripping with chains, a studded dog collar cinched around his neck. "Something tells me I won't find my dream guy here."

Piper rolled her eyes. "You've been saying you're going to find your dream guy all night, and I haven't seen you talk to a single man yet."

"Yeah, what's stopping you?" Addison skirted around the studded-collar guy. "Could it be that you're waiting for a certain musician to call?"

Zoe barked a "Ha!" over the music that grew louder as they dove deeper into the heart of the club. "What musician could you possibly be referring to?"

"Still haven't heard from him, huh?" Piper asked.

"Nope." She squeezed through the people around the edge of the dance floor who were too cool to dance.

"Maybe he never saw the letter you wrote for him," Addison suggested.

Zoe regretted writing the damn letter now that he'd clearly read it and ignored it. What had started out as a list of things she'd wanted to say to Levi, a way to organize her thoughts, had ended up as three pages explaining the night at her apartment and how she really felt about him.

Absence hadn't made her heart grow fonder. It only allowed her to listen to what was really in it, and that was deep feelings for Levi. She missed him. She wanted to be with him. And not just for a night.

She wanted him night after night after night. And the mornings too. She wanted to go on dates with him, to show him embarrassing childhood photos of herself, to make dinner with him, and listen to his serenading. It turned out her heart wanted *more* of Levi.

After no luck getting ahold of him, she'd driven over to his apartment the night before. Using the key he'd given her, she'd left the letter on his kitchen counter. The moment she got to her van, she'd come to her senses. She'd wanted to take it back, but she'd slid the key under the door after locking up.

"Maybe it slipped under a sofa, and he never even saw it," Addison said. "Just like when Leo DiCaprio didn't get Claire Danes's letter in *Romeo and Juliet*." She jumped up and down excitedly, as though that must be it. A guy in a Nirvana shirt clearly misinterpreted and jumped around her, trying to dance.

Zoe dragged her away, blocking the guy with her own body. "And all the calls he never returned?"

"Maybe he lost his phone," Piper said.

Addison gasped. "Maybe he accidentally dropped it into a mosh pit and someone stomped on it. That must happen all the time. Occupational hazard."

"Or maybe he just doesn't want to talk to me." He'd rejected her. Her friends just couldn't see it.

"But——"

She waved away any more arguments. "It's for the best. Trust me."

"Let's dance." Piper dragged her friends farther onto the dance floor until they were right beneath the stage among sweaty bodies pushing and jumping.

The next song began, slowly at first, then it built in heat and rhythm, infecting Zoe's body. Her hips swayed and her hands reached for the sky. As the intro peaked, out of the corner of her eye, she saw the lead singer lean into the mic to belt out the first verse.

The smooth, deep voice froze her gyrating body. Her head whipped toward the stage. However, she already knew who she'd see: Levi.

She suddenly felt exposed on the dance floor, static among a sea of waving hands and wriggling bodies. She wanted to hide; she wanted to run. Before she could move, his gaze that was scanning the crowd found her, as though he could sense her there.

His voice faltered, and it was a few seconds before he picked up the tune again. He closed his eyes as he focused on the song.

Their connection broken, Zoe found she could move again. She pushed against jostling, sweaty bodies. They pressed back, surging forward to fill her space at the front.

As she scrambled to get away, she got an elbow to the ribs, a heel to her shin, a flailing arm to the face. She forged on, not paying attention to the crowd or the music.

Levi had never called. He didn't care. She didn't even want to think about him at the moment, but there he was, headlining her night. And all around her, women screamed his name.

"Levi! Levi! Levi!"

Someone grabbed her arm from behind. "Zoe!" It was Piper. "Don't be upset. When I saw he was playing a gig here tonight, I thought if we came, you could talk things out."

"Now you can tell him how you feel," Addison said.

Zoe backed away. "I'm sorry. I need to get out of here."

She weaved her way through the crowded club, resisting the urge to throw punches to clear a path. Finally, she broke through to the back of the dance floor where the audience had spread out.

She picked up her pace, heels sticking to the beer-lacquered floor. Then the band hit the chorus, and the familiar words rang clearly through her head. Her breath caught in her chest.

> "You drive me plum crazy.
> Now it's 20-20.
> You are the one for me.
> So why can't you see?
> Miss Plum Crazy.
> You drive me plum crazy."

It was Levi's limerick he'd serenaded her with at the expo. But he'd improved it, made it into a real song.

The sticky floor seemed to make it impossible to keep moving. Zoe's feet felt glued to the spot. As he sang on, his voice thickened with emotion, with emphasis. His heavy words weighed down on her, holding her there.

And despite her desire to avoid him, to hide herself and her heart, there was a pleading tone in his beautiful voice that made her turn around. When she did, his tortured gaze locked on hers above the crowd as he sang the song he'd written about her.

The crowd faded away until only the two of them

remained. Levi sang just for her, telling her how he felt through his lyrics.

> *"Why do you hide behind your mask?*
> *I still see you.*
> *Take off yours and I'll take off mine,*
> *To be near you.*
> *So just let me in and we'll be all right.*
> *I need you.*
> *Miss Plum Crazy.*
> *You drive me plum crazy."*

Eager to hear more of the song, Zoe worked her way back to the stage until she stood below him again. Those piercing blue eyes undressed her. Not sexually, but as though he were removing her armor piece by piece.

When the song drew to an end, he still didn't remove his gaze from hers as he spoke to the audience. "Thank you, everybody. We're Reluctant Redemption. Thanks for coming out. Have a good night!"

The club erupted into cheers and whistles, but Levi didn't wait to take a bow or soak it all in. He leaped off the stage, landing in front of Zoe.

He grabbed her hand. "Come with me."

Hands patted his back, congratulating him on a good set. He tossed nods and thank-yous but didn't slow as he led Zoe through a door that said *staff only*.

The door slammed closed behind them, muffling the raucous sounds, shutting out the rest of the world. Their quick footsteps clicked loudly in the silence backstage. They slipped past spare mic stands and stepped around old speakers stacked against the wall.

Zoe could finally hear herself think about what she was going to say, how she would explain her feelings, her fears, her uncertainty. But despite all those things, her heart raced to have her hand clasped in his, to know he hadn't stopped thinking about her. Instead, he'd been singing about her.

They didn't speak. Not verbally, anyway. Levi's eyes said everything she needed to know as he cast glances over his shoulder. They drank in the sight of her, scraped over every inch of her tight purple dress. She knew he couldn't wait to peel it off of her.

He shoved open a door with a piece of paper taped to the worn wood. It read "Reluctant Redemption." The moment they slipped inside the small dressing room, their lips came together.

Zoe's hands caressed the contours of the face she'd missed seeing. Stubble scraped her fingertips. His arms locked around her, crushing her body against his.

Pressing his tongue into her mouth, he moaned as she caressed it with her own. She hungered to taste him again, like she'd been starved all week.

Raising his foot, he kicked the door closed. It slammed shut like a gunshot. They raced to have more of each other, to touch more, taste more. They tugged at clothes and pulled at buttons.

Levi's hot hands slid down her back. Her cocktail dress was so tight, he might as well have been feeling her naked body. Cupping her butt, he hoisted her up. Her legs automatically wrapped around him, locking behind his back.

He pressed her up against the door. The cool metal stung her back, making her realize how hot she was. Hot for Levi. Her skin blazed beneath his touch, his mouth like fire, his breath like steam as he ran his kisses down her neck.

Carrying her to a vanity on the other side of the room, he swept some of the clutter aside. Glass bottles crashed to the floor. When he sat her down on the surface, Zoe gripped his hips and pulled him closer. He pressed himself between her parted legs. Tugging her long hair aside, he ran his fervent kisses down her neck to the top of her low-cut dress.

"I need you," she breathed. Her desperate, groping hands reached for his belt. She unhooked the leather, sliding it free.

Levi's hand clasped over hers. He pulled away. His face screwed up as though it pained him to stop her. He tilted his head back and took a few labored breaths before answering.

"I want to, but—"

"I don't mean sex," she said. "I mean … Okay, I want that too. But it's because I want *you*."

His eyes closed for a moment. "What about your fiancé?"

She laughed, still a little breathless. "I'm not engaged. My mother wanted to arrange a marriage for me, and because I didn't want to upset her in the hospital, I agreed to a date. I don't know what she told him, but knowing her, she probably already had the venue booked. But I'm not marrying him."

"And your ex?"

"Still an ex. I accidentally ran into him the other day, but I barely talked to him. I don't know why he got it in his head to show up at my place." She widened her eyes, as though she could hypnotize him into believing her.

"It's just … I've thought about you all week. Obviously." He waved a hand in the direction of the stage. "And then I saw you here, and I thought, I hoped you came because you were thinking of me too …"

She winced. "Actually, it was a setup. Piper brought me here."

His expression fell, and he backed away.

She held him there. "But I'm glad she did," she said softly. "So, does that mean you didn't get my letter?"

Levi frowned. "What letter?"

"The one I left in your apartment."

"I haven't been back there. We got in from San Diego this evening and came straight here."

Zoe crossed her arms. "Well, I could have explained it all over the phone if you'd answered any of my calls."

He rubbed a hand over his scruffy jaw. "The band has a

no-cell-phone policy while on tour. It keeps our heads in the game. Our manager screens all our emergency calls."

She groaned, remembering he'd mentioned ignoring calls during practice too. "That would have been good to know before you left. That's the silliest thing I've ever heard."

He ducked his head. "Yeah. I'm starting to think that should change." He stared at her, apprehension creasing his forehead. "That night at your apartment … It just looked like—"

"Like I was a woman who didn't know what I wanted?" she finished for him.

"Exactly."

"I know what I want now. It's you," she said. "I never thought I'd want anyone ever again, but I want you. I *need* you."

The admission felt like removing a fifty-pound wedding dress from her body. And it wasn't just the acceptance of it within herself. It was the act of expressing it, tipping that bottle she'd filled for so long and letting it pour out.

Levi cupped her face and brought it close to his until their noses touched. "I'm all yours."

As he brought his mouth to hers in a gentle kiss, the door opened.

They jumped apart as a red-headed woman in a vintage polka dot skirt swept into the room. Zoe quickly tugged her dress back into place and slid awkwardly off the vanity.

"Oops. Sorry to interrupt." The woman practically bounced across the room, a little ball of energy. "Levi, you were amazing."

She stood on her tiptoes, and he automatically bent down so she could kiss him on the cheek. She made a loud "Mwah" sound as she slapped one on him, leaving a red stain on his skin.

Then she turned her bright eyes on Zoe and they widened. "Is this her?"

"This is her," he said proudly.

"You're the one in the song." She danced over to Zoe and slapped a kiss on her cheek too. "It's so nice to meet you."

"Zoe, this is Candi," Levi said. "She's our manager."

Not being much of a kisser, she waved. "Nice to meet you."

Candi spun to Levi. "And as your manager, I'm ordering you to get on stage. They're calling you back for another." She threw him a stern look before twirling out of the room.

"I'm coming!" He turned back to Zoe and gave her an apologetic look. "We've never refused an encore."

"It's okay. Go." She waved him away. "I'll wait right here."

He gave her one more lingering kiss before he headed back to the stage.

Once he'd left, Zoe checked the mirror behind her. She grabbed a tissue from her purse and wiped the lipstick mark off her face. When she pulled it away, she smiled at the shade of red, the same color she'd wiped off Levi's cheek at Juliet's wedding. Something told her she had nothing to worry about there.

She readjusted her dress and ran her fingers through her long hair. She was slapping some color into her cheeks when the door opened behind her again.

Zoe smiled into the mirror. "You'd better not keep your public waiting."

When there was no response, she shifted her focus to the door. It wasn't Levi. It was Chelsea Carruthers.

Chapter Twenty-Six

A SHAGGY DOG STORY

Zoe stared at the reflection in the mirror in disbelief, as though that must be someone else's pinched face sneering at her from the doorway, not Chelsea's. Maybe she'd had one too many shots earlier.

She closed her eyes and willed the image away. When she opened them again, metal glinted above her head: a mic stand.

She dropped to the ground. The stand crashed down. It caught the vanity, taking out the remaining knickknacks sitting on it.

Cans of hairspray and beer bottles rained down on her. She threw her hands up, protecting her face. When she looked up again, the stand rose above her.

She kicked out, catching a heel on Chelsea's leg. Her kneecap shifted beneath Zoe's shoe, and a *crunch* ran up her leg. Zoe shuddered. Chelsea screamed.

Adrenaline rushed through Zoe's body, pushing aside any lingering effects of the alcohol she'd consumed earlier. The door was still open. If she could get to it, she could barricade Chelsea inside and go for help.

Grabbing a can of hairspray, she took aim and fired. The

mist clouded around Chelsea's face. Coughing and sputtering, she clamped her eyes shut and rubbed them.

Zoe clambered to her feet and lunged for the door, but Chelsea blindly swung the stand, blocking her. She leaped out of the way just in time.

"Somebody help!" she screamed, but she knew no one would hear over the band's encore.

One red eye open, Chelsea hopped on her good leg, wincing slightly each time. She took a swing, and another, and another, forcing Zoe away from the exit.

With nowhere else to go, Zoe picked up a folding chair and hurled it. It caught Chelsea in the chest, and she stumbled onto her bad leg. Groaning in pain, she braced herself against the wall.

Taking the chance, Zoe dove for her. Her fingers wrapped around the mic stand. Clamping on tight, she tried to wrench it away.

Not ready to give it up, Chelsea twisted it to the side. Zoe tripped in her heels toward a tattered armchair. She grunted as she landed awkwardly, but she held on to the weapon.

Her rival bared her teeth and pressed down on the rod with all her weight behind it. Her teeth squeaked as she ground them together, face contorting with the apparent desire to squeeze Zoe's neck until her head popped off.

Zoe's arms shook. Inch by inch, the mic stand sank toward her throat. The cool metal pressed against her windpipe. She swallowed and felt it rub.

Desperately, she whipped her knee up. It connected with ribs in a *pop*. Chelsea doubled over, wheezing.

The pressure on Zoe's neck relaxed. She twisted the rod. The chair tipped over, sending them both flopping onto the ground.

Zoe tossed the mic stand aside. Throwing her weight on top of her rival, she wrapped her long legs around the ones trying to kick her. She tangled her arms with the ones clawing and punching and grabbing any part of her.

Once they resembled a human pretzel, all Chelsea could do was jerk and buck awkwardly beneath Zoe's body. She gave a few more futile wiggles before she gave up and settled on yelling and swearing in frustration.

Zoe kept her face tilted away in case Chelsea decided to bite or headbutt. Over the screamed threats, she heard laughing and chatting voices in the hall.

"Help!" she yelled. "In here!"

Footsteps quickened. People squeezed into the doorway. Levi's eyes swept over the destruction before they landed on the heap of tangled limbs on the floor.

"Zoe."

"Help me," she grunted. "I can't hold her much longer."

He dropped to the ground, replacing her hands with his own. As she untangled her legs, she saw Brody and Aaron grab Chelsea's ankles to prevent her from kicking.

Zoe rolled away and onto her back, gasping for air. Her pulse throbbed in her blossoming bruises. Her limbs shook, and she couldn't find the strength to stand until a couple of hands reached down to help her. She looked up to see Piper's and Addison's worried faces above her.

She let them help her to her feet and into a chair where she could catch her breath. It might have only been a two-minute fight, but she felt as though they'd wrestled for hours. She supposed that's what happened when your body gave it everything it had to survive.

"I'll go grab the bouncers," Candi said before taking off, vintage heels clicking down the hall.

Jett hung back in the hall and took out his phone. Zoe assumed he was calling the police.

"What the hell happened?" Levi asked her.

"After you left, Chelsea came in here with a microphone stand, wanting to play a game of T-ball with my head."

Bodies shuffled out of the way. The bouncer with the lip piercings pushed his way in, kicking the toppled chair aside. Another bouncer followed him, and they took over for the band. As they stood Chelsea up to get her out, she jerked wildly in their grip and released a carnal scream.

"You bitch!" she yelled at Zoe. "You just couldn't let me be happy, could you? You have everything, your successful business, your rock star boyfriend, your connections throughout the city. Why did you have to take what little I have?" Her hair escaped from its usual tight bun, falling in front of her face like a wild mane.

"What are you talking about?" Zoe asked.

"Sean. My *fiancé*," she spat. "You couldn't let me have him, could you? You had to steal him from me. Natalie said you came by the office the other day, that you spoke with him. What did you say to make him dump me? Huh?"

Zoe closed her eyes, gathering herself. "I went there to tell you to back off and to stop sabotaging me. I had no idea he would be there, and I don't care if you marry him. You two deserve each other."

Chelsea's narrowed eyes filled with tears, and when she spoke, her voice cracked. "Then why won't he marry me?"

Zoe pinched the bridge of her nose, the mother of all headaches forming. A hand rubbed her back comfortingly. It was Levi. She smiled up at him gratefully.

Chelsea's emotional outburst tugged at something inside her, drawing forth memories of her own wedding day, when Sean's sudden abandonment had thrown her off the deep end. She hated to admit that she had anything in common with this woman, but she could definitely sympathize with her. She was almost tempted to throw Chelsea a bone, to tell her things would get better if she let it.

"I don't know why he's not marrying you," she finally said, a little calmer. "But considering Sean's track record, I'd say it's him and not us."

"Everything was fine until you meddled with my life. You've ruined everything!" Chelsea burst into sobs, tears mixing with snot.

Zoe was fed up. Everything hurt, and she yearned for bed. "I haven't done anything to you. You've slandered my name all over town. You stole my assistant and my clients. And don't even start with your vandalized booth, because I didn't do that."

"Of course you didn't," she said, voice dripping with scorn. "I did!"

Zoe started. "What?"

"Holly Hart promised me that interview. I was supposed to be on the news. But all anyone cares about is *you*. Everyone's just so *plum crazy* about Zoe, Zoe, Zoe." She spat.

Zoe crossed her arms. "And you thought you'd blame me for it, get me kicked out of the expo, and ruin my reputation."

"Two birds, one stone." She said it like anyone would have done the same thing in her position.

Zoe thought back to when all her troubles had begun. If Chelsea had tried to set her up, then what else was she capable of?

"Tell the truth," she demanded. "Did you sabotage the Fisher-Wells wedding?"

"How could I? I wasn't even there. Natalie, on the other hand, was in the perfect position. And she was so eager to be a full-fledged planner that she was prepared to do just about anything."

Zoe got to her feet, suddenly finding the strength for round two. "Were you the one who broke into my van? Did you cut up Piper's dress?"

Levi stiffened next to her. "Did you cut her brake lines? Were you responsible for the explosion in her office?"

Addison gasped. "Did you try to poison Piper?"

Piper's eyes widened, then narrowed with a promise of violence. And Zoe didn't blame her. If Chelsea was responsible for all their grief, then she was to blame for Piper's wedding nearly derailing time and time again.

As everyone tried to put the puzzle together, Chelsea's head whipped around the room to greet each accusation hurled at her. Her hate-filled expression slowly transformed until amusement consumed it.

While a smile stretched over her face, her eyes were dead. Her body sagged against the bouncers. She'd lost her fight. Maybe because she had nothing left to fight for.

Zoe remembered that anger, that unquenchable anxiety and turmoil bursting to get out, and the frustration of not knowing where to place it—strangely, not at the man who deserved it for so recklessly toying with someone's heart. But in Chelsea's case, she'd found a target for that anger: Zoe.

The bouncers dragged her listless body outside to wait for the cops. For now, her fight evaporated, but it wasn't over. Zoe knew all too well that kind of anger wouldn't just go away. It would linger and fester if Chelsea let it.

In the shocked silence, her shoes scraped along the concrete floor as she was dragged down the hallway. Then her sharp voice rang out, echoing backstage.

"Just wait, Zoe!" she screamed. "You'll get yours! And I'm not talking karma!"

Chapter Twenty-Seven

SINGING THE SAME TUNE

Zoe peered out of Levi's apartment windows for the fifth time since they'd arrived. She wasn't sure what she expected to see. Maybe Chelsea standing in the street in the rain, just waiting for Zoe to go to sleep, to drop her guard.

She shivered. Clutching Levi's bathrobe closed around her, she backed away from the floor-to-ceiling view.

There was a knock on the door, and she jumped. Cautiously, she checked the peephole and then sighed in relief. It was just Freddy, or, more specifically, Levi holding the doxie up so his adorable face filled the view.

She unlatched the door and slid it open. Poking her head out, she eyed Levi up and down. "Secret password?"

He chuckled. "Sex in a pan?"

"Mmm, please." Smiling, she stepped aside.

Freddy raced inside, still geared up from their walk. He ran a few laps of the apartment as Levi slipped off his shoes.

After Zoe's battle with Chelsea, everyone had dispersed for the night. Piper and Addison went home for their beauty sleep before the big day. But Zoe wasn't eager to return to her small apartment, and she didn't want to drag her mother into any of her drama. Even though her rival had been arrested, she worried the police wouldn't have enough to hold her for long.

After the cops questioned Levi and Zoe outside the club, he'd driven her home. However, he refused to let her be alone that night, and she didn't put up a fight. She'd packed a few overnight things for her and Freddy and followed him back to his place in her van.

"Thanks for taking Freddy out while I showered," she said. "I think the hot water helped my sore muscles." She rolled a shoulder, receiving a sharp reminder of where Chelsea had dug in an elbow.

"Come here." He drew her to the leather couch.

Once she sat down, he positioned himself behind her. She moaned as he massaged and kneaded her aching back, wincing as he found each new knot.

He clicked his tongue. "She really did a number on you, didn't she?"

"She was definitely going for the kill."

A noise in the kitchen startled her. A moment later, Freddy skittered out, a guilty tail curled under him.

Levi reached for the stereo remote and switched on the local radio station. Like he'd been shot with a tranquilizer, Freddy jumped up on the low armchair across from them, worming his way beneath Levi's leather jacket for a nap.

"Now that Chelsea's behind bars, you have nothing to worry about tonight," he said. "Besides, you handled yourself pretty well."

Zoe gave a huff like a weak laugh, but even that hurt. "Because if I hadn't, I'd be in a coma right about now. It took a lot out of me."

He leaned in close, his body warming her back. "I'm sure I could rouse a little energy in you."

The words tickled her ear, and she already felt that energy tingling. "I thought you didn't want to do that."

He took up his kneading again. "You think it's weird that I turned you down for casual sex."

She shrugged, thinking it wasn't weird so much as a blow to her pride.

When she didn't answer, he said, "I'm just not a no-strings kind of guy. I think sex is more important than that. What two people have should mean something, and sex is an expression of that."

Leave it to a songwriter to be good at expressing himself verbally. She was glad she'd swiped the letter off his counter and tucked it into her purse before he could read it. It seemed so clumsy and inarticulate now. She wanted to say everything in person anyway.

"Don't get me wrong, though," he added. "I think it's hot that you're comfortable with your sexuality."

Stiffening, she looked over her shoulder. "What do you mean?"

"Well, look at you." He waved his hands over her like that was enough explanation right there. "You practically exude sex. Every man's jaw drops when you walk by, and you know it. You're knowledgeable and confident when talking about it. And then there's your sex toy business."

"Hold on a second." Zoe gaped. "Oh, my God. You think …"

He held up his hands. "No judgment here. I'm just saying that you're a little more … enlightened than I am. And that's totally cool."

She laughed. Oh, the irony. She spun on the couch to face him, not even knowing where to begin.

Levi must have misinterpreted her reaction because he rushed to explain himself. "Okay, let me start over. You're a sexpert, are you not? One would assume you'd have to have sex to claim that title."

She didn't blame him for thinking she had a lot of sex. That was what most people assumed. Hell, her closest friends suspected the same thing. And part of her wanted people to believe that. To believe she was some kind of goddess, confident and comfortable with her sexuality. Which she was. Only, she wasn't comfortable having sex with just anyone.

"Oh, I'm a sexpert, all right," she told him. "I know tricks that would make your toes curl." She leaned in, suckling on his lower lip before giving it a nip. "In theory."

He was reaching inside her robe, but his hand froze. "In theory?"

"Practice is … an entirely different matter."

"What do you mean?" he pressed.

She took a deep breath but found it difficult. It felt like the Fuzzy Friend conversation all over again. She supposed this was what sharing your secrets with someone felt like. And if she wanted to be with Levi, she needed to get used to it.

"I'm all talk," she said simply. Unable to meet his probing gaze, she stood up to move around the living room. The words threatened to choke her, but she swallowed and blurted them out. "I haven't had sex in six years. And even before then, well, I was with the same guy for four years. I've only had sex with three people in my life."

"Hold on." Levi jumped to his feet, coming close like he must have heard wrong. "You haven't had sex in six years? B-But you're a sexpert," he stammered. "You have a certificate and everything."

He ran a hand through his hair, staring at her with wide eyes as though for the first time, seeing the woman who was too heartbroken to connect with people emotionally or physically. Zoe bordered on the sexually innocent, not the "enlightened" woman she pretended to be. It made her more uncomfortable than when people assumed she was promiscuous.

"I-I just assumed," he said. "I'm sorry. I know I shouldn't have but—"

She waved away his visible guilt. "I'll let it go since I'd assumed the same thing about you."

He continued to stare at her in disbelief. "But why has it been so long?"

She fidgeted beneath his shocked gaze. "Because for a long time, I told myself I didn't need a man. And maybe because I think sex is special too. I wasn't just going to give it away to someone I didn't think I needed in my life."

"But that night you came over, you wanted to give it away to me."

"I suppose it's because I need you in my life." She reached out a tentative hand and laid it on his chest. "It was like my body knew before I even wanted to admit it to myself."

Levi took her hand and distractedly kissed each finger while he thought it over. He closed his eyes and inhaled, as though breathing in her words.

"Six years," he finally said. "Well, I don't want to deny you any longer."

Even in the dim light, Zoe could see his eyes darken, his pupils drink her in. He took her face in his hands and ran a thumb over her cheek, callused from so many years of playing guitar. He kissed her slowly and tenderly, his lips as gentle as silk running over hers.

His fingers caressed her face and then moved to her neck, following the collar of the bathrobe. Sweeping it aside, he exposed her chest to slide his warm palm over her.

Her skin tightened beneath his touch as it trailed between her breasts. When he reached the tie around her slim waist, he unfastened it. It slid off her shoulders and landed in a heap at her feet.

Levi pulled back, soaking up every swell, every curve of her long, lean body. His breathing changed rhythm at the sight of her, and he bit his lip.

After six years of loving her own body, Zoe had long since let go of any self-consciousness. Drawing him toward the spiral staircase, she let him gaze at her. Before they could climb to his bedroom, his eyes grew heavy with desire until he couldn't resist any more and reached out to touch her.

His hands slid down her flat stomach and around the contours of her back. Those hands that knew what buttons to press, what strings to strum, what keys to stroke. And stroke her he did. Soon, his mouth joined in, his stubble tickling her body, raising goose bumps.

She leaned against the cold staircase railing, her knees growing too weak to climb the steps. As he lowered himself to his knees in front of her, desire had him moaning with that sweet voice that made her melt each time he sang. He crooned his soft groans against her stomach and down her thighs, deft fingers strumming her like a guitar.

Zoe's legs shook, threatening to give out beneath her. One hand on the stair railing, she reached out with the other to brace herself. Her fingers landed on piano keys. Their tinkling filled the room, matching the high pitch of her tense body as her toes curled. Her hand came down again to make a different sound, as though trying to find their harmony.

Levi took her hand and dragged her to the music room carpet to begin the real performance. He'd only been warming her up before, tuning her. Now, his mouth and fingers moved in unison, playing her like an instrument until her moans and sighs crescendoed to her climax.

Wave after wave of pleasure washed over her until she felt like she might explode. But instead of bursting inside, she felt her bottle of emotions, which had been filling for so long, empty completely.

It left her body relaxed and yet strangely full, even as those bottled emotions leaked in the form of tears. She blinked them away. They weren't unhappy tears, but blissful, relieved. Tears of joy.

As Levi kissed his way back up her shaking body, he saw the tears running down her smiling face. He kissed them before kissing her. She could taste the salt on his lips.

Zoe removed his shirt, revealing a rock-hard rock star beneath, and tossed it aside. It swished against the cymbal on the drum set.

She ran her hands over him, exploring it all: the tight abs, the toned chest, those little dips above his waistband, taunting her like arrows pointing to what she really wanted. As she tugged off his pants, her foot thumped against the kick drum like a drumroll building anticipation.

He pulled out his wallet. Like he'd read the handbook for guys, he had his emergency condom tucked into one of the credit-card slots.

Impatient, she took it from him and ripped it open. A moment later, he grabbed her hips, guiding her down.

She closed her eyes, feeling each sensation as though for the first time: all the things her body had forgotten, that her heart had forgotten, everything she'd denied herself for so long and had refused to let in.

She couldn't deny herself anymore. Not just the sex but, most importantly, the love. She wanted all of it. All of Levi. Even if it meant opening herself up to pain.

His touch spoke of tenderness, his kisses showed understanding and acceptance, his eyes said love. With every roll of her hips and squeeze of her thighs, she returned those feelings, harmonized with him in a soulful duet until it burst out as a chorus inside of her.

Her body thrust against his like a striker hits a bass drum, deep and rhythmic. Together, they increased in tempo, banging and strumming faster and faster, their bodies making beautiful music together. And as their song climaxed and they sang out together, Zoe knew she'd finally found her jam.

And they were going to be a hit.

Chapter Twenty-Eight

TAIL WAGGING THE DOG

Zoe rolled over in bed, automatically groping for the softness of her Fuzzy Friends. When her hands fell on empty sheets, she opened her eyes in surprise. The night before came rushing back to her.

For so long, she'd gone to bed fantasizing she was with a man, so she thought she was imagining things. But she couldn't mistake the tingling in her body, and she remembered her jam session with Levi in the music room the night before. Her body still sang.

Below, the apartment door slid open with a scrape. A jingle told her Freddy was up and about downstairs. Crawling out of bed, she picked up Levi's crumpled shirt from the floor and slipped it on. As she wound down the spiral stairs, she inhaled eagerly. Coffee.

Levi was in the kitchen setting down a takeout bag and a to-go tray with two steaming coffee cups. Freddy spotted Zoe and skittered across the concrete floor, racing around her legs. She bent down to give him a good-morning petting. He responded by affectionately gnawing the length of her forearm.

Levi grabbed the remote off the counter, and a second later the speakers came alive with Aerosmith. Freddy trotted over to his favorite armchair—mostly because it was low enough that he could jump up on it. Grabbing the throw blanket on the back, he tugged it down onto the seat and crawled under it.

Zoe slipped onto a stool at the island, watching Levi. "You're up early."

"Big day today. Freddy and I picked up some breakfast while you slept in." He gave her a lingering kiss. "I figured you needed your rest after last night."

Warmth spread all the way to her toes. "It did take a lot out of me."

"I was talking about the attack." But the cheesy grin said he was kidding.

"So was I," she said, reaching for a coffee.

He slid his arms around her from behind, dipping his head to the crook of her neck. "Was it worth the wait?"

"The attack?"

He chuckled, his breath tickling her skin. "The sex."

She leaned back into his embrace. Tilting her head up, she kissed him. "Worth every second. I can't wait to do it again."

He smirked. "Why wait?"

"That's music to my ears." She sighed. "But I've got a busy day ahead of me. I should get to the venue to set up. I'm both wedding planner and maid of honor today. Not to mention I have to be on the lookout for sabotage."

"You have nothing to worry about. Chelsea's behind bars. And with everything she's done over the last couple of weeks, I'm sure she'll stay there."

Zoe took a sip of coffee and frowned. "I'm not so sure I'm out of the woods yet."

"Are you kidding? Vandalism, attempted murder—two times? Three if you count Piper's balls."

She laughed at the wording. "But we're not sure all that was Chelsea."

Levi dumped a packet of sugar into his coffee. "She didn't

exactly deny it either. Besides, how many enemies could you possibly have?"

She snorted. "You'd be surprised."

"Well, if anyone tries anything, they'll have to get past Killer over there first."

She glanced at the lump under the blanket. It shifted as though Freddy sensed they were talking about him. His head snaked out enough for his snout to show.

"And they'd have to get through me," Levi said. "But if you still feel uneasy, maybe you should spend a few more nights here. You know, just to be safe." He gave her a playful look, but she could see the hopefulness in it.

Before she could answer, the song on the radio faded, replaced by the DJ's voice.

"That was 'Dream On' by Aerosmith. You're listening to San Fran's best mix of today and yesterday. Popping into the station today, we have Channel Five's very own Holly Hart. Holly, what's on the agenda today?"

Zoe's coffee churned in her stomach. She picked up the remote and turned the volume up.

"Well, Stan," Holly said, *"if you follow me on my blog and social media, you'll know that today is the biggest wedding of the year. And I'll be working tirelessly throughout the day, giving you hour-by-hour updates on the latest gossip and news about the Summers-Caldwell wedding."*

"Tell us, Holly, are you on that exclusive guest list?" Stan's voice was flat with fake interest.

Holly sighed. *"Unfortunately, no. But I've got all the insider info on this doggy dream come true. My source tells me they'll use their dogs as the ring bearers. Isn't that sweet, Stan?"*

"Adorable." He yawned.

"I'm sure there will be some surprises throughout the day, so I encourage everyone to follow along!"

"Thanks for keeping us informed about the important matters in the world, Holly. Up next, we've got No Doubt. Stay tuned."

Zoe turned the volume down. "Something tells me Chelsea will be the least of my worries today." She chugged her coffee to boost her fortitude. "I should get going. I'm already running behind schedule."

"Zoe Plum running late?" Levi fake-gasped. "Who are you, and what have you done with the woman I first met?"

"You must be rubbing off on me."

He made a throaty sound. "Maybe later I'll rub off on you a little more."

She winked. "Sounds like a date."

"A date? Now I'm really worried." He glanced at the time. "I'd better get going too. Take your time and get yourself dolled up here." Metal clinked as he set the spare key on the counter in front of her. "You can lock up when you leave."

"Thanks," she said. "I'll slip it under the door when I'm done."

"Or you can hold on to it," he suggested. "You know, for emergencies." He threw his hands up. "No pressure, though. Not pushing. Totally relaxed."

She gave him a look. "We'll see."

He gave her a quick kiss before he grabbed a breakfast sandwich from the takeout bag. He waved on his way out the door. "And don't forget to eat."

"Sure thing. Thanks for breakfast."

Once he left, she cranked the tunes for Freddy and got ready. Instead of her bridesmaid's dress, she slipped on some comfortable clothes. She could change at the venue with the other girls once they arrived, but first, there was work to do.

Throwing her bag over a shoulder, she grabbed Freddy, who grumbled at being extricated from his warm blanket burrow. She slipped out of the apartment and locked up. But as she bent down to slide the key under the door, she hesitated.

She stared at the silver thing in her hand for a second. It felt much heavier than it had before, more than a key to a temporary office space.

After a moment, she slipped it into her purse. *No more holding back.*

Eager to put the finishing touches on the décor she'd set up the day before, Zoe drove to the Beaux Arts mansion where Aiden and Piper would kick off married life in style and luxury. The day was going to be perfect. Even if it killed her.

However, twenty minutes later, she thought her untimely death was a good possibility as she stood in front of yellow police tape fluttering in the morning breeze.

She gaped at the two fire trucks parked outside the mansion; their hoses stretched up the grand staircase and through the double doors. Soot marred the facade above the upper windows and along the ornate cornices. Blackened curtains drooped out of blown-out windows, dripping water on the sidewalk below.

Zoe swallowed hard, but her throat had gone dry from her panicked breathing. Freddy grumbled as she squeezed him for moral support. He shifted in her arms and licked her freshly applied makeup like he thought this would help.

Relax, she told herself. *Maybe it isn't that bad.* The fire could have been isolated to one area. Nothing a few strategically placed topiaries and curtains couldn't fix.

"Excuse me." A police officer approached her. "You need to stay behind the tape, please."

She glanced down. She'd taken several steps into the middle of the street, dragging the police line with her. *Well, technically, I'm still behind it,* she thought.

"Sorry." She backed up a few inches. "What happened here?"

"We're not releasing any information to the public yet." He shooed her back farther.

"But I'm not the public. I'm the wedding planner," she said, like this should grant her some kind of special treatment. If she could just get in there and start fixing everything, it would all be okay. Right?

The police officer stared down his nose at her. Zoe stared right back. She didn't have time for this.

"There's a wedding taking place here today," she explained patiently. But her panic returned when an incredulous look crossed his face.

"No one is getting married in that building today or anytime soon."

This couldn't be happening. She wanted to grip him by the uniform and shake him. What the hell was she supposed to do now? The venue doubled as the ceremony and reception location, not to mention there were romantic photo ops galore. And what about her newly replaced décor? She had practically nothing left now.

Zoe had worked hard over the last year to give Piper and Aiden the perfect wedding. She'd taken on most of it herself, so much of the stress, the details, right down to the hand-folded origami flowers carefully placed in each invitation.

God, Piper and Aiden were going to be crushed. And all those guests ... Piper's mother and brother had come all the way from Washington. In Aiden's case, people had flown in from all over the world.

She stared at the damage, at the chaotic collection of emergency vehicles. "But ... But what am I supposed to do? The wedding is today."

The police officer shrugged. "I guess you'll have to switch to a different location."

She choked. "But that's impossible. This is the best wedding venue in the city. Do you know what strings I had to pull to book this place? It *has* to be this venue."

"Why?" he asked. "Either they get married somewhere else or not at all. If they choose the latter, then I'd question their priorities."

Her mouth fell open as his words sank in. "Oh, my God. You're right."

She sounded exactly like Juliet, so focused on making everything perfect that she'd gotten wrapped up in the details and had lost sight of the bigger picture. The most important thing about this day was Piper getting married to the man of her dreams. Not where they did it, or how, or what dress she wore. It was about them and their love.

"Thank you," she told the officer. She hugged Freddy to her chest. "Come on, boy. We've got a wedding to save." And with less than four hours before go time.

She spun to head back to the van, nearly running someone over. She started to apologize before she saw the camera in her face.

"Zoe Plum," Holly said. "You're the wedding planner in charge of this year's most anticipated event: the Summers-Caldwell wedding. Now that the venue for today's momentous celebration has gone and blown up—"

"It blew up?" Zoe froze mid-swat at Hey You. "Are you sure it wasn't a fire?"

She rolled her eyes. "I have my sources. This isn't my first story."

Zoe assessed the destruction with new eyes. The glass, the chunks of stone, the bits and pieces of opulent furniture scattered across the road with little numbers marking them. Of course. It looked just like the scene after her office blew up.

But that didn't mean … Did it?

Destruction followed her wherever she went lately. Chelsea's threat from the night before still echoed inside her head.

Just wait, Zoe! You'll get yours! And I'm not talking karma!

But Chelsea was supposed to be in jail. Then again, she could have been released by now. Like the other attempts on Zoe's life, could this explosion be tied to her too? Had she somehow put the people closest to her in harm's way?

Holly nudged her with an elbow. "So, tell us. What will the lovebirds do now?"

Zoe shoved the mic out of her face. "No comment." Holding Freddy to her chest, she marched back to her van.

Holly gripped her by the arm. "Don't tell me the joyous

occasion is canceled." She beamed into the camera lens like she reported for an entertainment show, not Channel Five News.

Some of the people lingering around the crime scene gathered, attracted by the camera and Holly.

"Okay, I won't," Zoe told her. "Because it's none of your business."

The reporter covered the microphone and lowered her voice so her adoring fans wouldn't overhear. "Come on. You've gotta give me something here. I've built this thing up for weeks. It's going to embarrass me if I don't pull through on some kind of drama."

"Maybe you should have minded your own business all along," Zoe said.

"The things happening in this city *are* my business." She raised her voice so the surrounding crowd could hear. "It's my job to keep the good people of San Francisco informed."

A few people cheered at the false passion in her voice. Clearly, they followed her minute-by-minute social media updates.

"I'm a vessel," she said humbly. "A medium. San Franciscans want to know the latest gossip on their favorite couple. I'm just giving them what they want."

"Gossip?" Zoe narrowed her eyes. "And here I thought you were a hard-hitting reporter. I guess you'll always be a lowbrow gossip columnist. Maybe you should go back to your old tabloid."

Holly's face hardened, and she shook the mic in Zoe's face threateningly. "Tell me what I want to know, or I'll start a smear campaign against you that will keep you from any event this side of Nevada!"

"Bring it on," Zoe said. "But you're still not getting anywhere near this one."

The reporter's eyes lit up. "So, it's not canceled then."

"There *will* be a wedding, if it's the last thing I plan. But you're not going to have a clue where it is." With a triumphant grin, she wrenched out of the newshound's grasp and walked away.

"Mark my words, Plum!" Holly yelled after her. "It *will* be the last thing you plan!"

If someone really wanted Zoe out of the picture, the last thing she needed was Holly Hart discovering the new location of the wedding. The nosey newshound would post it all over the internet within seconds. For both Zoe's sake and everyone else's, the press needed to remain clueless.

She stomped back to her van, feeling her tweaked muscles knot up again. She craved the touch of her Fuzzy Friend in her purse, but her hands were already full of a much larger and fuzzier friend.

"Can you believe her?" she asked Freddy.

In answer, he leaned up and gave her another lick on the neck. *Believe who?*

She laughed and pulled away from the incessant tongue bath. "You're a special dog. Always good talking to you."

Despite her sarcasm, it was true. It might not have been like talking to Levi, but there was something comforting about having a friend always there, always happy to see her, to listen, to hug. And as she held him close, she found that by the time she got back into her van, her anger at the reporter had evaporated, and her muscle knots had melted away.

She gave him a scratch behind the ear before placing him on the passenger seat. "I'm sorry, buddy. Not much time to play today. You need somewhere to run around, don't you?"

The doxie whined like he understood her. And after two weeks, it felt like they were starting to "get" each other. Maybe seeing eye to eye wouldn't be so impossible after all.

"Don't worry. I'll find somewhere for you to play for a bit."

An idea hit Zoe like a bouquet to the face. Hopping behind the wheel, she dug her cell phone out of her purse and called Piper. It rang three times before she picked up.

"Hello?"

"Good morning, blushing bride," Zoe sang.

"Hello, maid of honor!"

The excitement in her best friend's voice made her cringe as she said the next words. "Listen … Piper. There's no time to sugarcoat things. I've got some bad news for you. The venue is a no-go."

There was a moment of silence on the other end, then a rustle of sheets like Piper had just leaped out of bed. "What?"

"It blew up."

"Blew up?" She exhaled a long breath. "Can we find somewhere else?"

Zoe smiled. "I thought that would be your response. It's doable, but I'm worried about everyone's safety. This explosion, after everything that's happened—"

"Chelsea is in jail right now," she said.

"We don't know that for sure, and this explosion can't be a coincidence. I was supposed to be in that building early this morning. I was running late. What if the bomb was meant for me, just like the one in my office?" Zoe laid her forehead against her steering wheel. Her head spun. "What if they try again and people get hurt? People we love?"

"Then they'll have to deal with me."

Zoe half-laughed. "I'm serious. Maybe I shouldn't be at your wedding. Not if it means putting everyone in danger."

"I will not have a wedding without my best friend," she said firmly. "We'll hire security. We'll keep the new venue quiet. Do what you need to do, but I'm going to marry this man today no matter what. And you're going to be by my side."

Zoe chewed on her lip for a moment before finally relenting. "Okay."

"What do you need me to do?" Piper asked.

"Do your bride thing. Relax, envision your perfect day, have some chai, and leave the rest to me. I'll let you know the plan as soon as I have it nailed down." She pulled her tablet out, already opening Piper and Aiden's file. "But I've got to go. I have an entire wedding to move in three hours and ... forty-six minutes."

Zoe hung up, hoping that if she pulled this thing off, the blow-out event wouldn't turn out to be a blow-up event.

Chapter Twenty-Nine

PUT ON THE DOG

- *Relocate guests*
- *Inform caterer and band of venue change*
- *Photographer*
- *214 chairs*
- *Flowers*
- *Dance floor*
- *Décor?*
- *A miracle*

Zoe scanned her list for the tenth time, making sure she didn't miss a thing. Who was she kidding? Of course she'd forgotten something, but as long as she had the bride and groom, that's all that mattered.

Fifteen minutes until go time, and, by some miracle, she'd pulled off the venue change. She cast an eye over the scene before her and smiled at the early 1900s farmhouse turned dachshund rescue center turned wedding venue.

Sweeping panels of organza adorned every entrance. Flowers exploded from the wraparound porch and dripped from the thick tree branches arcing over the yard. Twinkling string lights hugged every post, every tree, and the fence for the dog enclosure where the guests' pets roamed free.

Arms slid around her waist, and she felt a kiss on her neck. She leaned back into Levi's embrace, welcoming the reassurance.

"You pulled off a miracle today," he said.

She took a deep breath. All things considered, everything had turned out okay. "It's not perfect, but it feels good."

"They're getting married, and that's all that counts."

"You're right." She spun to face him. "You remembered your violin, right?"

"All tuned and ready to play The Beatles." At a look from Zoe, he raised his hands. "Just kidding. Canon in D."

She slapped him playfully on the chest. "Thanks for filling in. Mobile organs are hard to come by."

After a good-luck kiss, she hurried up the stone steps as fast as she could in her bridesmaid's dress. Sweeping through the French doors and into the reception area, she found Aiden and his two groomsmen seated around the hearth. They glanced up as the brass bell announced her entrance.

"Okay, gentlemen," she said. "We're almost ready. Please go take your places in the gazebo."

As they filtered out, sounds of clinking dishes drifted from the kitchen in the back. The caterer was making do with smaller facilities than expected.

Aiden stayed behind until only the two of them remained. He reached up to tighten his tie self-consciously. "How do I look?"

Zoe automatically reached up to tweak it. "Like Mr. Right."

"Thank you for everything." He leaned in and gave her a hug.

"Don't thank me. You would have been better off with a different planner. Things might have actually gone to plan."

"It couldn't have turned out better." But his grin said he would have been happy marrying Piper in a Chuck E. Cheese.

"Better hurry," she told him. "You don't want to keep your girl waiting."

He gave her a look, as if to say "Here we go," and slipped out the back.

She checked her watch. Ten minutes until go time.

Heading up to the second floor, she beelined it for the room at the end of the hall. Piper sometimes used it to nap when she had to stay overnight at the center to monitor sick pups. But today, the little wooden sign Zoe had hung around the doorknob said it was *The Bride's Room*.

Before she reached it, the door squeaked open. Piper's mother slipped out. Zoe had never met the woman before that day. She looked so much like her daughter, except her hair was darker and contained none of the natural red highlights that made up Piper's auburn locks.

She squeezed Zoe's shoulder on the way by. "She's ready for you."

"Thanks." She knocked and waited until she heard a response.

"Come in!"

She turned the handle and strode inside. The mid-afternoon sun filled the corner room with bright light. She squinted against the light bouncing off the bright ivory dress in front of her.

Piper twirled to face her. She literally glowed. The sun caught the delicate beading along the bodice, making her shine like the beauty she was.

Zoe gasped. "You look perfect."

"Thank you." She spun to take another look in the antique floor-length mirror.

Addison watched from the bed. "I went with a half updo."

"Very nice." Zoe ran her fingers over the soft curls. "Your

auburn hair complements the champagne lace on the skirt." She picked up the veil. "May I?"

Piper nodded and spun around.

Zoe set the comb into her friend's hair and fanned the veil around her shoulders. As she stood back and took in the results, she sighed.

She'd seen a lot of brides, but when she said, "You're the most beautiful bride I've ever seen," she'd never meant it more.

Piper's eyes widened. "Zoe! Are you crying?"

Zoe blinked rapidly, the droplets catching in her lashes. "I-I guess I am. I've been having all sorts of emotional revelations lately."

Piper yanked her close for a hug. Addison wedged herself into the huddle. When they all pulled away, they were sniffling and laughing.

Addison tossed tissues at them. "Don't ruin the makeup, ladies."

As Zoe dabbed at her tears, someone knocked on the door. She checked the time. Five minutes to go.

"Come in!" Piper called.

Zoe didn't know who she expected to be on the other side, but when the door opened, it was the last person she would have guessed.

And obviously Piper felt the same because her mouth fell open. "Ethan?"

Her brother hovered at the threshold. "I wanted to come tell my little sister good luck."

"Thanks," she said.

He rolled his shoulders and tugged at the collar of his shirt, but Zoe didn't think it had anything to do with his designer suit. She had to hand it to him; the man knew how to dress. But she supposed being a high-priced attorney in Washington and knowing how to dress went hand-in-hand. They probably offered classes about it in law school—Law*suits* 101.

An awkward moment passed before Ethan stepped into the

room cautiously, as though marbles littered the floor. His arms half rose, unsure if he should hug her. Piper eventually gave in and moved into the uncomfortable embrace.

Zoe and Addison shared a look. The siblings weren't exactly on hugging terms. In the ten years since their father's funeral, Piper had only seen him once or twice. Zoe remembered sending out his wedding invitation, but she didn't think Piper had even called her brother to ask him to attend. Maybe she'd hoped he wouldn't.

When they pulled away from the hug, Ethan shoved his hands into his pockets. "I also came up here to, well … see how you're getting down the aisle."

Piper's forehead creased in confusion. "My own two feet."

He glanced at the floor. "Well, I was just wondering, you know, since Dad isn't here, if maybe I could stand in his place."

Her eyebrows shot up. "You?"

"Yeah. I mean, I know we aren't exactly close anymore, but, you know, we're still family and … I don't know." He shrugged. "I guess, I thought it would be nice if I could walk with you."

Zoe hoped he was better at his closing arguments in court. However, she noticed how he didn't say "give you away," which was probably a smart idea since nobody owned Piper Summers. For her sake, Zoe hoped Ethan's offer was the start of them building a bridge, and not just because she was marrying a man who had Scrooge McDuck money.

Piper crossed her arms, and her eyes narrowed skeptically. "Did Mom put you up to this?"

He shook his head. "No. I'd really like us to be closer. I've actually been talking with Mom. We're considering moving down here to San Francisco. Wouldn't it be nice if we were all together? We're all we've got left."

Her hard gaze dropped. When it came back up, it was softer, if still a little guarded.

Zoe's eyes flicked between the two of them. Unable to help

herself, she checked her watch. Two minutes. Through the open windows, she heard Levi start up a classical piece on his violin.

Finally, Piper nodded. "All right. You can walk with me." She attempted a smile. "Thanks."

Zoe clapped her hands, startling everyone in the room. "Great. Now that that's settled, it's time."

Piper took a deep breath and followed her through the house to the back door where Marilyn waited to time everyone's exit. She practically glowed with excitement for Piper.

The mother of the bride went first, followed by Addison. When Zoe took her turn down the peony-lined path, she spotted a few guests out of place, a toppled vase, and a loose bow on a chair. However, she reminded herself she was the maid of honor and focused instead on Levi's beautiful music.

Head tilted against his violin, he grinned at her as she passed. She winked back before climbing the gazebo stairs and taking her place next to Addison.

Coming down the aisle behind her, Naia struggled to sprinkle petals onto the path while controlling the two ring bearers. Sophie and Colin stopped to sniff nearly every guest they passed, but Naia gradually coaxed the doxies down the aisle to Aiden, who helped her untie the rings from their necks.

Once Naia took her seat next to Felix, the porch door across the yard squeaked open. The congregation turned as one to watch Piper and her brother descend the steps. Zoe swore even Freddy stopped rolling around in the enclosure to stare—and that was really saying something.

Her best friend looked magnificent, off-the-rack dress and everything. By the way Aiden gazed at her, Zoe could tell he wouldn't have cared if she'd worn a dog-food bag to walk down the aisle.

Zoe followed the ceremony as though she'd never heard vows exchanged before. After what the almost-weds had overcome to be together at the start, how could even the biggest skeptic continue to believe it wouldn't work out? Or that every marriage was doomed to fail—or in her case, not begin at all?

How could she have denied herself for so long when a love like theirs existed in the world? Or maybe it was her newfound hope for her own future with Levi that had her singing a different tune.

"I now pronounce you husband and wife," the justice of the peace said. "You may kiss the bride."

Aiden reached out for his new wife and kissed her as though for the first time. When they finally pulled away, Levi started up a cheerful tune on his violin. The couple unceremoniously made their way down the stairs of the gazebo, the site of so many memorable Sunday pancake brunches.

The best man offered Zoe his arm, and she took it. They followed behind the bride and groom, barely making it halfway to the porch before the crowd swallowed the happy couple to congratulate them.

It was chaotic and spontaneous. And utterly perfect. The kind of intimate, laid-back wedding Piper had told Zoe she wanted, or at least she'd *tried* to tell her. It seemed that, despite all the setbacks and obstacles thrown at her, she'd pulled off Piper's perfect wedding—even if it was accidental.

As Zoe maneuvered through the crowd, Piper caught her eye and mouthed the words "Thank you."

She waved and moved toward the dog enclosure. Freddy saw her approach and pushed past the herd of dogs vying for attention, like *My ride's here, guys!*

She could already smell the appetizers being served on the other side of the house, drawing the guests away from where she needed to get the band set up. Then she had to assemble the dance floor, gather chairs, and set up tables for dinner. But if she was going to dive into wedding planner mode, she needed to grab her tablet from the van.

Clipping Freddy's leash on, she headed for the parking lot. When she unlocked her van and reached in to grab her tablet from the console, the screen glowed with a long list of recent social media notifications from Holly Hart. With a flick of a finger. She scrolled through them. She opened the latest one.

Hey, Holly's Hounds! Have I got a treat for you! The wedding is back on track with a new locale. It's the perfect fairy-tail ending for this puppy: The San Francisco Dachshund Rescue Center.

Zoe snapped the tablet cover shut. *Dammit.*

Now all the gossipmongers around the city would converge on them. Good thing she'd called in the best security company in town. Hopefully, they'd sent enough guards to cover the enormous property.

Marching for the entrance gates to check in with the head of security, she spotted two guests who'd strayed from the rest of the wedding group. When she got closer, she did a double take. What she'd mistaken as a dark suit was actually a police uniform. And the guest speaking with the cop was Bob.

The presence of a cop at the wedding couldn't mean anything good, especially after recent events. Zoe glanced around. She didn't see anyone else nearby. They obviously didn't want to be overheard.

This was Piper and Aiden's big day. Nothing could go wrong. Well ... nothing else. Not if she had anything to say about it.

She plucked Freddy off the ground and tucked him under her arm. "Now behave." She held a finger to her lips, like maybe by some miracle he would understand.

Holding him close, she slipped off her noisy high heels. The hot pavement burned the soles of her feet. Wincing with each step, she crept closer and hid behind the car nearest to them, a silver Mercedes—obviously a guest of Aiden's.

Crouching low, she inched her way to the front of the car, careful not to be seen over the hood, or, more importantly, soil her dress. Clearly going through some kind of Zoe withdrawal,

Freddy bathed her neck in slobbery kisses. She encouraged him with lots of petting—whatever kept him quiet.

"… we have patrol units parked out front," the cop was saying. "Do you think something will happen tonight?"

"I'm not sure," Bob said. "For now, let's just be prepared for anything. I'll monitor things here. I'd like you to call in more units, work with the security company to tighten up surveillance on the perimeter."

"Very good," the cop said. "We'll stand by and wait for your word before taking Miss Plum into custody."

Zoe gasped but covered her mouth before she gave herself away. They were going to arrest her? Did it have something to do with Chelsea? Maybe she'd set Zoe up again. Or it could have been about the venue bombing that morning. Inspector Warner had tried to pin the first one on her, so maybe a second bombing had him convinced.

"Unless something changes," Bob said, "I'll give you the go-ahead later in the evening so we don't arouse suspicion."

Zoe scowled. *Thanks, Bob.* Whose side was he on anyway?

However, if he wanted to arrest her, then whatever they had on her must be incriminating. But still, as her friend, she'd expected him to have a little more faith in her. Or at least give her a heads-up.

Freddy struggled in her arms, clearly bored with her little spy mission.

"Shh, Freddy," she whispered as she struggled to hold him. "Stop fidgeting."

She hummed the first song that came to mind: "Leaving on a Jet Plane." However, he'd hit his limit, and he wanted to play. Or maybe it was because she couldn't hold a tune to save her life. Squirming out of her arms, he flopped onto the ground and made a break for it.

Zoe lunged for the leash, but it slipped out of her grasp. The doxie skittered out from behind the Mercedes, veering for Bob and the cop, blowing her cover.

She swore under her breath. They couldn't know she'd overheard their conversation or they might slap the handcuffs on and take her away right then and there. If she hadn't already done enough to ruin Piper and Aiden's wedding, that would surely top their wedding cake.

Stooping low, she ran back a few vehicles, farther away from the men. Once she was hidden behind her van again, she slipped on her heels. She opened the driver's side door and slammed it before rounding the bumper at a jog. She slapped a smile on her face, hoping she was a good enough actress to pull one over on a cop and a veteran inspector.

When he spotted her, Bob held up Freddy's leash. "Lose something?" His expression didn't even flinch. Like he hadn't just been planning her incarceration.

Well, two can play that game, Zoe thought. "Yeah, thanks. I don't know where his energy comes from."

Now that she stood at the top of the property's driveway, flashes of movement outside the gates caught her eye.

"What's going on out there?" she asked.

"Just some party crashers," the officer told her. "Someone called to complain that they were blocking the road, so we came to check it out."

So that was the story they were going with. Her eyes automatically flicked to Bob. He smiled pleasantly. The man deserved an Academy Award.

Zoe chuckled. "Holly's got the city as amped up about the wedding as she is."

"Don't worry," the officer said. "We'll stick around to keep an eye on things. No one will get through those gates on our watch."

She wondered if that was a subtle message for her. But she wasn't going anywhere. She'd do her job, both as a planner and a bridesmaid, then she'd go quietly, hopefully unnoticed.

Taking Freddy's leash from Bob, she backed away toward the house. "Well, thank you. I'd better get back. Lots to do."

She sashayed back to the wedding party like the only things on her mind were centerpieces and photo ops. And right about now, that's all she could worry about. Because, despite socialite wannabes banging on the front gates, someone wanting to blow her to bits, and cops poised to arrest her for God knows what, she was still the best damned wedding planner in San Francisco. And she had a wedding to oversee.

Chapter Thirty

HEAR OF MARRIAGE AND YOU'LL DREAM OF A FUNERAL

Zoe watched from the edge of the dance floor as Levi belted out the most rock and roll version of "At Last" she'd ever heard. But it was strangely catchy. Freddy seemed to agree; he sat at her heels, enjoying the tunes. The extra-large dance floor was coming in handy because nearly everyone was on it. Even Marilyn and Bob shook their tail feathers. Reluctant Redemption knew all the crowd-pleasers.

Piper danced her way over in Aiden's arms. "Aren't they great?" she yelled over the music. "I'm so glad we hired them."

Addison spun by with Felix. "I bet Zoe is too!" She grinned devilishly and twirled away.

Biting back a smile, Zoe shook her head at her friend. She wanted to join them on the dance floor, but she gave into the temptation to check her social media for the hundredth time that night. She tugged on Freddy's leash, and he followed her to the snack table where her purse and bridal utility bag hid under the skirt. As the doxie gobbled up fallen cake crumbs, she pulled out her tablet and scrolled through the recent notifications.

Holly hadn't posted much since she'd leaked the news about the new venue. One post critiqued the newlyweds' first dance. And if she knew what the song was, then that meant she'd joined the crowd outside the front gates. But so far, things had been quiet—which Zoe took as a bad sign. What was Holly Hart up to?

The persistent reporter would probably stay all night, lurking outside the property, waiting for guests to leave so she could accost them with questions. But there was no point worrying, since Zoe would probably be arrested by then.

She wondered if they would arrest her in front of everyone. She preferred to hand herself over quietly and save her friends any embarrassment. Surely Bob felt the same way.

She was staring across the property at the driveway, half expecting them to come for her any second, when she heard a shout. Or was it a cry? Maybe a whoop of excitement for the band. It sounded like it came from around the side of the house.

She stashed her bag under the table again. Stepping out of the warm light from all the lanterns and string lights, she peered into the darkness. It could have been one of the guests. Perhaps a dog had escaped the enclosure or slipped off a leash.

As she stepped forward to investigate, someone grabbed her hand and tugged her back. She spun until she landed in Levi's arms.

"Hey, rock star." She beamed up at him. "Intermission already?"

"No. But the band was playing our song, so I thought I'd come steal a dance."

He hooked Freddy's leash on one of the dog-minding posts she'd pounded into the ground. The string lights sparkled in his eyes, and she dismissed the noise. It was probably just a small animal in the woods.

"We have a song?" she asked. "And what song is that?"

He swept her onto the dance floor, slipping into a free space. "Any song that will get you into my arms."

Zoe laid her head on his shoulder to soak it all in: him,

them, that moment. The band played a slow, surprisingly romantic instrumental version of "We Are the Champions" by Queen. Levi spun her a couple of times and pulled her close. Over his shoulder, something by the bar caught her eye. A flash of platinum blonde hair, almost white beneath the lanterns dangling from the trees.

He led her around to the other side of the dance floor, and the person disappeared from sight. She craned her head this way and that to see past the other dancers. When a man dipped his partner, she caught sight of the blonde woman again. She gave Zoe a cheeky smile and raised her martini glass in greeting. Or maybe a big old "Screw you!"

Holly Hart.

The reporter had dressed head to toe in black, as though this were a funeral, not a wedding. Maybe that was for the best since there was about to be a funeral: Holly's.

"Is everything okay?" Levi asked as Zoe stopped dancing.

"Holly's here." She pulled away, keeping her eyes glued to the reporter.

"Shall I call for backup?"

"Yes, get Bob," she said. "There's about to be a murder."

She maneuvered her way across the dance floor, all smiles at the guests. *Act naturally. Everything is fine.*

The reporter sipped on her drink, soaking in the ambiance. Her lazy smile dared Zoe to make a scene. Holly was an agent of drama.

The moment she was in reach, Zoe gripped Holly's arm, ready to drag her to the front gates. "What are you doing here?"

"I'm enjoying the festivities." She brushed her hand away. "This is quite something. I have to admit, I had my doubts after what happened to the first venue. But you really managed to pull it off." She gave her a sly wink and lowered her voice to a whisper. "That's why you're my favorite."

"Bite me."

She clicked her tongue. "Is that any way to treat a guest?"

"You're not a guest," Zoe spat. "How did you get in here?"

"Oh, it's a big property." She waved the details aside. "You didn't think a couple of police officers and some incompetent security guards would stop the likes of Holly Hart, did you? I always get my story."

Zoe plucked a leaf out of her blonde hair. "Yeah, I'm sure you get around."

Grass swished behind her. Levi and Bob were marching over. Even in dress clothes, the detective had an official air about him. The rigid stance, his hard expression. He carried authority even when he didn't carry his gun.

"What's going on?" he asked. "Everything all right?"

Zoe backed off; Holly was surrounded now anyway. "Miss Hart seems to have lost her way."

He addressed the reporter. "Will you come with me? Or would you prefer an officer to escort you out in cuffs?"

"Ooh, handcuffs." Holly bit her lip. "Sounds kinky. A couple of them looked pretty cute. I'll take that option." She giggled. "I like it rough."

"Now, don't make a scene," he said, like one would chastise a little girl.

"Who's making a scene? You ain't seen nothing yet. Just call your boys, and we'll see what happens then," she said, the threat as clear as crystal champagne flutes.

Zoe took a step forward. "I will take you down myself."

She raised her chin. "Let's go, stretch."

"Just leave her be," Piper's voice cut in.

Zoe turned to her friend, mouth hanging open. "What?"

"She'll do more damage to the evening if we kick her out." She marched up to Holly, looking her up and down as though she were a wild animal not yet tamed. "You can stay, on one condition. You hand over your phone until the night is over and delete any photos you've already taken."

"Deal." Reaching into her clutch, she drew out her phone and handed it to Zoe.

"I don't trust her." Zoe eyed her skin-tight dress. "She probably has a hidden camera on her somewhere."

"Who do you think I am? James Bond?" Holly threw her a withering look. "But if you're worried, I'm sure Aiden could frisk me." She bobbed her head around, searching the crowd for him. "Where are those handcuffs when you need them?"

"Don't make me regret this," Piper warned her.

Holly drew an imaginary halo above her head with a finger. "I'll be on my best behavior."

"That doesn't exactly ease my worries."

"Oh well, you can't please everybody." Holly downed her drink and popped the olive into her mouth. "Excuse me. I'm going to go mingle." She threw her black wrap over her shoulder and left.

Zoe watched her walk away. "I don't trust her," she said again.

"Neither do I," Piper said. "I just figured it would be less hassle to leave her alone."

"I'll keep an eye on her." She made shooing motions with her hands. "Go dance with your husband before Holly tries to."

Piper smiled. "Thanks."

Levi wrapped an arm around Zoe. "I'd best get back on stage. Any requests?"

"Britney Spears," she joked.

"Done." He kissed her cheek before sprinting back onto the wraparound porch to join the band.

She glanced down at the phone in her hand. Holly had handed it over too easily; she was up to something. No way would she give up recording everything she could. Which meant she had another way to do it. And since Zoe rarely saw the reporter without her cameraman to boss around, she had a hunch he was sneaking around the grounds too.

Holly's laugh carried across the yard as she rubbed elbows with a few of Aiden's wealthier guests. While she was distracted, Zoe moved away from the party and headed for the thick tree line encircling the property. After the dazzling lights around the house and dance floor, it was like walking into a black hole.

The ground dipped and swelled unevenly beneath her heels. She stayed out of the trees and thick underbrush to prevent a twisted ankle. She resisted the urge to go back and grab her tablet to light her path; she couldn't sneak up on Hey You if he could see her coming a mile away. Then again, considering the Channel Five News team she was dealing with, he probably had night vision goggles to do his snooping anyway.

The distant glow from the lights and paper lanterns reflected off the surrounding leaves. She imagined they were eyes watching her, winking as they rustled in the wind. It felt like she'd had eyes following her everywhere for the last few weeks.

Her ears strained for any sounds in the woods, a cracking twig, the whir of a zoom lens. But she couldn't hear anything over the distant sounds of Britney Spears. She chuckled but kept moving. She had a job to do.

The breeze picked up again, and the bushes scraped and hissed as they rustled around her. When it died down, she heard the rhythmic swishing of grass behind her. She'd been so focused on the thick trees, she hadn't been watching her back.

Her chest tightened. She spun around, squinting against the party's lights. Nothing. The swishing drew closer. She took a panicked step back. It was right in front of her, and yet she still couldn't see a thing.

A scream crawled up her throat.

Then it struck.

It pawed at her shins and licked her exposed ankles, relentless in its attack. Her scream escaped in a quiet grunt.

She bent down and gave Freddy a good scratch behind the ears. His leash dragged through the grass behind him. He must have gotten free of the dog-minding post.

"Freddy, go back. Go." She snapped her fingers and pointed to the house.

He whined, tilting his head to the side. *Who's Freddy?*

Zoe sighed. Of course, this was Freddy she was dealing with. He did the complete opposite of what she said.

So, she pointed at her feet and said, "Okay, stay."

Naturally, he took off. Only, instead of returning to the party, he dove for the trees.

"No. Freddy!" she whisper-yelled "Not that way!"

He rustled through the underbrush, crunching dead leaves, snorting and digging in the dirt as he sniffed around. *There's a mouse. I know there's a mouse. It's around here somewhere.*

So much for stealth, Zoe thought.

"Freddy, come back here. There are no mice in there. Come." But he was being his usual self and doing the opposite of what he should.

Groaning, she hiked up her floor-length dress and went in after him. She made a mental note to sign him up for obedience classes—just as soon as she got out of jail.

Her eyes slowly adjusted to the darkness. The nearly full moon overhead helped her avoid hidden roots and fallen branches as she followed Freddy's excited sounds. She doubted he'd found anything but a stick. The sounds grew louder behind the next bush.

"Freddy, come here, boy," she sang. "I'm making my voice sound really fun and lighthearted, but you're actually in big trouble."

She spotted his leash on the ground and bent to pick it up. A bright light caught her eye. A flashlight maybe, hidden beneath a bush. She'd likely discovered Holly's path through the property.

Zoe held the branches aside and reached for the object, but

it felt much bigger than a flashlight. It was the screen on Hey You's camera. But there was no sign of the weasel himself.

She dragged the camera out. It was still recording. She wasn't sure what he'd hoped to capture all the way out there from the bushes. Squinting against the screen's light, she found the stop button.

Over the years, she'd helped enough videographers film weddings, thanks to poorly timed bathroom breaks or illnesses, so she knew her way around professional equipment. Fiddling with the buttons, she found the playback menu.

A selection of past footage popped up on the screen. Very familiar footage. It was practically her last three weeks all laid out in video clips. Out of curiosity, she scrolled through them.

She searched back to the expo, when Holly had begun screwing with her life. Her fight with Chelsea popped up on the screen. Zoe cringed and skipped that one; not exactly her brightest moment.

There were lots of scenes shot around the Hilton. She flipped through those quickly until she stumbled on one showing the underground parking lot. Zoe's finger hovered over the button to switch to the next clip when it zoomed in on a van. *Her van.*

It was post break-in because the tendrils of Piper's shredded dress fluttered out of the open back. However, there weren't people hanging around it; no one had discovered the vandalism yet. Did Hey You first report it?

As she continued to watch, the van wiggled and rocked. Seconds later, a figure leaped out the back. But it was too dark, too far away to get a good look.

She skipped the next shot of her gaping at her destroyed van while Holly pestered her with questions. The next clip was something she'd watched on the news, along with the rest of the city. She hit play.

"This is Holly Hart coming to you from North Beach, where the San Fran Slayer has taken his next victim ..."

Zoe shivered and quickly scanned through what was practically a montage of her life, one epic disaster after another. And the news team was there for every one. Every ... single ... one ...

She rubbed the back of her neck. It tickled with a strange sensation. Suddenly on alert, she peered through the dark woods, straining to hear anything out of the ordinary. But the only sound was Freddy's grunting as he tried to drag his "mouse" out of the bush.

Mouse, mouse, mouse, mouse ...

Resuming her search, she found a clip filmed the day of their brunch at the restaurant. In fact, the time stamp told her it was shot while they were all still eating. Holly Hart stood next to a very-much-alive Chef Glazier.

Zoe hit play.

"This is Holly Hart, reporting from the restaurant House of Glass. I'm with Chef Glazier, world-renowned chef and caterer for this year's biggest event, the joining of our favorite devoted doggy duo, Aiden Caldwell and the dachshund rescue center spokesperson, Piper Summers." She turned to the chef. "Chef Glazier, can you give us a sneak peek of the wedding menu?"

"They haven't made a final decision yet. As we speak, they are sampling my signature dishes—"

Zoe frowned and pressed fast forward, skipping their banter. She'd had no idea this had occurred in the kitchen while they ate lunch. Holly must have come in after the interview, pretending like she'd only just arrived.

In the next video clip, Chef Glazier gave Hey You a tour. By the looks of it, they were in the delivery area where the body was found.

"What kind of stuff do you get delivered here?" a man asked.

Zoe realized it was Hey You from behind the camera. She'd never heard him speak before.

He continued to ask mundane questions until the chef insisted he return to his guests. She supposed that was why Holly asked the questions and he stuck to filming it. But when he continued to press the chef about wanting to see the bay door open, it was obvious; he was distracting Chef Glazier.

Fed up, the chef walked away. The scene jiggled as Hey You chased after him. When they returned to the kitchen, Holly stood at the prep counter.

"What do you think you're doing?" Chef Glazier demanded.

"I thought I might contribute to the momentous occasion," she said. "You know, I'm not half bad in the kitchen. I make a mean soufflé."

But the chef wasn't buying it. He swiped at something on his cutting board. "What is this?" He smelled it and touched a finger to his tongue. "Sesame seed?"

"This isn't what it looks like," Holly said.

He glanced from her to the truffles, freshly powdered with the deadly stuff. "You know about her allergy." He shook a finger in her face. "You plan to poison my customer."

"Okay, it's exactly what it looks like," she said. "But it won't kill her. It will probably just puff her up a little."

From the camera angle, Zoe couldn't see her face. Chef Glazier blocked the view. However, there was no hint of remorse or guilt in the reporter's voice.

"This is outrageous. Both of you are criminals." The chef turned to face Hey You. His cheeks flushed red, his eyes bulging with fury. "I'm calling the police."

Hey You didn't bother to aim the camera. The chef's chest filled the frame, the buttons of his double-breasted jacket shaking as he continued to rant, threatening jail time and lawyers. Then mid-sentence he trailed off, his voice gurgling in the back of his throat.

Chef Glazier fell forward. He crumpled to the floor,

revealing Holly holding the steak knife. It dripped with the chef's blood.

Zoe's stomach heaved, and she covered her mouth with a hand. She sank to her knees. The damp earth soaked through her dress.

She wanted to scream, to run. She suddenly felt so alone, but she couldn't seem to drop the camera, couldn't tear her eyes away.

"What …?" Hey You gasped. "Shit. You just stabbed him."

Setting down the knife, Holly pouted like someone just brought her a Pepsi instead of a Coke. "Well, I didn't plan for this to happen, did I?"

Though, for someone who hadn't planned it, she'd put on a pair of leather gloves at some point. That was why only Zoe's fingerprints had ended up on the knife.

Hey You placed his camera on the counter and bent over the body. "Oh, my God. He's dead. We have to do something."

The words seemed to change something in Holly. Her face went blank for a moment. "You're right. We have to do something."

"Good, okay. We should call the police and—"

But she wasn't listening. She reached down to the chef. "Come on. You grab his upper body. I'll grab his feet."

Hey You gaped at her. "What?"

"Well, I can't very well get blood on me. This is Dior for shit's sake." She tugged at her outfit. "Use your brain."

"But I don't understand," he said. "He's dead. We need to call the police."

"The police?" Her face fell. "But they're going to blame me."

"Yes." He nodded. "Because *you* killed him."

"You were here too."

"Tricking someone into eating a few seeds is one thing," he said. "But this … This is cold-blooded murder."

Holly covered her face with her hands. A sound not unlike

a sob came out of her, but Zoe thought it was far from the real thing.

"After working together for all these years." She sniffed. "After everything we've been through, you'd turn me in just like that?"

The reporter stepped over the body and placed a hand on Hey You's chest. When he didn't move, she laid her head against his shoulder.

"I thought you'd do anything for me," she said. "We're a team."

"Team? You do nothing but boss me around." But he sounded less panicky and more confused.

"That's only because I've been fighting my true feelings for you."

Hey You swallowed. "Feelings?"

"Don't deny it. I know you've wanted me since the first day we worked together. I've wanted you too." She pressed against him. "But we can't be together if I go to jail."

"Be ... together?" He seemed to forget about the body on the floor entirely.

"I can't take it anymore," she said. "I want you. Now."

"W-We can go to my place."

"No. I can't wait that long. We can do it in the van." She brought her lips close to his but kept them just out of reach. "But first ..."

Holly pulled away, disappearing beneath the counter. When she popped back up, she held a pair of feet. "Grab his arms. Hurry. Before someone comes back here."

Hey You did as she asked, grunting from the dead weight. "Where are we going to hide it?"

"Just shut up and lift with your legs."

They moved off camera. A moment later, the kitchen's double doors swung open, and the server came in with her tray.

"Chef Glazier?!" She scanned the kitchen for signs of him,

but didn't enter far enough to see the blood on the floor. When no one answered, she shrugged and loaded the desserts onto the tray.

The moment the doors swung closed behind her, Hey You and Holly returned to clean up the blood. He reached for the camera and the screen went blank.

Holly was the one behind everything: Zoe's van, the bombings. Even before the murder, Hey You had known she was up to something, or at had least suspected it. Zoe recalled chasing him down the alley after her office bombing. He'd been collecting footage of Holly. Evidence.

She knew she should take the camera and run. Run to the police. Run to Bob. Run to someone and tell them what she'd found, but something made her click on the most recent video. The last one.

With a shaking finger, she hit play.

The video was filmed from the very spot she kneeled on. The heavy breathing told her Hey You stood behind the camera. From his leafy hiding spot, he filmed the dance floor.

A twig snapped.

Zoe spun, scanning the trees. She was still alone. She returned her attention to the screen. The sound had come from behind Hey You. The camera spun to face the source. It was Holly.

She crossed her arms. "What are you doing here?"

"I came to stop you," Hey You said. "You can't do this."

She took a step forward, but he blocked her.

"Get out of my way." She glared at him.

"Give it up. It's over."

"It's not over yet," Holly told him. "I've tried too hard to fail now."

Zoe's breath left her in a grunt. The camera shook in her hands. This whole time, she'd assumed someone was out to get her, to sabotage her. But it wasn't about her. It was about Piper. Holly wanted to stop the wedding by whatever means necessary, by ruining the dress, hurting the wedding planner, landing the bride in the hospital.

"You've failed," Hey You said with finality. "You can't undo it."

Holly's chin rose. "There's one way."

And by the tone of her voice, Zoe knew what that "way" was. "Piper," she breathed.

Hands shaking, she dropped the camera. There was no point in watching more because she knew Holly had gotten past Hey You. She was already at the reception.

Zoe lurched to her feet. Was she too late? Would she find Piper in time?

The screen had been bright, the woods so dark. She tried to blink away the images burned onto her retinas, of Chef Glazier's body, his blood. Her heel caught on something, and she fell forward.

Pain exploded in her knee. Her shins scraped against rough bark. Her arms flew out, and she braced herself for impact. But her chest and face landed on something soft, cushiony.

Groping through the dark, she pushed herself up and found herself nose to nose with Hey You. His sightless gaze bored into her. He was dead.

A soundless scream escaped Zoe like a high-pitched whistle of wind through a broken window. She clambered back, clawing at the ground, shoving the body aside. It flopped away from her, the lifelessness making her panic all the more.

Freddy found her in the dark. She jumped as his tail slapped against her happily, like he'd found the biggest mouse ever.

Grabbing her doxie, she half crawled, half stumbled out of the woods, back toward the party. She just hoped she wasn't too late to warn Piper.

Chapter Thirty-One

I'LL GET YOU AND YOUR LITTLE DOG TOO

Zoe rushed onto the dance floor with Freddy clutched in her arms. Her muddy dress wrapped around her legs with each frantic step, threatening to trip her. Barging past dancing couples, she clipped a shoulder and sent someone spinning. She ignored their cry of surprise and pushed her way through more people. Finally, she spotted Bob dancing with Marilyn and beelined it for him.

"Bob," she wheezed, gasping for air.

He turned, eyes wide. "Oh, Zoe. You startled me."

Marilyn pulled away from her dance partner and gave her the once-over. "What's wrong, dear? You look like you've been dragged through a hedge."

Zoe gripped Bob's arm. "Go get the police."

"Why? What's happened?"

The gentle, older man transformed before her. The light-hearted boyfriend dancing with his sweetheart faded, and his look became unreadable. This wasn't the man they ate pancake brunch with every Sunday. He was the law now, and in his eyes, Zoe was on the other side of it, a criminal.

Despite the urgency of the situation, she became aware of the dancers slowing around them, forced to step past their frozen group. They eyed her with curiosity. Bob seemed to notice too. He drew her away from the dance floor, out of earshot.

It occurred to her that what she had to say could cause mass panic among the happy wedding guests. She lowered her voice and leaned close enough so not even Marilyn could hear. "Holly's cameraman is in the woods. He's been murdered."

He stepped back, and his mask slipped for a moment.

When she took her next breath, it almost sounded like a sob. "Look, I know the police are waiting to arrest me. But I didn't do anything wrong." She gripped him by the shoulders. "You have to believe me because there's something more important—"

He held up a hand. "Wait. Arrest you?" Understanding dawned on his face, and he shook his head. "They're not here to arrest you. They're here to *protect* you."

Zoe blinked, trying to make sense of what he was saying. "From what?"

Glancing around, he slid his arm through hers and led her around the side of the house, where the music faded. Marilyn followed anxiously, but he held up a gentle hand. The woman watched them leave, picking at a loose thread on her wrap.

When they'd walked far enough away, Bob took on the stance of a man having a friendly chat. He placed his hands in his pockets casually, as though everything were normal. But what he said next was anything but.

"They're here to protect you from the San Fran Slayer."

Zoe's legs trembled. She braced herself against the porch railing, but her arms shook so violently that she slid ungracefully onto the steps. Freddy slipped off her lap to sniff the ground in front of her. She held his leash tight.

"What?" she breathed.

Bob sat next to her, like they were taking in the night air together. It felt so wrong. As though they were relaxing while Piper's life was on the line.

319

"They found evidence on Chef Glazier's body consistent with the Slayer case," he said. "They know it wasn't you."

"Are you certain the Slayer killed the chef?" She shut her eyes. The images from Hey You's camera were still there, forever burned into her brain. If the Slayer killed the chef, then that meant …

"Yes, we're sure," he said. "Considering the attempts on your life recently, we're taking you into police custody for your protection after the wedding." He eyed the trees surrounding them. "But if you found a body, maybe the Slayer's already here."

"She is."

He drew back, staring at her in surprise. "How do you know it's a woman? We've never released information about the gender."

Zoe felt time slipping away. Every moment they sat there was another moment lost. They had to find Piper before Holly did something to her. Before a serial killer murdered her.

"The Slayer is Holly Hart."

"How—"

She held up a hand. "There's no time to explain. But it's not me she's after. It's Piper."

His wide eyes scanned the party, but his gaze was distant, as though realigning all the facts, all the evidence in his mind.

"And she's here now." He sprang to his feet with the energy of someone half his age. "I'm going to get the police from the property gates. You stay here."

He made as though to leave, but at the last second, he turned back. "And Zoe? It's important no one knows anything is wrong. If Holly learns we're on to her, it might make her act sooner."

"Act?" Zoe swallowed. "I have to go find Piper." She backed away, dragging Freddy with her.

Bob grabbed her arm. "It's too dangerous."

"She's after Piper, not me."

"But if you get caught in the middle——"

"Bob," Zoe said. "It's Piper."

"You can't help her if you wind up dead yourself." He squeezed her arm firmly.

But his words didn't convince her to stay behind. It only made her more desperate to find her best friend.

As Bob left to inform the police, she took a deep breath and pushed it all down—the fear, the anxiety, the guilt that, somehow, she could have prevented this. If only she'd figured it all out sooner.

All that mattered was saving the bride from a serial killer in Manolo Blahniks. She'd never thought she'd miss the normal wedding woes like ill-fitting dresses and drunk uncles.

Zoe spotted Aiden near the dance floor. Picking Freddy up, she crossed over to him, in a totally not-jittery or too-anxious way.

She laid a hand on his arm. "Aiden?"

He turned with a smile, but then he took in the state of her. "Zoe, what happened to your dress?"

"One too many tequila shots." She forced a laugh, but it sounded too loud even over the rock music. "Have you seen Piper?"

He frowned, glancing around. "Not for a little while now."

"Okay, no problem," she said as normally as she could. "She's probably in the restroom. I'll go check on her."

Before she turned away, she gave his arm a squeeze, afraid it wouldn't be that easy. That she wasn't simply going to find his wife reapplying her makeup.

Zoe calmly made her way to the snack table. She grabbed her purse with her tablet inside and slung it over her body. She would need to keep in contact with Bob somehow, in case she found Piper. Or in case Holly found Zoe first.

Pushing that thought aside, she entered the house. As she systematically checked every room and closet and still found no sign of the bride, she wanted to touch her Fuzzy Friend for support. Instead, she held Freddy tight.

His presence kept her calm and focused. She could get through this, just like she'd gotten through every other terrible moment in her life. But this wasn't a spelling bee or a broken limb. This was life and death.

Her frantic search took less than two minutes, but by the time she returned to the porch, her skin glistened with sweat, and she couldn't catch her breath. She scanned the yard; still no sign of a white dress.

She rubbed a hand over her face. She didn't want to think it, but she just knew Holly had gotten to Piper. As she stood there, heart rate increasing with each passing second, she wracked her brain. She scanned the dark tree line. Could they be in the forest?

Levi caught her eye from the makeshift stage on the porch. He gave her a wink and a smile between verses. Zoe felt her face move in what she hoped was a smile because no one could know, no one could suspect. Raise the alarm, and Piper might pay for it.

A little wrinkle formed between his eyebrows, and he tilted his head as though asking her a question. *What's wrong?* Of course, Levi saw right through her usual calm veneer.

Freddy squirmed in her arms—maybe he sensed her anxiety too. Before she could give away anything else, she turned and made for the dog enclosure. If she was going to search the woods for a murderer, she'd need her arms free.

The moment she set her doxie down on the other side of that gate, he raced away from her. Zoe frowned. *How's that for loyalty? First sign of trouble and he runs.*

Only a few dogs paced in the large, grassy area. She assumed the rest were in the doghouse, hiding from the loud party. And despite his love of music, that's where Freddy had disappeared to. Without a backward glance, he ducked through one of the doggy doors leading into the building.

Now that he was safe, she scanned the enclosure and the dark wall of trees on the far side. She hesitated, unsure where to begin her search. The property was so big. How would she ever find them by herself?

A moment later, a doggy door swung open. Freddy returned, dragging something behind him. It was long, whatever it was, because his short legs tangled in it. He went head over tail until he was a sausage in a blanket. Literally. Zoe realized he'd found a long piece of fabric.

She unlatched the gate and went to untangle the puppy. Frowning, she held the fabric up to the dim light. A black shawl —not unlike the one that had been wrapped around Holly's shoulders.

Beneath the vibrating bass, Levi's warm voice humming through the speakers, and the steady drumbeat, faint, chaotic sounds pierced the air. Shrill, urgent barking.

It came from the doghouse. The only place on the property where no one would hear anything over the dogs' barking.

Freddy took off without waiting for Zoe. Tossing the pashmina aside, she followed him. She snuck up to the building, searching for a way to peer inside without announcing her presence. However, the only windows were too high to reach, and the door was too obvious.

She watched her doxie disappear through one of the doggy doors. It was the best option. Getting on her hands and knees, she crawled up to one built to fit an English mastiff. With a hesitant finger, she nudged it open and peered inside.

A blast of excited yipping and howling hit her. While each enclosure had more square footage than her apartment's dining room, it was meant for only one dog at a time, so they had plenty of space to stretch out. However, by all the fur blocking her view, it seemed most of the dogs had crammed themselves into the few stalls not locked. And something had them agitated.

Between furry bodies jostling in front of her, she caught

glimpses of Holly Hart's blonde hair on the other side of the chain-link kennel. Her arms flailed wildly as she spoke, but whatever she said was drowned out by all the barking. While Zoe couldn't see who she was talking to, it must have been a pleasant conversation. Holly certainly seemed to be enjoying it, anyway, but that was probably because she was doing all the talking.

Zoe poked her head inside the dog door to get a better look. A border collie skittered out of the way, and she finally got an unobstructed view of Holly's captive audience. Piper was bound to one of the building's support posts with spare dog leashes, duct tape slapped over her mouth.

Chapter Thirty-Two

PUTTING THE DOG DOWN

I found Piper. Holly's got her in the doghouse. I'm going in.

Zoe's fingers shook as she sent the text message to Bob. Her stomach flipped, taking her heart with it. Gritting her teeth against the nausea and fear, she tossed her tablet on the ground beside her purse.

She didn't wait for a response; she knew what it would be. But she wouldn't stand by while her best friend's life was in danger.

She crawled through the doggy door, but it wasn't easy. No matter how she turned her head, Freddy kept kissing her face and chewing on her earlobe. His tail tucked between his legs as he let her know *I think there's danger.*

The chain-link enclosure didn't offer much cover. However, the reporter was facing away, and Piper was too distracted by the murderer threatening her life to notice Zoe. Between the dogs barking and Holly chatting up a gagged woman, she slipped in without notice.

"You know," Holly said to Piper, "Aiden was quite the player back in the day. But I told you that once before. Those were some of the best articles I ever wrote. He and I were practically made for each other." She pointed the tip of a knife at the bride's throat. "But then you came along."

Piper's eyes widened, and her jaw moved as she screamed against the duct tape. Zoe got ready to spring into action, but then the reporter sighed and waved the blade around dramatically as she continued her monologue.

"Ever since then, I've waited and watched." She laughed like she was remembering all the good times they'd had together. "Honey, I saw it all. You've got some moves in the bedroom, girlfriend. Very carnal. Kudos."

Zoe kept low, hiding among the shifting fur as the dogs danced inside the partitioned space. Inching her way to the kennel door, she reached up to the latch and slowly lifted it. She bit her lip, praying the metal wouldn't squeak.

Holly pouted and rested her head on Piper's shaking shoulder. "I never in a million years thought Aiden would actually go through with the wedding. Not with his scandalous history."

She scraped the knife along the base of Piper's neck. "I always assumed he'd come to his senses. That he'd finally see what's been right in front of him the whole time."

The blade changed angle, the edge puckering Piper's skin.

Zoe flung the kennel door open. The dogs flooded into the open space as she lunged for Holly and knocked her aside.

The reporter shrieked, tripping over a collie. She fell against a kennel. The knife clattered to the floor, lost from sight among the furry bodies.

As she regained her balance, Zoe brought up her foot and kicked her square in the chest. The air left the reporter's lungs in a grunt, and she fell back. She half stumbled and half slid into an open kennel.

Zoe slammed the door and dropped the latch.

With shaking hands, she slapped a padlock on the kennel door. The metal snapped home with a click of finality. The nightmare was over.

She scoured the floor until she found the knife. Grabbing it, she sawed away at the dog leads digging into her friend's wrists. Between her sweaty palms and Piper's shaking, she nearly cut her a dozen times.

Freddy pawed at their legs. *I'm helping. I'm helping. Am I being helpful?*

Finally, the last strands gave way, and Zoe yanked at the rope. Piper ripped the tape off her mouth. The second she was free, she threw herself into Zoe's arms.

"Am I glad to see you."

Zoe gave her a quick squeeze, but she didn't want to linger. "Come on. Let's go find Bob."

The kennel rattled behind them. Zoe spun around. The reporter casually leaned against the kennel fencing. A smile crept over her face as she slipped the barrel of a gun through one of the gaps.

"Did you seriously think I came unprepared?" She snorted at their ignorance. "You, in the white." She curled a finger in a come-hither motion at Piper.

Zoe shared a look with her friend. In such close quarters, Holly would hit one of them for sure, if not both. Piper's jaw clenched. Zoe could have sworn she heard teeth squeak, even above all the dogs barking and yipping at their heels.

Finally, Piper took a deep breath and reluctantly approached the kennel.

"Of course, I prefer using knives to guns," Holly said conversationally. "There's something so personal about it. Reporting on the gruesome things I see day in and day out, you get a bit desensitized to it, you know? The murders, the rapes, the car accidents. But taking some-one's life with nothing but a piece of steel between you? Now that's stirring. You can feel the sinew rip, the organs pop." She shuddered, a delicious smile warming her face. "But only an idiot leaves home without a gun. It's my plan B."

Piper appeared calm as she entered the code into the lock,

but as she unhooked it, it rattled in her hands. By the look in her eyes, it clearly wasn't from fear. It was rage.

Holly strolled out, tutting at Zoe. "You just had to come find her. You don't know when to quit, do you?"

She ignored her bounding heart and answered as coolly as she would any other day. "Should I have quit after you broke into my van and ruined Piper's dress? Or cut my brake lines? Or tried to land Piper in the hospital?"

"Hey." Holly held her hand up. "At the start, I tried to derail this wedding without anyone getting hurt. Well, except for that salsa instructor, but broken bones heal."

Zoe flinched in surprise. The manipulation went back much further than she'd realized. She scoffed. "You blew up my office."

"Oh … right. Okay, so you would have been a little crispy." She waved a hand like a trip to the spa could have buffed that right out.

Piper crossed her arms over her beaded bodice. "And the sesame seeds?"

"You would have been fine. It's just a little anaphylaxis. Nothing some modern medicine couldn't cure."

"Chef Glazier wasn't *fine*," Zoe shot back.

"Well …" Holly relented with a shrug meant for stealing the last cookie. "That was a little hiccup."

"And how about your cameraman? Or the jewelry designer a couple of weeks ago? Or the pizza delivery boy?"

Piper's head whipped from Zoe to the reporter. Her mouth dropped open. "What? You don't mean …"

Holly pursed her lips. "You know about those, huh? Listen, that jewelry designer was a crook. I swear she swapped out my diamond for a fake. And the delivery boy?" She groaned. "Thirty minutes or less, my ass."

Piper gasped, taking an automatic step back until she hit the kennel behind her. "*You're* the San Fran Slayer?"

Zoe dared to step forward. "And all those other innocent

lives you've taken in this city over the last couple of years? What are your excuses for them?"

She raised her chin. "I don't need to defend myself to you."

"You're right," Zoe said. "You just need to defend yourself to the police."

"The police?" She laughed. "Clearly, this is your first time being held at gunpoint, so let me explain. I have the gun." She waved it in the air. "That means I have the power. You don't have the gun. That means you die."

"The police already know about your cameraman in the woods," Zoe said, trying to make her second-guess her plan. However, she wasn't about to reveal she'd sent a text to Bob, in case Holly got trigger-happy out of desperation.

The reporter didn't look too worried, though. "If that were true, they'd be ripping this place apart, searching for me." She tilted her head, as though listening. "And I can still hear your glee club boyfriend singing out there. Sounds like the party's still on."

"Rock band," Zoe muttered.

She automatically tuned into the distant music, a song by Panic! At The Disco. But Levi wasn't singing. It was the original, which meant the band had taken a break.

Holly's face radiated confidence. She had it all figured out. Probably right down to where she'd honeymoon with Aiden. The fact that she had to murder people to get what she wanted seemed a minor inconvenience.

"Don't worry," she said. "I've got plenty of time to kill you and dispose of your bodies in the woods."

Zoe's eyes flitted around the building, but there was no escape. They would have a better chance of getting away out in the open. They just had to get out there somehow. "How are you going to drag our bodies out to the woods? I mean, now that you've killed your sidekick, there's no way you can manage it all on your own."

She frowned, glancing between the two of them, maybe estimating their weight. "You're right. It will be hard dragging your carcasses out there. Thanks for pointing that out." She picked up her knife and waved her gun toward the back door. "Get moving."

As they marched for the exit, Zoe glanced back at Freddy among the other dogs. He tried to follow, but the reporter kicked him aside.

"Hey!" Zoe yelled.

He yelped, but skittered away to safety. Ducking out a doggy door, he raced into the yard. She watched it swing shut behind him, wondering if this was the last time she'd see him. *At least he'll be safe,* she thought.

Piper threw her a look that asked *What's the plan?*

She grimaced and shrugged. *I guess we'll wing it.*

Holly jabbed her in the back with her gun as a reminder. "Run and I shoot. Yell and I shoot. Do anything I don't tell you to do and I shoot. Got me? Now, get the door."

As Zoe opened it, fresh air swept over them. She inhaled deeply until her panicked mind cleared a little.

Holly wouldn't shoot them early unless they forced her to. They were too close to the party; everyone would hear. They still had time to figure something out, to come up with a plan. And Zoe was nothing if not a good planner.

Holly forced them around the side of the building, hiding them from sight. People laughed and cheered above the blaring music, but Levi still wasn't singing. Was he looking for her?

She pretended to stumble in her heels and lurched forward. As she caught herself on the enclosure fence, she tore off the ribbon around her waist and balled it up in her hand. When Holly shoved her forward again, Zoe tossed the fabric back so she wouldn't see.

But Piper saw. And while Zoe didn't exactly have a surplus of outfit to leave behind as breadcrumbs, a bridal gown offered plenty of delicate details to tear off.

Piper began stumbling too, blaming the cumbersome dress. Each time, she tossed a little something aside, too small for Holly to notice in the dark: a string of beads, a ribbon, a chunk of lace.

As they dove into the thick woods that bordered the property, darkness swallowed them. Hardly any of the moon's glow reached them through the thick canopy. Surely, Holly couldn't hit targets she could barely see, Zoe reasoned. However, each time she gathered the courage to make her move, Holly jabbed their backs with the cold barrel of the gun, reminding her that at such close range, she'd be able to hit them with her eyes closed.

Eventually, the music faded to a dull beat in the distance. Even if they got the upper hand, how could they get anyone's attention? Zoe's eyes adjusted enough to see her friend's desperate expression. She looked fresh out of ideas too.

The reporter's footsteps slowed. "Stop here." She tossed Zoe a leash. "Tie Piper up to that tree over there."

She stared at the lead in her hands and then at Piper. When she took too long to respond, cool metal pressed against her neck. Enough said: do it or die.

Piper slowly backed up to the tree. Her eyes never left Zoe's, as though waiting for a cue. But Zoe just stared back as all thoughts fled her brain. She was usually the one with all the plans, the one in control, cool in the face of trouble. However, this was one wedding catastrophe she never could have predicted.

As she approached her friend, Zoe gripped the leash until it bit into her soft palms. Her breaths came faster, and her eyes prickled with tears.

This wasn't how it was supposed to go. The good guys should win. Holly should lose. It was Piper's wedding day, for God's sake. Was Aiden going to lose his wife of mere hours?

And what about Levi? Zoe had finally found the man she

wanted to be with, who made her whole again. Would he even know what happened to her?

No. It couldn't end like that. She could handle anything, including *The* Holly Hart.

She closed her eyes and imagined every ounce of her energy building in her limbs. She tensed her legs to spring and flexed her arms. Just as she prepared to attack Holly, leaves rustled behind them. Startled, they spun toward the sound.

"Who's there?" Holly demanded.

No one answered. Not a flicker of movement in the trees. The sound drew closer. Despite the situation, Zoe smiled. She knew who'd come to save her: Freddy.

She could practically sense his innocent excitement. *Hello! It's just me. Is this hide and seek? I found you!*

Holly searched the darkness. The gun twitched in her hand, and she waved it wildly.

Zoe took her chance and dove for the reporter.

Holly yelped and swung the gun around. Zoe grabbed her arm and drove her knee up. The elbow bent back.

Crunch. Pop.

The sensation echoed all the way up Zoe's leg. Holly screeched and dropped the gun.

"Help!" Piper screamed. She dropped to the ground and scrambled through leaves and grass for the weapon.

Holly snarled and dove for her. Before she could touch her friend, Zoe took the leash in her hands and looped it around the reporter's neck. She yanked, cinching it tight.

Choking noises sputtered from Holly's mouth as she clawed at the nylon cord. She jerked and thrashed. Zoe dug her heels into the earth. But Holly was stronger than she looked. Inch by inch she drew away. Suddenly, her head whipped back.

Crack.

Pain exploded in Zoe's nose. A flash of light burst across her vision. She could almost smell the pain. Hot liquid ran down her face, and she tasted metal in her mouth.

She stumbled back, holding her nose as she coughed and choked on her own blood. Holly wheeled around. Her fist drew back. Before it could connect, something flashed in the dim moonlight.

Twang.

A musical hum filled the woods. Holly cried out and hit the ground.

Freddy hadn't come alone; he'd brought Levi.

His face twisted with fury as he stood over the reporter. He raised his guitar over his head in true rock star fashion, ready to bring it down on her.

Beneath the hollow vibrations humming from the guitar, fallen leaves rustled as Holly scrabbled along the ground. Finally, she stopped like she'd given up, but then Zoe heard another noise.

Click.

Holly's arm rose, a finger wrapped around the gun's trigger. She aimed for Levi's exposed chest.

Chapter Thirty-Three

A LIVE DOG IS BETTER THAN A DEAD BOYFRIEND

As Holly pointed the gun at Levi, Zoe's breath left her in a sob. Her eyes filled with tears as she already grieved for what was about to happen. She couldn't stand to have her heart made whole again, only to be ripped out once and for all. It wasn't fair.

She lunged for him. A split-second later, the shot pierced the night air, echoing through the woods.

She could feel the sharp loss, almost as though she'd taken the bullet herself. As though Holly had aimed for her newly repaired heart and blown it wide open.

Zoe cried out.

Somehow, Levi found the energy to bring his guitar down on Holly. It twanged, and rang, and thumped, falling apart piece by piece until he held only the instrument's neck. It dripped with a dark liquid that glinted in the moonlight.

Grunting, he tossed it aside and fell to his knees, Zoe along with him. She wrapped her arms around him, holding tight.

That ache, it burned inside her. It was almost too much to bear, but she let it spill out of her as she held him. She didn't want to bottle anything up anymore. She didn't want to hold back. Because without the fear and pain of losing him, she couldn't give him her love. And she suddenly found she had so much to give. And she wanted it all, every feeling, every last painful second she had with him.

"Levi," she sobbed. "Stay with me."

"I'm not going anywhere." His voice broke, as though he could barely get the words out.

She heard Piper's screams fade as she ran back for the center. "Help! We're over here! We need a medic!"

Levi seemed to hold Zoe up as much as she held him. The damp soil seeped through her dress, making her shiver. She was so cold.

"I can't lose you," she said. "Not now. It's just … too short." She choked on her tears as another wave of grief ripped through her. It hurt so badly.

She shook now, breathing in quick gasps, unable to get enough oxygen between her sobs and that terrible heartbreak.

"Don't leave me," she said.

He laid a hand on her face, wet and hot with his own blood. He held her gaze, the moonlight reflecting in his blue eyes. His expression looked so pained that it hurt her to see him suffer.

Between her quick breaths, he kissed her. "I will *never* leave you. I promise. Never."

Those words made it a little easier to breathe. The constriction in her chest eased. After all the excitement, the energy trickled out of her body. She relaxed in his arms, feeling tired all of a sudden.

The sound of ripping fabric made her drooping eyes flutter open. Her blurry gaze landed on Piper. She balled up a piece of her beautiful wedding gown. Laying it against Zoe's chest, she pressed firmly.

Zoe screamed as hot pain shot through her body and rippled down to her cold toes. She bit her lip to stop from crying out again.

"Can you carry her?" Piper asked Levi.

Instead of answering, his hold shifted. The world spun as he stood—or maybe that was just Zoe's head. Every step he took stabbed her chest like a hot poker.

He grunted and huffed as he carried her back to the center. He held her protectively to his body as he picked his way through the rough terrain. She dazedly watched his face, focusing on the effort, the strain, the worry that creased it.

It struck her as odd that *he* carried *her*, when he'd been shot. When the dim lights from her wedding decorations glowed up ahead, it was even stranger that everyone called her name and not his. Especially when he was covered in so much blood. It coated his shirt, his hands, his neck.

The music stopped, replaced by agitated chatter, cries of exclaim, tinny voices over two-way radios, and distant echoes of sirens. It all sounded muffled beneath the buzzing inside her head, like a swarm of cicadas had gathered in there.

The light brightened, and Levi set her down on a cold, hard surface. She blinked. She was in the veterinary operating room.

Piper set something over Zoe's face. It hissed at her, blowing air. Annoyed, she raised a hand, trying to swipe it away. Levi's hand clamped over hers and held it still.

Metal clinked as Piper rummaged through tools. She then hung a bag of liquid overhead. Zoe watched it swing, almost hypnotized.

Her eyes drooped until something pinched the skin in the crook of her arm. She hissed. Levi held her hand tightly. However, she no longer had the energy to resist. Instead, she watched Piper fuss over her from the end of a really long tunnel.

The pain had dulled. Or maybe Zoe had become used to it. In fact, she felt like she'd left her body entirely. The only sensation remaining was the feeling of her hand in Levi's.

Only now did it occur to her that he hadn't taken the bullet. *She had.*

But that didn't seem like the most important thing right now. The only thing that mattered was that he had kept his promise. He hadn't left her. Only, as her vision darkened, she wasn't sure she could promise the same thing.

Chapter Thirty-Four

IN TUNE

Slimy wetness rubbed Zoe's cheek over and over again, working its way closer to her nose. She groaned, swatting it away. But this only made it worse. It increased in both speed and enthusiasm.

She brushed her hand in the general direction of her face, but her limbs didn't work as well as they should. She ended up slapping herself instead. Her nose throbbed as she hit it, taking her breath away.

Slowly, she halfway opened an eye to peek at her attacker. Freddy danced on top of her blankets—though, they couldn't be hers because she didn't recognize them. His wiry goatee tickled her face as he persisted in kissing her.

Zoe squirmed away, and pain shot through her chest. She froze, holding her breath. Her body might not have been cooperating, but she was able to aim a serious eyebrow twitch at the doxie.

Freddy jerked like he'd been shot, then flopped against her, exposing his belly in surrender.

Her eyes blinked one at a time while she took in her surroundings. A white ceiling and ugly green curtains stared back at her. Her nostrils stung, both from the scent of antiseptic and the dry air hissing into her nostrils. Noises overwhelmed her: beeping, whirring, chiming, and ... snoring.

She raised her head, grimacing as fire spread through her chest like she'd inhaled hot ashes. She found the source of the snoring halfway down her bed. Levi.

He sat on a stiff plastic chair, head resting on her raised bed. His arm stretched across her legs as though still holding onto her since ... well, since the wedding. Whenever that was.

She reached out a tentative hand and ran her fingers through his locks. They felt soft, no trace of his usual sticky gel. He inhaled deeply, and his eyes fluttered open. They looked bright and clean, not ringed with dark makeup.

Those eyes met hers, and he smiled sleepily, like they'd just woken up after a wild night together. Well, she supposed they had. It just hadn't been the kind of night Zoe would have preferred.

Levi blinked a few times before awareness seemed to hit him. Jumping to his feet, he reached for her face. "You're awake."

She closed her eyes, enjoying the sensation of his touch, the gentleness welcome after so much pain. The pain ...

As she took a few deep breaths, her head cleared, and memories accosted her: the wedding, the body, the woods, Holly.

Someone dropped something nearby. The *bang* made her wince. Her chest spasmed as though reliving the moment the bullet tore through her. Once she caught her breath, she raised the rough hospital blanket, tugging at the neckline of her gown to peek under it.

She wasn't sure what she'd expected to find. Blood and gore? A gaping hole in her chest, maybe? Instead, an oversized white bandage covered the left side of her chest. A thick, clear tube ran out from under it.

"The doctor said you were very lucky," Levi said, startling her.

She still felt a little dopey. Maybe the IV dripping into her arm had something to do with that.

"I should buy a lottery ticket," she croaked.

He ignored the joke. "It was just a small handgun, so the bullet didn't go all the way through. It hit just below your collarbone. Any lower and it would have gotten your lung."

Zoe's eyelids fluttered for a moment, imagining the bullet still in there, rubbing against her lungs with each breath. She'd had a lot of close calls in the last couple of weeks, but nothing closer than that. A centimeter, maybe a millimeter.

"How do you feel?" he asked.

"Like I've been shot."

"I can't say I know how that feels. But I almost did." Levi shook his head, his face screwing up. "Why? Why did you do it?"

"I know how you feel about pain," she joked. Reaching up, she ran a thumb over his naked eyebrow. There was not a glimmer of metal anywhere on his face. "But I'm tough. I can handle it."

"I know you are. I just wish it were me lying in this bed. It hurts to see you like this."

She gave him a wry look. "I'm so sorry for your pain."

He chuckled, and so did she. A jolt seized her chest, and she went rigid until it released her.

Levi passed her a cord with a red button on the end. "Hit this. It will give you pain medication."

She jammed the button three times. Her IV machine whirred, and a few moments later, she felt a little woozy. It wasn't enough to take the pain away, but it took the edge off.

"Maybe it's the drugs talking," she said, "but right now, I'm just happy I'm here. I have my friends, my life ..." She laid a hand on his cheek. "And I found my heart."

He pressed his palm over her hand to keep it there. "Thankfully, that's still intact."

She smiled. "It's better than ever."

Tired of being ignored, Freddy snaked his way up the bed, licking the oxygen tubing laying across Zoe's cheek. *I came too. I came to see you. Pay attention to me.*

She giggled, wincing with each shake of her chest. "How did you get Freddy in here?"

"The nurse let me smuggle him in," Levi said. "He is a local hero, after all."

"Is that so? Freddy, do you have an alter ego I should know about?"

He tucked his tail between his legs, but he wagged it hopefully, unsure if he was about to get praise or a scolding. She gave him a scratch beneath the chin. He nestled in the crook of her good arm, jutting his barrel chest out to make sure she got every last spot.

Levi pulled out his phone and cued up a video from the Channel Five News website. In front of the camera, as usual, was Holly Hart. Only, this time, she lay handcuffed to a stretcher.

As the camera zoomed out, the brunette who normally did the weather segment stepped into the shot, microphone at the ready. Although the scene was grim, her smile stretched big enough to reveal her molars; she'd obviously been promoted.

"What do a wedding, a wiener dog, and a rock star have in common?" she asked. *"They were the keys to uncovering the identity of the San Fran Slayer. AKA our own once-beloved Holly Hart."*

She turned, inviting the viewers to watch the downfall of Holly Hart's reign as attendants slid her into the back of an ambulance.

"I am happy to report the Slayer mystery has finally been solved at the location of this year's most anticipated event, the Summers-Caldwell wedding."

A photo from *The Gate*'s announcement section popped up on the screen. It was a snapshot of Piper and Aiden shortly after news of their engagement went public.

"After murdering her cameraman, Eugene Goodman, and crashing the

bash, Holly Hart attempted to take out the blushing bride in the hopes of replacing her as Mrs. Caldwell." The reporter walked slowly, and the camera panned with her until she stood in front of the dachshund rescue center.

"As we already know, the deranged ex-reporter had an obsession with the CEO of Caldwell and Son Investments. As it turns out, the obsession went beyond your average red-carpet crush. She's been stalking him for months, possibly years."

Zoe huffed. "That I can believe."

"Thankfully, the bride's maid of honor and local wedding planner, Zoe Plum of Plum Crazy Events, found Holly before she could do any harm. But when things didn't go as planned, local rocker and front man of Reluctant Redemption, Levi Dolson, tracked them down with the help of her dog, Freddy."

The scene cut away to a photo of Freddy, the one Zoe had posted on the center's website. Next to it was a video clip of Levi's band on stage at some club.

"Tonight, the lead singer performed the biggest hit of his life by taking down Hart, but not before Zoe Plum was shot and seriously injured." She paused dramatically. *"I'm happy to report that she's in stable condition and will recover from her injuries to plan another day."*

Behind the weather girl-turned-reporter, the ambulance sped down the rescue center's long, winding driveway.

"With Holly Hart on her way to prison, our city is safe once again, thanks to a wedding planner, a rocker, and a wiener. Reporting this rockin' ending for Channel Five News, I'm Fiona Fair."

She gave a sassy wink to end the segment, looking overjoyed. But that probably had less to do with the positive resolution of the mystery than it did the sudden job opening.

Levi tucked his phone into his pocket. "Did you hear? The reporter called me a rock star."

"I call you 'rock star' all the time," Zoe said.

"Yeah, but now the whole city knows. And she mentioned your business. Imagine all the brides who will want to hire you if you're willing to take a bullet for them. You can have a slogan like 'Zoe Plum, wedding planner. For when things don't go as planned.'" He used a deep, movie-trailer-guy voice, like she was the Arnold Schwarzenegger of wedding planners.

She snorted. "That's great. But I'm not sure I want to take bullets on a regular basis." The idea brought back the image of Holly's gun trained on Levi's chest. She swallowed hard. "How did you know where to find us in the woods?"

"It was Freddy," he said. "The boys and I were taking a break. When I couldn't find you, I texted you. I heard the chime from your tablet and followed the noise to the doghouse. That's when Freddy found me. He sniffed out your bread-crumb trail through the woods."

"Freddy. Did you hear that?" she asked him. "You're my hero."

His ears perked up at his name. However, he was too busy shoving his snout beneath her arm, seeking a hole to crawl into. She could tell he was growing restless.

"So, does that mean you're going to keep him?" Levi asked.

"Yeah," she said. "I think we're good for each other. A perfect match."

The doxie wedged himself beneath Zoe's blankets, burrowing down where it was warm. His tail slipped under until all she could see was a lump fidgeting beneath the linen.

Levi chuckled. "You'll need to get used to having music in your life to keep him happy."

"That's okay. I planned on having music in my life to keep *me* happy." She gave him a meaningful look.

His expression softened, the worry lines relaxing a little. "You know, I just so happen to be a musician. I could help you out with that."

"That's good. I'll need a lot of music, for a long time," she said seriously. "Maybe forever."

His face erupted into a smile. "I can do forever."

As Levi leaned over the bed to kiss her gently, the green curtain behind him swished aside. When they turned to look, her mother stood at the foot of the bed. If she was surprised to find them in the midst of a lip-lock, she didn't comment.

She rounded the bed, spreading her arms wide to embrace her daughter. "Zoe."

"Okaasan." She reached up and hugged her mom, ignoring the pulling sensation from her chest tube. When they drew apart and she saw the worry creasing her mother's face, she said, "Gomennasai."

"Don't apologize to me," she said in English. "You were very brave. Stupid. But brave."

Zoe rolled her eyes. "Mom."

"Baka," she teased.

"I'm lying in the hospital. You're not allowed to call me names." But Zoe was laughing. And somehow, she'd started crying at the same time.

"I'll leave you two alone for a while," Levi said. "Your overnight bag is in my van. I'll go grab it."

Junko watched him leave with a shrewd look. "I see you and the musician are close. What about Kimura-san?"

Zoe held back a sigh—mostly because she couldn't afford to waste oxygen. Leave it to her mother to worry about marriage at a time like this. "I told him it wouldn't work."

She sighed. "I had hoped ... Maybe if you give it some time?"

"I don't think he's the one for me. I'm sorry."

Zoe worried the conversation was about to become as painful as getting shot. Then her mother began ... smiling.

"Why do you look so happy?" she asked. "I thought you'd be upset."

"Because you make it sound like there is 'one' for you. That means we're making progress." Junko took her hand in hers, the way Zoe had when the roles had been reversed. "All I want is for you to have someone who will take care of your heart. Who will be there for you during tough times, as you have been for me?"

Zoe smiled as she realized that's exactly what Levi was doing. What he'd been trying to do all along. She'd just needed to learn to let him.

"Mom, how did you know Dad was the one?"

Her mother's gaze grew distant. "I remember the first time I met your father. He was brash, loud, arrogant, and thought himself very charming."

"He obviously charmed you," Zoe teased.

"I thought he was ridiculous." She chuckled at some memory. "I tried to ignore him. I told myself that he was wrong for me, that I was happy with my life just the way it was, surrounded by everything and everyone I'd ever known and loved." She sighed. "And yet, despite all the reasons why I couldn't be with him, it felt impossible to live without him."

"Were you scared?" Zoe asked. "To let yourself fall, I mean?"

"Oh, yes. But I was more scared to let him go. How can you ignore a feeling like that, like … destiny?"

"Destiny?" Zoe huffed. "How very unlike you."

Junko had given up everything to be with her late husband. Except for her sister, her family had cut all ties with her. To have leaped into the unknown, put her heart and her life in the hands of someone else, to have trusted him completely, that showed bravery. Meanwhile, Zoe had been afraid to go on a single date with Levi because she feared rejection. Maybe her mother had known more about love all along—not that Zoe would ever admit it out loud.

"So, does this mean you are considering Levi?" Junko asked. "Is he your destiny?"

Before she could answer, the curtains parted as Levi returned. Junko assessed him as he resumed his post next to the bed. After a moment, she nodded, as though it had been decided.

In Japanese, she whispered, "He will make me beautiful grandchildren."

"Oh, Mom!"

Levi nodded toward the open curtain. "Look who I found on the way here."

The ugly green fabric shifted before a parade of people still dressed to the nines filtered into the space: Piper, Aiden, Addison, Felix, Naia, Marilyn, and Bob. Piper wore a hoodie over her dress, but it didn't cover all the dirt and blood stains. Zoe's blood. She wondered how long it had been, if it was still the same night. Or maybe the next day, if Naia was there.

"Thanks for coming, you guys," she said.

Piper crossed her scratched arms, dirty manicured nails digging into her skin as she hugged herself. Her red eyes filled with tears as she took in the sight of Zoe. "Holly was after me the entire time. I'm alive because of you."

Aiden wrapped a protective arm around her. "Thank you, Zoe."

"It was a joint effort," she said. "Besides, I wouldn't be here if you hadn't taken care of me after I was shot," she told Piper. "Holly had been there all along, popping up every time something went wrong. I assumed she was being her nosey self. I should have put the pieces together a long time ago."

"You mean I should have," Bob said. "This city owes you a debt for uncovering the San Fran Slayer. Holly wasn't even on our radar. Her job was to report the crimes, not commit them. She had access no one else did and a reason to lurk around every crime scene. She had us all fooled."

Marilyn slipped her arm through his. She patted his hand, and his tense shoulders relaxed. He gave her a tight smile. Clearly, he'd been beating himself up over it.

He took a deep breath and shook it off. "We'll have more questions for you later, but for now, on behalf of the police and San Francisco, thank you."

"Well, it was in my best interest at the time," Zoe half joked. "What happened to Holly?"

"She's recovering. She ..." Bob glanced at Naia, clearly

choosing his words to keep it kid-friendly. "She won't be the same."

Zoe shivered, remembering the clang of the guitar strings as Levi brought the instrument down on the reporter.

"But either way, she'll never be a free woman," he said. "We won't have to worry about her ever again."

"And Chelsea?"

"She'll definitely face charges for attacking you. And while she wasn't directly involved in Holly's scheme, she provided her with copies of your former assistant's planner, knowing full well the harassment that lay in store for you. Maybe not the attempted murders," he said, "but she might be considered an accessory. At the very least, she actively aided in sabotaging your business. Your attorney will have more suggestions regarding her."

She rubbed her forehead like she could massage all the puzzle pieces together—which was tough to do while heavily medicated. "So, Natalie had nothing to do with it?"

Bob shook his head. "Apparently not."

Natalie probably didn't even call Astrid at the wedding dress shop. Holly could have posed as her ex-assistant. While Natalie wasn't in on the attempted murder, from Chelsea's confession, Zoe knew her ex-assistant wasn't exactly innocent, either. But that was a much smaller concern for another day.

She must have dozed off, because she couldn't remember anyone talking for a little while. Then Marilyn spoke up.

"Well, we'd best let you get your sleep." She patted her on the foot. "We're so happy you're all right."

People gave hugs, preparing to leave. Addison's hug was especially long. She still hadn't said a word, but by her pink nose and bloodshot eyes, Zoe suspected it was because, if she did, she might not stop crying—she'd seen Addison watch *The Notebook*, after all.

When Felix dipped close for a gentle hug, he whispered in

Zoe's ear. "You'd better hurry and get better. You'll have another wedding to plan soon."

She gasped. "Have you?"

He subtly shook his head, tapping his finger to his lips. He was going to propose soon.

The secret had Zoe grinning, happy for Addison, who was officially going to get the family she'd always wanted. Fairy tale-themed wedding ideas flitted through her head.

"And don't worry about a thing," Aiden told her. "You're going to get the best care money can buy. Physical therapists, chiropractors, acupuncturists. You name it, I've hired them. The next few months of your rehab are already coordinated."

Taking out his phone, he flipped through screens rapidly. "I've set the schedule into a calendar. It's color-coded, labeled, and alphabetized." His facetious look dared her to ask if it came with footnotes.

But Zoe smiled gratefully. "Thank you."

Junko had been silent, maybe a bit shy among the large group, but now she gave a somber head nod to Aiden in thanks.

Being a handshake guy, he stiffened a little before awkwardly returning the gesture. When he straightened, his hand reached for his tie out of self-conscious habit.

"It's the least I can do," Aiden told Zoe. "I owe you more than my life." He kissed the top of Piper's head. "I can send you a copy of your rehab schedule if you want to see it."

"That's okay," Zoe said. "I trust you did a great job. I'm sure it will all work itself out."

Levi's head snapped to her, but he said nothing. Once everyone had said their goodbyes and left, he laid a hand on her forehead. "Maybe you're not doing so well, after all."

"Why? What's wrong?" She craned her neck to look at the numbers and squiggles on the monitors.

"You're clearly very sick." He smirked. "What happened to things working out because you make sure they do?"

She recalled how much his laid-back attitude irritated her the first day they met. But despite all the things that had gone wrong since then, everything really did turn out for the best.

Piper's wedding was beautiful—well, except for the whole attempted murder thing. Zoe cleared her name; she finally owned a property; she'd adopted a heroic, lifesaving doxie; and she'd found her heart in the form of a rock star.

She laughed and pulled Levi in for a kiss. "Turns out, life doesn't go as planned. Sometimes, it's better."

~

She's seeking adventure. He wants to settle down. When the road gets rough, can they meet in the middle and map out a path to love?

Find all of Casey Griffin's books at

CASEYGRIFFIN.COM

THANK YOU FOR READING

I hope you enjoyed reading A Wedding Tail. If you have a moment, I would be so grateful if you could leave an honest review online at your retailer of choice. Reviews are crucial for any author, and even just a line or two can make a huge difference. I genuinely appreciate your time and support.

Thanks!
Casey

GET YOUR FREE SHORT STORY

He's a man controlled by rules. She loves to break them. She's just what he needs to find a new leash on life, but is he barking up the wrong tree?

Read the adorable meet-cute from *Paws off the Boss* through Aiden's eyes. Sign up for Casey Griffin's newsletter and receive your free short story now!

ACKNOWLEDGMENTS

I owe a *paw*sitively huge thank you to Rose Hilliard for helping me discover and unleash the best in this story. I appreciated all of your support and encouragement when things got hairy. Holly Ingraham, thanks for jumping on board this wiener with such enthusiasm and for seeing it through. And to Jennie Conway and the staff at SMP who have worked so hard to develop and promote the series, it was a real treat working with all of you. And I can't *fur*get Dayna Reidenouer, Jennifer Herrington, and Susan Keillor who stopped me from chasing my tail with edits.

To Devin, my inspiration, my rock, and my heart, I wouldn't have made it without you. Pooja Menon, my stories wouldn't have been heard if you hadn't stuck by me and believed in me. Thank you to my criminal subject-matter expert Pat McCormack and to my cultural expert Kacy Inokuchi. And finally, a shout-out to the amazing Fredwardo, the most unique dog I know. You've given me all the inspiration I could ever ask for.

And most of all, thank you to the fans of the series for your encouragement, dedication, and for sharing my silly sense of humor.

ABOUT THE AUTHOR

Casey Griffin spent her childhood dreaming up elaborate worlds and characters. Now she writes those stories down. As a jack of all trades, her resumé boasts registered nurse, heavy equipment operator, English teacher, photographer, and pizza delivery driver. She's a world traveler and has a passion for anything geeky. With a wide variety of life experiences to draw from, she loves to write stories that transport readers and make them smile. Casey lives in Southern Alberta with her family, and when she's not traveling, attending comic conventions, or watching Star Wars, she's writing every moment she can.

CASEYGRIFFIN.COM